A Drahma City novel

SUGAR
IN THE
BLOOD

L.M. Dodds

Book cover design and illustration by Idil Sukan.

Edited by Victoria Basnuevo at Red Loop Editing

First edition 2025

No AI was used to write this book; all em dashes are my own.

To anyone who has ever wished they could rip out the still-beating heart of their enemy but doesn't because they're not built for prison.

Corvid Sea
The Nest
Forlare Park
Fellkirk
Rettenness Building
Luminous Palace
DICKBALL LIVES HERE
Helport
Callahan's
Dravens Place
Petra's Place
Almaton
Istakia The Golden Circle
Roman's Place
City Hall
2nd Circle
Tradimento
Rikport
Lerendale
Lekotto Park
Nomads
Matt's Place
3rd Circle
East Bridge
The Fugue
West Bridge
The Hollows
Sugar's Place

Prologue
Sugar

The matronly nurse's uniform is unusual for me, but then again, so is the grown man dressed in a onesie with his thumb stuck in his mouth.

Kylie marches up beside me, her voice low and sharp as she says, "Reginald, you're supposed to be in bed. This is the third time tonight. We're going to have to get the paddles this time." His arousal spikes, but I don't need it. I'm already full from my first client tonight, one whose emotions were more to my taste.

Reginald runs across the room while affecting big, gulping sobs like a toddler. The illusion is somewhat ruined by the fact he's six foot five and sporting three days of beard growth and a massive erection. Kylie moves to the wall, where an impressive assortment of whips, paddles, and other toys hang.

I stride toward Reginald, my face one of unyielding austerity, as his brief requested. Our big boy doesn't want sympathy or coddling. And although my clients usually prefer me in leather and lace, this part is familiar. This, I know how to do.

Resting my hands on my hips, I give him a cold smile. "Did you think we wouldn't notice? Look at me," I snap, and his big brown eyes land on mine. Impressive. He's managed actual tears this time. "Do you think we're pushovers, Reginald? Did you really believe you could misbehave and Ms. Kylie and I wouldn't punish you?" His arousal surges, suffocating the room. Behind me, Kylie inhales, stifling a moan.

The door behind me opens, and I glance over my shoulder. Helen's wearing an identical outfit to mine, right down to the small cameo at her neck. Her tight bun looks better though, and I smooth back a few wayward strands of my silver hair. I didn't realize how long we'd been here. Time flies when you're having fun.

"Reginald," I say. "Turn around and put your hands against the wall. Nurse Helen is here to take my place. And no whining about it. She's very good at dealing with naughty boys." He immediately spins and slaps his hands against the wall next to the adult-sized crib.

Helen gives me a wink. "Where are your manners? What do you say, Reginald?" she demands.

"Thank you, Madame Writh," he breathes as Kylie drags a wooden paddle slowly down his backside. Helen grabs a riding crop off the wall and saunters toward him, smacking it against her palm.

I save my smirk until I exit the room, the heavy door falling shut behind me. There's only the faintest sound from the other private rooms in the Roman residence, but in the open seating area down the hall, a sensual melody accompanies the talking and laughing of the other guests. The subtle scent of tobacco and musk snakes through the hallway.

Last night, I had three of my regular clients at the Nest. I wasn't supposed to work Stanley Roman's party tonight, but Kylie's usual partner, Moira, was still healing after one of her clients got a little overzealous in his shifted form and bit her arm off. Unseelie heal quicker than Seelie, but even we need a week to recover from losing a body part. Unless it's a head. Nobody comes back from that.

Turning away from the noise, I head down the hallway, running my fingers across the black velvet wallpaper, toward what appears to be a dead end. One of the last doors pops open, and Estrella steps out and closes the door quietly behind her. She spots me and smiles. Her deep purple dress spills onto the floor. It's high-necked and skintight with long sleeves. As a necromancer, she doesn't really need to wear anything seductive, but it suits her.

"You off now?"

"Yes." I'm suddenly starving. Tipping my head at the door, I ask, "Everyone still alive in there?" It's a stupid joke, one she probably hears all the time, but she laughs anyway. Her palms meet in prayer, and she slowly drums her fingers together.

"Maybe," she draws the word out and grins. I snort a laugh and shake my head.

I don't bother asking her who's sleeping off their fun. Everyone who works these parties knows not to discuss the clients outside of the safety of the Nest. We're supposed to pretend we don't see our council members, judges, and teachers. A deep, recognizable laugh comes from the other end of the hall, and I purse my lips.

Estrella frowns and crosses her arms. The lights flicker against her bejeweled nails. "Is he still giving you a hard time?"

"Only when he sees me," I say with a wan smile. "It's not really that bad. I can avoid him well enough."

She huffs a laugh. "Wouldn't it be a little fun to work him, though?" She drops her voice until it's barely audible. "To make him crawl to you? Beg?" My gaze darts around the hallway, but the other doors are shut tight. "I bet it's a real rush."

It is a real rush. Watching some rich fae bend to my will with barely a thought? Or making a Seelie who might turn their nose up at me in the street, lick my boot? It can be downright addictive. Glass shatters, and there's a roar of laughter. Probably another ancient wine bottle. Stanley has quite the collection.

"No more than taking and bringing back a life, I should think," I reply as I step past her. These boots are starting to pinch, and now that the adrenaline of the job has worn off, I'm exhausted.

She wrinkles her nose. "Meh. It's practically clinical, especially with the better necros." Estrella fans herself to imply she considers herself one of them and steps away from the door. She bumps my shoulder in goodbye as she walks toward the noise of the other guests, calling over her shoulder, "Get some rest."

At the very end of the hall, a bouquet of peonies and dahlias sits in an ornate vase inside an alcove. I give the wall behind the flowers a gentle push. A latch clicks, and the wall pops open.

Pulling the handles of the vase to open it wider, I step through and shut the door behind me. It's a small, plain stairwell, meant to allow the servants of this house to move about unseen. It's also freezing down here in the sublevel, but I'll be warm enough once I climb to the third floor.

Various sounds reach me through the wood. It's almost six in the morning, and members of the household who haven't been enjoying the party downstairs—or more likely, those who serve them—are starting the day. Just as I reach the exit for the second floor, there's a crash, as if someone has upset a tea service. No voices reach me, not even apologetic-sounding murmurs, as I climb the last flight and step out onto the third floor.

Mostly servants live up here. But there are a few guest rooms, so the rugs are expensive and orbs glow in gold sconces. After leaving the stairwell, I give myself a moment to sink back against the wall beside it. I lean down to untie the laces of my high-heeled boots, then sigh in relief when I slip them off. As I pick up my shoes, I fantasize about the enormous breakfast I plan to eat once I bathe and change. I want a pile of scrambled eggs heavy with pepper and cream.

"You alright there, Sugar?" Cari calls out as she exits her room, adjusting her cap and apron. "Want me to bring breakfast up to the room?"

I give her a grateful, if tired, smile but shake my head. "Not today, but thank you." I often eat breakfast here with Linnea, but I need to get back home to the Nest, to my own bed.

"See you later, then." She gives me a playfully over-exaggerated curtsy and grins before heading past me into the stairwell.

Shoving myself off the wall, I head down a long hallway. The sunlight brightens a little more with each window I pass. By the time I get to the room I use whenever I work one of Stanley's events, I'm barely awake.

Putting my hand on the doorknob, I pause, the hairs on the back of my neck standing on end. I look around, trying to pinpoint the source of my unease. There's nobody in the hallway. When I push open the door, nothing is amiss. My regular clothes are right where I left them when I got here.

"Linnea?" I call as I walk into the bathroom.

She hasn't filled the bath. That's what's missing—the scent of oranges and vanilla, or lavender and rosemary, or whatever she's chosen that day for me. She's been here, though. Her array of bath products is lined up on the counter. There's even a teapot and two cups for us. The ceramic is still hot to the touch.

I trail hairpins and items of clothing as I go back into the bedroom. Never once in all the time Linnea has been helping me has she not been here when I've arrived. Surely it was bound to happen, though. Mrs. Roman probably demanded some service. She's always moody during her husband's parties. Not a fan of his particular entertainment, Jaqueline Roman prefers to get her kicks exercising pointless authority over the servants.

I throw my boots into the open bag on the floor and remove my dress. Crossing my arms over the silk slip I had underneath,

I sit on the edge of the bed. The bronze clock on the wall ticks audibly.

Standing, I pace back and forth. The prickly feeling won't go away. My cuff moves on its own, sliding around my wrist in a mirror of my agitation. The rug muffles my footsteps as I leave the room and turn down a different hallway. I pause when I reach the room at the end.

The door is slightly ajar, revealing only a sliver of the space beyond. There's a familiar smell. The smell of rooms where clients want things really rough. Thick, slithering dread roils through my stomach. My nerves vibrate, and my power jumps inside me, unsure of the threat.

I can't hear her. Linnea is in there—I can feel it—but I can't hear her chatting to herself or singing or moving about. My fingers are damp as I push them against the dark wood.

The door swings open easily.

Chapter 1
Sugar

As anniversaries go, this one has to be the worst. Three years. And what do I have to show for it? Crappy patrols nobody wanted to take, mountains of boring paperwork, and, my favorite, the constant suspicion and wariness from my coworkers. At least it wasn't hard to get promoted. Unless you're on the take, the job is pretty undesirable.

Years of bad pay, worse hours, and chasing down dead ends, and I'm no closer to finding Linnea's killer than I was when I first found her small, lifeless body. I should have left like I'd planned, should have known my foolish career change would come to nothing. Nobody cares about one dead human in a place like this.

"Have we met before?" The man's brown eyes are slightly unfocused as they roam over my face. He attempts to lean casually on the bar, but his elbow slips on the well-polished wood.

As he clumsily rights himself, I search for that distinctive tug, the spark that calls to my unique preferences. But there's nothing. He's not aroused either, so he wouldn't even qualify as a light snack. I shudder at the thought he's genuinely interested in getting to know me.

"Yes. Best we don't do it again. Keep the mystery alive," I deadpan. A ribbon of green smoke from someone's water pipe meanders through the air, and I wave it away before taking a sip of my drink.

Callahan said it was wine, but it tastes like vinegar. Or maybe it's just my attitude. Coming here usually cheers me up. The moody bar in the Second Circle is popular with pretentious assholes, and there are always a few among them who can satisfy my needs.

"I don't get it," he slurs, smiling like I've told a joke. Judging by the eagerness emanating from him and the faint smell of kibble, I'm guessing he's a Seelie dog shifter. Seelie look almost human. Unseelie tend to have more distinguishing characteristics, such as a vampire's fangs or a butterfly's wings. I can extend and retract my claws at will.

"Story of your life, I think." I let my navy eyes flash enough to let him know I'm dangerous. "I'm not interested, Sparky. Go find someone else to play with." He rears back but doesn't leave, still too curious for self-preservation. I turn away, letting my hair fall like a curtain between us.

"Are you sure I can't b—"

I twist, intending to violently insist on his departure, when a hand with perfectly manicured red nails snakes over his shoulder. Petra shakes her head at him in reprimand. "Pretty sure she said she wasn't interested."

She releases a torrent of air, tossing him across the room. He tumbles over to where his friends sit at one of the bar's midnight-blue velvet booths. The singer on the small corner stage doesn't miss a beat despite the sudden disturbance. Her sultry voice continues to float across the dimly lit room as the horns blow a languorous beat.

"Fancy meeting you here," Petra says as she slips onto the barstool next to me, bringing an enticing cloud of citrus and neroli.

The shifter grins and shakes himself as he climbs into a seat. His friends pat him on the back and order another round from the server, a beautiful siren who flutters his eyelashes as he props the tray on his hip and laughs with the group.

"Yes, it's almost like you were following me." I sigh. "Your surveillance skills need work. I clocked you the minute I left the department." Petra might be a good lawyer, but she's a terrible sleuth. I really shouldn't tease her, though. Before I became a corner, what passes for law enforcement in Drahma City, my job was to draw eyes toward me, not away.

Callahan, a Seelie with the power to create any beverage, approaches us and asks, "Can I get you something to drink?"

Petra smiles at him, showing off her straight white teeth and cheekbones that could cut glass. "Sweet Tina, please. And another round for my friend."

He raises his eyes at me in question. I incline my head, and he twists his hand, the drinks appearing before us on the cherrywood bar. Not for the first time, I wonder whether Callahan even wanted to be a bartender or whether his power decided for him.

I suppose what I am doesn't leave me a ton of options either.

When he's left us alone again, Petra speaks. "I wouldn't have to resort to such things if you'd return my messages." She tosses her long dark hair over her shoulder. The lights play against her honeyed skin, and a few heads turn her way from around the room.

To the normal eye, she looks like any other rich, beautiful fae, but she treats her bag too preciously as she adjusts it on the hook below the bar. She doesn't toss her coat on the empty barstool beside her but stands to hang it on the rack. I haven't known her for very long, but I'm certain she doesn't come from money.

"Wouldn't want to come across as too easy," I say. "And also, I want nothing to do with your little project." I grab a handful of pickled popcorn from the bowl between us. It's delicious but not what I want, and I scowl a little at the snack before taking another look around the room.

"Hungry?" Her light brown eyes scan the room. "Nobody here catch your eye?"

"Yes and no. Apparently, they're all doing their evil things at home, selfishly depriving me of a good meal." I replenished myself a few days ago. I shouldn't be this ravenous. Perhaps self-pity is increasing my appetite.

Petra drums her nails on her glass. Her polish matches the plump cherry inside. "I can't sit by and do nothing, Sugar. It's not in my nature."

I throw back my drink and start on the second one. Petra has been hounding me about the crown prince of Eddahn—CP, as everyone calls him—for almost three months. "What you're asking is impossible. He's untouchable. They all are." I use a cocktail stick to spear a piece of popcorn. "Trust me."

She pulls out a blank piece of paper and beckons to a sullen-looking Seelie with a septum piercing, green platform heels, and a black corset. She slides off her stool in the corner and walks over, looking supremely put out.

"Yeah?" she says when she reaches us. I can't blame her for the attitude. It must be profoundly boring to sit in a bar all night waiting for someone to request the news.

"Top stories, please." Petra pushes the paper toward her with one hand while holding out her money with the other. Septum Piercing touches the paper, and it fills with today's current events. She drifts back to her seat, stuffing Petra's money down her top. The band starts up a new song. A few couples revolve on the dance floor, their faces tinted blue by the lighting.

"Congratulations," I say, nodding toward a story about her latest win in court. It was a defense case. Despite Petra's hard-on for taking down CP, the Crown's criminal attorneys are a single pool, from which they're randomly selected for either prosecution or defense.

"Thank you," she says dismissively. She taps a different story.

I'd already seen it, but I read it again to buy time. A butterfly went missing from one of CP's booze- and drug-fueled parties. The party was two months ago, but the reporter probably only just got someone to talk.

There was no doubt in my mind the corners knew about it and hushed it up. There were probably more fae in my department who were in the Crown's pocket than out of it. Then again, it could be sheer incompetence as well.

"Well?" She looks at me expectantly.

I ignore her and let my gaze drift over the rest of the paper. There's an article about repairing the West Bridge, a project that's been dragging on for years. And someone robbed a local apothecary.

Petra's stare practically burns a hole in the side of my face. It's not that I don't understand what she wants—or why she wants it—but it's pointless. Most Seelie with royal blood are as corrupt as they are powerful. Nobody knows that better than I do. And at four-hundred and thirty, I'm not so old that I'm not still irritated by a waste of my time.

"F. Jasper," I say finally, noting the byline on the story about the butterfly. "There's a name I'll no doubt soon see in the obituaries."

It wasn't the first story the reporter had done on the crown prince or other members of the royal family. His weren't the same as the obviously purchased puff pieces the others did. The king and queen might not spend much time in D.C., but their public relations people likely know all about F. Jasper.

"If only," Petra grumbles. I raise my eyebrows as her malevolent feelings call to me. My blood hums. It's not strong, but in my current state, even a shred of ill will is better than nothing.

"You know my ability works on women too, right?" My eyes travel over her skin involuntarily, and the empty well inside me growls.

She shakes herself, and the ripple of ill intention disappears. "I need your help. And don't pretend you're afraid. The Nest offers enough protection that you might be one of the few people who can help me bring him down."

"He's still young. Maybe he'll mature." CP and his three siblings are all only in their early hundreds. The king and queen waited a long time before they brought their potential rivals into the world.

She purses her lips in disdain. After another moment where neither of us says anything, she snaps, "I'm just asking you to do your godsdamn job."

I scoff and shake my head. "I can do my job. But you'd need more than just me to tackle something like this." She needs good people, people who don't have self-destructive habits and constant simmering anger.

"Who?" She sips her drink, eyes on the antique-finished mirror behind the bar.

Sighing, I tick off my fingers, counting the people we'd need on our side to build a solid case against the crown prince. "The evidence collectors, the death examiner, the chief." I push the paper back toward her. "And that's if the Crown doesn't come in and squash the whole thing the minute they get wind of it. You're better off joining forces with this reporter and trying CP in the court of public opinion."

"I'd rather be your dinner." The venom in her voice smells delicious, and I have to stop myself from leaning in.

Smirking, I say, "So it *is* the reporter. Bad date? Unflattering news story?"

She ignores the question and turns to face me. "I know you didn't leave the luxury of the Nest to be a corner for fun. I'm giving you the benefit of the doubt by assuming you had some good intentions."

"You're wrong," I say, frowning. "I was just bored. An incredibly long life will do that to a girl."

Petra and I are not friends. My reasons for becoming a corner are not public knowledge. And while I don't think she'd interfere, there were too many powerful people in the Romans' house that night. I can't risk Linnea's killer finding out and deciding to tie me up like a loose end.

She looks at me for a long time before pulling some money out of her purse and dropping it on the bar. "Fine. I don't know why I bothered."

She retrieves her bag, pauses as if she might try one more time, then snatches up her coat. She storms out in a huff, leaving me with the dregs of whatever animosity she has for the reporter. My need sharpens painfully, the cavern of my magic begging for relief.

The door opens again. Four people walk in, bringing the brisk November air with them. Two do nothing for me, but there's one with a sharp nose and an even sharper jawline. He's got his arm thrown around a petite blond girl. He looks too clean. His pristine white shirt has freshly ironed creases. She's got a proud little tilt to her chin as she surveys the room. The girl thinks she's bagged herself a good one. She has no clue of the danger she's in.

Regardless of whether it's arousal or my unique preferences for anger, hatred, and ill intent, the feeling starts in my neck. Chills begin just below my ears and roll down my shoulders. Desire strokes down my back and over my hips. I roll my neck and exhale in relief at the promise of a good meal.

"Finally," I breathe, closing my eyes and relishing the smell of cruelty coming off him.

Luck is on my side. A message appears in the air in front of the girl. Her face drops as she reads it. Something urgent apparently, as she hastily scoots out of the booth. Her words tumble out. She has to go—so sorry. It's a scene I've watched before—and sometimes orchestrated.

When she's gone, the man's eyes turn hard. He searches the room hungrily, his other companions forgotten. His gaze snags on me, and I give him a sweet but seductive smile. The predator in him scents what he thinks is blood in the water. He gives me a well-practiced, endearing smile, shrugging ruefully at the loss of his date.

I'm about to slide over to him when a note materializes on the bar in front of me. "Damn it."

Only one person I know sends notes with that blood-red paper. Clenching my jaw, I pick it up despite already knowing it won't have any words. When the Dame wants you, she sends only a single kiss. When she's angry, there are two.

If three X's appear? You're dead before you finish reading.

A single kiss. I turn back to the man. His attempt to pretend he hasn't been watching me is laughable. I give him a flirtatious little wink before making my way to the back of the bar. Callahan catches my eye but wisely goes back to cleaning glasses.

I don't have to wait long. The man follows me right into the bathroom. He's trying to play it cool, but his eyes gleam with desire. If I had to guess, his usual method is drugging drinks. He's fae but strikes me as low-powered. Probably works in finance.

"Meet me in the alley," I say, feigning tipsiness, to his reflection in the mirror. He grins, practically panting at how easy it's been to get me alone.

When I walk outside, he's leaning against the wall, foot propped up and arms crossed. He tries to do it surreptitiously, but I catch the way he checks to ensure we're alone in the dark. I don't bother. Inhaling just a taste, I push my hands against his biceps and watch as fear rolls over him like fog. The blood drains from his face as he freezes, trapped. Poor thing tries to resist, but he was too excited about taking advantage of me. Now he's putty in my hands.

Trying to savor the anticipation, I ruffle his perfectly styled hair. I push up on my toes and flick my tongue against the tip of his nose. Oh gods, the rage coming off him. A neat freak. I love being right.

"It's hard, isn't it?" I coo. "You're gliding through life, on top of the world, and then something tilts." I run my nails across his scalp. "Nothing big, just a little shift." I grab his hair—hard—and twist his neck to the side. "And all that power comes tumbling down." I'm close enough he can feel my breath on his cheek. "Suddenly, you find yourself at the very bottom of the food chain."

His eyes widen, and a muscle jumps in his jaw.

"Shhh, I know." I wipe my thumb across my lips and drag it down his white shirt, leaving a long smear of red lipstick.

He emits the faintest squeak, and I chuckle as I lean in. I inhale all his bad intentions, his sadistic thoughts, and his autonomy, at least for the next few hours. Taking his free will for that long isn't required—I could simply feed off him and restrict his useless attempt to fight me off until I've left—but he deserves it. I might even check up on him in a few days.

My power swells, and I groan with satisfaction as it floods my veins. I don't need a mirror to know my skin is practically glowing, the navy in my eyes becoming rich and my cheeks turning a lovely shade of pink. Crackling energy sweeps through my body, fueling my strength and my senses.

I pull back, releasing him, and he stumbles a little. I run my hands down my body and exhale, relishing the tingling after-shocks of full power. The man gives me a vacant stare, and I can almost see him behind those eyes, struggling to get out.

"Run along and be a good boy. I'm done with you." I adjust my coat and pull my hood up to hide my distinctive—and now much shinier—silver hair. He gives me a dutiful nod and marches back into the bar.

Chapter 2
Sugar

The Nest, Drahma City's most famous hotel and pleasure house, sits in the Third Circle. But instead of an avenue of overpriced mansions that should stand between it and the First Circle, there's only a wide inlet from the Corvid Sea.

The moon tonight is just a thin coffee ring in the sky, barely enough light to illuminate the fortress across the dark water.

A boat emerges from the low-hanging fog, gliding under its own power, and bumps gently against the dock.

"Long time no see, sister." Helen grins. "I've missed you." She waits for me to step onto the boat, her straight black hair perfect even in the sea breeze. She's dressed in a charcoal gray sheath dress with the Nest's insignia embroidered in gold on the front.

"Missed you, too." I step aboard, and we exchange a quick hug. Helen and I aren't related by blood, but we're sisters in the way everyone who works at the Nest is family—blood of the battlefield and all that. "Any idea why she sent for me?"

"No clue." Her expression darkens. If Helen, one of the Dame's most loyal and longest serving employees, doesn't know, the Dame is keeping this close.

Interesting.

When I became a corner, I knew it was only a matter of time before she'd come calling. And she has, but it's all been minor stuff, nothing as bad as what I've already done—what I'm already doing. I've managed to keep my nose pretty clean at work so far—no small feat for someone with the ability to control anyone who gives me a dirty look.

The power inside me stirs as we push off into the inky water and head toward my former home. The Dame creates concoctions on the lighter side of legal to heighten her guests' experiences and therefore strengthen the magic they generate for her staff. I know her blends well, having used them myself during the years I worked for her. Despite my recent meal, my skin shivers at the potent emotions reaching out from inside the stone mansion, seeking what they crave most.

"Meet anyone interesting lately?" I ask Helen. "Any tragic poets?"

All concubi, both succubi and incubi, can draw power from sexual excitement—it's why we often run pleasure houses—but some of us, like Helen and me, get an even better boost from other emotions. After years of frequenting coffeehouses and art exhibitions, Helen discovered she has a special taste for hope and wistfulness. It sounds mind-numbingly dull to me, but who am I to judge?

"Nothing but a bunch of affected whiners," she says. "It's worse because they don't even know they're affected," she grumbles. "People just don't feel their emotions like they used to."

I give her a sympathetic smile as we hit the other side of the inlet and hop off. It's a common lament among the older concubi. Emotions are so complicated now, all of them tinged or watered down with something else. Nobody feels true love, or true anything.

The Nest's austere exterior belies the opulent furnishings inside. The Dame prides herself on making anyone who comes here feel like they belong to this world of class and indulgence—for a price, of course. Everywhere you look is a sumptuous buffet of jewel tones and metallics. Soft lighting glows from beneath amethyst lamps, and an enormous fireplace spreads warmth along the swirling indigo and green rugs. Hints of magnolia and jasmine float through the air.

There are about thirty customers drinking wine and sampling delicate appetizers as they meet with the hosts. It's not just concubi. The Dame employs a variety of fae to meet every need.

I wave and smile at a few friends as I pass through the guest area, headed for the guarded doors leading to the Dame's office. We pass some customers admiring the paintings as we walk down the corridor.

"That's what I'm looking for," a blond man says. "Someone wild and unrestrained." He and his friends are eyeing a painting of a succubus wearing an elaborate and scintillating leopard costume. All the paintings in the hall show the hosts in various animal forms, each with thin metal bars painted over them to give the appearance of a caged wild animal.

Helen and I share a knowing smile. The paintings are a private joke among the staff. If anyone bothered to look closely enough, they'd see the lock is on the wrong side. It's the viewers, the customers who follow their wants and desires into the Nest, who are locked inside.

"Good luck," Helen says, stopping before enormous engraved metal doors. "I'll wait here to take you back when you're done."

I give her another smile and step inside. The floral scent is stronger here, layered with something deeper. Crossing a plush red rug, I approach her desk.

The Dame isn't sitting. She stands before a wall of mirrors enchanted to show every room in the Nest. In one, a man crawls on his knees before a butterfly and a succubus, both clad in black leather masks. In another, an incubus bathes a woman in a bathtub filled with deep purple rose petals.

Considering the concubi's ability to control anyone whose emotions match their needs, the mirrors are less about security and more about customer satisfaction. I consider myself pretty good, but nobody reads body language like the Dame. She always knows how to make those little tweaks to ensure someone's experience is truly memorable.

"Dame," I say, "you called for me?"

She holds up a taloned finger, leaning forward to squint at a mirror. She waves a hand in front of it and speaks to the hosts inside. "Kylie, you could be a lot rougher. He can take it." Her words will flow into the room but be inaudible to the customer, a portly bear shifter wearing nothing but rags. Kylie leans down, absorbing his lust but leaving him his control, before smacking him hard across the face. He shudders in pleasure.

My former boss and mentor turns; the movement casts a sea of sparkles against the walls from her diaphanous white gown. I let myself feel the awe I know she likes. Her body looks like someone took the softest down pillow and cinched a belt tight at the center. If she were human, I'd put her around fifty, but she's closer to seven hundred. As she walks around the desk, her hips and honey-blond hair sway like a warm current.

The Dame's eyes appraise me. "I was going to ask if you've eaten, but now I won't bother. You look gorgeous."

It's more of a professional assessment than a compliment, but I take it. "Thank you."

A beat passes. Her brow furrows as if she's deciding whether it was worth bringing me here. Finally, she says, "The Crown has asked for my help with something. What I'm about to tell you cannot leave this room."

"Understood." A sick feeling creeps into my gut. What has CP done now? Did they find the butterfly Petra was talking about? Did he do something to her?

"It concerns Princess Lira," the Dame says.

"Lira?" My eyebrows shoot up. Princess Lira, fourth in line to the throne, barely spends any time in Drahma City. Her sister, third in line, was married to the neighboring country of Traeva twenty years ago, and Lira splits her time between her sister's home and Zavrik, Eddahn's capital. I've only seen her a handful of times in the last ten years. Fenrik always said Lira was the smartest of the royal children.

The Dame leans back against her desk. "She wants to be Made."

"What?" I grimace in incredulity. "Why?"

Seelie fae possess a base level of power in addition to their unique gift, like shifting or elemental control, and they can only reproduce the old-fashioned way. Unseelie, like succubi, vampires, and butterflies, don't have that same base magic, but we have other abilities, including the power to turn others, to Make them like us.

Long ago, some Seelie thought they could get the best of both worlds by being Made by the Unseelie. Most of them died, and those who didn't drastically reduced their lifespans. The practice was outlawed and is punishable by death. Only humans can be Made safely.

Does that mean it never happens? Of course not. But why would the princess risk it?

"She has her reasons," the Dame replies. Meaning either Lira hadn't told her or she wouldn't be providing them to me. "Have you spoken to Fenrik recently?"

I still at the mention of the man second in line for the throne. Walls I've spent years perfecting rise inside me. "No. Obviously not," I say, my voice glacial.

The Dame's eyes, framed by long lashes, merely blink in response, her expression unbothered. Only years of practice hiding my emotions from my clients keeps me from fidgeting.

"You know, when you told me you were leaving us for a job with the corners, I could have taken that as an insult. After I welcomed you into the Nest, gave you a roof over your head, and allowed you the freedom to take only the customers you wanted, I could have considered it a slap in the face. But I didn't. Do you know why?"

I hold her gaze as if doing so will keep her from seeing through me. "Because you know why I did it."

She exhales, her eyes distant. "I didn't realize dying was the only way to ensure your continued loyalty. I guess everything else I did was a waste of time." There's no bite in her tone, only resignation. The Dame never even met Linnea. She was shocked when I told her I was leaving her, leaving the Nest, to become a corner.

She straightens and sashays toward the fireplace on the opposite wall. I frown, discomfited, as she retrieves a long cigarette holder, inserts a deep red cigarette, and lights it on a tapered candle.

"I'm sorry, Dame."

She inhales deeply before tapping the ash into a crystal bowl. The candlelight caresses her golden hair.

"What do you want from me? To cover up the Making?"

"No. Obviously not," she says, mimicking my earlier dismissive tone. "If we do it right, it shouldn't need covering up. What I want is a candidate. I don't want anyone associated with the Nest."

I scoff. "Trust me, I wasn't about to volunteer."

She continues as if I haven't spoken. "And not a butterfly, for gods' sake."

We both cringe. Butterflies literally turn people to goo to Make them. Historically, they have the worst rate out of all the Unseelie for keeping their intended progeny alive, even the humans.

"Lira doesn't have a preference?" If it works, she'll get the best of Seelie and Unseelie power. While I have no love for vampires, the enhanced strength would be nice.

"No. But we'll need to choose carefully." She takes a long drag before blowing pink smoke in the shape of a perfect heart.

I snort, earning a disdainful look. Choose carefully, indeed. The Unseelie would have to be desperate enough for the money but not so desperate they'd become a liability. Even if they succeed and Lira doesn't die, the Crown can't be trusted. Our Maker might still end up dead. This person would need to be either smart enough to protect themselves or too naïve to realize the danger.

There's a candy dish on her desk with pastel-colored sugared almonds inside. I poke around, looking for the violet ones and trying to suppress my curiosity. I fail. "Who asked you?"

She makes her way back to the desk and sits down. "Lira herself."

"She was here?" I pause, my hand halfway to my mouth with the sweets.

"I was summoned to Zavrik," she says. "I met with Lira alone. Not even the guards were present." I give her a pointed look.

"If you're asking whether I know whether the king and queen approve of her request, I only have her word for it."

"But you're still willing to risk it?"

"I may have implied you were my first choice for the assignment." She blows another heart of smoke while she throws a glance at the wall of mirrors.

Right. Of course. Lira knows all about my history with her brother. She and Fenrik are close. Hopefully, she knows nothing of my current activities. Lira would expect me to check with Fenrik. But why then wouldn't she bring the king and queen to the meeting with the Dame? Or her brother?

"I think it very unlikely the king and queen would risk being seen with me," the Dame says, reading my mind. Her lips twist into a smile. She loves her unsavory reputation.

I push my hands into my pockets, casting about for the right thing to say. "She could *die*. We could be responsible for the death of a royal."

"You say that as if I did not consider the request before I asked you." She arches a perfectly manicured eyebrow at me.

"Just figured one of us should say it out loud." I exhale. "I'll consider it, but..." I shake my head. Why would Lira want this? Making a human will cure them of existing illnesses, but I don't know if that works for the Seelie.

The Dame writes something down before sliding it across the desk. "She's prepared to pay quite the finder's fee if the Making is successful."

I pick it up and inhale sharply. "That is a lot of zeroes." But my mind isn't on the money, despite missing the luxuries of the Nest. My train of thought suddenly shoots sideways and up, to a small room on the third floor of Stanley Roman's house. Hope picks up its head inside me, sniffing at the possibility of finally getting momentum on Linnea's case. "I want half for finding a willing candidate and the other half if it's successful."

The Dame nods. "Naturally."

"And I want a favor."

Chapter 3
Draven

"Gather round, children!" Captain Gibson's voice cuts through the chatter, followed immediately by a chorus of groans. Kurt and I play a quick game of rock, paper, scissors to decide who has to get up. All around the department floor, the other corners are engaging in a similar back-and-forth with their partners. I lose and begrudgingly make my way across the long rectangular room.

I sidestep two uniformed corners herding an irate-looking man wearing a top hat and monocle into one of the temporary holding cells along the back wall. Probably an actor. Drahma City is lousy with them. I stop by the coffee station to grab a cup as the other on-duty detectives line up in front of the captain.

"Oh, sorry," Tindra says as she reaches past me to take a napkin and drops it. It floats to rest on the worn beige-and-maroon-checkered floor. She bites her lip before saying, "Mind grabbing that for me, Draven?"

"Of course." I avoid looking directly at Kurt, who is pretending to swoon, as I bend and snatch it from the floor. She lets her fingers brush mine as she takes it out of my hand.

"You want?" Tindra pulls a cinnamon roll from the tray next to the coffee. She uses her ability to grow the pastry until it's twice the size. She winks, and it takes all my willpower not to look at my partner, who's probably giggling like a child at this display. "It's not the only thing I could grow. But you probably don't need any help in that department, do you, Draven?" She pointedly looks at my crotch.

Clearing my throat, I say, "I'm good, thanks," before quickly sidestepping her and heading over to everyone's least favorite annual event.

Gibson holds a glass jar filled with little slips of paper and shakes it menacingly as he yells, "That's right! Step right up for this year's cold case lottery!" I take my place in line, sipping the perpetually burnt coffee. "I want a close rate better than last year's pathetic two percent, you hear me?"

Lief Cowper, an Unseelie siren with bluish-gray hair, reaches into the jar and pulls out a slip. He squints at the name and date and mutters under his breath as he shuffles back to his desk. Samantha Pike, a fellow vampire and friend, goes next. She and others each react with varying degrees of dismay as they draw their aged cases.

"Get us a nice, easy one, partner!" Kurt calls from across the room, his constantly bloodshot eyes gleaming with encourage-ment. "Something from this century would be nice."

Despite the hound shifter's permanently weary look, he's endlessly upbeat. Our partnership is a source of amusement for the rest of the precinct since my species is not known for our warm and cuddly vibes. For him, I make a show of swirling my hand in the jar before finally pulling a slip.

Linnea Faroe

The date is only a few years ago, which makes me think this is going to be harder than the ancient cases. With something this recent, if it wasn't solved, there was a good reason. Or, more likely, a bad one. I grimace at Kurt, who shrugs good-naturedly.

Once the last case is drawn, Gibson barks, "Get your case files from Research & Evidence by the end of the day!" He turns and carelessly tosses his office door shut behind him. The beveled glass with "Captain" printed on it rattles on impact. He's broken it half a dozen times since I became a corner.

"I'll grab it," Kurt says, holding out his hand for the slip. I pass it over as a flurry of notes appears in the metal tin I use for an inbox. I check for any marked urgent.

Twenty minutes later, Kurt returns holding a disappointingly thin file.

"That's it?" I groan, eyeing the slim folder. "Where's the evidence?" The question is rhetorical. If there isn't a box with clothing, weapons, hair, etc., it likely means it was never collected or was deliberately "lost."

Kurt sighs, flipping it open. "Body was found at Twelve Roman St., First Circle, home of Stanley Roman." He slides an image of the stately mansion across the desk—a palace of marble columns and massive windows.

His nose twitches as he quickly skims the report before letting out a low whistle. "Any guesses how long the corners had to investigate before the Romans lawyered up and they were kicked out?"

I lean back, steepling my fingers. The Romans are one of the oldest, wealthiest families in Drahma City, rivaled only by the royals. Officer Beadle walks behind Kurt on his way to the bathroom, and I frown. I'm pretty sure Beadle and one other officer in the room take bribes from people like the Romans. For a death, a likely murder, on their own property, they would have paid handsomely to keep the investigation short.

"Twenty-four hours?" I guess.

Kurt grimaces, holding his hand up and wiggling three fingers. "Try again."

"Shit. Three hours?" I rake a hand through my dark hair. "Who alerted the corners?"

"Anonymous note," he replies, cocking his head as he scans the page. "Nobody claimed it. Detectives on the scene said the occupants didn't even know anything was amiss until the corners knocked on their door." He pulls out the remaining documents and organizes them neatly into statements, images, and reports. He growls. "Oh, look. According to this, CP stumbled out of the house right as the detectives showed up. Refused to answer any questions, of course."

"Was he ever questioned?"

Kurt flips through a few more pages. "Not sure, but there are a few other reports. Maybe he's in one of those."

Shaking my head, I pick up the first image. It's surrounded by a fuzzy black border, a requisite for all recorders who work for the department. Linnea Faroe, a small woman with mousy brown hair, lies on her side, eyes closed, blood pooling beneath her stomach. The sight shouldn't bother me. I've seen many dead bodies, even before I became a corner. But my jaw still clenches at the stark image.

"Stabbed," Kurt supplies before I can ask. "Human. She was some kind of maid."

"Who was first on the scene?" I take in the bare wood floor beneath her. A dilapidated dresser sitting in the corner of the images catches my eye. It's filled with books, many of which I recognize as fae and human folklore. Another image shows the rest of the room, just a chair and a single orb light. The Romans likely never set foot in her sparse bedroom.

"Cowper and Peterson," he replies. Peterson retired three years ago. Glancing at Cowper, I discover he's already looking my way. I raise my brows at him, and he turns back to his desk. Kurt doesn't look up as he says, "He's not bad. He'll talk to us."

More notes materialize on my desk. I skim the first one and push to my feet. "We have to go. Looks like another ulgashen attack in the Hollows."

***

Kurt leaves the file in his desk, and we grab our gear and head downstairs to the gates. Drahma City is walkable. And there are transport fae who make their living using their abilities to get you where you need to go. But many of the busier buildings, including the corners' department, have stone-rimmed portals, which connect to critical points around the city.

The portal lets us out among a copse of trees within the thin forest that lines the edge of the water, just before the East Bridge. There's no point in using West Bridge. It's one strong breeze from collapsing.

On this side of the Fugue River, in the upper city, things are orderly. Once we get across the bridge, it's as if the city shifts, sliding into chaos. In the Hollows, the streets are alive with their own volatile magic, warping and reshaping seemingly at random.

Rushing through, we pass shops that spill out onto the sidewalk and teetering apartment blocks. Some streets dead-end on Tuesdays but not on Fridays. Others look long and straight but will trap you in an endless loop until they see fit to release you. Most believe it's because the Hollows is part of the original city, the part that hasn't been paved over. The old magic twists and combusts into the maze-like streets favored by humans and low-powered fae.

We smell the blood a few minutes before the first ulgashen appears. She's thin as a reed and almost ten feet tall. It's like someone grabbed a hairless cat at each end and stretched before setting it back down on two legs. Her leathery black skin reflects the light from the nearby shops.

Ulgashen are mindless feeders. They roam in packs but will quickly turn on one another if food is scarce. This is the third attack this year, which makes zero sense because the creatures are slow to breed and avoid big cities. They usually stay in their caves in the mountains along the river. And despite having claws as long as my fingers, they don't normally hunt, preferring dead fish and whatever else washes into their lair.

My fangs snap out, and I unsheathe two short swords from my leather shoulder holster. Kurt grabs his own weapons and prepares to circle behind her when someone whistles somewhere above us. A young man leans out the window and points to our left, where another ulgashen lumbers out from behind a dumpster.

"Shit." I stow my weapons to fire off a note asking for backup. By the time I've rearmed myself, a third ulgashen has appeared, dragging a motionless body caked in blood. "Damn it."

I run forward, sliding under the legs of the female and slicing my blade across her ankle. She shrieks, a blood-curdling sound that probably woke anyone who wasn't already watching the fight. The street creates a high bank on one side, tossing me back toward the others as Kurt bounds forward.

"Over here, asshole!" He jumps and drives his dagger deep into the thigh of a male, dragging it down and narrowly avoiding the ulgashen's claws as it lashes out at him. It loses its balance, toppling over onto the street. I use my extra speed, darting beneath the female again and slamming my baton across her knee. She goes down with a snarl as I sprint toward the third.

Like all Seelie, Kurt has some ability to move objects without touching them. He pushes the male into the female, and in their panic and pain, they turn on one another. A sickening crunch comes from the male as the female bites into his shoulder.

I put on another burst of speed and aim for the third one, jumping on his back and wrapping my hands around his spindly neck. He reaches behind, grabbing for me. Pain ignites as he drags his claws up my back. "Fucking Helva!" I grab his neck and use my enhanced strength to rip his head from his body. We both fall to the ground.

Kurt is darting back and forth beside the other two, waiting for an opening, but they're doing all the work themselves. The female jabs her claws into the male's chest. The sound of his cracking bones bounces off the brick walls as she snaps his elongated spine. While she's distracted, Kurt drags his dagger through her throat.

The two of us stop to catch our breath and wipe the ulgashen's inky purple blood from our skin. It has a sickeningly sweet scent. There's a halfhearted clap from above, and I turn to the kid who warned us before. He gives a final single clap, looking unimpressed in the way only teenagers can, before disappearing from the window. Even the streets flatten out, sensing the show is over.

"Thank you, thank you. We'll be here all week," Kurt says, hands on his knees as he catches his breath.

I stow my weapons and retract my fangs. "What the hel? Where are they even coming from?" I furrow my brow. The ulgashen never attack the upper city, and I doubt it's just because they don't like crossing a bridge.

The two of us step over the twig-like bodies to reach the dead man. The ulgashen abandoned the body when the fight started. His head lies at an unnatural angle, courtesy of the lethal gash to his throat. But the blood on his neck is dry. There's dirt covering every inch of his clothes. Did the ulgashen dig him up?

"Human. Looks like he's been dead for too long." Kurt kneels by the body, fishing through the man's clothes for ID. He shakes his head when he comes up empty.

"There goes that lead." Necromancers have the power to truly steal someone back from the dead if they've only been gone a short time. But most of the time, and the main reason they're employed by corners, they can only bring them back for a brief period to provide witness testimony.

"You call for backup?" a uniformed officer calls out to me. Her name tag says "Sawyer." She and her partner both look green as they warily take in the surrounding streets. The magic vibrates in the air, ripples that distort buildings and refract the light. Somewhere in the darkness, a bike bell trills.

"Took you long enough." I walk toward them, frowning at the way the road suddenly steepens, slowing my steps.

"We got stuck in a roundabout right after the bridge. Damn place is like a funhouse." She shudders. Before I can reply, her eyes widen, and she shouts at something behind me.

I'm fast. Faster than most fae and even faster than many vampires. But when I turn, it's like pushing through molasses. The movement of Sawyer's mouth falling open as she stumbles back takes a lifetime. It's hours, days, before I'm even facing the right direction. An orb light in the corner dies and lights up again, in time for me to see every awful detail.

I'm not sure I manage a single step before the claws of an ulgashen slowly and audibly pierce Kurt's chest. My partner's face goes white, the color draining as the female we thought was dead takes her parting shot. She pulls back her claws with a horrible squelching sound, taking half of Kurt's insides with her before collapsing behind him.

"Kurt!" I shout, my heart hammering and the worst sort of dread consuming my everything thought as time suddenly speeds up. The air is thick with my fear as I rush over to him, uselessly putting my hands against his wounds. His blood pours out from holes thicker than my wrist.

He's frozen, balancing but not standing of his own will. The muscle and sinew holding him together is shredded, pulling apart like melted cheese while his hands twitch at his sides. Kurt gives a final exhale and falls against me as I drop to my knees.

Chapter 4
Sugar

"Bet you're glad you wore pants today?" Matt says. I snort as I stare down through the clear glass dance floor to the exposed rooms beneath us.

A few thousand years ago, there'd been a sprawling metropolis in this same spot. But an unhealable plague had taken out eighty percent of the population. The remaining twenty percent were so overwhelmed at the thought of cleaning out the city that they simply built right over it, leaving a dark warren of rooms, tunnels, and bone dust.

Other buildings display the ruins of the city below for a bit of historical character. At Tradimento, a popular nightclub, circular beds and plush pink couches fill the lower level, giving the patrons a salacious view of anyone dancing above.

"Is he down there?" I ask. Matt had received the message just after ten. Male, dead, possible stabbing.

"Not sure." He strokes his impressively bushy mustache as we walk further into the club. At his height, it should take me two steps for every one of his, but my partner takes his time, absorbing everything. "Damn it." He scrapes his shoes against the floor as we leave the dance floor and cross into a carpeted area. "Stupid glitter. Sticks to everything."

A short staircase leads to a large set of metal doors. Above them hangs an illuminated sign that reads "Theater." A man with slicked-back hair, wearing an impeccable black suit, exits the doors just as we reach the top of the stairs.

"Detectives?" he asks, adjusting his cufflinks, square-cut diamonds and probably worth about ten grand each.

We nod, pulling out our badges. "This is Detective Writh," Matt says, gesturing to me, "and I'm Detective Diaz. You the owner? Mind showing us to the body?"

"Yes, I'm Horatio Stone. Per your request, I've sequestered all the guests and staff in the theater. Is there a chance you could question some of them first so they can go home?"

My eyebrow quirks. The way he says "some of them" makes me think there are some very specific guests he wants gone.

"Some VIPs getting antsy?" I let my power loosen, feeling out the emotions inside the building. It's a chaotic mix, but a few stand out, calling to my need.

Stone clears his throat and crosses his hands behind his back. "CP is here with his friends. He's not yet bothered by this inconvenience, but his moods are...mercurial."

I frown. *Mercurial* is putting it lightly. He's probably high as a kite, but as soon as he comes down, he'll level this club if he's not allowed to leave.

"Show us the body first. Then I'll get His Highness squared away." I resist the urge to roll my neck at the thought of dealing with the crown prince right now.

"Right this way. I'm going to take you through the staff area. It's quicker than using the guest route." He beckons us to follow.

Tradimento is still beautiful inside, but seeing it under the harsh glare of the white orb lights instead of their usual sultry gold is jarring. Dirty glasses and empty bottles clutter the tables. Matt rolls his eyes as we pass a pair of red panties dangling off a lamp. The air reeks of heavy perfume, booze, and sweat.

Stone leads ups behind the green-and-gold bar, and my shoes squelch on floor mats sticky with spilled alcohol and mixers. He glances back apologetically. "I didn't have anyone clean, assuming you wouldn't like it."

"Thank you," I reply. A bar doesn't even crack the top twenty messiest crime scenes Matt and I have seen.

We step through a door marked "Employees Only" into the staff area. The gray walls are covered in signs reminding employees how to treat the customers. We pass several unmarked doors, and Stone explains they lead to private exits from rooms for better-paying patrons. We round a corner and exit back into the public area, beside a stairwell with green marble steps that shine under gold metal banisters. Each landing has glass doors leading to balconies or, at this level, the street.

"Emergency exit?" I ask as we step out through the glass doors into an alleyway. Staff circle the body, protecting it from prying eyes.

"Guests may leave through it, but the door locks from the outside so no one can enter. A bouncer is usually stationed outside to make sure no one sneaks people in."

"Usually?" Matt says, glancing back toward the stairwell.

Stone runs a hand down his neck. "Kosta is in the theater with the others. A guest was ill on the sidewalk, so he left his post to bring her inside to wait for a healer. When he returned, he saw the body through the door."

"Nobody else saw? Wouldn't there have been a lot of people in the area?" I ask. The staff part for us as we approach.

Our victim is a Seelie man in a vibrant blue suit. He lies on his front, his blood dark in the dim alley light. Crouching, I pull his jacket open and search for ID. His head is turned to the side, revealing a six-inch gash across his neck. Fae heal faster than humans, but not that fast. And whatever his base healing power might have been, he doesn't look like he'd have been conscious to use it.

"It was ten o'clock," Stone explains. "Most people on this side of the club would have been watching the show." He snaps his fingers, summoning a blond with cat eyes. She hands me a piece of paper with a detailed schedule with showtimes, employee names, and shifts. There must be more than thirty names on it.

"Thank you," I say, handing the paper to Matt. We exchange a knowing look. Stone went through a lot of effort to get us this level of detail so fast. He clearly wants us gone as quickly as possible. Fae love a scandal, so murder is good for business, but only if the club is open. Flipping through the victim's wallet, I note the name but don't say it out loud.

A faint snicking sound in my pocket announces a message. I pull it out, along with a few others I'd missed from today. "The evidence collectors are here." Turning to Stone, I say, "Could you show them back here, please?"

"Yes, of course." He sweeps away, leaving me to size up the employees, scanning for any ill intent. Matt checks the area, noting the streets on either side of this alleyway and the surrounding businesses. Tradimento is pretty big, but there are two other clubs and some restaurants within walking distance. It's also in the Second Circle, near Lekotto Park, so there are more than a few places into which our killer could have disappeared.

Matt and I wait until the evidence collectors appear, a team of fae with powers conducive to gathering and cataloging everything from fur to blood, before we head into the theater. The city has more than a hundred theaters showing a range of performances. Tradimento's is decorated with leather couches, black velvet curtains, and flickering red orb lights.

Stone stopped the performance, but the band keeps playing softly onstage. The club's patrons are still drinking and laughing, nearly oblivious to their confinement. CP is easy to spot, surrounded by a swarm of admirers, one of whom is paying him some "special" attention while he plays cards with a few of the actors.

"Detective Writh! Here for the show?" he calls, turning toward me with a malicious grin and adjusting his dark gray suit jacket, which likely costs more than my apartment. The fae on her knees quickly repositions herself. "Maybe you'd like to join me. Rita can make room." Rita, a butterfly, flutters her gossamer wings indignantly at the potential competition.

His pale blue eyes are glassy but still hold that mean edge. I estimate we've got ten minutes before he turns violent, twenty before his slimy lawyer shows up.

"Did you know him?" I ask. "Carter Fox?"

The name draws sharp inhales from a few people. Behind me, I know Matt is marking anyone who doesn't look surprised.

"Seen him around." CP flicks his fingers, and a vial floats out of his pocket and dumps itself on the table. One of his lackeys rushes forward to cut the pink powder into four thin lines. CP snorts one before adding, "Does fashion shit. Has his own paper."

"You ever see anyone fight with him?" I'm careful not to cross my arms or touch any of my weapons. If I make a single defensive gesture, he'll see it as weakness. I'm not afraid of him, and I don't have time for him to showboat for his followers.

"No fucking teeth!" CP roars suddenly, grabbing Rita by the neck and flinging her across the room as he rises from his chair. She tumbles through the air before regaining her balance and leveling out. She tries hard to feign indifference as she drifts to the ground.

I hold the prince's gaze as I repeat my question.

He prowls toward me, zipping his pants. I'm not short, but he has a good six inches on me. He slides a hand around my waist, pulling me closer, and drags his nose up my neck. I hold back a sigh at this unnecessary display of his power. Short blond stubble grazes my cheek as his lips come within a breath of mine.

"Nope," he pops the P before stepping back with a cruel smirk. "We're out of here!" His entourage springs to life, following him out. As he passes, he drops his voice to a threatening whisper. "See you around, Writh."

"A wellspring, as always," Matt grumbles when he's gone. I rub my thumb against my thigh in frustration, willing myself not to take out my irritation on any potential witnesses.

We start with the women who accompanied Fox to the club. He'd brought two recorders with him, fae with the ability to transmit what they see into words and pictures, to help document the night for his fashion paper.

"We met him here at nine. He was his normal self, excited about the evening. We were led to a VIP table, and after chatting with a few people, he went outside to answer some notes. That was the last time we saw him alive," the woman named Sarah says.

"You two always come as a pair, or can she also speak?" Matt asks, gesturing to Cathy, the other woman. He looks tired, probably dreaming of shifting and getting a good night's sleep at the bottom of his pond.

"Yes, she can speak," Sarah snaps. "I was trying to be efficient. We were together the whole time."

I tilt my head toward Cathy. "Would you mind showing us?"

Cathy shrugs. "Sure." She pulls a large notebook from her bag. As she stares at it, it fills with a description and pictures of their night with Fox, right until the moment we begin questioning them. She tears off the pages and hands them to me.

"And you?" I ask Sarah. She huffs but repeats the process, handing me her own set of notes and images, which contain far fewer pages than Cathy's.

"Thank you. We may need to ask you some more questions, but you're free to go for now." I offer them both a polite smile. Sarah grabs Cathy's arm and marches off.

The staff are far chattier. More than a dozen servers, bartenders, ushers, dancers, and actors tell us all they know about Fox. He's a regular at the club. Nicer than some of the other VIPs, but still kind of a dick sometimes.

"He was a good tipper, and that's all that matters here," a blond server named Sigrid says. She sits on a swing suspended from the ceiling, wearing a bodysuit made entirely of tiny black crystals. "Carter wasn't here to party; he was here to work. He didn't care if you got his drink wrong, but if you messed up his pictures or his interviews, he'd get pissed." An usher and another server standing next to her nod in agreement.

"Anyone he get particularly pissed at?" I ask.

Sigrid and the other server, Candy, who wears pink crystals, shake their heads, but the usher, a stout guy with "Bradley" written on his vest, tips his head up, thinking about it.

"Not really. But he had some publicity deal with Horatio, and I once saw him walk out of the office like he was annoyed."

"Annoyed?" I ask.

"Yeah. Not angry, just kind of irritated," Bradley clarifies.

"And what about Horatio?" I ask. "Was he also annoyed?"

Bradley shrugs. "Wouldn't know. I was in the hall. I only saw Carter leave, and he shut the door behind him. But Horatio isn't really the type to kill someone like that. He would never get blood on his suit." Both servers laugh. The movement causes their outfits to emit a tinkling sound.

"Did either of you speak to him tonight?"

Candy shakes her head, but Sigrid says, "Sure. I waited on him downstairs. Just drink orders. Oh, he asked whether CP was going to be here. I said I didn't know."

I nod. Someone like Fox would definitely want to be seen in the same place as CP.

Bradley shrugs. "I only said a few words to him. Just showed him where his seats were."

"Well, thank you both. We'll be in touch if we have any other questions," Matt says. Once they've left and we're alone on the stage, he turns to me. "You get anything from anyone? Other than the dickball set to inherit the throne?"

"No," I say. "But I wouldn't expect to. If the killer's still here, they've already scratched that itch."

Chapter 5
Sugar

It's after three in the morning when I make my way over the Fugue. The bridges are more like ramps descending from the elevated city proper down into the lower level of the Hollows. Looking across from the old city, one can only see the face of a great, looming wall. It casts everything into twilight well before the sun sets. Even my hair dims here, blending in with all the other shadows lying in wait.

The muddy cobblestones shift beneath my feet, creating an incline where none was before. Sighing in frustration, I speak aloud to the magic. "I appreciate the warning, but I know he's there, and I'm going in anyway." The street refuses to level out, clearly disappointed in me.

When I open the door, Alaric is sitting on my couch, one arm slung over the back, drinking the last of my good booze. He throws back the dark brown liquid and grins. I ignore him as I go into the kitchen, pour myself a glass of water, and rummage in the cabinets for something to eat. He comes up behind me, grips my hips, and grinds his cock against my ass. The same cock that, only a few hours ago, was shoved down the throat of a butterfly who'd dared to graze him with her teeth.

Before tonight, I hadn't seen the crown prince in months. He disappears for a while but always returns to terrorize his favorite playground. His presence is like a clock, a reminder of how much time has passed and how little I've achieved.

When I refuse to react to his attention, he says, "Oh, are you mad at me, Sugar? I love it when you're mad." He bites down on my neck before snaking a hand between my legs and rubbing me through my jeans.

Internally, I curse as my power surges, salivating over the ruthless thoughts he's clearly thinking, dying for a taste. Such a delicious meal being just out of reach... The prince's talented fingers... The heady mix sends a forbidden heat cascading through my body. It's bordering on addiction at this point. At least, that's how I justify it.

I shut the cabinet door and step out of his grasp. Turning to him, I demand, "Did you kill Fox?"

Alaric acts as if he didn't hear the question, prowling forward and relieving me of my jacket. He tosses it on the floor before running his hands over my chest. My hunger sharpens as he chuckles darkly. He's angry too. Whatever he's thinking would definitely have someone spilling blood.

He pops open the buttons of my shirt. "Why the fuck would I tell you if I did?"

My traitorous body responds to his touch. "It would save me some time and paperwork. Why should I bother investigating a crime that won't result in a conviction?"

I push away from him to the drinks cupboard and pull out a bottle of red wine. Alaric watches in silence as I pull down a glass, pour myself a sizable amount, and take a long drink. It's delicious but does nothing to slake my thirst.

The Dame wasn't kidding when she said she put a roof over my head. When I came to Drahma City fifteen years ago, I was broke and didn't know a soul. Concubi tend to live in groups, but I was without a nest. She was the one who helped me understand which emotion would satisfy me more than any other and taught me how to charge for that experience.

Alaric and I met when I was still working at the Nest and giving men like him the taste of something they'd never experienced before—submission. But not him. Even under the shitty attitude and worse behavior, some part of him remembered he was a prince and would not submit to me or any of the doms.

"Yeah right, baby. Where would the fun be in that? Besides, don't you need to run around after the bad guys? To at least pretend you're not one of them?" He leans back against the counter, crossing his arms and smirking. Whatever sadistic fantasies he has in his head increase, and every nerve in my body screams at me to take what I want from him. "I know what Lira asked you to do." His voice is icy, and my blood purrs.

Raising an eyebrow, I say, "Oh?" Lira isn't stupid. Alaric, with his partying and bed-hopping, is a liability. I'd be surprised if she told him anything they didn't want him accidentally disclosing in a drug-fueled haze. "And what's that?"

There's that anger again. This time, it flashes through his eyes, the tick of his jaw. "You're going to Make her." He stands up, crowding me against the counter, a wall of muscle and cruelty.

"No. I won't be Making anyone," I say. Alaric has his own network of spies. I suspect all the royal children do. It's impressive he found out, but it's clear he doesn't have the whole story. "Why does your sister want it done?"

I'd tossed around a lot of theories since I'd heard. Scientific discovery, incurable disease—all of them were less likely than the last.

"What does it matter? You're going to do it anyway." He brushes nonexistent lint off his shoulder as he says it, the suspicion clear in his eyes. He doesn't know. "Or did you suddenly grow a backbone? Or a conscience?"

The glass thankfully doesn't crack when I slam it onto the counter. "I'm the one without a conscience? Fuck you, Alaric."

The speed with which he moves is a testament to his power. In one breath, he spins me roughly and shoves me face down on the counter. I hiss as he grips my hair and twists my head to face him.

"Exactly. Your soul is as black as mine, Sugar." He yanks down my pants, then makes quick work of his own buttons. He slides along my skin, and my nipples harden against the cold countertop. Guilt consumes me even as my arousal spikes.

"Did you know some of my thoughts make you wetter than others?" His voice is a low threat in my ear as he touches me.

I bite my tongue hard enough to draw blood to keep from moaning.

He never tells me what he's thinking about. Different thoughts change my craving, alter the taste. It's the difference between devouring a dripping piece of meat or a tart cherry pie. But the prince would never reveal what horrifying thoughts make my power want him so much, too afraid I'd be able to replace him.

I'm not sure I'll ever be able to, no matter the reasons I started this or how sick it is. He'll never willingly give up control and let me feed off him. But he knows I could, knows if I really want to, I could use my power to make him my bitch. He gets off on knowing I wouldn't, couldn't. His family would have me executed on the spot.

Would they, though? The thought regularly pushes itself into my head. It throws my willingness and treachery into stark relief. Even if I can't use my power, I don't have to be here, don't have to keep allowing this to happen. A familiar unease crawls through me along with the growing pleasure.

He tightens his grip before slamming into me. I cry out, clutching the countertop and knocking over the wine. The bottle smashes against the counter, splattering red droplets all over the walls and cabinets.

"This is what you deserve, isn't it, Sugar? You're not meant for precious Fenrik. This is what you're good for. This is what you want." He bites hard into my shoulder, and my claws snap out at the pain. I drag them down, leaving deep gouges in the tile.

"Does it kill you, knowing you could be the one screwing me over but can't? Does it make you seethe with rage and lust, knowing I own you and not even someone with all your power can get the tiniest taste of me? Does it?" he demands.

"Yes," I said, my hip bones rubbing painfully against the wood.

"Yes, what?" He pounds into me faster.

"Yes, my prince."

***

Afterward, he buttons his pants in silence, and I try to pull myself together. Familiar shame burns in my throat, but I never let him see it. Anger or indifference are the only safe emotions. He grabs his jacket from the couch and leaves without a word.

I'm staring into my darkening kitchen, wondering again why I keep doing this, when a message appears on my kitchen table. The letter is magically sealed. Meant for my eyes only. That wouldn't have meant a thing to Alaric if he'd still been here when it arrived.

With trembling hands, I rip open the envelope, surprised when it's not from Lira. The familiar handwriting fills me with bittersweet longing.

I know you're probably confused, but it's for a good reason.
Fen

My eyes fall closed, and I slide down to the floor, forehead on my bent knees. I can almost hear him, see his mouth move with the words. No wonder Alaric had been so angry tonight. Despite being first in line for the throne, he's insanely jealous of his younger brother. Alaric's antics are good for selling papers but not for ruling countries. All of Eddahn knows Fenrik would make a better king.

It makes me wonder why he's never told Fenrik about us. The thought haunts me—Alaric getting drunk and throwing it in his face after Fen receives yet another award for humanitarianism. Maybe he'll bring a recorder next time he pays me a visit. Let them watch while he forces me to show his brother how truly vile I am. Or maybe he's already told him and Fen is just too kind to mention it to me. Not that he mentions much of anything to me anymore.

At least Alaric's spies didn't learn of the favor I'd asked for in addition to the money. Knowing something like that would give him leverage I can't afford.

I haul myself to my feet and wipe the wine from the walls. Pulling out the case file, I spread it across the table. I'm not sure what compelled me to grab it from the unlocked drawer. I can recite everything in it from memory. When I went to Gibson to see about a cold case, he said this year's had all been taken. The list of assignments stared at me from his desk. I'll put it back tomorrow.

I need to solve this case. It's wishful thinking, but part of me still believes I just need one solid lead. And then, maybe, I'll get

out of Drahma City and away from the entire godsdamn royal
family.

Chapter 6
Draven

The problem with necromancy is that nobody wants to stay dead. It's not the raising, it's sending them back that's the problem.

A good necro can save lives if the person has only been dead for a short time. They're invaluable for accidental or wrongful deaths. For the adventurous, they can provide a daring experience, letting people die and calling them back before they've gone too far. I've heard it's a real high. Once they've been gone too long for permanent recovery, though, they can only give them a chance to say goodbye. I'm sure it makes them feel powerful and useful, but I don't envy the aftermath.

One has to have a serious level of clinical detachment to raise someone—watch them absorb what happened to them in real-time, grieve, rage, and then coldly let them go. I guess that's why the chief has such a hard time keeping necros employed here. Why torture yourself raising crime victims when you could make more money working the party circuit or just getting a normal job?

The one in front of me looks about twenty-five, pale and bored. He scratches something on his clipboard before pulling away the sheet, revealing Kurt's lifeless face. Years of watching this same scenario play out still haven't prepared me for this—seeing him lying there, his body shredded by the ulgashen. My chest tightens, and heat gathers behind my eyes as I remember the relieved look on his face when we thought we'd caught the last one.

Kurt didn't deserve this. He was a good corner, honest, and a loving father and husband. And now, he's just a body.

"Detective?"

My head snaps up. Victor Anistemi, the necromancer, is staring at me. "Sorry, did you say something?"

"Where's your witness?" he asks. His face looks young, but his dark brown eyes seem far older. This job would do that to anyone. Necros only live to be about a hundred anyway. Payment for all the lives they snatch back from Helva, I suppose.

"My witness?" I know I sound clueless, but my gaze keeps drifting to Kurt's face. It's completely unmarred. Not even a scratch from our fight with those monsters. At least Maria won't have to see the blood and gore when she finds out her universe has been shattered.

"Two corners for a raising. That's the policy." He puts the clipboard down on a nearby table and picks up a glass of water.

"Never heard that before." Then again, why would I? Kurt was with me at every raising I've attended.

Anistemi just gives me a pointed look, and I don't have the energy to argue. I march into the hallway, determined to commandeer the first person I see. The bathroom door down the hall swings open, and I think luck is on my side—until I see who it is.

My shoulders and fists tense automatically. With her silver hair and *fuck you* attitude, Detective Sucrelia "Sugar" Writh has a venomous sort of beauty. She gives me a dismissive glance before turning toward the stairs.

I search the hall, looking for anyone but her, but it's glaringly empty. Damn it. "Wait," I call out, charging toward her.

Her body turns as a three-strand, coiled black cuff on her wrist slips from beneath her sleeve. She narrows her eyes, warning me not to get any closer.

"I need someone to witness a raising." I spit the words out, unable to lower myself to actually asking a succubus for a favor.

Writh's blood-red lips turn down in a frown as she tips her head up at me. "Don't you have a partner?" Her hair practically glows as it slips over her shoulder.

"He's the one being raised," I snap.

Her eyebrow arches, and she pauses like she might say something, but the determined look in my eye must stop her. Instead, she just jerks her chin for me to lead the way.

I hesitate. Turning my back on a succubus is the last thing I should do. And she's not going to let a vampire get behind her. One of us is going to have to give. Desperation wins. I turn and head back toward the morgue, and her precise footsteps follow me. Kurt is more important than my pride or safety right now.

Normally, vampires and concubi are *on sight*—have been for as long as anyone can remember. The concubi's power doesn't work as well on vampires. Combine that with them having uniquely delicious blood, and you get some especially catastrophic and gruesome battles.

I've never said two words to Writh before. The only place I've seen her is at her desk or maybe a departmental meeting. I would love to take my fury at Kurt's death out on someone, and a succubus would be an excellent option. A familiar face bracketed by dark blond hair pushes into my mind, sneering at the thought of me disgracing my family by asking her for help.

Instead, I clench my teeth and—gods help me—hold the door open for her behind me. My ancestors, the ones who are actually dead, are probably turning in their graves. Anistemi glances up as we enter, then picks up his clipboard and writes something—probably Writh's name—before handing it to her to sign. I watch her gaze move over Kurt, cataloging his injuries, her expression calculating.

Pure violence surges through me as she lifts the sheet—without even asking—to see the rest of his body. Fucking succubi. They think they know everything about you with their creepy emotion magic. At least vampires are honest about our coercion. We don't have to fuck with your libido to do it. She replaces the sheet and gives me a look like she finds my outrage tedious.

The only thing that stops me from reaching for her throat is the sight of Anistemi raising his hands over Kurt's body.

Blue light emanates from my partner's skin as the necro works. Anistemi's eyes are closed. It doesn't seem difficult for him yet, but the magic takes a toll. I wonder how long he has to rest between each raising to recover. I've seen necros puke from the effort before, but that's usually with older bodies, ones too far gone for the magic to work well.

It takes everything I have to hold back my grief as Kurt's eyes flutter open, his gaze locking on mine. "Draven?" he whispers. Before I can respond, he notices the blue light and the bloody gashes on his chest. His face crumples. "No, no, no. I can't die, Draven. Maria and the kids—oh hel, I can't leave them like this."

Grabbing his hands, I repeat, "I'm so sorry, Kurt. I'm so sorry." I don't care if Writh can feel my emotions. "We don't have a lot of time. Just tell me anything you want me to say to them."

Kurt is inconsolable, and for a moment, I'm not sure he'll be able to speak. But he takes a shuddering breath and says, "Tell them I love them and I'm sorry. Tell them I'm so sorry. I was going to turn things around. But—oh gods—how will she keep the house, Draven?" He breaks down again, and from the corner of my eye, I see Sugar take a step back.

"What do you mean? What did you do?" My brow furrows, but my heart sinks. I've seen Kurt tracking down the reporters, getting the latest on the horses or dogs or whatever else there was to bet on. It was a harmless hobby, or so I thought. And I wasn't about to confront my best friend.

"It was going to get better. I was going to quit. Please tell her I'm sorry. Tell her I love her. Tell my girls I love them so much and that Daddy is going to miss them forever." His words dissolve into sobs as the gashes on his chest split further, squeezing out errant drops of blood spurred into life by the necro's magic.

"Kurt, how bad is it?" I lower my voice, wishing Writh wasn't standing right next to me, hearing all of this. She's going to judge him, and I hate her for it. Can't she read my emotions enough to know I don't want her there? Surely policy doesn't require her to revel in my misfortune.

"It's really bad. The debt collectors have already come to the house twice." His voice is so small, so unlike the boisterous man I know, and I nearly crumble. We've worked together for five years. It's not fair this should happen to him and not to me. He has a family, a wife and two beautiful daughters. His hands grip my arms, still wet with his blood, and I hold on to him. "Please Draven, don't let them lose the house. I don't want them to end up in the Hollows."

Next to me, a sound escapes Writh's throat. It's barely audible, but my hearing is better than most. When my face snaps to hers, though, she's looking at Kurt with confusion and possibly a little sadness.

"I can't hold him much longer," Anistemi says. The strength of the fae and the necro determines how long someone can be dead before a raising and the duration of their revival. The blue light surrounding Kurt is dimming. Anistemi is sweating.

"I'll take care of it, Kurt. Don't worry about anything. I'll take care of them." My grip tightens, but I can feel his hand slackening beneath mine. Kurt's spirit—his soul, whatever the hel it is that makes Kurt, Kurt—is dissolving under my touch.

"Thank you, partner. I love you, buddy." His eyes close, his tears drying in eyes that will never produce them again. The blue light fades and dies.

Kurt is gone. Again.

Anistemi stumbles away, grabbing a huge bottle of water and downing it in one go. I bow my head, steeling myself for the worst conversation of my life. Beside me, Writh's jacket rustles. Her pale hand holds out a tissue.

I inhale sharply and stand. "I'm all right." Vampires can't cry like other fae. Our blood pumps too slowly. It's the same reason we survive serious injuries. No big risk of bleeding out when your blood moves at a sloth's pace. Not that I'll share any of that with her.

She pockets the tissue. "I'm—"

The door slams open, and Samantha barrels in, her face mottled red.

"I just heard! I can't believe it—not Kurt." She shoves past me, staring in horror at his body before looking up, her jaw tight with emotion. Her gaze lands on Writh, and her expression swiftly transforms from surprise to anger. "What the fuck are you doing here?" Pike's fangs extend as she squares off against the succubus.

Writh's blue eyes flash, but she blinks, and the fire in her gaze is gone. With a bored expression, she turns toward the door.

"Thank you," I manage. She doesn't respond, walking out without a word.

Chapter 7
Sugar

At around two in the morning, the rotted posts of the West Bridge finally gave way, and it sunk into the Fugue. Gibson ordered Matt and me, along with a few other corners, into a last-minute security detail for the early morning press conference at City Hall.

"Councilor Nichols, what do you say to the allegations that your office repeatedly failed to address safety concerns?" The reporter's auburn hair catches the light as I glance his way. He's one of a dozen reporters here for the press conference, all clamoring to get the best quote.

For years, Drahma City officials claimed they were going to repair it, but it was a low priority to them, considering it was one of four ways into the Hollows. But unless a fae could fly or swim, most inhabitants used the East Bridge. The city is like a giant cove, water on one side and surrounded by mountains on the others. A natural stone wall horizontally bisected the Fugue, a convenient stopping point when they paved over the city. On either side, wide plateaus jut out from the mountains, parks that have winding stairs down to the Hollows.

Nichols shakes his head, a practiced look of remorse in his piercing blue eyes. I wonder if the councilors drew straws to see who had to appear this morning and pretend to give a rat's ass. "Only that I'm relieved nobody was hurt and that we all still have sufficient ingress to the Hollows."

There are more than a few snorts of disbelief in the crowd but no true ill will toward the councilor and his obvious pandering. I glance at Matt across the crowd. His mustache twitches with amusement. Councilor Nichols lives in the First Circle, aka the Golden Circle, and has almost certainly never set foot in the Hollows.

"Do you plan to rebuild it?"

"Not at this time. As I said, we still have multiple avenues across the river."

"Will the shifters who live in the river be provided compensation for this disruption?"

"We currently have inspectors assessing the underwater damage, but as yet, it doesn't appear significant enough to warrant such a thing."

Nichols patiently answers question after question. We're standing on the steps into City Hall. The beige monstrosity takes up an entire city block in the Second. Five floors of windows look down on the square used for press conferences and inaugurations for the rotating council of seven elected officials.

The redhead raises his hand again. Nichols points to him. "Yes, Mr. Jasper?"

I shift to the right to get a better look at the man who raises Petra's hackles so much. He's tall and holds himself like he knows the difference between a salad and a dinner fork.

"Shoes are worth at least five hundred," I murmur to myself, earning a sideways glance from the corner next to me. I've been sensing a low level of animosity from him since we got here.

"Where will you divert the money previously earmarked for its repair?" Jasper asks. He has dark brown eyes and, like a few other reporters, isn't holding a notebook. He must be a recorder, able to commit everything to paper after he leaves. It reminds me I need a second look at the notes from Cathy and Sarah, Carter Fox's recorders.

"Well, there are always a few projects around here that could use a little extra." Nichols grins and gets a few perfunctory chuckles from the crowd.

"But nothing specific? Not maintenance for East Bridge? Are you intending to allow it to fall into disrepair as well? Would it have anything to do with the fact that residents of the First through Third circles rarely need to cross into the Hollows?"

Jasper's voice is strong, carrying out to the rest of the crowd. He's not giving Nichols an inch, and now I'm even more interested in knowing what happened between him and Petra. She left me another message yesterday: CP held a server suspended upside down for the entirety of his meal for bringing him a wine he didn't like. I roll my neck as the other reporters wait in silence for Nichols's response. Jasper and Petra certainly have unfailing determination in common.

"We haven't yet decided," Nichols says with finality. "Thank you all for coming. Special thanks to our corners, who I know are feeling the loss of their friend and colleague today." He nods sympathetically at a few of us. My lip curls at his use of Detective Kurt Copper's death to end Jasper's line of questioning. Images of his shredded chest, his sobs as he confessed his sins, and Draven Flint's grief-stricken face flash into my mind.

I touch the black mourning band around my arm, the same one all the corners wear today, as I move in front of the podium to keep the reporters back. There's no reason, though. Nobody is trying to question Nichols any further, and he strides back up the steps into City Hall without incident.

Matt ambles up beside me. "That felt pointless. Where do politicians learn how to say so much and so little at the same time?" He mops his dark skin with a handkerchief. It's not hot, but as a manatee shifter, he prefers cool water to nearly everything.

"Maybe it's a natural talent. Just like certain powers. If you're born being able to talk out of your ass, not much choice but to become a politician," I reply.

"Or a lawyer," a familiar voice says from beside us.

I take my time turning to Jasper and appraising him before responding. "I don't know. Some lawyers are alright. What's the F stand for?" I ask, recalling his byline.

"Fitzwilliam." Matt and I wince, and he says, "Yeah, that's why I go by Jasper. You're Detectives Writh and Diaz, right?"

"I prefer Detectives Diaz and Writh myself," says Matt. He's got a few inches and many years on Jasper, but he doesn't stare him down, choosing instead to gaze across the street in disinterest.

"Really can't argue with the alliteration," I add. I keep my eyes on Jasper's face, letting my power reach out to him. "Something we can do for you, Fitz?"

There's a sliver of annoyance at the nickname before he speaks. "Any promising leads on the murder of Carter Fox?"

"Did you say murder?" I ask Jasper, frowning.

"Did you say murder?" Matt asks me.

"I didn't say murder. He said murder." I motion to Jasper.

"I don't think either of us said murder," Matt says, his voice flat.

"So, you believe it was suicide?" Jasper arches a brow disdainfully, and I'm again struck by his aristocratic demeanor.

"Hard to understand the demons that drive people these days," Matt says somberly, shaking his head.

"Indeed. Everyone is a stranger, even to themselves." Jasper audibly exhales, clearly unamused by our antics. "How do you know Petra Kohl?"

His eyebrows rise at my sudden change of topic. "I never said I did."

"Did she put away one of your friends? Run over your cat? Bad date?" His animosity doesn't surge like Petra's did when I mentioned a date. Maybe only she thought it was bad. Or maybe she's angry because she thought it was good.

He tries again. "Carter Fox?"

"You'll find out when we do," Matt says as he turns to leave.

I'm about to walk away too when Jasper says, "Did you know he met with CP and Councilor Nichols before he died?"

We both pause. Matt crosses his arms. Tilting my head at the reporter, I say, "Did someone provide you with Fox's schedule?"

"I've interviewed Carter before. I'm on good terms with Issa, his personal assistant."

"Really? Why was a fashion blogger interviewing the crown prince and a councilor? His content veers toward gossip, clothes, and fashion, not politics, doesn't it?"

"Issa said he didn't document his notes for her before he died. She wasn't sure exactly what he discussed with either of them."

Matt squints into the sun and flaps his suit jacket to cool himself down as he asks, "She have any theories?"

"A few." Jasper's face relaxes as he speaks, and his words come quicker. "She thought he was discussing a business venture with CP. And Nichols's daughter is Carter's intern. Maybe it was a progress report."

"Anything else?" Matt says.

Jasper opens his mouth to speak but closes it, crossing his arms. "This conversation feels a little one-sided."

"Because you're not telling us anything we don't already know," I drawl. "But good to see Ms. Collins immediately ignored our request that she not speak to the press." According to her, besides meetings scheduled with CP and Nichols, Fox also had a lengthy workout, visited a new club that had yet to open, and wrote four articles. It sounded exhausting.

"I told you," Jasper grits out, "she's a friend."

"Did he say 'friend?'" Matt asks me, and Jasper huffs a breath through his nose.

"No, he didn't. He said he was on 'good terms' with her. She was promoted halfway through our conversation. You know very well we're not going to comment on an active investigation. If you have information about Carter Fox's death, I suggest you disclose it now."

There's a long beat as Jasper stares between the two of us. He's got a good jawline, with a little dent in his chin. It's the kind of face that begs you to kiss or punch it. "I'll let you know if I learn anything of use, Detectives."

"You do that," Matt says as we turn and walk down the steps.

***

We arrive back at the department to find it near empty. Almost everyone has already left for Copper's funeral. I take the opportunity to head down to Research & Evidence. I can hear Nelson, who handles evidence, and Catriona, the archivist, fighting before I've made it down the stairs.

"I swear to all the gods now and who have ever lived, Nelson, if you touch my stapler one more time," Catriona hisses. She's almost eight feet tall and stoops slightly as she leans over her desk, glaring at Nelson.

"Oh, pipe down, you histrionic shrew. I never touched your stapler," he tosses back. He's half her height and stares menacingly up at her as he throws his arms wide to show his desk is absent of said stapler.

"Your lies are as big as your ass, you cretin!" she shrieks, stepping out to the line painted straight down the middle of the room. The chief had the line painted after their vitriol moved from words to actions, and now neither of them can cross it.

I clear my throat, leaning over the half door that leads into the room. Beyond their desks, towers of shelves sit behind an iron cage. They each have keys that must be used in tandem to access the department's archives and evidence storage, but for obvious reasons, only one of them goes into the cage at a time.

"Writh? What are you doing here? Not going to Kurt's funeral?" Nelson glances up at me but goes back to processing paperwork on his desk as he speaks. Catriona takes a piece of jerky out of her desk and tears into it. Nobody is sure if she likes jerky or just does it to annoy Nelson, who, despite being a cheetah shifter, is a vegetarian.

"I am. Wanted to put in an order now while there's no line."

Catriona walks over, pulls a clipboard off the wall, and hands it to me. "You know the drill."

First, I write a request for everything Fox published in the last year. I add on a separate request for any murders committed in the vicinity of Tradimento within the last three, even though I've made so many similar requests over the years that I probably know them all by heart. My eyes snag on Kurt's request from a few days ago.

Linnea Faroe, all available evidence. K. Copper.

After all this time, the sight of her name, or the lack thereof, still sends me straight back to that room, the blood, the silence.

The Romans, who'd been Linnea's employers, are still some of the Dame's biggest clients. But they never visit the Nest. We always had to go to their house. The first time I laid eyes on Fenrik was in Stanley Roman's office. I'd arrived to get payment for the party the night before, and he was collecting a donation for one of his many charities.

"Can I help you?" Fenrik's brown eyes light with warmth as he opens the door wider for me to enter. "I honestly don't know why I said that. This isn't my house or my office, so I'm not sure what help I can be. Stanley said he'd be right back." He speaks quickly, and I don't miss the way his gaze darts down my body before settling back on my face.

"Oh, I don't know about that, Prince Fenrik. I can think of a few things you could do for me." I walk over and sit on the edge of the desk, crossing my legs at the ankles under my sleek red dress.

He doesn't respond but cocks his head, his expression thoughtful. The longer he looks at me without speaking, the more unnerved I become. "Does she teach you to speak like that? To turn your every word into an invitation?" he asks.

I glance away. It didn't sound like an insult, but with the royal family, who knows? "We don't have to speak, Your Highness. If you don't want to."

"No, I'm sorry." He steps forward, palms up. "I meant no offense." He stumbles over his next words. "I've always been interested in language. The way your words and speech complement your profession is fascinating to me." He pauses as if unsure how to go on. "And how you use your power but not your body to do...what you do...it's also fascinating."

My lips tilt. "I thought you didn't know who I was, but it seems my reputation precedes me."

Fenrik grins and runs a hand down the back of his neck.

Stanley's heavy steps sound outside the door, followed by a familiar soft shuffling. The door opens, and he holds out his hands at the sight of us.

"Ah. My favorite royal and my favorite succubus." He walks behind the desk, Linnea following close on his heels. He pulls a cigar from a dark lacquered box, holding it out for Linnea to cut and light. "I'd pay good money to see the two of you together." His eyes swing between us, and his arousal reaches out to me. Fenrik's cheeks color, embarrassed on my behalf, and he glances toward me in apology.

"Stop your waffling, Stan," I say. "Give the prince his money before we taint him any further with our unsavoriness. And get mine while you're at it."

Stanley grins and lays the cigar on a diamond-studded ashtray. He takes off his deep plum dressing gown, leaving him completely nude and at half mast. Fenrik blinks rapidly before averting his eyes. Stanley hands the dressing gown to Linnea, who *hangs it over her thin arm while handing him a fresh shirt, silk briefs, and dark gray pants.*

Her hair is pulled back in a low bun, and I squint at the yellowing bruises on her neck.

"All done?" It's Catriona's turn to clear her throat, taloned fingers waiting expectantly for the clipboard as my eyes snap up.

I bury the memory with a strained smile. "Sure neither of you wants to give me a little top-up? Something to tide me over?"

Catriona snatches the clipboard out of my hands while Nelson frowns at me from behind his desk. "It'll be ready tomorrow, smartass."

Chapter 8
Draven

The clearing Maria chose for the funeral is lovely, bordered by thick trees and carpeted by wildflowers. Kurt would have loved it. My steps are heavy as I escort her and the girls to their seats. Keisha and her mother share a similar look, pale and drawn. Sloane, the younger one, hasn't stopped crying. It's luck of the draw when fae and humans reproduce. It's usually one or the other, although sometimes you might get a human with a fae characteristic like horns or minor levitation abilities. Kurt's children are both human like their mother, something that has never been more apparent than now.

Sadness rushes through me as I remember again how Kurt should have outlived them by hundreds of years. I haven't told Maria about what Kurt said, the gambling, the debt. She knew he had a problem but probably had no idea of the extent. Typical fae, thinking there'd always be more time to fix his mistakes.

There are over two hundred people here, friends, family, and dozens of corners sitting in the back rows. As I step up to the podium, my eyes snag on a flash of silver in the back. Sugar Writh's hair dares to stick out among a sea of black, and anger surges inside me. My fangs threaten to extend, and I force myself to take several calming breaths. Everything is brittle and too close to the surface. I nod to the musicians, who play one of Kurt's favorite songs. Maria and the girls sob as six people move forward with Kurt's canvas-wrapped body.

They place the body into a nest of leaves and wildflowers and arrange him until he's curled neatly inside. Sloane breaks away from her mother and kneels by her father's body, pleading with Helva, the goddess of the afterlife, to send him back. Maria sinks down beside her, clutching her by the shoulders, but nods at me to begin.

My throat threatens to close, but I speak anyway. "Kurt Copper was more than my partner. He was my friend. He was the first person in the department to buy me a cup of coffee, to invite me to dinner, and to tell me when I was being a dumbass. Of course, he was also the first person to tell me when all of *you* were being assholes," I say as I start the story of my first few weeks as a corner.

"You know, being this high isn't as impressive if you can just fly away." A lanky man with chestnut hair and red-rimmed eyes approaches my position on the roof ledge.

I roll my eyes, repositioning the enchanted spyglass. "How that rumor persists is beyond me. Vampires cannot change into bats."

"Fine, fine. Keep your secrets." He shakes his head and smiles. "He's not gonna show."

I squint up at him. "How do you know?" Gibson assigned me surveillance detail. I was watching for a heavyset frog shifter to exit the beauty parlor across the street. It was my first assignment, and I wasn't going to screw it up.

"What's the perp's name?"

"Guy LeNeaux."

"Reverse that for me." Kurt grimaces.

"LeNeux Guy...the new guy." I sigh in realization. "Fun," I grumble as I stand and shove the spyglass in my pocket.

"Don't take it too hard. I was up here for six hours." He grins and sticks out a hand. "I'm your new partner."

The crowd laughs as I finish retelling the bittersweet memory. "Of course, I'm not going to stand up here and tell you he was a paragon of virtue or some bullshit like that." Laughter trickles through the crowd again. "He was a real person, with real flaws as well as his good qualities. Kurt was a methodical and patient detective, a generous friend, and, most importantly, a loving and devoted husband and father. He was loved in return and will be sorely missed."

My heart squeezes as Maria manages to tear Sloane away, and they sit down again. I turn toward Kurt's body, ignoring that flash of brilliance in the corner of my eye. I want to tear down the aisle and force her to cover her head, to stop distracting my grief. Instead, my jaw ticks as I say, "Please rise."

I descend to stand next to Maria. She holds Keisha on one side, Sloane in front, and leans against me as I put an arm around her shoulder. She takes a deep breath. "It's okay, Draven. Tell them to do it," she whispers, her voice hoarse from crying.

"Please accept this soul, Helva," I intone, wrapping my arm tighter around Maria.

The crowd murmurs back as one. "Keep and protect him."

Two fae step out of the crowd, raise their hands, and engulf Kurt in flames. It's over in an instant, leaving nothing but a small circle of ash.

***

Mourners flow steadily through the Coppers' house for hours. Maria does her best, but she disappears every so often to check on the girls, who choose to remain in their bedroom with friends. I don't blame them. I'm trying to do right by Kurt, but of the two of us, he was the extrovert. But I persevere, pouring drinks, replenishing the tiny sandwiches, and asking people to give their memories to the recorders, who will document them for Maria to keep.

Samantha wanders over to me as I put out another pile of clean plates. "You think there will be this many people at your funeral?" she asks, taking a bite of a cucumber and salmon sandwich before using the other half to gesture at the packed room. Her short blond hair is up, revealing the undercut.

There would probably be many people at my funeral, but few who would actually care about me and none I want to mention to her. "Doubtful. You?"

Sam snorts. "Not likely. Normally, I'm deeply suspicious of anyone with this many friends." She exhales, looking around. "But he really was a good guy."

I nod, pouring myself another healthy measure of liquor. Is this my third? Or my fourth? "That he was."

"Of course," she says, her tone dropping, "he could have been a little less friendly."

I look up from my glass and follow her line of sight to the far side of the living room. Writh is speaking to two other concubi.

"Do you know them?" I ask. They don't look like corners.

"Don't recognize the other two." Her eyes narrow on Writh. "I can't believe they let concubi join the department. It's un-ethical. Those mind-fuckers wiped out my entire great-uncle's family." She sneers and tears into another sandwich.

Writh turns and looks directly at Sam before leveling her gaze at me. The challenge in it makes my blood heat. Sam tenses and takes a step before Maria appears at the bottom of the stairs.

She spots us and comes over, the exhaustion evident in her gait. "Hello, Samantha, thank you for coming." Maria gives her a hug, nearly disappearing under the detective's muscular arms.

"Of course. I'm so sorry, Maria. Kurt was good people." Sam releases her and steps back.

Maria nods. "Thank you."

"Is there anything I can do? How about I go check out the kitchen and see if there's any trash to be taken out?"

"That would be nice of you. Thanks."

I hand Maria a glass of wine, and she waves me away. "I'm afraid if I keep drinking, I'll be sick as well as sad."

"There's more than enough fae here with healing ability. Drink all you want."

"Hey, Draven." A young corner, who I think is named Paul or Mark, appears at my side. "There's a guy out front asking for you. Said he didn't want to disturb the party."

"Thanks." I squeeze Maria's arm gently. "Probably just more food being delivered." She nods like it takes a lot of effort to do it, and I head through the crowd to the front door.

When I get outside, I don't immediately see him. But as my eyes adjust to the sun, I spot the stocky fae across the street wearing a mud-colored suit with a matching brown hat. He's chewing a toothpick and leaning against a thick tree trunk, blending in perfectly. A gold incisor flashes in his mouth as he tips his chin up to beckon me closer.

"What are you doing here, Puck?" I ask when I'm close enough. Puck Rogers is a low-level grifter and go-between for some of the city's more unsavory businesspeople. He's been known to drop helpful information to the corners now and then—if he thinks it won't be traced back to him and you can make it worth his time.

He pulls the toothpick out and says, "Didn't want to be disrespectful now, but some people are a little qualmish about the source of their remuneration being nothing but ashes."

"Are you fucking kidding me right now?" My hand snaps out, and I grab him by the shirt, struggling to keep my fury in check. "Did you really come to a man's funeral to collect a debt from his grieving widow?"

He holds his hands up in surrender as I lift him high enough that his toes barely graze the ground. "Hey, I'm just here to convey the inclinations of my clients, Flint. And I've been right genteel about the situation in not imposing my personage into the house."

I glance back at the house, hoping Maria isn't watching. Then, I pull him close so he's at eye level with my fangs as they slowly descend. "They'll get their money," I growl. "I'll make sure of it. But until then, if you so much as sneeze in Maria's direction, my teeth will leave so many holes in your body your clients will use you as a colander. Do I make myself perfectly clear?"

He swallows and bobs his head. "Completely perspicuous, Detective."

I shove him back. Puck grabs his hat where it's fallen and dusts it off before taking off down the street.

My nerves are as taught as a bowstring when I return to the house. Maria gives me a questioning look as I join her side. "Work stuff. Sorry."

She gives me the barest smile and shakes her head. "You don't need to apologize."

Guilt squirms inside me. How long can I keep her in the dark about this? Can I take care of Kurt's debts before she has to know? I'm not even sure how deep the hole is.

Several more people approach to offer their condolences, and suddenly, I'm face to face with Detective Writh. Panic rises inside me, afraid she might tell Maria about Kurt's confession. Before she can say a word, I jump in.

"Who are your friends?" I jut my chin toward the concubi who are still talking in the living room. Three more have joined them, and they've moved to the couch. "Making themselves pretty comfortable."

She doesn't take her deep blue eyes off me, and Maria responds instead. "Those are my neighbors, Draven. We've known them for years." Maria gives Sugar a look, apologizing for what she thinks are my poor manners. If only she knew her neighbors probably aren't any better than Writh.

"My deepest apologies, Mrs. Copper. I didn't know your husband well, but it's clear he was loved and respected," Sugar says, her voice convincingly sympathetic.

"Thank you..." She trails off, and I can tell she's waiting for me to make the introduction, but I can't stop being irritated at the sight of that shining hair. Her dress is ridiculous too. It's made of some kind of soft material and hugs every curve of her figure. For gods' sake, it's a funeral, not a fashion show.

"Sugar Writh." A line has formed behind her. The two of them shake hands, and she gives Maria an upside-down smile before moving away.

"Something wrong?" Maria whispers to me between accepting condolences. "Did she do something to you? Or Kurt?"

The words catch in my throat, and I curse myself for making her worry about one more thing today. "No, sorry. I didn't mean to give you that impression. I just think it would have been more respectful if she'd covered her head. It's not...appropriate for a funeral." We shake a few more hands, but I can feel Maria's eyes on the side of my face. When I turn, she's giving me a bemused smile. "What?"

"There are butterflies here with incandescent, multicolored wings; sirens with blue hair; and multiple bird shifters in their animal forms. Why is it so important that Sugar Writh cover her silver hair?"

I open my mouth but close it again. Finally, I grumble, "Concubi and vampires don't get along."

Maria raises her eyebrows knowingly. "Ah."

The afternoon wears on into the evening, and everyone relaxes. There are dozens of stories told about Kurt, some of which make me very glad his children are upstairs. I'm in the kitchen cleaning up when Maria comes in dabbing her eyes. They're tears of laughter, though, not sadness, and my chest relaxes for the first time today.

"Don't tell me. The zoo story?" I ask, grinning.

She chuckles. "Kurt told me, but he glossed over some parts. Samantha's version is much more embarrassing." I chuckle as she heads over and begins opening a stack of mail.

I'm thinking of getting one of the Seelie in here to use their cleaning power when I remember why I didn't want Maria to open the mail. "Wait, you don't need to—"

She throws a glance over her shoulder. "Don't need to what? Have my house recolored?" She's holding several advertisements. "So much junk today."

"Maria, I need to tell you something." Before I can finish, a crash reaches us from the living room, accompanied by the splintering sound of breaking glass. The two of us share a look of surprise before rushing toward the noise.

"I told you to back off, leech." A succubus, one of Maria's neighbors, is in a fighting stance. Sam is picking herself up off the floor and the shattered remains of an end table.

"What the—" I don't even get the words out before Sam launches herself at the succubus, slamming her fist into the woman's face.

"I'll back off when you make me, mind-fucker!" Sam yells as Maria gasps.

There's a moment when I think it will be just the two of them before complete chaos erupts. Other vampires attack the concubi. The concubi release their claws, and blood splatters onto the couches and carpet. Another end table meets its demise, and a mirror is smashed before I can act.

I wrap my arms around a succubus from behind, pulling her off a vampire I think is Kurt's cousin. She flails, trying to get loose, and kicks over a tray of drinks. It hits a butterfly in the face, and he releases a cloud of venom into a group of three corners. They cough, stumbling back, and their eyes shrink and dilate in confusion. Through the mayhem, I see Sam put the first succubus in a headlock. A flash of silver in my periphery tells me Sugar is standing near Maria. Is she using Kurt's widow as a godsdamn shield?

"EVERYBODY KNOCK IT OFF!" Matt Diaz's voice booms. He grabs Sam and the succubus by the neck and pulls them apart. Everyone else freezes. "Everyone who threw a punch, go home. Anyone with a cleaning or repair ability, sort this shit out. Now!"

There are mumbles of apology and guilty looks at Maria, who doesn't look mad, only mildly confused. The room is dutifully put to rights, followed by a sudden mass exodus.

Several people are sporting bloody noses or ripped clothing. Sugar is standing beside Matt now. She can't have been fighting. Not a single strand of that silver hair is out of place.

"Sorry about that, ma'am," Diaz says to Maria as he and Sugar head for the door. She smiles apologetically at Maria but doesn't spare me a glance.

"I'm so sorry, Maria," I say once everyone has gone. "I can't believe I let that happen." She hands me another towel. Between venom residue, blood, and alcohol from the spilled drinks, I'm a mess.

"Oh, it's quite all right," she smiles. "It was a nice distraction. For a few brief moments, I wasn't thinking about Kurt, but about how even someone as old as you can still be an idiot."

Chapter 9
Sugar

Matt leans back against the interior windows in the morgue, blocking the view of the recorders on the other side. He feigns ignorance of their increasing irritation at not being able to see beyond his prominent body until they bang on the glass to get him to move. He chuckles and pushes off.

"Why do you insist on antagonizing them?" I ask as he makes his way across the spotless stone floor to stand next to me. The room is entirely devoid of soft furnishings, and his footsteps echo in the cavernous space.

"Gotta liven this place up somehow." He grins before pulling a cinnamon hard candy from his pocket and popping it into his mouth. It's the only smell in here, what with teams of fae coming in to clean the place every half hour. "Get it? Liven up the morgue?"

"If you have to explain it, it isn't funny." I shake my head at him as our necro, Anistemi, walks in. His skin always looks a little dull. The bluish-green orb lights don't flatter anyone, but he looks even more drawn today. It has been a busy week. Besides the usual murders, jealous lovers, and power experiments gone wrong, there was another ulgashen attack—two dead and multiple injuries.

"Afternoon." Anistemi yawns. "Body, names, and badge numbers?" He holds out a clipboard.

"The body of Carter Fox. And seriously?" Matt says, dipping his head at him. "You don't recognize us yet?"

The necromancer just looks at us, and I honestly can't tell whether he's following procedure or really can't tell one corner from another. I suppose he does see a lot of faces, and he's only been here a few years. The role has a poor retention rate.

"Writh. Eleven thirteen," I say, signing the documentation before handing it to Matt. The necro didn't ask me for ID during Kurt's raising, but I don't bring it up.

"Diaz. Oh-nine twenty," Matt huffs.

Anistemi nods in response and takes the clipboard from Matt before tossing it onto a nearby table. It clatters noisily against the metal. He walks over to one of the many steel cupboards in the wall and pops open a door. Inside, a dull red glow emanates from a kylan demon. Most people get away with hiring fae to freeze rocks for cold storage. The more affluent citizens—and places who need longer storage, like the morgue—will use a kylan. The demons don't have faces; they're basically a frigid, amorphous gel.

The necro pats the interior wall and says, "How you doing today, boss?"

I cock my head, trying to see if the red goo reacts, but there's nothing.

Anistemi floats Carter Fox's body onto a long rectangular table and pulls the blue sheet down to his shoulders. Fox was a dekken, a Seelie with the ability to change his appearance. His skin has grayed, his hair thinned, and even his eyes are a different color. All his glamours are gone. He looks younger. Seelie age faster than Unseelie, but he couldn't have been more than a hundred and fifty.

Death removes all magic except a person's natural core. Anistemi will reach out to that core—the soul, if you worship the gods—and tug it to the surface one last time before sending it to the afterlife. The necro takes a long drink of water from an enormous bottle before holding his hands out over the body. A shimmering blue light lifts from Fox's skin, and he opens his eyes.

He blinks and struggles to a sitting position. Fox places a tentative hand on his gaping neck and winces. "Godsdamnit!" His eyes widen, and he looks around like his assailant might still be lurking.

Some corners find it hard to jump right in. They want to give the dead time to grieve, to process. I don't have that problem. "We're very sorry for your loss, Mr. Fox. This is Detective Diaz and I'm Detective Writh. Did you see who assaulted you?"

Fox continues to examine the rest of his head, cringing as he touches a bald spot. "This is so unfair! Why me? I've never done anything wrong! I did nothing but bring beauty and fashion to the people of Drahma City," he says indignantly. He catches sight of himself in the glass-fronted cabinets and inhales sharply. "Oh my god, I'm going to be sick."

"Please don't," Anistemi says mildly, jutting out his bottom lip to blow a piece of hair out of his eyes. He looks tired but relaxed.

"Mr. Fox, we're not sure how much time we have with you. Do you know who attacked you outside Tradimento?" I ask. I'm really hoping he can last a little longer than Kurt did.

"I heard someone behind me but didn't see them. I remember the pain, and then nothing." He flexes his hands, examining the blue light. There are tears gathering in the corner of his eyes. He sniffles. "Who would do this? Everybody liked me."

"That seems unlikely, given the circumstances." The reply is out before I can stop it. Fox looks deeply offended. Matt rolls his head toward me in an *are you kidding* expression, and I shrug in apology.

"Tell us what you remember." Matt says in a comforting voice I've never mastered. "Start from when you got to the club." I try my best to look remorseful but take a small step back, out of arm's reach. My power doesn't work on the dead, and Fox still looks pissy.

"Sarah and Cathy, my assistants, met me outside. We entered through the VIP entrance." He waves his hand in an "obviously" gesture. "We picked up our tickets for the show. Originally, I'd planned to head straight into the theater to have them get some ambiance images but decided to go downstairs instead."

"Did you speak to anyone before you went to the sublevel?" Matt asks.

"No." He shrugs, and I motion for him to go on. "I'd had a busy day. We ordered some drinks and relaxed for a bit. There was a necro there I'd seen before at a party. I was really considering dismissing Sarah and Cathy and just having some fun." He winks at Anistemi, who purses his lips in irritation.

"Name?" Matt asks.

Fox blows out a breath and pulls up his feet to sit cross-legged. The sheet slides off his body, and Matt catches it before it hits the floor.

"Thank you," Fox says, absentmindedly laying the sheet beside him instead of covering his lower half. "His name is Somefun."

"Some fun?" I say.

"Somefun, all one word. I think it's a stage name."

"You don't say." Matt's lip quirks as he writes it down. His notebook is filled with sketches and doodles, including a very detailed starfish.

"He works at the Nest. But we didn't end up doing anything. Sarah kept reminding me I was on a deadline. So, we went back upstairs." Fox rubs his hand over his eyes. "Can't believe I'm dead because I chose work over deadgasms."

"What did you say?" Matt asks, frowning as he looks to confirm I'd heard the same thing.

"It's when a necro asphyxiates you and brings you just past the point of death before bringing you back during sex," I reply.

Matt squints as if he's trying to work out the logistics of my statement. Our necro clenches his jaw and rolls his eyes.

Anistemi may sneer, but there's no denying it's a real talent. We only had a few necros at the Nest who could do it properly. When fae die, the necro only has thirty minutes—an hour tops—to revive them. Otherwise, the only thing they'll be bringing them back for is the same testimony Fox is giving. For a human, you only get about ten minutes, so most necros won't risk a deadgasm on them. And forget about bringing them back to testify. I've never heard of it being done successfully.

Fox snaps his fingers and points at me while nodding emphatically. "Think of the most aroused you've ever been. As you climb the peak, your heart rate increases because you're not only turned on but fighting for your life. You're climbing as fast as you can. You're almost there when you black out, suspended in mind-blowing pleasure, but wait! Light flickers behind your eyes, and you're yanked back into the present, blood pumping, air rushing back into your lungs, and every sexual nerve exploding with pleasure and gratitude." Fox exhales wistfully. "You really gotta try it."

Not a smidgen of arousal reaches out to me from Matt, and I smother my smile. My partner just nods slowly and says, "I'll be sure to do that. Now you're back upstairs. What then?"

"We went into the theater. I'd only sat down for a minute when I got some notes from my intern, Bellanie. She's Councilor Nichols's daughter. I left, went outside, and now...I'm here." His face falls, and he wipes his nose on the sheet.

Three other corners walk in and head for the bay next to us, waiting for another necro. I don't spare them a glance, focused on getting as much out of Fox as I can before Anistemi loses him. "Did you see anyone when you left the theater? Anyone in the stairwell or outside?" I hand him a tissue, and he takes it, wiping his eyes and dabbing his forehead.

"There were a few staff, I think, but they were all headed toward the theater because the show was supposed to start soon. There was nobody outside when I walked out."

"A few minutes," Anistemi says. His pinky finger trembles a little, but his hands are otherwise steady.

Matt picks up a tray and hands it to Fox. "This is what we found on you. Anything missing or wrong?" The tray holds a wallet, some breath mints, a small vial of cologne, and a few notes from Bellanie we'd already read, confirming Fox's various appointments and reservations.

Fox's chin wobbles as he picks up the vial and smells it. "No. I didn't have anything else on me." He sniffs and wipes his nose again.

"Issa said you were scheduled to meet with CP and Councilor Nichols. Anything you can tell us about that? Anything unusual happen?" I say rapidly. The blue light is weakening.

"The councilor just wanted to ask how Bellanie was doing. I guess it's her first job. She's a good kid. Her dad's kind of a piece of work, though. Between you and me, I think he wants the West Bridge to fall into the river."

"Why do you say that?" No need to waste our precious few minutes explaining to Fox that West Bridge had already fallen into the Fugue.

"When I arrived, he was in a meeting with CP. I spent some time answering my fan mail, but after about ten minutes, I heard Nichols laugh really loudly. Said he wasn't going to waste money on an invisible bridge. Which was weird. Made me think he might make it 'invisible.'" Fox makes air quotes around the word.

"Did you ask him about it during your meeting?"

"It was just a feeling. I wasn't about to accuse him of any-thing. When I told him I was thinking of building in the Hol-lows, I joked about how not everybody wants to swim to get into a club. Just to see if maybe he'd bring up repairing the bridge. He didn't seem to appreciate my humor."

"How did you know he was speaking with CP?"

"I saw the prince walk out. We had a meeting set up for later that day. I'd been feeling him out on investing in a nightclub, and he'd been giving me the runaround for months." Carter's face turns sour. "I guess seeing me reminded him to blow me off again since I got a note right after I left the councilor's office saying he couldn't make it."

"One minute," Anistemi grits out. Sweat beads on his upper lip.

Fox's face collapses in anguish. "This is so fucked up. Tell Bellanie to take care of my plants."

"Thank you. May Helva keep and protect you," Matt says.

The blue light dims further before disappearing altogether. Fox's body slumps. Anistemi doesn't move to float him down gently, so I grab his shoulders, easing him back onto the table. The necro stumbles backward and grabs some water. He gulps it down before taking several deep breaths. Matt pulls the sheet out from under Fox and repositions it over his entire body.

Seelie power confuses me. They cannot, like the Unseelie, actively refill it. If they use too much at one time, they just have to rest and wait to wield it again. Their talent, be it necromancy or shifting, and their base magic, like healing, levitation and cleaning, rely on their overall health.

As an Unseelie, if I use a lot of power, I can just replenish myself. However, if I don't feed, I will die. There is no substitute. Absorbing others' emotions keeps me healthy and youthful and gives me enhanced speed and strength. The claws and control are leftovers from our time as beasts.

I'm sure the control was meant as a paralyzing agent, to give us time to feed, not to make powerful fae crawl to me from across the room. Of course, during my years at the Nest, I often didn't even exercise control when absorbing my clients' baser impulses. Most just needed an excuse to do what they already wanted to do.

"You okay over there?" I say to Anistemi, who looks extremely pale. The kid could definitely stand to eat more.

He nods, the hair falling back into his eyes. "Yeah. I'll be okay."

"Did it bother you? His remarks about the necro from the Nest?" I ask. Matt is taking notes, but he pauses and looks up, waiting for Anistemi's answer.

His brown eyes harden. "It bothers me when people assume I use my power for sex."

Matt coughs and gives Anistemi an awkward grimace.

"Do you consider that kind of work beneath you?" I keep my voice light. It's not the first time someone has tried to make me feel bad about working for the Dame.

He gives me an odd look. "I heard you used to work at the Nest, but now you're a corner." He puts his hands on the table holding Fox, and I'm glad to see the color return to his face, although his brown hair still looks like it could use a wash. "You must have gotten tired of it."

"Who told you I worked there?"

His eyes bounce between me and Matt. "The other corners, they've talked about you once or twice during raisings."

"I'll bet they have," Matt mutters under his breath.

I huff a laugh. "Maybe I wanted a change. But I didn't leave because I was ashamed of what I did." He jerks his head in a nod and bounces on his feet a little. The necro is like a skittish pet. "It's Victor, right?"

"Right." He thrusts out a hand, and Matt and I shake it. "But don't think just because we're on a first-name basis that means I won't make you follow protocol and give your names and badge numbers." He offers a hesitant smile. Does he think we're going to bite him? Matt doesn't even have canines when he shifts.

Matt groans dramatically, and I hold up my hands, my lip twisting. "Who, us? Nothing but a couple of law-abiding citizens here."

Chapter 10
Sugar

"How do you get in and out of this without me?" Linnea asks, smiling as she unlaces the tight knots at the back of my corset. "Are succubi weirdly flexible?"

I laugh. "No. And I don't get out of it without you. If you weren't here, I'd throw on a coat, head home, and find someone else to unravel me." I groan in relief as the last of the laces come undone and I peel the sculpted leather off my damp skin.

She reaches around and takes it from me. "Long night tonight." She nods toward the window, where the sun is peeking over the horizon. We're in a bedroom on the third floor of the Romans' place. It's the same one I've dressed and undressed in for the past two years. The walls are a cheerful yellow, and it's got a gorgeous four-poster bed, but I only care that it's quiet. The party is on the sublevel, and not a single sound can reach us up here.

"Too long. And I don't have the stomach for the stuff they all take to keep going." About twenty guests this time, all of them high as dragons. Stan always pays the Dame to send two hosts for every guest. It's good for business, and I've raised my prices twice since I started working these private events, but it is exhausting. "Paolo was there again."

We both give exaggerated grimaces at the thought of the ridiculous siren. He's good for a laugh but can really grate on you after an hour.

Linnea hands me a fluffy robe as I discard the rest of my outfit and the tourmaline earrings a satisfied client shoved in my hand in a lust-addled haze.

"Was the prince there?" she asks, dropping the earrings in a silk bag.

I snort. She doesn't mean CP, who attends all the time. "No. You know he doesn't come to these things." I turn to face her. She looks all right, no bruises, but there are smudges of purple under her eyes.

"I keep thinking he'll show up and sweep you off your feet and you'll come back as a guest next time," she says, her brown eyes wide with hope as she folds my clothes and packs them for me to take back to the Nest.

Tossing in my last few things, I sigh, "Linnea, you are a hopeless romantic." I drop my voice. "And I would never set foot in this house without getting paid." I tap her nose with my finger and start for the bathroom before she tugs the back of my robe, beckoning toward my wrist. Smiling, I pull off my cuff and hand it to her. She takes it gingerly in two fingers and sets it with the rest of my things.

Sinking into the copper tub, I inhale the scent of oranges and vanilla and smile. Fenrik didn't come to the party, of course, but he'd snuck away and met me at the Dame's house in town a few days ago. It's a gorgeous white townhouse, with a stunning view of

Forlare Park. He hadn't been able to stay long, but I replayed the stolen moments over and over again in my head.

Linnea slips in, bringing in my clean clothes and whatever lotion she's made for me to try. When I first discovered she liked to create bath products, I offered to front her the money to start a side business, but she brushed it off. When would she find the time?

I squeeze the bubbles through my hand but don't look at her as I speak. "You look good. Are things better?"

Her tiny body closes in on itself, shoulders hunched and her eyes shuttering. "She's stopped hitting me."

It's not really an answer. "She" is Jacqueline Roman, Stanley's wife. Mrs. Roman doesn't attend the parties and takes out her anger at Stanley on the staff. I sigh. Marrying for money is the sharpest double-edged sword.

"Linnea..." I start, but she flicks the bubbles at the foot of the bath in my face.

"Stop worrying. Now hurry up, or they'll be ready for another round before you get out of here." She flits out the door, and it clicks softly behind her.

My eyes snap open. The smell of orange and vanilla lingers from my memory. I try to grasp the fleeting feeling of that moment before everything became so much heavier. It's like holding sand, the laughter and easy talk falling through my fingers, leaving only memories more bitter than sweet.

The morning light is weak. Dawn is still half an hour away, but I can see the disarray in my room well enough. I sit up and run my hands down my face before glancing around at the piles of clothes, discarded shoes, and half-read books littering my bedroom.

I'd been working the Romans' parties for a few months before I started changing and bathing upstairs before going home. Linnea had been assigned to help me. We'd done that same routine dozens of times over the years. We'd had conversations like that multiple times, too. My memory won't let me forget them. The first time I saw her bruises, watched her limp, saw her lip split open again when I accidentally made her laugh. Each one is a perfect picture of my cowardice, my failure to be the person I should have been.

The dreams have only gotten worse since the Dame made her request, grabbing at me like drunks at a bar.

My memories of the parties themselves are a blur. It's one reason I've had such a hard time finding Linnea's killer. The guests were usually the same core group of ten, but with their guests rotating in and out, along with different hosts from the Nest. It all became so mundane after a while, one face the same as the next. It's made it that much harder to remember anyone.

Pushing back the blankets, I untangle the hair caught in my necklace before getting out of bed. Outside, the people of the Hollows are already starting the day. The sounds of shopkeepers greeting delivery people, awnings being raised, and displays being carted to the sidewalk float through my window.

I stumble out into my living room. There's an empty tumbler on the coffee table. Alaric had let himself in again last night. And

I hadn't turned him away. I rotate my arm, healed from where he'd grabbed and twisted it last night.

Ignoring the glass, I walk over to the table and pick up the bills I stole from Maria Copper's kitchen. Kurt hadn't been lying. The money situation was dire. All the envelopes were addressed to him alone. He must have handled their finances. And Maria must have believed that at two-hundred and twelve, he was mature enough to do so. I toss the bills back on the table.

Humans are so naïve.

Fae are the worst with money. There's always more time, another job, another chance to do the right thing. I have a storage room full of clothes, shoes, and jewels at the Nest to show for my earnings. And what's the point of them now? At least the books, the only thing I brought here other than the furniture, were worth it.

Most of the apartments in the Hollows are built to accommodate humans and low-powered fae—those of us without that convenient base power. Once a month, an ice wielder freezes the pipes that run through the cabinets for cold food. Some of us pay him a little extra to cool the place down when summer hits and the undercity becomes a swamp.

We get year-round deliveries of stones imbued by fire wielders for heat and cooking, but I like to use the wood-fired stove when I bother to make my own food. I set my percolator on top and wait for the bitter aroma of coffee to fill the air.

The anguish on Kurt's face wasn't a lie. Hope and good intentions are the worst traits for a chronic gambler. I stir milk into my coffee and stupidly take a sip even though I just saw it boil. I hiss as the blistering heat touches my tongue. Does Maria know yet? How long will Draven wait until he tells her? What if he finds some way to fix it and never does?

I've felt every bit of animosity Draven Flint has aimed my way from the moment we met outside the morgue. All during the funeral, even when he was giving his eulogy, I could feel the tendrils of hatred slipping from him and searching out my power. Those gray eyes of his hardened to steel each time they landed on me.

We can still sense and use vampires' emotions, but our control over them doesn't last nearly as long as it would with any other fae or human. Of course, even a few seconds can make a world of difference if you're fighting for your life, so historically, vampires would train to control their emotions, to thwart our power.

His distaste for me is irrelevant, though. He's a corner. That gives him some protection, but that's not the only reason I'm considering him as a candidate to Make Lira. I've done my research. Draven, with his bleeding, wounded heart and his helpful connections, is not untouchable, but he is in a far safer position than anyone else I might consider.

"She's stopped hitting me."

I pull out Linnea's case file, which I still haven't returned, and spread it on the kitchen table. Every word and image are burned into my brain. In one image, Jacqueline Roman stands next to her husband as the detectives question them. She wears a self-satisfied expression, while Stanley's is blank, focused on something beyond the recorder.

Their answers to the corners' questions were perfunctory, only enough to say they did their duty before kicking everyone off their property. Their lawyers stepped in, and the case was buried. If this works, I'll only get one shot at it. Jacqueline Roman has been at the top of my list for a long time. Before Linnea died, the list was anyone whose neck I wanted to squeeze until their head popped off, just for fun. But now it's a list of suspects. She may not be Linnea's killer, but she was upstairs when someone drove a knife through my friend's stomach.

My eye catches on Alaric's empty glass again. I walk toward it as if it'll uncoil and lash out. I've never truly eliminated him as a suspect, but I knew better than to interrogate him when I was still reeling from her death. After we slept together, I gently pulled and prodded him until I told myself I was confident he didn't do it. But a sex-filled shame spiral can really cloud one's judgment.

He'd been there that night. Although, I'd avoided him. I've replayed my conversation with Estrella over and over again, intent on nailing the timing of his laugh, whether he'd had enough time to get upstairs and back, whether he would have even stooped to kill Linnea himself. Alaric knew about my friendship with her. He could have done it just to hurt me for dating his brother. Then again, he's never needed much motivation for his cruelty.

My claws extend as I snatch up the glass, and I stop myself from crushing it in my palm. There's mud on my coffee table where he put his boots. My clothes are all over the floor and couch, and not just from last night.

Clenching my jaw, I drop the glass in the sink. It clinks noisily against the rest of my dishes. I grab the worst of the bills, shove it in a blank envelope, and address it to Maria Copper. Still in my pajamas, I march out my front door and up the stairs. I step gingerly around a bucket of water between the third and fourth floor. There's a steady drip from the ceiling, and I make a mental note to harass Marco about it.

The sound of Ms. Plichen moving around in her apartment reaches me as I head for apartment 4F. She opens as soon as I knock, revealing her cheerful living room. It's a riot of color, each piece of furniture decorated in a different floral pattern.

"Good morning, Sugar. You're up early for someone who stayed up so late." She narrows her watery brown eyes at me in knowing disapproval and adjusts the net holding in her hair curlers.

Ignoring the accusation, I say, "Morning, Ms. Plichen. If you're not busy, could I get my apartment cleaned today?"

She stares at me for a beat before saying, "You have two hands, don't you?" Behind her, her granddaughter toddles over, reaching out and twisting her hand in Plichen's flowered skirt. The little girl has pink wings and holds a half-eaten apple in one hand.

"I do," I concede. "I'm just...busy. And with your power, you're obviously faster. And better at it. You don't want the job?"

Plichen is a few inches taller than me on a good day, and those curlers add another three. I use this as an excuse as to why I'm always a bit intimidated by her, even though her power pales in comparison to mine. Or perhaps it's because she could probably smack me across the face and my magic wouldn't even react because she wouldn't be doing it out of malevolence, but for my own good.

She thinks about it as she tenderly runs a hand over the little girl's head. "Seems like you might want to do the work yourself, but sure. I'll have it done by the time you get home." There's a flash of pity in her eyes as she looks at me. It morphs into judgment as she takes in my disheveled appearance again.

"Thank you," I say before she can lecture me on keeping up appearances. I give a quick smile to them both and turn to leave just as the girl angles her body toward her grandmother, revealing a six-inch-long scar on the back of her right arm. My eyes jump back to Plichen. "What happened?"

"Ulgashen. Nearly ran right into it as we came home last week. The street shifted and tossed her back to me, but not before the beast got its grimy claw in."

The little girl gazes up at me with defiance in her eyes, daring me to ask more about it.

"I'm sorry." The Seelie in the Hollows aren't powerful. Matt probably has more base power than the ones who've set up shop here as healers. Plichen must have barely any, or else the girl wouldn't still have that angry scar. She's a butterfly, and they're not defenseless, but she'd lose against the towering beasts. "I'm sorry," I say again, uselessly.

Plichen nods and closes the door. I rock back on my heels, thinking as the dripping water continues its mindless beat. There's an apothecary near the department. There's probably a protection charm I can afford for her. Shaking my head, I head back downstairs, skipping my apartment and putting the letter to Maria in the outgoing mail before I can think about it too much.

Chapter 11
Sugar

Matt gazes at the elaborate water feature with visible envy. It takes up an entire wall, a vertical river complete with fish and plant life. He looks like a naughty child as he checks to see it's still just us before he lets his fingers trail through it. The water doesn't fall down even as it drips off his hand, but sideways, back to where it belongs. Underwater lights glow blue when he dips his finger in again. He sniffs it before tasting it.

"Not bad. Not bad at all. Mostly fresh, but just a hint of brackishness. How much you think this thing cost?" he asks without looking at me.

"Well, there are probably several enchantments besides the obvious one for gravity, exotic fish, filtration system, design…" I tick them off on my fingers before squinting at the ceiling in thought. "It'll probably come to about…a fuck ton more than either of us can afford."

Matt gives a low chuckle. "Asshole."

I smirk as I continue inspecting Councilor Nichols's bookshelves. Award after meaningless award, with images of him with the royal family and the other councilors. There's even one with him in front of the water feature Matt's so impressed with, cutting a ribbon and grinning. He's a crocodile shifter, so his obsession with water makes sense. A bigger image shows him with a stunning woman with a near-identical daughter.

A note appears in my pocket.

Dame wants a progress report. Also, Daphne accidentally trapped someone in the stirrups. Again.

— Helen

I snort a laugh before blowing out a breath. One of the best benefits of being a corner is the privacy we get for messages. Normally, it's just the rich or the royal who can direct them to a pocket or bag instead of having them appear midair, forcing you to snatch them up before they fall to the ground. Of course, no guarantees the power would work as well outside Eddahn since it's not natural to any of us but due to a wide enchantment provided by the royal family to every citizen.

The door opens, and Matt and I look up to see Councilor Nichols smoothing back his steel-gray hair. He's got a chunky ring on his right ring finger, far more elaborate than the simple gold wedding band on the left.

"Good afternoon, Detectives. Sorry to keep you waiting." As he approaches, I catch the lingering smell of lust. His assistant? Another councilor? "I just met my wife for lunch."

Interesting. I figured him for a cheater. "Thank you for meeting with us."

He sits down at his sleek black desk, and I take a seat in front of it. Matt remains standing.

"Of course. Bellanie just sent me a note. She'll be along short-ly. Examining my river, I see." He grins indulgently at Matt, who couldn't resist touching one of the little trees poking out of the water.

"Yes, it's pretty amazing," Matt replies, nodding at me to begin.

"Can you tell us about your last meeting with Carter Fox?" I ask.

"Yes, I was very sad to hear about his passing. Bellanie was inconsolable." He shakes his head, and his gaze flicks to the photo of his family. "She was so excited to work with him. I asked him to stop by to let me know how things were going."

"And how were things going?" I ask.

Nichols waves his hand before standing and going over to a side table. "Apologies. I forgot to offer you a drink. This is thrice-clarified water from the Syvald Sea. Would you like some?" He pours a glass and holds it out to Matt, who takes it, looking suitably impressed.

I decline with a shake of my head. "Bellanie?"

Nichols nods apologetically. "He said she was doing well. Very organized. To be honest, I'm not sure how challenging the job was. It sounded to me like she was a glorified plant sitter. But who understands the whims of the young?" He takes a drink of water before sitting back down. "She really liked him, though. Said he was a good boss. Any leads on who might have done this?" He folds his arms on the desk and leans forward.

"We're working on it," Matt replies, putting his empty glass on the side table. "Did your daughter ever mention anyone who didn't like Fox? Anyone he might have had a falling out with?"

"She occasionally talked about him fighting with his recorders. Don't know their names, though."

My eyes flit to the water feature as a fish does a dramatic perpendicular jump. "Did the two of you discuss anything else during your meeting?"

"He said he had a meeting with CP afterward." Nichols smooths down the front of his shirt. "The prince and I had been discussing some infrastructure projects when he arrived, so it's possible he only said it to try and impress me." He shrugs as if the thought of him being impressed by CP is laughable.

"Did he say anything about the substance of their meeting?" I ask.

Nichols cocks his head before shaking it. "No. Not that I recall. Oh!" He snaps his fingers. "I do remember someone else my daughter mentioned. She said Carter and a reporter, F. Jasper, got into it once over an article. That's as much as I remember, but you can ask her the rest." He beams as if he's handed us the killer on a silver platter.

Bellanie Nichols floats through the door without a sound. Her hair is a blond, smooth sheet down her back, and her light blue eyes are round as they look from me to Matt.

"Come in, Bell." Nichols stands and walks toward her, then puts an arm around her shoulder. She tries to go left, but he leads her away from the water feature as if he's afraid she'll break it. She chews her lip before sinking into her father's high wingback chair.

"Hi," she says, sitting on her hands.

Matt smiles at her. "Thanks for talking to us, Ms. Nichols. This is Sugar Writh, and I'm Matt Diaz. We're detectives investigating the death of Carter Fox."

The girl's eyes immediately fill with tears. "I still can't believe he's dead," she sniffs.

"We're very sorry for your loss. I hope it's a comfort that he thought of you during his raising," Matt says, giving her a bracing look. Matt had sent her the message about taking care of Fox's plants. I wouldn't put it past him to have made it sound more heartfelt than it was. "Can you tell us about anyone that might have wanted to hurt Carter?"

"No. Not really. He had disagreements with people, but nobody ever got so mad I thought they would kill him." Her voice cracks on the last word. "He was a beautiful soul." She waves her hand, and the water disappears from her face.

"Who did he argue with the most?" I ask.

She takes a long inhale. "He and Sarah bickered a lot, but not really fighting. She just had ideas about how the paper should be run, and he thought she should stick to recording." Bellanie shrugs. "I can get you a list of people he did publicity for if you want."

"Thank you. That would be very helpful. Did he ever argue with Cathy?" Matt asks, mentioning the other recorder.

"No. Never. Cathy is super quiet. She never says much of anything. They've both been with Carter forever." Bellanie put her hands on the desk. Her nails are expertly done, with little charms and even delicate swirls of smoke that curl around them as she moves.

"What about rivals? Competitors in the fashion and beauty world?" As far as I can tell, the world Carter Fox inhabited was just as cutthroat, pun intended, as anything else in Drahma City.

She cocks her head to the side, thinking, before shaking her head slowly. "Nobody that springs to mind. I mean"—she lowers her voice and gives me a conspiratorial look—"you read the fashion papers. Nobody really came close to Carter."

My lips twitch at the thought of Matt reading the fashion magazines as he jumps in with, "Ms. Nichols, your father mentioned something about the reporter Mr. Jasper?"

Her eyes pop open, and she looks at her dad and then back at us. "It's not a big deal, but I did once overhear him and Jasper arguing over a piece. Jasper was publishing an article on some stupid robbery at the art museum, but Carter was planning on doing a full page on the art show that had taken place there the same night. Carter wanted Jasper to wait a few days to publish his piece. It would obviously be kind of depressing to see those awful images from the corner recorders—no offense—before the nice ones Carter got. Jasper was totally unreasonable about it." She gives a little huff of disapproval.

"I see." Matt bobs his head at her before looking down at me.

I recross my legs and tap a finger against my knee. "Did you and Carter ever fight?"

Nichols snaps his head up. "Now wait a minute. You can't honestly think Bell had anything to do with this."

"What? No!" Bellanie says, aghast. "It was my dream to work with Carter. I would never have hurt him."

Unlike some fae, I don't have the ability to detect lies, but there's no animosity coming off her. She's probably not tall enough anyway, considering the angle of Carter's injury. "Just ticking all the boxes. Thank you," I say, standing. "We appreciate your time. Please, just send that list to my attention and contact us if you think of anything else." I leave my card on his desk.

Nichols escorts us to the door, and we step out into a light-filled circular atrium. Nichols's assistant, Jahnara, who let us into his office, gives us a friendly smile and a glimpse of her fangs. Her skin is deathly pale beneath her red hair, so unlike Draven.

I'm not at all confident he won't report me if I ask him to Make Lira. But having had nothing to go on for so long, I'm too impatient to look for another candidate. Guilt pricks at me for taking advantage of Maria's situation, but then again, she has her husband to blame for that.

As we walk down the stairs, Matt pulls a note from his pocket and sighs. "All the chef's knives at Tradimento are accounted for. Unfortunately, they don't keep track of the knives they give the customers to eat. Killer could have taken it with them or just put it with the others to be washed."

I make a disgusted face. "Remind me never to eat there."

***

After finishing my notes on the interview with the councilor and his daughter back at the department, I head downstairs to go to the Nest. I step out of the front doors and run straight into Petra. It's unlikely she's here to shoot her shot again about CP. She prefers to do that away from prying ears.

"Here to see someone?" I ask. The street is bustling with people. The sun is hazy, covered by a layer of thin cloud. Fall is almost over, but the memory of the sun's warmth draws the city's inhabitants outside to walk and eat at the various sidewalk cafes. There's a strong smell of roasting meat coming from the place on the corner.

She adjusts her coat, smoothing down an errant lapel. "Trial prep with Detective Pike."

I snort, imagining the hotheaded Samantha Pike losing it on the stand. "Good luck with that. All the defense needs to do is put a few succubi in the gallery and she'll completely unravel."

Petra narrows her expertly lined eyes at me and drops her voice low. "Well, let's hope nobody on the defense team heard that, Sugar. Then again, you are rather lax in your approach to enforcing the law, so I suppose I shouldn't be surprised."

"Really? A guilt trip? Things must be getting desperate if you're resorting to such childish tactics." I cross my arms. A transport Seelie appears out of nowhere on the curb in front of us. A woman in a gray suit and an incubus both call out, rushing toward her at the same time. They smile politely at one another before going back and forth as to who should go first. After watching their interaction with increasing frustration, the transport fae grabs both their arms and disappears to deposit them at their requested locations.

"Things are getting desperate," she replies. She opens her mouth to say something but pauses, her eyebrows shooting up. Even though she's been berating me, there's been no malevolence in it. Not like now. Finger-like tendrils trail down my neck as my power rises in response to the unfettered hostility coming from Petra. Her light brown eyes flash, and I nearly lean forward for a taste when she bites out, "Jasper."

I twist to see the auburn-haired reporter walking toward us. Chills run over me, and I have to stop myself from tipping my head back and groaning at the emotions flowing from both of them. His are somewhat tempered, but there's no doubt these two absolutely loathe one another.

He gives us a curt nod. "Ms. Kohl. Detective Writh." He turns to me. "I was hoping to ask you a few questions. I understand you raised Carter Fox yesterday."

I pull my lower lip into my mouth, inhaling. "I'm on my way out." The Dame is probably already irritated at my timekeeping, but I can't help asking, "Tell me, how do you two know each other?"

"We don't," Petra snaps just as Jasper replies with, "Not up for discussion."

My power flexes and reaches for both of them, and I can't decide who I want to taste first. "Oh c'mon, tell me. Childhood sweethearts?" My skin is buzzing, and my fingers flex. The cuff at my wrist loosens slightly with muscle memory.

Petra's expression hardens while Jasper clenches his jaw. She tilts her head up and exhales. "Get your kicks somewhere else, Writh," she says before pushing past us and into the building.

I turn involuntarily to watch her before refocusing on Jasper. "I would love to skim a little of that anger off for you. I'll even tell you what Fox said about his assailant."

Jasper hesitates for only a second before nodding. "Fine. But no control."

"Excellent," I sigh, leaning into him and inhaling just enough that my power purrs in response. My smile widens. "Thank you. Please feel free to tell me, in detail, about your history with Petra whenever you feel like it." I start to walk away, but Jasper reaches out and grabs my arm. My eyes snap to his grip, my tone glacial. "Take your hand off me if you want to keep it."

"Sorry," he says, releasing me immediately. "But we made a deal."

"Oh, yes." I tilt my head to the side. "He said he didn't see who hit him." Jasper, to my surprise, doesn't look surprised or even angry at my revelation.

"Interesting. Do you think that implies the attack was not personal?" As he speaks, he steps closer to the street to allow a hunched siren to pass on. The woman gives him a flirty smile.

"I think hitting someone hard enough to kill them is always personal."

"But it sounds like there was no argument immediately before he was killed?" His face is earnest as he steps back.

I wrinkle my nose at how he's still managed to glean something from that small piece of information. "Clever. But that's all you get, Fitz."

Jasper's irritation at the nickname is weaker this time, and he doesn't respond. He gives me an appraising look before nodding and heading into the department. Part of me really wants to follow to witness any more interactions with Petra, but I turn and head for the Nest.

Chapter 12
Draven

"How long have you known?" Maria asks.

Her light blue eyes are wet, but there's fury in her voice. She holds a crumpled bill in one hand. The rest are scattered over the worn kitchen table, where she's methodically ripped into them. I'd been collecting the mail and putting it all in Kurt's office upstairs, telling her I'd check it for anything important. The pile of overdue notices stares at me, evidence of dishonesty from both me and Kurt. Her expression bounces between hurt and rage.

"Just since the raising, I swear." I hold up my hands, my gut twisting. "I knew Kurt gambled. We both did. But I had no idea it had gotten this bad, Maria." I sit down across from her, gently prying the paper from her fingertips and flattening it onto the table. I wince. It's the worst one, the one from the loan sharks who let Kurt borrow against the house at an astronomical interest rate. The fae in D.C. deal in money and power, and Kurt didn't have much of either.

Her gaze darts from me to the bills before ricocheting around the kitchen as if the house might disappear into a puff of smoke. "Do you know how bad it really is?" Her voice is hollow, and I shake my head, though I have a pretty good idea. "It's every-thing," she whispers. "I'm going to have to start all over again."

Maria jumps up from the table suddenly, frantically search-ing the surfaces, picking up items and putting them down again. She moves a bright yellow bowl of fruit and peeks under a stack of the girls' schoolbooks.

"What are you looking for?" I croak out, rubbing a hand over my face. Gods, how long has it been since I shaved? Vampires are notoriously vain, and I'm no exception. I can't even remember the last time I looked at myself in the mirror. It's just been one long situation after another, with the fallout from Kurt's death.

"The newspaper." She rushes from the kitchen and into the living room, returning with the sheet. "Classifieds," she mur-murs to the enchanted page, and it responds to her request. The letters change, rearranging themselves into the listings for everything from furniture to charms. "We'll need an apart-ment." Her eyes are manic as she pushes her reddish-brown hair away from her face.

"Maria, don't." I gather the bills and stand up. "You don't need to move."

She wipes haphazardly at her face with the back of her hand. The tears are flowing fast. I doubt she can even see the ads. "What am I going to do, Draven?"

"Please." I put a hand on her shoulder. "Just leave it with me. I'll figure something out. Don't worry about it right now."

"You can't do that. You're not responsible for any of this." She shakes her head but trades the paper for the handkerchief

I hold out. "I'm so mad. I miss him so much, Draven, but I'm livid!" She yells the last word before inhaling and gulping down another sob. "How could he do this to us? To you? Making you feel obligated to help us?"

"Hey now. I don't feel obligated. I'm happy to help. So please, leave it with me. Try not to think about it while I get a plan in place." I squeeze her shoulder again. "Okay?"

She doesn't look convinced. Maria isn't the waiting type. She was the structure to Kurt's slow and easy style, and I can sense her need to do something, anything, to fix this. But she gives another long exhale and nods.

***

Daylight is just turning from dusk to dark as I leave Maria's house. The temperature drops like a stone once the sun melts into the horizon. I pull my collar up against the chill as I travel across the darkened cobblestones.

The problems I need to solve are escalating at an alarming rate. An errant strand of thought floats just beyond my consciousness, and I pinch the bridge of my nose, trying to grasp it. When it still refuses to materialize, I blow out a breath. It'll come back to me.

I'd shoved all the bills into my bag, hoping the lack of easy access might let Maria relax a bit. But I can't. The muscles in my neck tighten as I again review my options. Going to my quench is out of the question. Those vampires wouldn't lift a finger to help a human. I probably have enough to help Maria out with the smaller stuff, but my uncle locked my access to my accounts as punishment for leaving home. If I ask him for access, he's going to want something in exchange, like my return to him in Ensame.

The thought of my uncle dredges up other memories of my past. Eliza's throaty laugh travels through my memory, her lips wet with blood, her eyes limpid with desire. I rake my hands through my hair before shoving them into the pockets of my gray wool coat.

A flash in the corner of my eye has me looking up and into the dimly lit windows of a diner. Sugar Writh sits on her own, calmly flipping through a menu in a booth by the window. A wave of irritation crashes through me.

Before I've even made the conscious decision to do so, I stride to the entrance and swing open the door. The smell of roast chicken and bread assaults me as I stalk over to her table. I stop beside her booth, the sight of her hair fueling my indignation.

"You know, I was just thinking it was weird running into you, of all people, outside the morgue, when I don't think I've ever laid eyes on you outside our floor in my entire time with the corners. And then you not only came to Kurt's funeral but also to the reception afterward, even though you didn't even know him. And now, here you are again, only a few blocks from his house."

Her eyes stay on the menu the entire time I'm speaking, which sets my teeth on edge. Only once I'm finished does she calmly twist her head up to look at me. I lean over her, putting one hand on the table and the other on the back of the booth.

"Feels like more than a coincidence," I say, lowering my voice. "That's *four* times in two weeks."

Writh slowly rolls her eyes as she says, "Your powers of addition are truly astounding."

"Are you following me?" I demand. An older-looking couple sits at the next booth over, and I ignore their looks of disapproval. Someone who didn't know better might see a bigger man threatening a defenseless woman. But the succubus and I know better.

She flips the menu over on the table and looks at the breakfast items before giving me a cursory once-over. "For what? Impeccable grooming tips?" she deadpans.

I grind my jaw, resisting the urge to run a hand across my unshaven face. I'm about to reply with something equally insulting when she unzips and removes her jacket, revealing a dark green top with thin straps. Her silver hair spills over her shoulders and dips onto the smooth skin of her chest. Three freckles trail down her right arm, each a perfect finger's width apart.

"See anything you like, honey?" The server appears behind me, and I jolt upright, causing the two overturned coffee cups on the table to rattle in their saucers.

"I'll have the number five, please. And a lemonade," Sugar says, continuing to ignore me as she hands over the menu. "Thank you."

"And for you, dear?" The server doesn't look anywhere near old enough to be calling me "dear," but she could be a thousand for all I know. She sets a glass of ice water on the table.

My attention jumps to Writh, who leans back before lifting the glass of water to her lips and taking a long drink. Her brows raise in a challenge. Condensation runs down the glass, and I instinctively reach out with my tongue to feel the sharp points of my fangs.

"I'll have what she's having," I say, sliding into the booth and removing my coat. "But with coffee, please." Before I've finished the sentence, the server flips the cup over in its saucer, waves a hand, and it fills itself with hot coffee.

When she leaves, there's a long beat of silence. Finally, I ask, "How do I know you're not using your power on me?"

"How do I know you're not using your coercion on me?" she volleys back.

We fall into another silence, during which I have to try very hard not to look at the straps on her top. The left one is loose, teetering on the edge of her shoulder. Nothing would happen. Logically, I know the top is snug enough not to depend on the wisp of silk balancing on her skin, but it irks me, like a glass too close to the edge of a table. One careless move would send it shattering to the floor.

I turn away from her, leaning my back against the window so I'm facing the rest of the dining room. Once she's out of my line of sight, my agitation for her returns with a vengeance. My gut tells me her presence isn't a coincidence, but if she wants to pretend, I'll play along. If she wants something, I'll give her the opportunity to ask.

The older couple leaves, passing our table, and the woman shoots me an impressive glare. I want to call after them, to tell them what Sugar is, what she's capable of. Discomfort settles over me like an ill-fitting coat when I realize I don't really know.

She interrupts my imaginary defense. "How are Maria and the kids?"

"How do you think?" I snap. I almost apologize for the response, but Sugar doesn't flinch, just continues to regard me in that cool, dispassionate way of hers. "Do you ever smile?" That earns me a glare, and inwardly, I grin in satisfaction.

"You're suggesting I smile?" Her glacial expression could turn a weaker man to stone.

"No. Just idly wondering if you're capable." My eyes scan the room, force of habit after this long as a detective.

In a blink, the food and Sugar's lemonade appear in front of us. I wasn't sure what I'd ordered—what we'd ordered—but I'm not picky. I'm pleasantly surprised it's grydstel, a bread bowl filled with roasted meat and vegetables.

"What are you doing?" I ask, my lip curling in horror as Sugar dumps an obscene amount of pepper into her food.

"As a general rule? Nothing that concerns you." She takes a bite and chews thoughtfully before adding, "Did you know Kurt's gambling issues were that bad?"

Gripping my fork so hard it bends, I close my eyes and resist grabbing Sugar by the neck and telling her to shut her godsdamn mouth about my late partner. "That's none of your business. And I'd appreciate it if you didn't repeat it."

She shrugs, and the strap slips lower, taunting me. I stab my food with my maimed cutlery. "How long have you worked with Diaz?" I grumble.

"A few years. His other partner retired just after I started."

I grunt in acknowledgment. "Been there a long time." The manatee shifter is good. And I realize with some annoyance that a lot of his solved cases and conviction rates I've heard about from other corners are actually a credit to both him and Writh, but she's never mentioned. Vampires earned the concubi's hatred, and we've returned it for millennia, but for the other fae, it's just good old-fashioned fear.

"What'd you do before becoming a corner?" she asks, and I risk a look upward. She's leaning back. Her nails do a slow drum on the table as she takes a sip of her lemonade.

"That's a pretty long period of time. You looking for my life story?" Suspicion flares inside me. If she's keeping tabs on me for my uncle, she can scurry back and tell him to go fuck himself.

"Did you fight in the wars?" she asks as she dips her fork into the bread bowl and takes another bite of her food.

I don't need to ask her which wars she's referring to. Twelve hundred years ago, there was both a Seelie and an Unseelie court in Eddahn. But, due in large part to our inability to play nice amongst one another, the Seelie court overthrew the Unseelie.

And now someday, we're all going to have to swear fealty to Alaric, the crown prince of meaningless fuckery.

"Not that old. You?" She shakes her head, and my eyes involuntarily dart to her shoulder. The strap is still holding on for dear life. "I lived in Ensame for most of my life." No point in hiding that. "I've been a builder, an architect, a teacher…" I wave my hand at the endless jobs I've done. "What about you?" Was she human once and Made, or born of Unseelie parents, like me.

"Ensame. Not a lot of concubi there," she muses.

Of course she didn't answer the question. I snort in response. The vampire-controlled province is a secluded peninsula with a razor-thin isthmus and a dozen outlying islands in the southwest of Eddahn. It's not a safe place for a succubus. Especially not while my uncle and his charming wife are in power.

"I worked for the Nest."

"Hmm. Why'd you leave? I'm sure you made more money." From everything I've heard, the Dame is more than good to her employees.

Sugar shrugs. "You know how it is. Wanted a change. You talk to Gibson yet?"

I swallow another bite of the stew and shake my head. "Monday. He'll probably assign me to some godsawful desk job to 'take it easy' for a while." I'm not sure why I just told her that. She doesn't need to know the details of whatever the captain is going to do in some well-intentioned but pointless attempt to help me get over Kurt's death.

"Why did you leave Ensame? Did you have family there?"

And there it is. I push my bowl away and fold my arms. "You done a little background check on me, Writh? Or did my uncle find you? Are you his honey trap?" The thought of him paying Sugar to seduce me so he can drag me back there sends a river of anger racing through my veins.

She cocks her head, examining my face almost as if she didn't hear me at all. Her eyes slowly circle the room as she lightly chews the inside of her bottom lip. They're stupidly nice lips. I don't wonder why people paid for her company. I wait patiently to discover whatever angle she's playing.

Writh toys with her napkin for a moment before saying, "I have a proposition for you. It has nothing to do with your uncle."

My lips twist in a "yeah right" gesture, but I say, "Go on."

Chapter 13
Draven

I must be out of my godsdamn mind. That's the only explanation for why I am willingly following Sugar Writh across East Bridge and into the Hollows. Maybe grief has addled my senses. I can almost picture Kurt walking beside me, gawking at me in confusion. No, he wouldn't be confused. He'd take pleasure in mocking me. I smirk. All that bad blood between our vampires and concubi, and it only took a single silk strap to turn my head.

Sugar notices my smile, and I hastily remove it. It's increasingly stupid that I'm ignorant of what it would feel like to have Sugar use her power on me. I should go to the Nest and hire a succubus just to find out. How can I ever be sure of my own actions when she's around?

Despite what she might think, coercion isn't one of my strengths. Most vampires aren't naturally good at it. You need to really want it. And while my venom has a similar incapacitating effect, it only works while I'm drinking and isn't nearly as strong. From everything I've read about concubi, they use their power quite effortlessly. They need to intentionally not use control over their victims—excuse me, *donors*. The irony that I have my own donors is not lost on me.

The small houses become apartments, and the apartments squeeze closer together as we head deeper into the old city. There are no streetlights, not like across the river, where orb lights nestle between baskets of flowers that bloom even in winter. There are more humans here, children who will never have an ounce of power unless they purchase it. They play games in the street, teasing the magic into creating goals for their ball games or stone walls to climb.

The streets don't mess with me like I'm used to. They lie flat, unassuming, as we walk deeper into the neighborhood. The power here has never been outright hostile to me— it was actively trying to help the night Kurt was killed—but I find it suspicious all the same. Like the ancient energy is circling us, wondering what to make of our unlikely alliance.

"It's not an alliance," I mutter. Just idle, and probably harmful, curiosity. She said her proposal could help Maria and the kids. I owe it to them to at least hear her out.

"What did you say?" Sugar surveys me from where she's stopped in front of a squat, sand-colored apartment block. A narrow, pale green door sits at its entrance just below worn black lettering that reads "Nevian Mews." She presses her hand against the thin wood, and it swings open as she waits for my answer.

"Nothing." I make a show of studying her building. I know a few newer corners who live in the Hollows, but none of the detectives. From the way she mentioned her prior career, I didn't get the impression she left on bad terms. But she couldn't live further from the Nest if she tried.

She shrugs and steps through the door. I follow her into an interior courtyard littered with bikes, mismatched outdoor chairs, and a few personal shopping trolleys. There's a circular stone fountain with a worn statue of Neve, the goddess of dreams, in the center. The orb light above it emits random sparks. They sizzle on the water that erratically fills and drains as we cross to a stairwell.

A skinny man in a short-sleeved, collared shirt flashes a smile at Sugar as he descends from the second floor. "Oooh, new boyfriend, Sugar? Need another imprint made for your door?"

"No, Marco," she says loud enough so she knows I heard it. "He won't be here again." Her voice is direct but not unkind.

Marco, presumably the landlord, gives me a mock pout and a wink as I pass him. "Too bad."

Another imprint? I blame my corner's training for the way my brain snags on that word. It's just useful information, knowing that Sugar has someone in her life, someone who warrants regular access to her place.

"How long have you lived here?" I ask as we hit the third floor and she leads me to apartment 3D. She unlocks it with a press of her hand and opens it halfway. A smug sense of satisfaction rolls through me as she hesitates, as if she's just realized who she's letting into her home, before she steps in and opens the door wider for me to enter.

The smell of lemon and apple blossom lingers over everything. The place is spotless. Magazines and papers are stacked neatly on the coffee table, and there's not a speck of dust. She has several full bookcases. My eyes wander to the other side of the room. There's an expensive round dining table with clawed feet. Something she kept from the Nest? A small glass jar sits on top, filled with camellias.

"It's very clean." I don't hide the surprise in my voice as my eyes meet hers. Something, perhaps the flowers, tells me she finds different ways to spend her time.

Sugar pauses as if she might take offense to the implication. "My neighbor cleans it for me." She drops her bag on the table but seems to think better of it and hangs it on a hook by the door. "Coffee?" she asks, and my face must show my shock at the unexpected courtesy because she adds, "I'm making coffee for myself. Would you also like some?"

"Sounds good."

Sugar appears oddly nervous, her movements less deliberate, and the sight is so unsettling I almost ask her what's wrong. But then she removes her jacket and hangs it next to her bag. The strap has fallen. As expected, the top remains in place even as the thin silk hangs loosely below the curve of her shoulder. I stick my hands in my pockets to keep myself from doing something stupid like sliding it back up.

Once she's gone into the kitchen, I sit on the couch instead of inspecting the books like I want to. It'll look too much like

I'm interested in learning more about her. I already feel like I've given something away by coming here.

"Here," Sugar says a few minutes later, handing me a mug before sitting down in a small wicker chair next to the couch with her own. She rolls hers in the flat of her palms for a few moments before announcing, "What I'm about to ask you is illegal. Very illegal. I want your word that if you decide it isn't for you, you won't ask me any further questions or speak to anyone else about this conversation."

I take a slow sip of my coffee. Part of me thought the reason she didn't want to discuss it in the diner was because it was for the Dame. Not illegal, but perhaps...nuanced. Wishful thinking, I guess. She's in someone's pocket and wants me there, too.

I'm disappointed. Diaz is a good corner, never given me any reason to suspect he's on the take. Does he know Sugar is dirty? It's not hard to hide things from your partner; Kurt is proof of that. And the Nest walks a delicate tightrope between keeping its business license and serving patrons who are only too willing to pay to bend the rules.

Putting down the coffee, I place my hands on my knees. "I'm not interested in taking bribes, but thank you for the coffee." I start to stand, and she touches my shoulder before quickly pulling her hand back.

The coiled brown cuff on her wrist rotates once before settling down. Sam has a broach that turns into a small explosive. I'm not sure what Sugar's cuff does, but something tells me I might not want to find out.

"It's not like that. I'm clean." She thinks about it. "—ish." The corner of her mouth quirks, and my brow furrows. Was that a smile? "This has nothing to do with the corner's department, other than it's illegal. I'm not asking you to do any favors in your official capacity."

Leaning back, I rest my ankle on my knee and throw my arm over the back of the couch. I'm strangely relieved. I put the feeling aside to unpack later and raise an eyebrow at her. "In what capacity are you asking me for a favor?"

Her eyes flick briefly to my neck. "First, it's not a favor. You'd be paid. And second, do I have your word?" She takes another sip of her coffee, and her tongue darts out to grab an errant drop on her lip.

Succubi are disgusting. Nothing but vulgar, emotionally manipulative whores.

I shake the sound of Eliza's voice from my head. She'd despise me for this. The thought makes me sit up straighter. "Okay, you've got my attention, Writh. I give you my word to never speak of this again if I decline your proposal."

"Good." She looks down at her coffee cup and frowns. There's a long pause before she says, "Actually, how about something harder?" Before I can respond, she strides into the kitchen and pulls down a bottle of dark liquor but puts it back, instead pouring us both a glass of wine. If I wasn't concerned before about what she's into, I certainly am now.

"Thank you, again," I say, taking the glass from her and giving her a wry look.

"I need someone to Make a Seelie."

The glass has barely touched my lips, and I rear back in surprise, causing the contents to slosh up the sides. "I beg your pardon?"

"You heard me." Sugar leans back in her chair, crossing her legs and looking far more relaxed now that she's actually said the words. "A person of means has asked me to find them a Maker. They're willing to pay more than enough to help Maria and the girls." She fishes in her pocket for a piece of paper. "You'd get twice that amount."

The paper smells like jasmine and money. Looking at the numbers, I exhale like the wind's been knocked out of me. It's more than enough to help Kurt's family. It's enough to ensure Maria never has to work again—at least for her brief human life. "Is this person in their right mind?"

She taps a short nail against the side of her glass and purses her lips. "That, I can't say. But they are good for the money."

There's music playing somewhere outside and muffled laughter from next door. The small yellow orb lights on each side of the couch are working hard to dispel the increasing darkness.

"Hard to be good for the money when you're dead." I put my glass down, lean forward, and prop my elbows on my knees. "Seriously, who is this stupid? It's extremely risky, and for what?" I'd witnessed the Making of a Seelie once before. They were in unimaginable pain for three days before dying.

Sugar tenses at the sound of someone coming up the stairs, then relaxes as the footsteps continue to the next floor. She looks back at me and says, "I've been told they have their reasons. And wouldn't you ask for some of the money up front?" She cocks her head as if she's questioning my intelligence.

"Who are you worried is going to show up? Your boyfriend? Is he the jealous type?" I ask, tipping my head at the door. There's a flash of irritation on her face before she schools it back to ambivalence. Is it another corner? An incubus? Is Diaz married?

"You'd also receive a release, of course, from any liability should something go wrong. And an agreement never to disclose your involvement to the authorities."

"Why would I be worried about them telling the authorities? Wouldn't they be punished too?" The music outside is louder. It's a lively tune, something with horns, completely at odds with our conversation. She's not only asking me to do something illegal, but something that could get both me and my intended progeny killed.

She tips her head in a "maybe" gesture. My eyes lock on her fingers as she runs a hand up her arm and pushes the strap back into place. "Just a little extra insurance, I guess."

"Why don't you do it yourself?"

She hesitates but says, "I can't. I've never been good at it. It was a great disappointment to my Maker since I was meant to be part of a repopulation effort for the remaining members of my nest."

Sugar used to be human. It explains why her coloring is so different, more like a siren's than the concubi who originate from the south. Just like the vampires. Neither group wanted to share their territory, hence all the fighting. I file the rare fact about her away.

I stand and cross the room to release some energy. "This is ridiculous. There's no reason anyone should want this. Unless they're power hungry and stupid, extremely ill, or…"

I head toward the window. There are more people in the street, talking and eating. A few are dancing while kids race over the sidewalks. I turn away and look back at her. I'm behind her chair, and she hasn't turned around to watch me.

With one step, I could have her head bent to one side, my fingers pressing into those freckles on her arm and my fangs sinking into her lush vein. Her pulse reaches my ears, slow and steady, mesmerizing. I can practically taste her, can almost see the contrast between my tan skin against her pale throat.

The memory of our first meeting in the morgue comes back, the jerk of her chin as she made me lead the way. She's a succubus and a corner, and she's willingly leaving her back exposed to a vampire.

Like bait.

My eyes fall closed, and my head tips up. Manipulative little demon. She's playing me. With her abilities, I bet she's felt it every time my attention has fallen to the strap of her godsdamn top, too.

My voice drops. "No. I'll keep my word about this conversation, but no," I say with finality. I stride across the room and grab my coat from where I left it on the rack.

She doesn't speak, doesn't rise from her chair, doesn't try to stop me. Sugar remains in her seat, sipping her drink, gaze holding mine as I close the door behind me.

Chapter 14
Sugar

The water at the Fugue's edge is a muddy gray, a stark contrast with the butterfly's lime-green wings, vivid even in death. My eyes sweep up the towering wall that meets the upper city. A natural spring, deep within the mountains, feeds the Fugue, pushing it under the city's two parks. The water flows in and out of a network of caves before traveling out to the Corvid Sea. Must have been more rain this year. The watermark is unusually high, exceeding the normal water line by at least a foot.

To my right, the remains of the West Bridge are just visible above the water. Slightly closer, the East Bridge ascends from the Hollows across the water at a forty-five-degree angle. Corners circle us at a respectful distance, keeping any lookie-loos from getting too close to the crime scene. The burnt red of Jasper's hair is only just noticeable under his black hat as he huddles with the other reporters on the bridge.

Matt crouches by the body, speaking softly to Corinne, the evidence collector. A biting wind whips off the water, and I tie my hair back to keep it out of my face as I step closer to them. My partner stands with a groan and bends his head to speak to me. He covers his mouth to be sure nobody reads his lips.

"Killed elsewhere and dumped. Corinne thinks she's been dead a while." He pauses, his eyes despondent as he looks over the butterfly's injuries.

"Like a few months?" I murmur. I recognized her immediately. Tonya. The one in the newspaper Petra showed me, who went missing from CP's party. My gaze flits again to Jasper before landing on the group of fishers who found her body. There's a low stone wall bordering the sand. Beyond it is a road and a row of shops. They mostly sell bait, fishing equipment, or waterproof items for fae who choose to live in the river. It'd look almost cheerful if the beach wasn't permanently in shadow thanks to the wall. At least the lack of sun keeps the rotting fish smell to a minimum.

The fishers found the body at first light and bravely fought off the two ulgashen who'd followed the scent. One escaped. The other beast lies dead only a few feet away. A rusty trident sticks out of its chest, the tines covered in blood that looks and smells like rotten blackberries. A few fae have popped out of the river, only their heads visible, and watch us in curiosity.

"Anything unusual, Corinne?" I ask as I crouch next to Tonya's body, frowning at the unnatural angle of the woman's limbs.

Corinne is a trained examiner, but she's also a Seelie with an enhanced sense of smell. "She's definitely been dead for some time," she replies. "But she's well-preserved and colder to the touch than she should be. Someone kept her on ice." The three of us share a look. They kept her long enough so she couldn't be raised. Corinne reaches out and delicately touches Tonya's wings with two fingers, dusting her dark skin in a light layer of green powder. She closes her eyes as she sniffs. "No venom."

The mud squelches under my boots as I lean forward to examine the discoloration on Tonya's neck. Her head lolls to one side, no longer supported by an intact spine. Someone grabbed her head and twisted hard. When threatened, butterflies can release a toxin from their wings that confuses their assailant. They can also release powerful pheromones. They replenish their power through physical touch, which is why there are so many working at the Nest. If there's no venom residue on her wings, Tonya didn't or couldn't fight back.

"Attacked from behind, then, you think?" I ask.

Corinne nods. "Most likely. I'll have to get her back to the lab to see if she was drugged. But there aren't any defensive wounds I can see. She's got several broken nails, but those could have happened on the way down from the bridge. And, of course, the wings."

Matt's somber expression matches mine as we regard Tonya's broken wings. The left one has been snapped on three sides and hangs down like a folded piece of paper. The other cradles her body, pierced by several sharp rocks on the shore.

Two morgue assistants appear with a long rectangular box floating between them. One of them holds it aloft as Corinne and the other assistant float Tonya into it. I step back, startled, as her face transforms into Linnea's for a split second. My friend stares at me with empty eyes, and my heart beats loudly in my head. I wrench my eyes away as they close the lid.

"Detectives?" a voice calls out.

I turn to see a young man in a suit approaching us, delicately picking his way across the beach.

"Stop right there," Matt barks. "Back up and go back to the line. You're disturbing the scene." He glares at the other corners, who aren't doing anything to stop the man from coming closer.

Ignoring the stranger, I turn back to where Tonya's body left a defined imprint in the wet sand. My gaze catches on something shiny, and I crouch down, brushing the sand away.

Matt mutters, "The nerve of this guy."

"Idiot." I glance back in irritation before returning my attention to the sand.

The man freezes for a moment but now continues toward us with an apologetic grimace. "Sorry, but I need to speak to you both."

"Get back to the line now!" Matt yells again across the shore. I uncover a tiny jewel. Could be from Tonya but could just as easily have washed up on the beach.

I rise just as the man gives us another look of chagrin. He glances back toward the stone wall, where the corners and the reporters watch his progress with interest. "I just need a moment." He takes a few more tentative steps.

I flex my hand, and my cuff spins in readiness, but before I can do more, Matt takes three of his extra-long strides forward and grabs the man by the lapels with one hand. His voice is dangerously conversational. "What's your name?"

"Boltier," the man squeaks, his toes clearing the mud as Matt raises him aloft.

"Hi, Boltier. I'm Detective Diaz. You might remember me as the guy who told you to Get. Back. To. The. Fucking. Line."

"I…" He trails off as I step toward them both, my eyebrow raised in a threat. "Here." He fumbles to pull a piece of paper out of his pocket. I grab it while Matt continues to stare daggers at Boltier, who looks at risk of running out of oxygen.

Ice coats my veins as I read the precise handwriting and note the royal seal. "It's an order to vacate the Crown's property. Says we can take the body, but any further presence on the beach will be considered trespassing."

"What?" Matt carelessly tosses Boltier to the ground, and he falls on his ass in the mud. "Let me see that."

I hand him the paper and glower at Boltier, who despondently takes stock of his dirty clothes. "Who told the Crown?" I scan the bridge. Several of the reporters who write those fake puff pieces about CP are already here.

"I'm not at liberty to say." He tips his head up at me from his ungraceful position on the ground. There's no animosity coming off him; he's just another lackey following orders. I wonder if he sleeps with a picture of the monarchs, maybe jerks off over the royal portraits.

"Bodies from the Hollows have been dumped here plenty of times. How come I've never heard of the Crown stepping in before?" I ask.

"Again, I'm not at liberty to say," he responds primly as he struggles to his feet. I keep my eyes locked on his. His cheeks color as he fumbles over his next words. "I'll be waiting over there to ensure you vacate the premises."

Matt and I stare at Boltier's back in silence as he picks his way back to the line of corners who dutifully part for him. I turn back to the bridge, where Jasper's eyes meet mine. Holding up my hand, I crook a single finger and beckon him.

The other reporters clearly give him shit as he pushes through them and meets us off the sand, beyond the rock wall and away from anyone else.

"It's her, isn't it? Tonya?" he asks when he's about four feet away. Unlike Boltier, he doesn't seem concerned about his expensive shoes getting dirty.

"I can't confirm that officially, but since we need your help, I'll just say it's highly likely," I reply. "Since you're here and the corners who covered her disappearance aren't, please refresh our memories on the circumstances of her disappearance." I don't say, "since the corners who investigated her disappearance did fuck all and are most likely in the Crown's pocket," but he nods as if he hears it anyway.

Jasper runs a hand through his hair, and his eyes flit from side to side as if he can see all the memories in his head, neatly alphabetized. As a recorder, he probably can.

"She went with a few friends to a party in a suite at the Hotel LeMar. According to the hotel, CP rented the suite. They showed up just before midnight. Around three in the morning, her friends said they tried to find her to leave, but she wasn't in any of the rooms. They sent her a few messages but assumed she'd gone home with someone. When she still hadn't answered any of them the next day, they called the corners."

"I read your article." Jasper blinks at me in acknowledgment. In the article, he mentioned someone saw Tonya go into a room with CP. However, considering how many girls throw themselves at him, it wasn't suspicious on its own. But coupled with the Crown strong-arming us out of the crime scene? "Did you leave anything out?"

"Not at the time, no. But I've been tracking down anyone else I can find from that party, and they all said CP partied for hours in the main room. And in typical fashion, he wasn't shy about his activities with several of the guests, many at the same time." Jasper says it all rather clinically, just a reporter reciting facts.

A familiar shame rolls through me at the thought of CP's "activities." My temples pound, and a buzzing fills my ears, making it hard to concentrate on Jasper's words.

"But by all accounts—from those who remember, anyway—he only went into the bedroom with one girl, and she wasn't a butterfly. Nobody else was allowed in. There was a guard posted to make sure of it."

"So her friends were lying?" Matt asks. His eyes flick toward me, and I take a breath, smoothing my face into calm, professional interest.

Jasper sticks his hands into the pockets of his black raincoat. "Or mistaken. And only one of her friends said that. She could have had the bedrooms mixed up. There were four to choose from. She was pretty certain, though. Said Tonya had been trying to catch the prince's eye for a while."

There's a creaking sound, and we all glance over in time to see a small part of the collapsed West Bridge sink further into the water.

"Didn't turn out so well for her," Matt says, his voice quiet in the salty wind.

***

"Do those two ever stop?" Matt groans as we reach the door to Research & Evidence.

"You were gone for two hours!" Catriona shouts as we round the corner. "Why do you even need to take a lunch break? Can't you just live off the happiness you suck out of me every day?"

"Happiness?" Nelson scoffs from behind his desk. "If I could live on that, a miserable wretch like you wouldn't even qualify as an appetizer!"

I'm already on edge, and their bickering isn't helping. I slam my hand down on the bell, and it lets out a shrill dinging. It's a jerk move. Nelson and Catriona swing their heads my way in surprise, and I can feel Matt giving me a similar look.

"If you two wouldn't mind taking a break, we need some help." I rub the bridge of my nose between two fingers. Nelson and Catriona share a look, but neither gets up to see what we need. When there's another long beat of silence, I huff, "Please?"

"There. That wasn't so hard, was it?" Catriona smiles with feigned warmth as she crosses the room in two steps. She pulls out a clipboard and hands it to me.

Seeing I'm about to snatch it out of her hand, Matt reaches out and gently takes it from her. "Nothing too difficult. We just need the last known address of Tonya Penn, and criminal record, if any."

Catriona smiles sweetly at him as she takes back the clipboard. "Of course, Detective." She sways her hips a little as she walks toward her desk. I'm about to apologize when I feel the lust drift off of Nelson. I back away and walk down the hall to cool off before I give away their secret and add two more to the list of people who hate me in this department.

I haven't spoken to CP since the night before I asked Plichen to clean the apartment. My place is still clean. An image of him callously snapping Tonya's throat makes my stomach cramp with disgust. How many times has he been at my place since that night? I chew the inside of my lip, letting the pain distract from my nausea. He hasn't tried to come over, so none of my efforts mean shit. If he showed up tomorrow, would I have the strength to throw him out?

The other night, he told me I was just like him. And I've always told myself it wasn't true, but what does that even mean if I tacitly condone all his horrible behavior? It was sheer narcissism to believe anything I did would stop CP from doing whatever the fuck he wanted, but shouldn't I be doing the bare minimum to try? If I keep letting him into my bedroom, shouldn't I be doing something, anything, to mitigate his cruelty?

My mind is flung back six months before Linnea died.

"I can do something. You could run away," I plead with her. An hour before, I had Stanley Roman thank me for letting him lick the riding crop I'd used to turn his ass red. "I can help."

"Would you stop it? There's nothing you can do. Now turn around so I can unlace you."

It was the first time I'd ever heard her irritated. And I used her irritation as an excuse. Like a comfy blindfold. I should have pushed harder, should have stolen her out of that godsforsaken house whether she liked it or not.

Matt joins me, holding out a piece of paper. "No record," he says in his deep, soothing voice. The voice that makes victims and witnesses open up while mine makes even seasoned corners flinch.

I frown at the address. The puzzle of her death momentarily drives away my self-hatred. Tonya was a resident of the Third Circle. Hotel LeMar is near the Luminous Palace.

Glancing up at Matt, I ignore the look in his eyes that says he's waiting for an explanation for my behavior. "If she didn't die in the Hollows, why did her killer dump her body there? It would have been easier to toss it from the other side. Especially since it would have been more likely to drift into a cave and be eaten by an ulgashen."

"Maybe the killer thought one of the water residents would find it before that happened?" he says.

"What's the difference if they were going to dump her in the sand for the fishers to find?"

"Fair point. Sending a message?" Matt suggests as he taps his fingers against his chest in thought.

"To who?" I blow out a breath, and my heartbeat calms a little.

"It's 'to whom,'" Nelson calls from down the hall.

"Fucking cheetah shifter," I mumble under my breath. "Keep it up, Nelson. My apartment could use a nice rug!" I yell back as Matt snorts a laugh.

Chapter 15
Draven

There's no tinkling bell as I walk into the apothecary. Instead, a giant parrot squawks from the perch of her floor-to-ceiling cage beside the counter.

"Tricky, tricky, little Mickey. Sure you wanna do that?" She ruffles her feathers, purple and black, with a shock of red on top.

"Hello, Sacha," I say as I walk past the overflowing shelves stuffed with tins, boxes, and bottles. Bags of powders and salts line the floor, spilling into the aisles. A mix of smoke and spice fills the air, layered over the unmistakable smell of Duft's cologne. Half the orb lights are dark, but I'm pretty sure I'm the only one in the shop. "Where's your boss?"

"You don't have the cards. You don't have the cards." She bobs her head eagerly as I approach.

"I've got four aces," I whisper as I poke a finger through her cage. She sidesteps along her wooden post to let me scratch her head.

"Dirty cheat. Lousy, stinking, dirty cheat," she croaks as she leans into my hand.

Duft got her from the Dame years ago. Sacha used to sit in the gaming hall, overseeing the endless exchange of coin in the

Nest. Unfortunately, she picked up a little too much of the banter. Gamblers are superstitious sorts and didn't appreciate her exclamations regarding their poor chances.

"Stop molesting my bird," Duft's sandpapery voice calls from back. He appears a few moments later, lugging a blue patterned jar nearly as big as his expansive chest. He's practically spherical and not a tall man, with dark eyes and a shaved head. When I move to help him, he shakes his head, setting the jar on the floor. "Every year, I promise myself it's the last time I order this expensive shit, and every year, I do it anyway." He wipes his sweaty brow with his sleeve.

"What is it?" I open the top and examine the fine gray sand inside. There's nearly no odor to it. Might as well be chalk.

"Crescenite." He shuffles back behind the counter, grabs a half-finished mug of tea, and downs it in one go.

My brows knit as I look up at him. "Isn't it normally blue?" Crescenite is a growth enchantment mix. Parents buy it to give to their human children. It bolsters their immune system and physical strength so they have a fighting chance against their fae peers.

Duft avoids my eye as he answers, "The kids don't like the taste of the blue one."

I nod smugly. "Ah, and I bet you're charging the same price? How much money are you losing on this, exactly?"

"Shut up," he grumbles.

"Silence for the Dame!" Sacha screeches, angling her head toward me for more pets. I stroke her soft feathers, and she gives me an affectionate nibble.

"How you holding up?" Duft turns away from me as he speaks, grabbing the kettle and filling it with water. He opens the belly of a small stove and turns the heated stones inside over so the hottest side faces up before shutting the door and setting the kettle on top to boil.

I often brought Kurt to the apothecary to get tonics for the kids and Maria or to ask Duft to identify illegal enhancement mixtures. The apothecary knew what it had meant to me to have made a real friend. Someone I could trust.

Duft and I knew each other in Ensame. He'd come to Drahma City before me and is the main reason I picked it instead of somewhere else in Eddahn. He used to run an apothecary there too, a place I found myself going more and more after he hired a vampire with long dancer's limbs and blond hair.

I hurl the thought of Eliza from my mind and say, "Fine. Okay."

"Fine, or okay?" He pulls the kettle off the stove and begins pulling down half a dozen jars from the nearby shelves. He mixes the concoction into two metal strainers, places them into mugs for each of us, and pours over the boiling water. The steam smells of licorice and something spicy I couldn't identify if you paid me. But Duft can. His power is the ability to pick out the components and their exact amount from any mixture.

When he places the mug in front of me, my shoulders slump, and the words spill out of me. "Kurt was in debt up to his eyeballs. Maria is freaking out, justifiably, terrified she's going to lose the house. An insidious succubus just offered me a way to help, but it's completely ludicrous. And dangerous. And illegal." I release a breath, relieved to have told someone. I wish I had a recorder's ability. Then I could show my entire bizarre meeting with Sugar to Duft.

"So not fine or okay." He deadpans before taking a sip of his tea. I follow suit. "What are you doing hanging around with a succubus?"

"Sugar is a corner. She was at Kurt's raising." Her name sounds strange on my lips. It might be the first time I've ever said it out loud. I have the inane desire to say it again, to sound it out.

Duft pauses, the mug halfway to his mouth. "Sugar? Sugar Writh?"

My brows raise. "The one and only. You know her?"

He coughs and actually blushes. "I've met her once or twice. She's a very talented woman."

I narrow my eyes at him. "Were you a client of hers, Duft?" The thought of it causes a storm of emotions inside me. Surprise, curiosity, and the tiniest spark of...envy.

"It was a long time ago. You know I was incredibly angry when I left Ensame. Bitter at the whole world. She, uh, helped me make use of those feelings." He rubs a hand across his chest. "It's a heady thing, to give up control. You should try it."

"Winner! Winner!" Sacha interjects from her perch. "Take home a prize!"

As my eyes flick to the bird, the thought of giving up control to Sugar isn't what flashes through my mind. It's the thought of what it would take for her to lose control, to let that permanent mask of ambivalence drop. It wasn't really a joke when I told her I wondered if she was capable of smiling. I want to dislike her; I *do* dislike her. But she strikes me as a deeply unhappy person. An awful, deceptive, rude, unhappy person.

Duft floats a few items toward him from the shelves and begins weighing and mixing on the counter. His fingers, thick as they are, are nimble as he takes a pinch of this and a sprinkle of that. "You're considering it?" he asks, head down.

"No. Maybe." I drag a hand down my face and take another sip of tea. "I promised Kurt I would take care of them."

"You could ask your uncle," he says quietly. "Would mean a bit of pride-swallowing and some serious strings attached, but he'd give you access to your accounts."

The anger claws up my spine. My teeth extend before I pull myself together and rein in my emotions. Half the time, I feel like a child throwing a tantrum. The other half, I think I haven't punished them enough for what they did to me, to Duft, to everyone in Ensame. And then I feel guilty for not doing more for my people, for not marching back there and burning the whole place to the ground. I consider whether Sugar's power could make me feel calm about the whole situation, if only for a moment.

"No," I breathe. "No, I won't do that."

He looks up from where he's filling vials with the concoction he's just made. "Do you have any other options besides Madame—Sugar's proposal?"

I ignore his little slip. What did he call her? Madame Writh? Some stage name? "Not at the moment. And the creditors are already getting persistent."

"Why'd she come to you?" Duft taps the glass vial to level out the powder inside before weighing it on an ancient scale.

"She needs a vampire." I shake my head at him, telling him I can't give him more than that. "I agreed not to tell anyone about the offer if I didn't take it."

"How about best-case/worst-case? Can you give me that?"

I tip my head up to the ceiling and eye the weird brown stain that's in a different place every time I come in. "Best case, it earns me enough money to set Maria and the girls up for life. Worst case, I die painfully and publicly."

He blows out his cheeks in a loud exhale. "Well, those are some options. Can you tell me what she gets out of this?"

What *does* Sugar get out of this? Frowning, I replay the conversation in my head and come up with nothing. "I don't know. Money?" It's a big risk for money. She probably makes as much—or as little, I should say—as I do as a corner. And the Dame pays well. If Duft's wistful look is anything to go by, she must have been good at her job. Then again, the fae really are shit with money. She could be in as much debt as Kurt.

Duft rearranges several jars, digging into the back of the shelf, before finding the one he wants and setting it down. He leans against the counter and crosses his arms, a thoughtful look on his face. I know he misses Ensame. This shop is only a third of the size of the one he had before. Starting over is rough.

"Look," he says. "I know it's going to be tough for you to trust anyone, let alone a woman, after what happened. And I'm not over the moon about you having your fangs ripped out in public, but it sounds like you have two choices and have already decided against one of them."

Gods. Would they really execute me like that? Rip out my fangs and let me starve to death? Watch as my power dwindles to nothing and my body shrivels to dust? I grimace in disgust.

"I don't like the idea of it either." I pause and let out a long exhale. "My uncle probably wouldn't let it get that far. He still needs me alive. And I guess there is a third option, and that's to give Maria what I can and help her and the girls find a cheaper place they can afford on her income."

Duft raises his eyebrows at me and nods like he's considering it. "Yeah, you could do that too. No beautiful, devious succubus required."

The pained look on Maria's face as she tore through the house looking for the paper flashes through my mind. Those girls lost their father, and now they were going to lose their house? The place where they had birthday parties and family dinners? My expression darkens.

He notices my look and huffs. "Looks like you're not a fan of that option either."

"Time for the run! Place your bets and watch out!" Sacha announces as someone enters the shop.

A small woman with light brown hair approaches. Her appearance triggers that tingling feeling in my brain, like I've forgotten something. She waves a hand absentmindedly through the air, and the mud on her shoes disappears. It must have started raining since I've been here.

"Good evening," Duft calls. "How can I help you?"

"Step right up! Step right up!" Sacha echoes.

The woman gives the parrot an indulgent smile and asks, "Good evening. Where are your protective charms?"

"Back left," Duft says, pointing into the dim aisle behind me.

"I'll show you." I give her a polite smile. "Follow me, ma'am." I weave my way past the cosmetic enhancements and temporary clothing tattoos until we reach the section on protective charms. As one of the best ingredients to bind a protection charm, the smell of charcoal is nearly overwhelming.

"Here you go. Everything from tonics that will last around forty-eight hours to charms that'll work for six months."

"Oh, thank you," she says, her eyes widening at the options. "I've never bought one of these before. I had no idea there were so many kinds." She levitates a purple box off the shelf and studies the ingredients.

"I don't mean to pry, but I'm a corner. Is there anything I can do to help?"

Her face falls before twisting into anger. "It's the ulgashen. I live in the Hollows. It's gotten so bad lately. I don't want my family members going out without something extra. And then this business with the dead butterfly." She shudders. "It's just not the same place anymore. In the last week, three families I know have just up and left. Moved away."

The orb flickers out above us, casting her face into shadow. Behind her, the shelves become dark, angular mountains. Duft bangs something, and the light comes sputtering back to life.

"I'm sorry." My chest constricts as the image of Kurt's shredded chest rips through my mind. "You're completely right," I say with ferocity. "It has gotten worse."

"We don't want to leave. My family has lived in the old city for seven generations. So..." She holds up the box and shrugs.

As much as I admire her for wanting to stick it out, Kurt's words about not wanting his family to move to the Hollows hang in my head. What if the ulgashen keep coming?

"This one is good." I grab one I know several corners use and hand it over. "You heard about the butterfly?" The discovery of the Unseelie girl who'd last been seen with CP was big news at the department this morning, as was the Crown muscling Writh and Diaz out of the crime scene.

"We own a bait and fish shop on the Fugue," she explains. "My husband was the one who killed the ulgashen. That poor girl, dumped like trash. Who does that? Terrifying creatures. I don't know why the council or the Crown can't get rid of them." She sniffs and pulls down three more of the charms I suggested.

I already know she was there, so I'm not sure why I ask. "Did you happen to see a detective with silver hair?"

The woman lightens and nods emphatically. "Detective Writh, right? She and her partner came into the shop to take my statement. Both of them were very irate at that vile little slug from the Crown." She abruptly stops speaking, and her gaze darts around the shop before coming to land on mine.

Snorting, I say, "You'll find no snitches here. People who follow bad orders commit two evils, the act itself and being too stupid to think for themselves."

She chuckles in relief as we turn and travel back up toward the front. "They were very nice. Thanked my husband for his bravery. Detective Writh even offered to give my daughter a tour of the department. Maya wants to be a corner."

"Really?" I say in confusion. Sugar didn't strike me as the type to willingly endear herself to anyone, even children.

We get to the counter, and she puts her purchases down for Duft to bag and total. "The other detective seemed surprised too." She laughs. "Detective Writh said I reminded her of an old friend."

I smile at the woman and give her my card after she pays. "Please contact me if you have any more trouble with the ul-gashen."

"Well?" Duft asks once she's gone. "Made a decision, have you?"

"Go for broke, handsome. All in! All in!" Sacha chants, puffing herself up to three times her size and shaking her tail feathers.

"Unfortunately, yes. And she never said I had to keep it a secret if I agreed, so listen up, because I'm going to need your help."

Chapter 16
Sugar

The Rettirness Building sits in the Third Circle, in the neighborhood of Fellkirk. It's a stone's throw from the Nest, which makes sense since so many of the employees patronize the Dame's establishment. From my vantage point in the deli across the street, I've got a clear shot of the front door.

Judges, lawyers, clerks, and corners all stream in and out of the black marble building. It should be beautiful, but not even the wide veins of gold can stop it from sucking up all the sunlight. It's cold and imposing, like an oversized mausoleum. My eyes scan the dome on top, with its shining statue of Rett, the god of justice, holding his sword in one hand and a loaf of bread in the other. His eyes have been following me since I set foot in the deli, waiting for me to chicken out.

My sandwich was excellent. I had a top-up from a donor. We closed two other cases this week and might have a lead on someone else who could have seen Carter Fox leave the club before he bled out next to decaying lettuce leaves. I should be in a good mood. Instead, I'm sick to my stomach.

Petra exits the building with her customary stride. She crosses the street toward me before turning the corner. I walk out the back door just in time to see her stop in front of a laundry. She's inside for about ten minutes before walking out with her various clothes and suits. She's paid for them to be shrunk to make it easier to walk home, so none look large enough to fit even a small child.

When she takes another turn, I dart across the street, watching her reflection in the windows so I know when she's far enough away for me to follow. Petra keeps her head up, smiles at a few people, and doesn't stop again until she reaches a swanky apartment building. The door attendant cheerfully opens the front door, a wide pane of glass enchanted to show images from around Eddahn with an ornate bronze handle.

Just as Petra moves to step inside, I move, sidling up beside her. "Room for one more?"

She gives a satisfying startle at my sudden appearance but disappointingly doesn't clutch her purse to her body or cry out. "Sugar?" A wrinkle appears between her eyes. "What are you doing here?"

"I happened to be by Rettirness. Figured I'd follow you home." The door attendant's eyes widen. She even takes a bold step toward me before I stop her with an arched brow. "Thought you might be up for some takeout and girl talk."

Despite being shorter, Petra looks down her nose at me, her expression brimming with contempt. "Girl talk? Really?"

I shrug.

"Couldn't you have just looked up my address?" she asks.

"Probably."

"So you followed me home just to prove you're better at it than me?"

"Maybe."

"Haven't you received extensive training in surveillance? Wouldn't it be pretty pathetic if you weren't better at it?" She switches her laundry to the other arm. They must have only changed the size, not the weight.

"Yes," I sigh. "Enough with the cross-examination. Are you inviting me in?"

"Would you like me to call anyone, Ms. Kohl?" the attendant asks as she shifts her weight from one foot to the other. She's certainly a brave one.

"No," Petra says, smiling kindly at her. "That won't be necessary. Detective Writh would never do me any harm." She says the last part like a threat and beckons me to follow her with a jerk of her head.

We don't speak at all as we ascend a staircase that's really more of a piece of art. Its curves are light and fluid, the complete opposite of the Rettirness. Petra's apartment is on the second floor. It's clean and organized, with a subtle floral scent, and filled with the kind of elegant touches I'll never achieve.

She places her bag on a blond wood desk in the corner of the open-plan living room and pulls out three case files, one green and two blue. Blue is for prosecution, green for defense.

I wander freely, snooping through the knick-knacks on her mantel and the fancy leather-bound legal books on her shelves, even stopping to peek in her fridge. Petra pretends she's ignoring me, but her eye twitches when I pick up the framed image on her desk of her with a similar-looking woman. Her sister? Her mother?

"Not going to offer me a drink?" I ask, turning to face her.

She's removed her shoes and leans against the pristine island countertop. "I'm still deciding." Finally, she huffs and pulls out two bottles of gyllino, a sparkling fruit drink, and hands one to me.

Popping the cork, I take a long sip. It's good. I didn't even realize how thirsty I was. "Thank you."

She nods, continuing to assess me. "Well? Get on with it." She walks toward the living room and sinks onto the couch. "Are you here for legal advice? Done something bad?"

"Those things are not mutually inclusive," I say as I shrug off my jacket and sit down next to her. "I'm actually here to help you. I was thinking about your offer. Or demand, I should say, to work with you and build a case against Alaric."

After a brief look of surprise, Petra schools her face into casual interest. She plays with a gold charm on her necklace and takes another drink. "Is that right?"

"I'm willing to help you, on one condition." She frowns but nods at me to go on. "I'll do it if you tell me what went down between you and Jasper."

Petra's power makes her feelings tangible as her anger instantly swirls around her like a literal storm. Wind lifts the hair from her shoulders and ruffles the edges of my collar. "No," she says flatly.

"Wow." I lean back into the comfortable cushions. "Not even to take down the worst man in Eddahn? Must be an awful story. Well, it was worth a try. Where do you want to start?"

She startles. "Wait, you still want to help me? Even if I don't air my dirty laundry for your gratuitous perusal?"

"*Your* dirty laundry? So you're the villain in this story?" I resist sliding closer to her and inhaling her outrage, doubtless at Jasper and me.

Petra ignores me, stands, and marches over to the desk. From a deep drawer at the bottom, she pulls out a file, then another, and another. There must be at least twenty-five by the time she's done. They're not green or blue, but beige. These are clearly her personal collection. She waves a hand at them. "These are the incidents I've collected on CP."

"That seems...light?" It's a lot, but Alaric has clearly done more than twenty-five awful things.

"These are the ones I have the best chance of proving because the victims are willing to testify. With the right help." She pulls one out and opens it. "Three and a half years ago, CP burned down a restaurant when the owner refused to kick out other guests to make room for his large party." She flips to a different folder. "Two years ago, CP beat a recorder nearly to death when he tried to get images of CP during a party." She picks up another. "And last year, he got high in the park and threw a child's dog into the river. When the kid cried about it, he threw him in too."

There's a lead weight sinking fast in my stomach. Bile crawls up my throat, and I struggle to swallow it down. "They found that kid, though, right?" I surreptitiously wipe my palms on my pants.

Petra gives me a perplexed look. "They found the kid," she says slowly. "Doesn't excuse what he did."

"No," I say weakly before clearing my throat. "No, it doesn't." These are big things. Incidents where there would be lots of witnesses. There's no excuse for him not to be charged. But he wasn't, not for any of the ones she's just mentioned. "You probably already have this, but here." I grab my jacket and pull a piece of paper from the pocket. "Alaric's background check. People have tried before to charge him. A few things stuck."

She pulls it from my hand and scans it with her eyes. It's not much. And his last conviction for anything was twenty years ago. Her hand falls to her side, and she stares off into the distance, thinking. "I did wonder if it had something to do with his power. Some ability he has?"

I shrug. "It's possible." That would be a very convenient excuse for my behavior.

The members of the royal family are all Seelie, of course, and they do their best to keep their specific powers under wraps. During the war, it was a strategic decision. Now, it's tradition more than anything, and sometimes it comes out anyway. King Alistair is an enormous bear shifter. And Lira is a tidakos; she can absorb knowledge from books and objects. Most people suspect Queen Cassandra has some kind of elemental power.

Fenrik, Alaric, and Isadora are all completely unknown. None of them need to use their power when there are always enough servants and groupies to do it for them.

I try to think back on my every interaction with Alaric, an exercise that makes me more ashamed by the second, to see if I remember any particular power manifesting. It's something I've considered before. I don't think he's a shifter. Some more powerful shifters can tap into certain elements of their animals without shifting completely, but there's usually some visible sign. Considering all the stuff he snorts, it'd be a miracle if he'd never lost control of his animal form.

Shaking my head, I say, "I can't think of anything I've seen."

"Why would you have seen it? You spend a lot of time clubbing with the crown prince?" She snorts. I inhale sharply, about to make some excuse, when she snaps her fingers at me. "Sorry, that was rude. You're referring to when you worked at the Nest, right? Did he go there often?"

I hide my discomfort by taking another sip of my drink. "He didn't. Not often. But he hired hosts for private parties. And he went to parties I attended when I worked there."

Petra nods, her eyes distant as she thinks. "The most important thing," she says, coming back to sit down beside me, "is he cannot know about this. We need to be airtight before bringing charges, and I don't want any of the Crown's spies getting wind of this and thwarting our efforts." She gives me a pointed look.

"Heard about that, did you?" I drawl, referring to Tonya's crime scene and that pissant, Boltier.

"Everybody heard about that. I want CP to walk into court thinking he's there to get a godsdamn massage and walk out in a prison jumpsuit."

I blow out a breath. "Do you really think we can do this? You think the king and queen will let us put their firstborn behind bars?"

Petra's eyes are alight with determination. "There's a reason they fuck with everything before it gets to trial, before it gets too public, when they can still quash the rumors and send CP away to 'recuperate' until people forget about it. A trial, with all those recorders and everyone watching? Fae memories are long, particularly the Unseelie's." She points at me. "They won't let them just refuse. Especially when he's going to live another eight hundred years." She scoffs. "He can afford it."

A shiver goes across my shoulders while the tiny hairs on my arms stand on end. This would be public, very public. If I stand next to Petra while she's dragging Alaric across the coals, he will fight dirty. He'll make sure everyone knows about me, about us.

"I—" Before I can get another word out, a note appears in my pocket. I pull it out, grateful for the reprieve from disappointing Petra.

I accept.

316 Vermeer

—D

Relief cascades down my body like someone pulled a plug. I stand, grabbing my jacket and hastily shoving it on.

"You're leaving? We haven't even started." Petra says in surprise.

"When do you want to meet next? I've got a lead I need to run down now," I lie. "And do you want to keep meeting here?"

She looks around her apartment, considering. "I definitely don't want to do this at the office. The Crown has ears on every floor of Rettirness. But people might wonder why we're meeting here when we're not friends."

"None taken," I say drily.

Her lip quirks. "You know what I mean. It looks suspicious. I'll think about it. Expect my note. Oh, and Sugar?"

"Yes?" My hand is on the doorknob, and my mind is on getting to Draven before he talks himself out of it.

"You keep calling him Alaric. I don't like it—it's too sympathetic. Stick to CP," she says dismissively, turning back to her desk.

I turn away and open the door before she can see the color in my cheeks. "Noted."

Chapter 17
Draven

There's a knock on my door less than thirty minutes after I sent Sugar the note. The speed of her response makes me even more curious to know what she's getting out of this. I cross the living room and pull open the door.

"Got your note," Sugar says, her face the same unruffled mask it was when I left her at her house. She steps into the entryway without waiting for me to invite her in.

"Hello to you, too," I drawl, shutting the door behind her. I almost ask to take her coat, but I don't need the distraction. Instead, I brush past her and motion to the living room. "Please have a seat, and we can discuss this plan of certain death."

Sugar freezes. Her eyes widen with shock as they roam over my apartment. "Do you live with someone?"

"No. It's just me." Is she worried about someone hearing us? My apartment is on the top floor. We should be perfectly safe.

"You decorated this apartment? Like this?" Her eyes travel up the red and gold patterned wallpaper and across to the ornate gold and black velvet loveseat with matching side chairs.

Her brow is furrowed in confusion, and I finally catch on. "No, I didn't decorate it like this. It came furnished. I'm renting it. The owners say they plan to come back at some point, but they've been traveling for years now."

I suppose seeing the apartment through her eyes would be pretty weird. When I first moved in, I figured I'd change a few things, but it just never seemed necessary. There are places to sit, sleep, and eat. Why do I need to mess around with window treatments? But watching her cautiously run her fingers over the brass, life-size crane balancing an orb light atop its head, it does seem a little much.

"Is your bedroom full of mirrors?" she murmurs as she removes her jacket and moves deeper into the apartment. I lose focus on her question while I confirm, with some relief, that she's wearing a long-sleeved turtleneck.

She doesn't stop at the couch but walks down the hall, toward my bedroom, and I'm mindlessly following. I guess we're allies now, so some trust is warranted. I'm not sure why I don't stop her. She pokes her head in and takes in my non-mirrored and, thankfully, bird-free bedroom before turning around to face me.

Her eyes are level with my mouth, and I'm pretty tall. I resist looking down to check the heel on her boots. "Satisfied?" I ask.

"Not remotely." She heads back and takes a seat in a side chair. "I'm going to need your word again. I'll give you the details, but you need to promise me—"

"Slight problem there," I say, cutting her off. "I told a friend of mine. An apothecary. He has a few things that should help the process." Sugar needs to remember I'm not someone she can easily control.

She rolls her eyes toward the ceiling before closing them and exhales through her nose. Her gaze snaps back to me. "You weren't supposed to tell anyone. You gave me your word."

"I gave you my word I wouldn't tell anyone if I didn't accept. I'm accepting." Sinking onto the couch, I give her smirk. There's the slightest purse to her lips, and I file it away like I'm hoarding her every expression.

"Fine. Who is this apothecary?" Her fingers curl around the ends of the shiny armrests. She looks like a queen, straight-backed and imperious.

"A former client of yours. The name Duft ring a bell?"

To my complete surprise and extreme irritation, she smiles. Actually smiles. It's small and without teeth, but it's still a damn smile. For Duft.

"It does." The smile drops, and she's back to business. "You're going to be Making a Seelie female. She's rich and important enough that she may be able to keep you out of trouble if this is discovered, but that's not guaranteed. So we're going to do everything we can to ensure it isn't."

"You're not going to give me a name?" I cock my head to the side. If I am caught, my uncle might let me stew in jail for a while, but he'd probably have some minor heartburn over my execution. I'm holding on to that hope, slight as it is.

"No. The fewer details you have, the better. She's young and knows the risks. You get half the money up front and half when it's successful. I'll message you with a time and place when she's ready. Is there anything else you really need to know?"

"Yes, there is." I lean forward, my eyes locking on hers. "What's in it for you?"

"Why is that relevant?" There's an almost imperceptible tightness in her shoulders, a slight hitch to her cheek.

I don't know why I want to push so badly. Why every tiny crack I see in that stone-cold veneer is so thrilling. I'm pretty sure underneath it all, Sugar isn't sweet and helpless. She's never going to show up at my door, crying and saying she made a terrible mistake. She'd never beg for my forgiveness. But she's hiding something. What would make Sugar Writh break?

"So it's not about the money?" I draw my eyes down her figure, to the nice jacket, the well-made shoes. Not fancy, but not cheap.

"Didn't realize you were so concerned about my financial situation. But yes, I'm being paid." She gives a small huff of irritation or boredom.

"You didn't answer my question." I give her a pointed look, but she doesn't respond, just continues to stare at me.

The sound of notes being delivered to both of us at once breaks the silence. We pull them from our pockets. I have two. One from Captain Gibson, which it looks like Sugar has as well. And one from Marisol, the woman I met at the apothecary.

"Ulgashen attack," I say, rising from my seat. It must be serious. I'm supposed to be on bereavement leave and doing only boring administrative tasks.

She nods. "Yes, I can read." I restrain myself from responding and we quickly pull on our coats. As we head to my door, she throws over her shoulder, "Do you need to let the crane out before you go?"

It takes me a full second to realize she's making a joke and another few seconds to get over my shock. I grab my jacket and follow her out. "He's housebroken."

***

When Sugar and I step out of the portal closest to the Hollows, someone slams into my shoulder. Residents are running over the bridge, away from the under city. Corners are everywhere, herding people or running toward the chaos. The sky has darkened, and raindrops plink on the metal bridge supports as we hustle across the Fugue.

I turn right toward Marisol's shop, surprised when I find Sugar next to me. Then I remember what Marisol said about Sugar's offer to her daughter. The door is locked, and I pound on the wood frame. A window beside me creaks open.

"We're in here! We're safe. They're over there!" Marisol stands at the window, a large man with a weatherbeaten face behind her. They both look worried but calm.

"Stay inside. Board your windows up if you can. Don't come out until we sound the all clear," Sugar orders. They nod in the affirmative, and we take off.

The street declines, speeding our way, and we somehow skip several blocks. With my vampire speed, I'm faster than Sugar, but I keep pace with her anyway. "Why does the magic here like you so much?"

"What?" she says. She's running fast and shows no sign of tiring.

"It's helped me out, but it responds to you differently. I thought so when we came to your apartment." We take a sharp turn and have to dodge several more people. "And now it's definitely helping us get there faster."

Sugar wipes the rain off her face and pushes her wet hair behind her ears. It's darker here, still silver and shiny, but like a blade instead of a diamond. She curses as she barely avoids hitting an overturned cart in the street. "The magic protects the Hollows, Draven. It's not being nice to me. It's helping us so we'll move our asses and save its people."

I disagree but say nothing as we arrive at a larger cross street. The ulgashen are everywhere. I've never seen so many. Did they all come from the sea caves? And what the hel is driving them onshore in such a mass?

Everywhere we look, the streets are thick with fighting. There's black and red blood spattered over a child's chalk drawing on the sidewalk. A bird shifter flies up before shifting back into a corner and wrapping her legs around an ulgashen's neck. The fae sticks a short sword straight through the top of its skull. Sam nods to me as she rushes past in a blur, fangs extended and a long rip through her shirt. An ulgashen roars, its teeth bloody, at a fox shifter who bites it on the ankle before dashing away, baiting it to follow. Matt spots us and whistles.

"Funnel formation," he says as we approach. "Half of us are pushing them down the side streets and alleyways, where there's less room for them to maneuver. The others will meet them there and take them down. You two take that alley. I'll herd them your way." Matt holds a baton in one hand and a short sword in the other as he heads toward a group of ulgashen, readying for the fight.

Sugar nods, and we sprint off into a small offshoot between two taller apartments. Several of the residents in the higher windows are hanging out, watching the action like we're the evening entertainment. We position ourselves a third of the way down. A slight flare of panic rises in my chest at the thought of getting myself killed before I can help Maria.

Flicking my eyes to Sugar, I shout, "How do I know you've got my back?"

"How do I know you've got mine?" she replies. Her tone is dark and determined. She holds her short sword in her left hand and extends her right out to her side and flexes her fingers. The brown coiled cuff rotates once, then twice, and on the third rotation, it extends and slides into her hand until she's gripping it like a handle. It lengthens and grows like a fuse burning in reverse until it's ten feet of corded leather.

A whip.

Sugar warms up her arm, circling it at her side and around her head. She catches my stunned expression and says, "Eyes forward, Flint." But even in the darkening alley, with rain and shadow drenching her face, I swear I see a tiny smirk and a glimpse into why just her name makes Duft blush.

Matt runs forward, leading two ulgashen our way before slipping back behind them. They catch sight of us and charge, their long black arms swinging out with lethal claws. Sugar rotates her arm and snaps out with the whip. It wraps around the ulgashen's thigh, and she pulls hard, sending the creature tumbling backward. She runs up and impales it on her sword when it hits the ground.

I run toward the wall, using my speed to climb six feet up before leaping off and onto the other ulgashen's back. With one hand, I stab its chest, and with the other, I cut off its airway until it falls forward, plummeting to the ground. I leap off before my legs get trapped beneath it. Beyond the entrance to the alleyway, Matt and other corners fight off others, stemming the tide, but there are three more coming toward us.

One jumps forward, grazing Sugar with its claws. My heart pounds as I turn toward the other two, shoving one into the other. These ones seem less interested in fighting each other than taking a chunk out of us, and they both turn back to me. Leather wraps around the one closest to me, and Sugar drags it back while I battle the other.

A steady flow of them tears down the alley, and I'm lost in the scent of their sickly black blood and the endless sound of bodies falling. Sugar's hair flashes in my periphery. The sight only barely calms my panic at having to bury another friend, coworker, whatever she is. One of them shoves me back, and I roll to the side just in time to see another charge toward her.

Her face is pure vengeance, and something tells me she's not seeing the ulgashen as she hacks off their limbs. One falls on top of me, and I'm holding him off, my arm against his neck when I see an enormous ulgashen sprint down the alley, the creature's long strides carrying it straight to Sugar. It backhands her across the chest, and she flies through the air. When her back cracks against the brick wall, I feel it in my spine.

With a grunt, I twist the neck of the one on top of me and run toward her. Another steps in my path, and I barely see it as I stab through its gut. The giant one reaches her as I leap over the bodies trying to get closer. It grabs Sugar by the shoulders and lifts her into the air. Her whip has disappeared, but she doesn't raise her sword. Her hair glints like steel, and she pushes the palm of her hand against the beast's chin.

Footsteps sound behind me, and I twist, trying to focus on my new attacker. When I'm able to turn back, my mouth drops open. Sugar has holstered her sword.

What the hel is she doing?

She pulls her arm back and punches through the ulgashen's chest, ripping out his sticky black heart. The beast freezes, its arms falling. Sugar drops back to the ground, crouching to cushion her fall. Our eyes meet as she flings the heart to the side and casually shakes the blood from her hand.

It might be the sexiest fucking thing I've ever seen.

When five come down the alley at once, we push through. Blood and water drench every part of me. Gore covers my forearms as I behead another beast. I stumble back as I pull my swords from the creature's flesh. A searing pain drives into my shoulder as one of them catches me with its teeth. I shout in pain, but before it can bite down further, there's a sick popping sound. I turn to see Sugar's whip unwinding from its neck, having squeezed the head clean off.

Matt rushes in behind another two. "This is the last of them!" he shouts. He takes his baton and slams it hard into the knee of the beast rushing Sugar while she's distracted with another. Instead of going down, it pivots, pushing across the wall and reaching for Matt when he's mere inches away.

"Matt!" she shouts with fear I didn't think she could feel. She pushes her attacker off with a burst of strength, slamming its skull into the ground. She's scrambling for the one attacking Matt, but I get there faster.

Matt holds its jaws open as it tries to sink its teeth into his head. With as much strength as I have left, I move toward them in a blur, driving my sword up and cutting off the entire front of the thing's face before Matt kicks it hard in the chest. It tips backward with a gurgled protest before falling to the floor, splashing us all with more blood and filthy groundwater.

It's strangely quiet for a moment, only the sound of our labored breathing filling the alley. Even the rain has stopped, and there's no more shouting from the streets. Sugar crosses the last few feet to get to her partner. She touches his sleeve, as if to be sure he's still standing there, her throat bobbing.

He pats her fondly on the shoulder. "I'm all right. You're all right." He smiles.

Her jaw clenches, and she nods. "You're all right."

Matt chuckles. "Getting soft on me, kiddo?"

Her face transforms into her typical insouciance as she snorts a laugh, the tension in her eyes draining away. "Kiddo? I've got more than eighty years on you, man-child."

"Yeah, but you Unseelie age so slow. Mature slow too." He grins at her rolling eyes before holding out his hand and shaking mine. "Thank you."

"No problem." I catch Sugar's eye, but she quickly twists her head, examining the carnage surrounding us. The alleyway is filled with dead ulgashen, their blood congealing into a disgusting tarry mass.

"Everyone okay down there? Need a healer?" Victor Anistemi calls from the end of the alley.

I let out a low whistle. "The necro is here? Damn. They really called in everyone."

"Man looks like he couldn't heal a bloody nose," Matt murmurs.

It's true. Victor's skin is waxy, and he looks like he hasn't slept in days. But as a necro, his healing power is slightly stronger than most. Raising someone from the dead returns them to a sort of stasis, but the wounds can still bleed. Necromancers have something extra to heal people if they're saving them after a recent death or, if it's too late for that, keeping them alive long enough to testify. But the corners rarely use them as healers.

"Either of you want the healer?" I ask. Sugar is sporting a busted lip, and Matt is favoring his left leg, but they both shake their heads. "We're good," I call out to Victor. "You look like shit, by the way."

"That's rich coming from three people who've bathed in ulgashen viscera. I'm glad you don't need healing, so I don't have to smell you." He gives us a weak smile and a wave before walking away, hopefully to go home.

Matt holds his hand above my bitten shoulder. "I doubt I have much, but could try?"

I rotate my arm. The bite stings. Once the adrenaline wears off completely, I'll be feeling it, but it's manageable. "Don't worry about it. It's not deep, and I heal fast enough. You should get some rest." I've got some blood back at my apartment that'll suffice until I get a donor. I resist looking at Sugar's bloody lip again. Who will she get to replenish her power?

The three of us climb over the dead ulgashen into the bigger cross street. The cleanup crew is arriving, using their powers to burn the ulgashen or render their bodies into smaller versions to be bagged and destroyed.

Captain Gibson stands talking to several people. He pauses when he sees us. "Not dead?" We shake our heads, and he smiles. "Good. You can give me your reports tomorrow. Get outta here."

We turn away, and my eyes widen. The street has created an opening that wasn't there before, leading directly to Sugar's block. I can even see Marco, her landlord, standing outside and talking to some of the other residents. They all look concerned and will probably pepper her with questions as soon as she arrives. For a moment, I lose my mind completely and consider offering to walk her home.

Before I can open my mouth and say something pathetic, she says, "See you guys tomorrow," and gives us a mock salute. The innocuous cuff and her unreadable expression are firmly back in place.

When she's halfway down the street, I turn to Matt. He pats me on the shoulder, much like he did to Sugar, and gives me a look of amused pity. "Good night, Flint."

Chapter 18
Sugar

The office is somber today. Matt, like most of the Seelie corners who were on duty last night, is at home, resting and letting his power recover. The conversations are only murmurs. Nobody is slamming their drawers or arguing over whose turn it is to make coffee. Even the sunlight streaming through the windows is weak and cold.

We lost twelve people yesterday, three of them corners. When I left my apartment this morning, another family was packing their things into a wagon. A fae wearing the uniform of a moving company leaned against it, patiently waiting to transport them instantly to somewhere else in Eddahn.

My cuff twirls anxiously around my wrist, sensing my mood. I've been here for hours, reviewing everything we have on the cases for Tonya and Carter. I rub a hand down my face, forcing away the image of the ulgashen's teeth bearing down on Matt's face.

If Draven hadn't been there...

"Stop it," I mutter to myself.

If Draven hadn't been there, the entire situation would have been different. Still, I'm grateful he was there, and there's no denying his skill. In the brief moments I had to watch him last night, I couldn't help being impressed. He moves like a fighter. Every step flows seamlessly into the next. No wasted energy, precise and controlled. If I'm being honest, the sight of his well-defined muscles moving under his soaking wet shirt was a little intoxicating, even if he was covered in blood. He's definitely been trained and has honed his skills over decades, centuries.

Unlike me.

I didn't really know how to fight before. I learned to use my whip at the Nest because I didn't want to accidentally take the eye out of my best clients. Once I joined the corners, they taught me to use my sword and baton and basic hand-to-hand. I practiced with the whip since I was already familiar with it. But I rely too heavily on my power, which doesn't help with the ulgashen. Even if their aim was malevolent and not pure survival, my power doesn't work on animals.

Most of my nest died in the war but I wasn't trained for battle. I was part of a failed effort to repopulate. The memories of my human life are gone, written over by newer experiences. I'd just been bouncing from place to place before I wound up in Drahma City. I followed the pull of all those delicious emotions straight to the Dame's front door. To the Nest, the one that would become my home, my safe space.

Until Linnea.

Her death was like seeing Tradimento in the daytime. A harsh light that revealed everything I thought was exciting and beautiful as nothing but illusion and theater.

"Citizens of Eddahn, please give a round of applause for tonight's honoree, Prince Fenrik!" The announcer gives everyone a dazzling smile as Fenrik approaches, a lopsided smile on his face. He doesn't hate being in front of a crowd, but he's too worried about disappointing people. I can see it on his face, how much he wants to remove the stuffy tuxedo and run for the nearest fireplace and a good book.

"Thank you, thank you, everyone. I'm truly honored. And so grateful we've raised so much tonight for charity. You should all feel good about what you've done for your city." His gaze finds me at the back of the room, and his smile widens. I give him a wink and relish the way he tries to keep his eyes off me as he continues his speech.

A chair clatters to the floor somewhere behind me, and my jaw tightens. Alaric's emotions crash into me as he stands at my shoulder. So much anger and hatred. He downs his glass of wine and leans in, his voice hot on my face.

"Why are you even here?"

I take a steadying sip of my drink, refusing to show any reaction to his presence. "Your brother invited me."

Alaric snorts. The lust rolls off him as he takes in my long, fitted navy dress. It matches my eyes perfectly. He toys with one of the diamond straps, and I have to stop myself from slapping his hand away.

"He wouldn't be caught dead with you in public," he hisses. "Fenrik's not going to ask you to dance. Or introduce you as anything other than the Dame's stand-in." He slips a hand around my waist and pulls me closer. His lips nearly touch the shell of my ear. "Don't you have any fucking pride, Sugar?"

Fenrik catches my eye, his expression worried. He's off the stage now, and people have swarmed him for attention. I subtly roll my eyes at his brother's behavior, and his shoulders relax.

"Why are you here?" I say, injecting as much nonchalance as I can. "I can think of a thousand things you'd find more fun than a charity gala."

His hand moves a little lower to the swell of my ass, but he doesn't speak. Not until Fenrik begins making his way toward us. Alaric grabs my wine and downs it before shoving the glass back into my hand. "If you ever want to be with someone who will treat you how you really deserve, let me know."

"This place is like a fucking morgue." Nelson's voice snaps me from my memories as he walks up to my desk. He leans against it, staring out at the mostly empty office.

My eyes lazily follow his gaze before turning back to him. "What are you doing up here? Got something for me?"

I lean back in my chair, stretching my back. My stomach grumbles, and my power feels weak. I really need to feed soon. Unlike Draven, I can't just pick up a bottle of blood. I need to get my emotions from the source.

"Sure do." He pulls open an evidence envelope and dumps it out on my desk.

A small transparent bag falls out. Inside is the square jewel I found under Tonya's body on the beach. I'd thought it was dirty when I first picked it up, but even after a clean, it's still black. Now, however, I can see the silver backing and tiny bits of metal sticking out on each side.

"No blood. Corinne smelled traces of perfume and alcohol," Nelson reads off the back of the evidence envelope.

"Like cleaning alcohol?" Corinne could still smell traces if the killer cleaned it manually or with magic, but it would be harder. I squint at the jewel. It's probably only because I was just thinking of my dress with the diamond straps, but it looks like clothing, not jewelry.

"Drinking alcohol. There was no blood on it. And none of Tonya's venom." Nelson reaches across me and grabs the container of mints on Matt's adjoining desk. He grabs one and pops it in his mouth. The tin rattles as he closes the lid and puts it down.

"Hand me that, will you?" I point at the magnifying glass at another corner's desk. Nelson floats it over, and I grab it from the air. Holding it over the jewel, I get a closer look. The metal bits sticking out on each side are loops. All of them are bent at an angle, revealing the small gap at the top, as if they were wrenched apart.

I inhale sharply.

"What is it?" Nelson peers into the magnifying glass. "It looks...like it was part of a chain?"

"Not a chain," I say as I stand and pull on my jacket. "An outfit made of these little black jewels. For a fae who would definitely smell of perfume and booze."

***

Matt raises his fist and knocks three times in quick succession. We wait a moment, staring at the locked door to Tradimento. He's about to knock again when a voice calls to us from the side of the building.

"Can I help you, Detectives?" It's Bradley, the usher from the first night. He's wearing an apron over his uniform and holding a trash can full of empty bottles.

Tradimento is massive. Too big to have the normal staff use what they have to clean the place. They have professional cleaners. Seelie with enhanced cleaning powers, like my neighbor, Ms. Plichen. We had to make Horatio promise not to use them until we'd processed the scene where Carter died.

"We need to speak to Horatio," I say.

Bradley nods. "Sure. Come this way." His hair has been cut since the last time I saw him. Close-cropped and black, with a tinge of blue. He levitates the trash can until it dumps the bottles into a bigger bin in the alley before leading us through a service entrance. It's only a few feet from the exit where Carter was killed.

"Who's working today, Bradley?" Matt asks as we enter an enormous kitchen. There are five prep chefs at various stations, chopping vegetables or preparing sauces. It smells mostly of garlic and tomatoes. One chef reads a paper, using his power to relieve potato after potato of its skin.

Bradley drops the trash can next to a sink and removes his apron. "The shift sheet is here." He waves a hand at a notice board on the wall. There's a large calendar with the names and shift times for each day. "Only about ten of us right now. The rest won't arrive until seven."

Matt and I scan the names. Sigrid, the wolf shifter we questioned the night of Carter's death, isn't working today. And it doesn't look like she's been scheduled for over a week. We continue to trail Bradley through the hallways before reaching Horatio's office. Bradley knocks but doesn't wait for his boss to answer before opening the door.

Horatio looks up from where he's writing at his desk and raises his eyebrows at the sight of us.

"Detectives here to see you," Bradley says to Horatio. We thank him, and he walks out.

Horatio leans back, his eyes sharp. "How can I help you? Did you find Mr. Fox's killer?"

"Not yet," I say. My gaze darts around his office. It's not big, but it is organized. The filing cabinets have labels with precise script. Papers are neatly stacked on his desk. On the wall to my right is a detailed mural of the exterior of Tradimento, complete with people lined up to get in.

"Do the servers and performers take their costumes home, or do they keep them here?" I ask.

Surprise lights up Horatio's face for a moment before he answers. "They keep them here. Otherwise, I might never get them back. And I can't count on them to clean them properly."

"So there's a dressing room? Mind showing us?" Matt says, opening the door to the office as he does so.

"Of course." Horatio stumbles over the words a bit but recovers and stands. "Can you tell me what this is about? Do you suspect one of my people in the attack against Fox?" He buttons his suit, and those diamond cufflinks wink at me.

"It's possible," Matt says. "We're working on a theory."

I knew Matt wouldn't stay home once I told him, regardless of how low his power still is right now. He's probably at fifty percent. On my way over, I stopped at a donor cafe and got a top-up from a horse shifter going through a divorce.

I'm almost certain the jewel I collected from Tonya belongs to an outfit like the one I saw Sigrid wearing the night Fox was killed. And if it is, our two cases are linked.

We head downstairs this time, to the sublevel. But instead of turning right, toward the circular beds and opulent decorations, we turn left, toward a metal door. Horatio puts his hand on it, and it unlocks. Inside is a massive closet. It's not as big as the one at the Nest, but there's still a sizable amount of clothing hanging on racks. Tuxedos, dresses, costumes, uniforms, and one entire rack of the jeweled lingerie worn by some servers.

"Is there something I can help you find?" Horatio asks, eyeing us warily. I'm sure he thinks we're about to confiscate all his clothes as evidence.

I don't speak but flip through the outfits, looking for a black one with one or more jewels missing. There are eight in various colors, including two black ones. They're all completely intact.

"Have you sent any of these out for repairs recently?" I ask.

"No. Why?" Horatio moves to stand by me, inspecting the outfits as if he might see what I'm searching for. "Is one of them damaged?"

"What do you do when they break?" Matt asks as he examines a wall of props for the stage show.

"We have a tailor who comes in. Human. But very talented. He comes by once every two weeks. Sooner if we need it." Horatio crosses his arms, his gaze bouncing from me to Matt.

"Are any of these missing?" I motion to the rack. "Any of the black ones?"

His face relaxes in realization. "Yes," Horatio says. "Sigrid left sick during her last shift. Went home in her outfit. Normally, I'd make her change, but she's worked here a long time. I trust her to bring it back."

"When was this?" Matt says, stepping closer. "How long has she been sick?"

Horatio thinks for a moment. "About a week. She usually only works the busiest nights."

Healers can fix most things, but there are illnesses unique to certain abilities or animal forms. I rack my brain for illnesses particular to wolf shifters.

"And she didn't check in with you?" Matt says, and Horatio shakes his head.

"Isn't that unusual?" I say.

"No. She's my employee, not my friend. She wouldn't contact me unless it was to tell me she was still sick and couldn't make her next shift."

"Did you see her before she left? Did she look sick?" I say, a familiar dread growing inside me.

"No. I was managing the floor. She sent me a note. I had no reason to distrust her word."

Matt gives me a look, and dread pools in my gut. He looks at Horatio. "We're going to need her address."

Chapter 19
Sugar

Sigrid's apartment is not far from the club. We rush up the stairs like we both already know what we're going to find. I pound on the door, hoping I'm just annoying a very sick woman. When nobody answers, I try the knob and find it unlocked.

Matt and I unsheathe our short swords. I press the door open, and my stomach clenches hard at the memory it revives. Pushing past the feeling, we stalk into the apartment, announcing our presence.

If I live another thousand years, I'll never get used to the smell. Earthy and acidic. It hangs over everything, the true specter of death. There are clothes and papers everywhere, but it's all the normal detritus I associate with a young person. Matt clears the kitchen, and I check the small bathroom. We head down the hall to the bedroom, where decay squats among the scents of perfume and hairspray.

This door opens easily too, revealing a large bed with a violet comforter. There are flowers dying in a glass jar by the window.

We both suck in a breath in shock and immediately regret it. The stench is palpable in here. Matt checks the closet and under the bed, while I blink in horror and approach the body.

Someone beat her beyond recognition. She's so bruised and broken it looks like a piano fell on her. Dried blood flakes from her skin. Only her right leg appears untouched, the bones where they should be, the skin devoid of abrasions. Her black jeweled outfit hangs off her; crystals litter the bed.

"I'm sending for the team," Matt says, firing off several messages. "Sigrid could have been another victim, or it might be a partnership gone bad. Tonya and Carter were both a lot less messy. This feels personal."

"And she isn't cold like Tonya. Killer knew someone would find her, eventually." I stand as the sound of voices reaches us from the hall. Based on the smell, Sigrid died the night she left Tradimento. "Considering she's still wearing the outfit, she could have been murdered at work or on her way home."

Matt nods and purses his lips in thought.

"If she was killed at work, the killer could have sent the note telling Stone she was sick," I add.

"In the back," Matt yells before lowering his voice for me. "You think there's a leak in the department? Does the perp know we connected her to Tonya?"

"That's certainly possible. But if they know and wanted to hide the connection, the killer could have kept her on ice somewhere. And even if they don't know, they have to assume we'd consider the two deaths at Tradimento related. Leaving her here could be intentional or accidental."

Matt frowns as the room fills with people. Three other corners, plus Corinne, the evidence examiner, and Victor, the necro. "We need to keep an open mind. We could be looking at separate perps."

We know the jewel from Sigrid's uniform somehow ended up on Tonya, and Sigrid and Carter both have a connection to Tradimento, but Matt is right. They were all killed in very different ways.

"If it is the same person, the violence is escalating," Matt says. "Could be a serial, coordinated hits, or they're sending a message." His voice is barely a whisper so the other corners can't hear.

I dip my head to acknowledge I heard him before looking up at Victor. "How long until we can raise her?"

The necro runs his hands over her body, the faint blue light focusing over her chest. "She's got some power. Which is handy because I don't have room on my schedule for a few weeks."

He still looks like crap. Like Matt, he can't possibly be at full power yet. I'm not sure how killing ulgashen compares to healing on the power-suck scale, but I don't want Victor raising Sigrid until he's back to full strength. I tell him so, and he nods in agreement.

"I'll message you with the date," Victor says, the relief clear in his voice.

"Thanks, Vic," Matt says. "How about you, Corinne? Anything jumping out?"

Corinne's face is so close to Sigrid her nose is practically touching her broken jawbone. She inhales the way I might absorb someone's emotions. How she can smell anything beyond the rot is beyond me.

The other corners step out of the room, watching from the hall to keep their scent away while she works. I'm sure she can smell them all anyway. Even from here, I can sense the blond one is uneasy around Victor. Of course, I could probably figure that out without my power, considering the stink eye he's giving the necro.

A lot of corners are creeped out by necros, despite how useful they are to law enforcement. They think their power is unnatural, some weird affront to Lysandra, the goddess of life. Or is it Helva, the goddess of death, they think is being insulted? I can never remember.

"I think the jewel is a match. Same mixture of perfume and alcohol. I'll want to go over her again back at the department, but she smells similar to Carter. Like herbs and smoke."

That makes sense. Carter's body was found only a few feet from Tradimento's kitchen door, near the trash bins in the alley. There's no blood around the body. Seems unlikely the killer would go through the trouble to clean the surrounding blood but not the body, but I ask Corinne anyway.

She sniffs the sheets and moves in a slow circle around the bed before shaking her head. "I don't think she was killed here. No blood anywhere but on the body."

"Anywhere else in the apartment?" Matt cocks his head at her. She walks to the front door and back, making a detour into the kitchen and bathroom.

"No. There are a few other scents, though. I'll need my shelves to be sure," Corinne says, referring to her laboratory shelves. They contain a thousand tiny vials, each containing a small amount of various substances she uses to compare against what she smells in the field.

The other corners bring the box for Sigrid and begin bagging up the sheets and things from the bed. Matt and I walk out, both of us concentrating on what we know from each case.

"We need to start from the beginning," Matt says, squinting into the dying sunlight as we step out onto the street. "Tonya was killed first. Let's start there." He stops at a cart where a red-headed fae is filling a fluffy pocket of bread with flame-broiled chicken. Matt holds up two fingers. "Put an unhealthy amount of pepper on one of those," he says, tilting his head toward me.

The fae throws marinated raw chicken and onions onto a square metal plate before lifting his hand. A rush of flame streams from his fingertips, instantly charbroiling it all. My stomach growls at the smell of smoke and meat. The vendor separates the pile and throws a slightly less-than-adequate amount of pepper on mine before pushing them into the bread and handing them over in folded napkins. Matt covers his in garlicky white sauce while I take a satisfying bite of mine.

"I'll talk to Gibson. See who worked the disappearance originally. I think it was someone new," I say around a mouthful of food. "Probably only went over the basics." There were always a lot of high-profile people at CP's parties. A lot like the Romans' events. It's inevitably why it took so long for Jasper to track down anyone who would talk.

Matt pays before turning back to me. "And we need to talk to CP."

***

Matt knows about Alaric, but we don't talk about it much. When I tell him the crown prince might speak to me if I meet him alone, he doesn't ask why. He only tells me to be careful.

"I was wondering when you were going to crawl out of that hovel again," Alaric drawls as he leans back in a beautifully crafted armchair with hand-stitched cushions. There are burns on the armrests from where he's put out his cigars. We're in his townhouse, not far from the Luminous Palace. He hungrily drags his eyes over my body.

"Doesn't seem like you missed me too much," I say as my gaze lands on the naked sleeping woman sprawled on the couch next to him. Her eyelids flutter, and she lifts her head for a moment before it falls back and she turns over, presenting her gorgeously ample backside to us.

Alaric scoffs like the idea of missing me is ridiculous before he stands and prowls toward me. He's shirtless, wearing nothing but loose black pants. He and Fenrik have similar body types. Both are tall and broad-shouldered, with light brown hair and blue eyes. But where Fenrik's eyes are kind and full of warmth,

Alaric's eyes look back at me with everything that makes my power sizzle with need.

He wraps an arm around my waist and pinches my chin with the other hand before slamming his lips into mine. The kiss is hard and punishing. My skin stings where he holds my face, but I don't pull away. There's so much fury in him. My knees practically buckle from the waves of emotion spreading from his body toward mine. The tiny voice in my head, the one that dares me to just do it, to stop leashing my strength, to tip back his head and steal whole days of his time, is so loud today.

As if he can feel my willpower weakening, he breaks the kiss. Before he can do anything that might lead me to the same position as the woman on the couch, I say, "The night of your party at LeMar, a butterfly went missing. That same butterfly showed up dead on the beach the other day. And then your cockroach, Boltier, kicked us off the scene. I take it you killed her?" My voice is devoid of emotion.

There's venom in his grin. "Butterflies can be such bitches, you know? I'm sure there are lots of people who found her just as annoying as I did." His eyes are a little unfocused, and I press my advantage before he sobers up.

"So you spoke to her? At the party?" I take off my jacket and lay it on a nearby table, and he watches the movement. "Her friends said she was pretty desperate to be with you. If only they knew."

His eyes narrow. "You trying to bait me, Sugar? Think if you get me mad enough, I'll spill all my dirty secrets for you? Confess to a murder?"

I slip out of my shoes and kick them over toward my jacket. Lust spills over Alaric's anger as he watches me peel off my top. My voice is a low purr as I say, "I don't need to do anything to make you mad. You do that all on your own."

His breath quickens, and his hand snaps out with preternatural speed. He fists the top of my pants, his fingers trapped between my skin and the material. I refuse to stumble as he yanks me closer.

"I never laid a finger on her. But if someone taught her some manners, it's her own fault." He pushes me backward, forcing me down the hallway as he eyes my body with predatory intent.

"Since when do you care about manners?" I scrape my claws against the wall as I walk backward, leaving deep, uneven scratch marks.

"I care about what's mine—what's owed to me," he growls.

He reaches for me, and I jump out of the way. "What's owed to you?" I tap a finger against my lip. "What could that be? Not money, of course. Sex, maybe. Did you fuck her?" I ask, feigning just the tiniest amount of jealousy.

But Alaric doesn't seem to hear me. His eyes are far away as we reach his bedroom and he throws me roughly onto the bed.

"Did you?" I ask again as he rips off my pants. His eyes are still glassy.

His expression is distracted as he says, "No." He might actually be telling the truth. Or that might be my guilt talking.

Before I can blink, Alaric reaches over to the nightstand and pulls out a belt. He wraps it around my wrists before securing me to the headboard.

"Can't leave now, baby. This is what you like, right?" He lowers onto me, licking and sucking my skin. The pleasure rolls through my body even as the malice inside him ebbs. He bites down hard, and I cry out, not ready for it for once. "That's right," he whispers. "You know you deserve this. For everything you've done, you deserve worse."

"I do," I say, but the words don't come out as easily as they normally do. "Did you see her with anyone?" I pull my legs back and kick him hard in the chest, sending him stumbling into the wall behind the bed. His face turns feral. And for a moment, I think of Petra and search his eyes and body for any signs of another power but find none.

He leaps on top of me again, gripping my hair until I reward him with a wince. His smile is evil. "I saw Tonya with lots of people. She probably should have stuck with her friends. My parties can be dangerous, but they can also be a lot of fun. You might even come to them soon. Once you stop running back to that shithole across the river."

I open my mouth to ask him more, but he slaps his hand against my mouth and drives into me, silencing anything but the sound of his skin against mine.

Later, I slip away, collecting the rest of my clothes from where I conveniently left them outside his bedroom. Couch Girl is still fast asleep. When I get far enough away, I send a message to Matt telling him everything I learned.

There are a lot of things CP might feel he's owed, but only one that might make him this concerned.

The crown.

Chapter 20
Draven

I haven't even had coffee, and Sugar Writh is pounding on my door. Her note arrived fifteen minutes ago, just enough time for me to roll out of bed, brush my teeth, and throw on some dark clothing.

What does one wear to potentially kill someone?

I open the door, and a strange expression lights Sugar's eyes. Surprise? Relief? "What?" I ask, opening the door wider so she can step in. "Never seen a vampire with bedhead before?" I'm joking, but when she walks past me, I run a hand through my hair.

"I was expecting you to back out," she says. And this time, there's no mistaking the expression in her eyes, regardless of how she's trying to hide it. It's fear. She was *afraid* I was going to back out.

And that's when I realize I might be totally fucked when it comes to Sugar, because she's a succubus, incredibly unlikeable, and might get me killed; but right now, I want to wrap my arms around her. I want to comfort this dangerous and surly creature in front of me.

Eliza was sweet and desired me, and she still ripped out my heart and drove a stake through it. Sugar couldn't be further from sweet and doesn't like me at all. She could cause me untold pain if I make the mistake of wanting her. It's an alarming prospect.

"No. I wouldn't do that," I say, clearing my throat. That familiar mask slides back over her face, and she nods. "But..." She arches an eyebrow at the word, her face going hard. "I want to know what you're getting out of this. Because I know it's not just money."

Sugar's hand flexes at her side, the cuff making a single slow rotation.

Holding up my hands, I say, "I'm not asking for you to bare your soul, Writh. I'm taking the bigger risk, and I'd just like us to be on slightly more even footing."

She rubs a thumb against her thigh as she turns to examine the crane lamp. Whether she's gathering strength to answer my question or trying to resist choking me to death with her whip is anyone's guess.

"Your intended progeny is going to do something for me. She's going to help me speak to someone I might not otherwise have access to."

"There now, was that so hard?" I say, hiding my surprise that she actually answered the question. Her chest rises as if it's taking her a lot of strength not to snap back. Who does she want to speak to so badly? Who wouldn't she have access to as a corner and someone tight with the Dame?

I finish getting ready, and the two of us slip out of the apartment.

It's still dark outside. Too early for even the shopkeepers to be out. According to Sugar's note, our mystery Seelie is ready to be Made. I haven't had a moment to process it yet.

"You want to slow down there?" I whisper as we exit the Second Circle and head into the Third. The air smells like snow. Sugar is wearing a heavy wool coat, her silver hair back from her face and hidden under a hood.

"You're a vampire," she replies, scoffing at me. She turns the corner, heading deeper into the neighborhood of Fellkirk. The orb lights are further apart here, and it's near pitch black between them.

"Yes. I am. Which means if I knew where we were going, I could use my excellent vampire speed and be there in half the time. But since I do not, I'm walking normally while you are going at a pace best reserved for things with wheels or wings."

Sugar grumbles something that sounds like "whiny child" but slows her pace.

"So considerate. Thank you," I say as I come level with her. "Are you planning to tell me who this person is yet?"

"No. You'll see when you get there."

"Exactly, so why not tell me now?"

Sugar huffs, and her breath is visible in the cold air. "Who trained you to fight?"

"That's an abrupt change of subject, but fine. I was raised to fight. All the vampires in my family were. A lot of my quench died in the wars."

"Most of my nest did too." The words come out of her mouth like a reflex, and she snaps her mouth shut like she regrets them. It's not uncommon among the Unseelie to have lost family members in the war with the Seelie. I wonder if Sugar's family members were older, or young and naïve like mine.

The sky is still dark, but around us, the orb lights flicker off in anticipation for the day. The smell of baking bread wafts through the air as we turn down another street. My stomach growls at my lack of breakfast. We walk in silence for another block before I speak again. I'm not entirely sure why I'm making conversation. There's no reason for either of us to speak to one another again after today. Unless we're arrested, of course.

"Heard you caught a break in the Fox case?"

"Yes, it's going well. Instead of one dead body, we now have three." She pauses on the corner of a street, holding up her hand for me to stop. A fae steps out of their house before disappearing, and we continue walking.

"Wow, that's more bodies than I have. Got any tips?" As we step under an orb light hanging above a wrought-iron gate, I swear I see the corner of her mouth lift. "Seriously. It seems like you could be getting close."

She sighs as we pause again, this time for two humans who've arrived in a horse-drawn cart. The sky lightens from black to blue as one of them hops out. He grabs a crate from the back and drops it in front of a house before getting back in and driving away.

"The cases appear connected. We have some theories." She pauses, her face tightening, before continuing. "And CP may be involved."

"That asshole is always around when bad shit is happening." That damn errant thought tugs at me again when I mention the crown prince. I'm forgetting something. It's driving me crazy. I mentally walk through the last few days, searching for what my mind is trying to tell me.

"This is it," she says, stopping in front of a small blue house with white shutters. It's on the very edge of the Third Circle, overlooking the river. I can smell the water from where we stand. The gulls are waking up, calling to one another above our heads.

I guess it's showtime.

Sugar opens the door, and we walk into a combined living room and kitchen. It's clean, with well-loved furniture. "She was going to wear a tattoo," Sugar says, referring to the tattoos one could buy to create the illusion over your face or body, "but we didn't want anything to interfere with the Making."

I frown. "What does it matter if I know what she looks like? Not like I can turn her in. Also, how come I wasn't offered the option of a disguise?"

She leads me to a staircase. "Because it wouldn't matter. They know me. A disguise wouldn't help if her family is trying to find you."

"Her family?" I ask as we reach the top of the stairs. Sugar opens the door, and my mouth falls open as I come face to face with Princess Lira of Eddahn.

***

The princess looks at me with calm blue eyes. Her shiny, dark hair tumbles loosely about her shoulders. She wears no crown, and even her clothes are something you might see on any fae, albeit a more expensive version. She's sitting on a bed covered with a white and green quilt. Instead of orb lights, a glowing kinrock rests on the small nightstand.

My heart, usually so much slower than any non-vampire's, beats rapidly in my chest. The princess. I'm getting paid to Make a princess. I might *kill* a princess.

"Sucrelia," Lira says, smiling as she rises. She's a few inches shorter than Sugar. "It's good to see you again." I almost reach out to stop Lira from getting closer—whether to protect Lira or Sugar, I don't know. Sugar notices my slight movement and raises an eyebrow as she leans in to shake hands with Lira.

"Good to see you again, too. This is Draven."

She tips her head toward me, and I give a small bow. "Pleasure to meet you, Your Royal Highness."

"I think, considering the circumstances, we can dispense with the titles," she says, and I nod in acknowledgement.

"I'll admit the request came as a surprise, Lira," Sugar says, curiosity in her tone.

Exactly how well do the two of them know one another? I'm trying to remember everything I know about Sugar and whether she's mentioned any close ties with the royal family.

"Yes, I'm sure it did. I have my reasons." It's an answer and a silent command to ask no further questions. She motions to a box on the nightstand. "Half the money for both of you is in there. You'll get the other half in a month. If I'm still alive." Lira's words are not quite joking but certainly casual.

"Thank you. I have every hope you will be. And not just for the money." Sugar's face softens.

There's some kind of friendship there, and I'm definitely feeling out of my depth. Sugar's words come back to me about how Lira might be powerful enough to protect me if this goes sideways. I assumed it was a rich family, like the Romans, who could make the corners look the other way. That would have been better. A private citizen is one thing. The people of Eddahn would definitely have something to say about such a blatant violation of the law by those tasked with upholding them.

"Yes. Your other request—"

"We can talk about that later," Sugar says, cutting Lira off in a voice too sharp to be casual.

"Very well." She turns to me, and there's the tiniest hint of mischief in her eyes. "Would you like me on the bed, Draven?"

I don't have it in me to rise to her teasing. Instead, I focus on Lira waking healthy and whole. I picture the other humans I've successfully Made. But the image of Maria and the girls knowing they'll never have to leave their home and won't want for anything is at the front of my mind as I pull open my bag.

"I have a friend, an apothecary. He's been working on some blends for me—you." I pull out a vial of pale orange liquid. "This mixture isn't strictly legal but..." I give her a playful grimace, and Lira huffs a laugh. "It should help."

The princess steps forward and reaches out to take the vial, but I hold on to it, our fingers just barely touching. "Why are you doing this? Really?" I ask, letting her hear the sincere concern in my voice. "I can't guarantee your safety, no matter how much I wish I could."

"Why are you doing it?" she whispers. Her eyes search my face as she looks up at me before moving closer.

From the corner of my eye, I can feel Sugar watching us. "I lost a friend. I promised I'd help take care of his family."

Lira's fingers dance over the vial like she's trying to read it with her eyes closed. "And you always keep your promises, don't you, Draven." It's a statement, not a question. "Because someone broke your trust? Not this apothecary." She slips the mixture from my palm, her hand small and warm. "He trusts you. He wants this to work for you, and he's very talented."

I swallow. "Yes, he is." I search her eyes, but there's no artifice. She doesn't appear to be a power-hungry Seelie, but can any of the royals be trusted? My gaze flicks to Sugar. She's looking at the vial as if it's her key to everything. Her eyes return to mine, and she tips up her chin in challenge.

I turn back to Lira and explain the process. She says nothing but nods along in understanding. "Once this starts, we won't be able to heal you. You understand?" Not only does healing not work on a Making, but even if it did, we'd just have to start all over again. "I promise to do my very best."

She smiles. "I know you will." A look I don't understand passes between the two women. "Ready?" The princess sits on the bed, uncorks the mixture, and swallows it. Several minutes pass in silence when she suddenly blinks like she's trying to focus. "I feel so warm," she murmurs.

"Yes. My venom will be cold. This will balance it out," I murmur.

Sugar discards her coat on an overstuffed armchair and climbs onto the bed next to Lira, ready in case she lashes out once I've started. Her eyes meet mine over Lira's head, and there's so much unguarded hope in them it nearly takes my breath away. She watches in anticipation as my fangs extend, something that probably shouldn't arouse me as much as it does, considering what I'm about to do.

The princess makes only a small gasp as I bite into her neck. Her hands dart out to hold my arms as I begin draining the blood from her body. She leans against Sugar, who pulls the hair away from her neck and rubs small circles on her upper back. I'm not hurting her. I've been a vampire long enough to know how to make this as painless as possible.

In less than a minute, I pull away and bite into my wrist. Lira is still conscious, and she latches on, sucking my blood, knowing how important it is to take as much and as fast as possible. I bend over her neck and start drinking again, ensuring the rate at which I take her blood matches how fast she's swallowing mine.

An hour goes by, at which point I'm confident I've taken all of her blood while the venom in mine has spread throughout her body, transforming her into something new and hopefully healthy.

Lira looks like death, hair limp and tangled, blue veins visible beneath her damp skin. She passes out, and Sugar gently lays her on the bed, arranging the pillows to support her neck. She checks her pulse and cleans her wounds. My venom will close the marks made by my own teeth, and I watch to be sure the skin on her neck knits together as it should.

Sugar sits back on her heels, the palest sheen of sweat gracing her forehead in the dawn light, and says, "And now we wait."

Chapter 21
Sugar

"Do you think you're clever? You think you've won something?"
Jaqueline Roman's voice bleeds from behind the door to the parlor
on the second floor.

I shouldn't be here. I'm allowed a certain amount of freedom
within this house, but it doesn't include traipsing through the
hallways when I should be working.

"No, ma'am," Linnea answers. Her voice isn't quiet, but there's
a slight tremble to it. It takes all my willpower not to bust down the
door and wrap my whip around Jaqueline's neck. Instead, I hide
behind a hideous plant, with an ear out for any other servants.

"You think you'll be left alone because I can't discipline you
anymore? How stupid can you be? What I've done will seem like a
dream compared to what he'll do to keep you two in line." There's
a soft thud and the sound of something falling to the floor. "Oops,
sorry, my foot must have slipped." Jacqueline laughs, but it's forced
and angry. "Stupid human."

There's a sound of fist against fabric, and Linnea begins to
scream.

No. That's not right. Linnea didn't scream that day.

I jolt upright, throwing off the blanket. Lira is screaming, moaning and keening like a tortured animal. I rush upstairs to find her bent over on the floor, vomiting blood all over the soft gray rug. I half lift, half drag her to the bathroom. She can barely raise her eyelids. Bloody tears track down her face as she heaves again, covering us both in blood.

Once she's near enough to the toilet, I grab for the tinctures on the nightstand. My fingers slip over the glass as I look for the right one. Duft made us one for everything: pain, delusions, even bloodlust. I find the metal tin with thick yellow salve. There's no point in trying to shove anything down her throat while she's puking everything up.

"I've got you, Lira. It's going to be okay. I'm going to help." I rub the salve over her neck, back, and stomach, not caring there's a bit of blood mixed in. It smells strongly of pine and juniper. My fingers heat and tingle, but she still won't stop shaking. Have I put on too much? Too little?

Lira throws out an arm, and I'm not ready for it. Her fist connects with my chest, and I slam into the wall behind me. Broken tile rains onto my head as I struggle to catch my breath. Her eyes move rapidly, as if she's in a dream, and she lunges for the door. I launch myself at her, wrapping my arms around her shoulders and squeezing.

Slowly, the tremors lessen, and her stomach stops convulsing. She clings to me as I slide down to the floor beside her and rock her back and forth. "See. You're okay. Everything is okay." I pull a towel off the rack and wipe at the blood on her face and neck.

The cheery yellow bathroom looks like a murder scene. I inhale through my mouth and let it out slowly. Lira's head drops back against my shoulder. I free one of my hands to lift her lip. Two new teeth are pushing out her canines.

"Sugar?" Draven calls from the bedroom door before he rounds the corner and finds us. He looks concerned but not surprised by the state of the room. He's only been gone an hour to get blood. I went out around four in the morning to replenish my power. "Sorry, I thought I had a few more hours before we got to this stage." He reaches out and inspects Lira's eyes and her growing fangs.

"Is that a good sign?"

"I really don't know." He shakes his head. "But her fangs look about right." He bends down and lifts Lira out of my arms. I feel strangely untethered without her.

"We need to clean her off." I wince as I hoist myself up and turn on the shower. I was already barefoot, just in a shirt and pants, so I step into the shower with her, letting the water rinse the blood and vomit off both of us. Draven and I slowly peel off Lira's clothes. He told her what might happen, and she gave us permission to do whatever needed to be done.

Nevertheless, he avoids looking as the last of her clothing goes into a wet heap on the floor, keeping his eyes fixed on the wall or on me. He hands me a towel, and I dry her off as well as I can before wrapping her up. Draven lifts her and carries her to the bed.

It's midday, but all the curtains are closed. The kinrock gives off a soothing pink glow. I braid Lira's clean hair, swallowing back the memories it brings. Linnea's hair was always a little too fine for braids, but I did my best. The hope I've been trying to tamp down until Lira is in the clear rears up. It's going to work. And I'm finally going to get some godsdamn answers.

"You should have a real shower," Draven says from behind me when I've finished. "It'll make you feel better." His eyes are soft and full of questions I don't want to answer. I feel the ghost of his fingers on my back, where the tile cut into my shirt.

Water from my hair and clothes drips onto the floor, and the bruise on my chest smarts. I jerk my head in acknowledgment, grateful for an excuse to leave Draven and his searching eyes.

Downstairs, there's another small bedroom and bath. I remove everything, even my cuff, and scrub myself raw.

"Please let this work," I whisper into the dark gray tile as pink-tinged water spills into the drain. There are gods I could pray to—the god of luck, the goddess of healing—but instead, I just repeat the words. "Please let her live. Please let her live."

Instead of feeling better, I feel like I've aged a thousand years when I step out. I consider just collapsing on the bed and going back to sleep, but Draven will need my help if she has another episode.

He seemed nervous when we started but, since then, has been entirely composed. It's almost military-like, the way he's given me instructions and tended to her needs. He's been keeping notes and asked me to update them with her temperature, physical appearance, and anything else I notice.

A few times, I've caught him looking at me, and while I don't hate it, I don't want to give him the impression this makes us friends. It'll be best and safest for both of us if we never speak outside of work again if—*when*—Lira's transformation is successful.

Even if I do like the look of him in rolled-up shirtsleeves and the random touches of his skin against mine. We're both in this shitty situation together, worry and stress suffocating us like a noxious plant. It's only natural to scramble for a distraction. It doesn't mean it's a good idea.

I inhale deeply and let it out.

The downstairs bedroom has only a single bed and a small empty closet. My clothes are in my bag in the living room. I became very comfortable with nudity while working at the Nest, but since I've felt more than just a sliver of lust from Draven over the last few weeks, I wrap myself in a towel before stepping out.

My heart seizes in my chest as Fenrik looks at me from beside the kitchen table.

"Hello, Sugar," he says, giving me a sad smile. The curtains are closed down here, too. Thin beams of sunlight stab through the gaps, illuminating the dust particles and tinting the room bronze. A ship's bell is ringing outside as it travels down the river.

Draven's arms are crossed. His eyes flick suspiciously between the prince and me. Considering how he reacted when he saw Lira, he must really be confused now.

"Hi," I say. It's more of a breath than a word. "Have you seen your sister?"

This is the first time I've seen Fenrik in more than a year. And even then, it was from a distance. I told him it was better that way. We're not anything to one another anymore. Just occasionally brought together by his brother's misdeeds or my side projects for the Dame.

"Yes. Just now. Detective Flint showed me upstairs. She looks like you both have been taking good care of her." I doubt that's true, but he always was a diplomat.

"Looking for this?" Draven says, holding up my bag. My eyes dart from his face to his knees, which are damp with blood. He must have been trying to clean up when the prince arrived.

"Thank you." I take the bag. "Upstairs is kind of a mess. Do you think you could—"

"Already did it," Fenrik says, and his weak smile grows. But Draven frowns, and there's an awkward pause. "Sugar, do you think we could speak in private for a moment?"

A chill runs across my skin. I'm not sure I want to be alone with him. But I find myself agreeing. I avoid looking at Draven as I lead Fenrik to the small bedroom. I go into the bathroom to change, if only to give myself a moment to breathe.

"It's really good to see you," Fenrik says when I come out. His eyes look tired, as if he hasn't been sleeping. There's something different about him, older.

I steel my spine, reminding myself of all the reasons we're not together. One of which includes the fact I was recently tied to his brother's bed. He may have ended it, but I drove the nails into the coffin.

"Are you here to check on Lira? We're doing everything we can. Draven has done his best." The words come out too rushed.

His eyes flash with hurt, and he swallows. "I did want to check on her, of course. And I know you'd never let any harm come to her." He pauses as if he's struggling with the next words. "Lira's so stubborn, you know? We never could tell her to do anything. That's the baby of the family for you, I guess." He gives me that rueful smile, the one that always makes my heart flip.

But instead of returning it, my brow knits. It sounds almost like he's apologizing for her choice. "Do you know why she wants this, Fen?"

"I do, but I can't tell you." He hesitates, then takes a step forward. My body lights up as he runs his hands down my arms. His warm hands engulf mine, and I resist looking down to see if they still fit as well as I remember. "Sugar, I miss you. I know I have no right to say that, but I do."

Tears I refuse to let fall gather behind my eyes. This isn't the first time he's tried to have this conversation, and I don't seem to be getting any better at handling it. "You should go. I'll send you updates on her progress."

But he doesn't let go of my hands. "Sucrelia," he breathes, holding a hand up to my face. "I don't want us to be strangers."

His skin is so familiar. The memories are jagged and painful—the warm breeze flowing over our skin while we lounged in the afternoon sun, his fingers trailing over my back as he peppered kisses on my skin, the look on his face when he told me we couldn't be together only two months after Linnea's death. And of course, the ever-present voice of his brother, reminding me of my place in their world.

"You can't fix this, Fen." I yank myself away, hastily wiping at my eyes. "Please, just go." He takes a step like he might touch me again but stops when I whisper, "Please."

He rubs a hand down the back of his neck and blurts, "I'm sorry. I really am."

I want to hit something or scream. How can being with someone make you feel so good and so awful at the same time?

I take a deep breath, closing off my emotions like the Dame trained me to do, letting ice seep into my voice and my other persona take over. Internally, I sigh in relief as my voice comes out cold and measured. "Thank you for your help. I'll let you know as soon as Lira is safe."

Draven isn't in the living room when I enter, but a breeze ruffles the papers on the table, and I suspect he's used his speed to dash back upstairs. Nosy fucking vampire. I really don't need Draven Flint rifling around in that part of my life.

I march over to the door and hold it open, avoiding Fenrik's gaze. The prince continues to give me a troubled look, and it takes everything in me not to break and look back at him. My heart squeezes again, like he's bruising it with each of his fingers. I need this to work. I need Lira's help, and my issues with Fenrik and his brother cannot get in the way. From the corner of my eye, I catch him opening his mouth to speak, but he closes it and shakes his head before walking out.

Chapter 22
Draven

Sugar's footsteps above me are loud in the silent house. Fenrik brought one of their transport fae, who whisked Lira and him away a few minutes ago. It's been four days of tending to our patient and catching bits of unsatisfying sleep when we could. Sugar's been working on her cases from the kitchen table, and we slipped into a bizarrely domestic routine. I'd gone from knowing Sugar mainly by reputation to spending a significant amount of time in her personal space, constantly resisting the urge to touch her.

The princess seems okay. Weak, but that's to be expected. Exhaustion claws at me as I turn to face the stairwell. Sugar didn't come down to see them off. Fenrik was nice enough, if a bit...polite. There was clearly something between them, and I'm irrationally pleased at her choice to distance herself.

"All good?" I ask as she appears at the bottom of the stairs. Her clothes, a soft cotton shirt that hugs her curves and gray pants, are wrinkled. Her silver hair escapes from a messy bun, and whatever makeup she usually wears is long gone. She's still unfathomably stunning. Her eyes are like cool, fathomless lakes against her pale skin.

"Yes. More waiting?" she asks, walking closer. Her hips have the most amazing curve. It looks like they'd fit perfectly under my hands. I rub a hand down my face, trying to move my thoughts in a more rational direction.

I blame lack of sleep when my voice comes out like gravel as I reply, "A month should be enough time to know where we stand." I hazard another step toward her, my mind drowsy and easily tuned to thoughts of what Sugar's inner thighs would feel like against my face.

We're mere inches from one another as she leans forward. I frown in confusion as she keeps going until her head is level with my chest. Then she stands, holding the bag she grabbed from the armchair next to me. I mentally punch myself and walk away, gathering my stuff from the kitchen table.

"We should probably limit our contact as much as possible. We also shouldn't message Lira or Fenrik unless it's an emergency." Sugar stands at the door, one hand on the knob.

I look up, halfway to shoving my daggers back in my shoulder holster. "Of course. Understood," I say, returning my attention to packing. I know she can feel my arousal. Considering how she looks, I wonder if the attraction of others is just a low-level hum to her now, barely worth noticing.

The door opens and closes again without another word from her. I run a hand down my face, cursing my continued stupidity when it comes to the succubus, before walking out into the early afternoon.

As I approach the streets near City Hall, the sound of raised voices carries over to me. The plaza in front, where they usually hold press conferences, is filled with people. They carry signs and shout in unison at the councilors' windows. I catch sight of a sign with an expert rendering of an ulgashen covered by a red X. Grief pierces my chest, and I have to stop moving for a moment until it ebbs.

I school my expression and head over to the corners doing crowd control.

"What's going on?" I ask a young corner, whose brown eyes flit nervously over the crowd.

"People from the Hollows protesting the ulgashen attacks. They don't think the council is doing enough to stop them because it's not happening up here," he says, gesturing at the surrounding streets.

An older corner with a nose that's definitely been broken a few times, snorts. "We send people out every damn time. Haven't we done enough?" He gives me a pointed look, like the two of us have something in common. "Bunch of ingrates."

I give him a contemptuous expression that'd do Sugar proud. "They don't get paid to be grateful. You get paid to protect them. And they're right. The people in the upper city don't care unless it's on their front doorstep."

Broken Nose rolls his eyes and turns away from us, but the young guy nods. "It's not just the ulgashen either. Did you hear about the flooding?" When I shake my head, he says, "A big part of the cliff face on the Lekotto side broke off, causing a wave of water to flow down into a bunch of houses."

"A bunch of *vacant* houses," the older guy mutters.

The young man shrugs. "They were closest to the caves where the ulgashen live. With all these recent attacks, of course people moved out. But now, even if we get rid of the ulgashen, they don't have a house to go back to—or at least not one that's not sitting in six inches of water."

Shaking my head, I turn back to the crowd. They're calling out the councilors by name, demanding they do something. I'm not sure what can be done about the flooding. They put parks on top of the mountain plateaus that border the Fugue because they weren't considered stable enough for housing.

A note appears in front of me, and I grab it, afraid it's something from Lira. Seeing Eliza's familiar handwriting, I crumple it into a ball and toss it into a nearby trash bin like I've done with all the others. Definitely something I don't need to deal with right now. She's been sending me letters for a while now, pretending everything is normal and I'm just away for a brief vacation.

I wade through the chanting crowd until I get to Duft's shop. The smell of smoke and spice assaults me as I step through the door. Sacha squawks from her perch. "Read 'em and weep!"

"Oh, I didn't even recognize you, Victor. How's it going?" I say, surprised to see the necro browsing as I walk toward the counter. He looks less tired than usual, his hair isn't as lank, and his brown eyes have more light in them.

He puts a box back on the shelf and grins. "Hey, Draven. I thought you took time off?"

"I did."

He gives me a a puzzled smile. "How come you look like you haven't slept in three days?" Before I can answer, he adds, "Oh, it was that kind of time off. I got you. Who is it? Anyone I know?"

I shake my head, amused. He must be well-rested to be this cheerful. "Didn't take you for a gossip, Victor."

"Why not? I spend a lot of time hearing people's secrets. It's always good to hear them when the person isn't about to die on me." The words are out before he realizes what he's said. He pauses awkwardly while we both remember Kurt spilling his secrets before taking his last breath. "I'm sorry. That was careless of me."

"It's all right. And I never thought about it that way. You do know everyone's secrets. I should be asking you if you have any good gossip."

"Well, that depends. Can I trust you not to go blabbing to your friends?" He picks a few more things up off the shelves and puts them back as we wander together toward the front.

"I'm incredibly trustworthy. Just ask this guy." I jerk my thumb at Duft as he comes out of the back.

Sacha scratches her head with an incredibly long talon and croaks, "Blinds are up!"

"Pipe down, you." Duft throws her a treat from a jar on the counter.

She snatches it out of the air with her beak. "Aces and eights!"

"What lies is he telling you?" Duft asks, rubbing a hand over his bald head.

"Just about how trustworthy I am." I roll my neck, the exhaustion weighing heavier in my limbs now. I need to eat and sleep. There's a donor den a few stores down. I'll grab a quick top-up and crash.

Duft squints like he's really evaluating the question before shrugging. "I suppose that's true."

I look at Victor expectantly. He huffs a laugh. "Next time you see Sugar Writh, ask her why she never feeds from Nelson and Catriona." He raises both eyebrows suggestively. "I've got some more browsing to do. I'll get out of your way." Victor nods to Duft before wandering back into the depths of the shop.

It's my turn to squint as I attempt to fathom Victor's meaning. It can't be consent; that's a normal reason for her not to feed from them.

"Well?" Duft asks, breaking into my musings about the gazelle and cheetah shifters. "How did it go?" He keeps his voice low and the question generic.

"Good. I mean, awful, but I think you really helped, thank you."

"And your coworker? That working out?" He throws another treat to Sacha, who doesn't bother to catch it. Instead, she watches it fall to the floor as if Duft gave her a pebble and not the food she gobbled down moments ago. "Damn bird," he mutters.

"Also good and also awful." My head is all mixed up about Sugar. I'm hoping it's just novelty and physical attraction. I look over at Victor. He's on the other side of the room, examining the section on food enhancements. The shop is otherwise empty. "Do you know—did she have a thing with Prince Fenrik?"

"Yeah. It was in the papers." He shrugs. "I don't think they're still together, if that's what you're asking."

I shake my head and glance through a stack of flyers left by a local band. "She feeds on arousal, right? That's what you gave her?"

That dreamy look Duft had the first time I mentioned her passes over his face. "Yeah, she can. But that's not what I gave her. Or at least not the only thing. Sugar feeds off anger and hatred. So when you're a new resident of D.C., fresh off of getting kicked out of the place you've called home for a century, you've got a lot of rage to spend."

My brow furrows. "Anger? Really?"

"Yeah, I mean, I don't know the specifics, but emotions like that. She can feel them, feed from them, and use them to make you do things you didn't know you wanted to do." He clears his throat, eyes clearing. "Anyway. I take it she didn't feed from you?"

I snort. "No. Could you imagine the look on my uncle's face if I let a succubus feed from me?" The odds of Sugar having siren in her ancestry are looking better if she can feed off more than lust.

"Red 23! Red 23!" Sacha says, bobbing her head.

A thought pushes to the front of my mind. "Duft. You know all these ulgashen attacks? Is it possible to lure an ulgashen? What kind of power would that take?"

"Just enough power to carry the bait," He scratches the side of his cheek. "Ulgashen are just animals. They're going to follow their food source. And they already like to nest in those caves across the Fugue."

"So all it would take would be dropping some carrion?"

He shrugs. "Pretty much."

The door opens, and Sacha screeches a welcome. If it's that easy, it'll be much harder to prove that someone lured the ulgashen to the Hollows. If that's even what's happening. It's not like there aren't butchers and graveyards that might draw the beasts. My eyelids sag, and I step back from the counter.

"I gotta get something to eat and then crash. Just wanted to let you know you might be on to something with those special blends." We shake hands. I give Victor a casual salute as I exit the shop.

An hour later, after I've drunk from a very chatty human donor, I stand under the shower, letting hot water beat against my shoulders. My mind, or more accurately my cock, won't give Sugar up. Images of her sliding her thigh down mine while we lay tangled in my sheets and what she might look like with her head tipped back and shouting my name keep playing in my head.

It's pure lunacy to think about her like this. She's shown no interest in me. But I take myself in my hand anyway, imagining her looking up at me from her knees with those big navy eyes, mouth parted in invitation.

Would she let me drink from her? I can almost feel my fangs sinking into her inner thigh while her hands tangle in my hair. The water is going cold, but I don't care as I pick up my pace. Her indifferent expression flashes in my head, and I'm filled with an insatiable craving. Would she be so aloof if I made her tell me every one of her darkest fantasies while I worshipped her with my mouth? Would she use her power to stop me?

A vision of her in this shower with me, water dripping from her sparkling hair to the tips of her breasts, has me coming hard. Once my breathing slows, irritation claws at me. Sugar is my coworker and coconspirator. She was very clear on what she expects from me—only distance and silence. I need to shut off these thoughts. Maybe it's time for me to be with someone. Or maybe I'm still not ready, which is why my mind is hung up on a succubus who barely speaks to me on a good day.

As I towel myself off and collapse into bed, I fall asleep idly wondering why Sugar never feeds from the pair from R&E.

Chapter 23
Sugar

There's nobody in the restaurant. Not unusual. It's ten in the morning on a Tuesday, and Nomads is really more of a dinner spot. It's in the Third Circle, in Almaton. Heavy, rust-colored silks drape across the ceiling and down the walls, tied back with tasseled rope, giving the illusion of being in some exotic camp. Star-shaped orb lights hang above each table, swinging listlessly. It's like Draven's apartment but less gaudy.

The look on his face when Lira and Fenrik left us at the river house floats through my mind. He had a hungry expression, his arousal snaking around me, testing the waters. It would have been so easy to give in to the powerful body I've seen fight ulgashen and carry Lira. He strikes me as the rough now, gentle later type, and I can't deny the attraction.

But I know, better than most people, your body can lie to you just as well as your mind. Attraction is only one of those lies. Draven might want me now, but he'll figure out what I did eventually. I can at least spare him the regret of sleeping with me.

The black tea warms my throat with the subtle taste of oranges. I ordered some kind of meat skewers to snack on. Petra arrives just as the server sets them on the table. Garlicky steam rises from the plate.

She orders a tea as well before sitting down beside me. I push the appetizer toward her, and she lets out a breath. "Yeah, why not?" she says before grabbing a skewer and taking a bite. "That's not bad at all." She dabs her hands on a napkin and begins pulling out her files, spreading them across the table like the world's least fun game of cards.

The meat is sweet and spicy and makes this feel more like a casual lunch than a clandestine meeting to discuss the crown prince of Eddahn and all his sordid habits. Of which I am only one.

"We're going to start with a list of witnesses. You'll procure their statements. They need to be official, but obviously, I don't want Captain Gibson knowing about this yet." I nod in understanding. There's a flutter of curtains as the front door opens and someone else steps into the restaurant. Petra freezes at the sight of the tall man's silhouette.

"Relax," I say. "It's not CP. But someone you like probably almost as much."

Jasper steps away from the sun beaming in through the door and walks toward us. Petra unfreezes and angrily hisses at me, "What is he doing here?"

I ignore her as he makes his way to the table. He shrugs off his coat and sits down, rolling up his shirtsleeves and revealing lightly freckled forearms as he does so.

"Sugar, Petra," he says in greeting. His animosity toward her has only cooled slightly, but he's better at hiding it. Hers is still as high as ever, and the ornate metal orb light above us spins in the slipstream of her magic.

"I know the two of you have some issues, and I don't care." I cock my head, pausing. "Well, that's not true. I'm actually dying of curiosity, but I'm selflessly willing to put that aside for the greater good. Petra, you need more than just me. Jasper can get into places and interview people I can't. And he's been investigating CP's misdeeds for years. Plus, I've recently discovered he's quite well off, so that always helps."

The anger I'm getting from both of them spikes, and I file that away with the rest of the hints I have at the reason for their tension.

It took no time at all to track down the source of that aristocratic air. Jasper's family is loaded. He's got the kind of money that has its own genealogy chart. During my digging, I learned the two of them went to school together. They're both only thirty-five, basically infants. It explains why they feel their emotions so strongly.

Jasper pins me with an annoyed expression. "Exactly how does that help?"

"Exactly something a rich person would ask." I say as Petra side-eyes him. "Money always helps. Expenses, bribes, protecting you from a sadistic prince who throws people and their pets off cliffs for fun." I shrug.

"Did you know they never found that kid's dog?" he asks. But the look in his eyes as he stares at me says he's not really asking about the dog.

"We *know*," Petra replies. She's staring at the ceiling like she's wondering what she did to deserve this while her hand maintains a death grip on her pen.

"And I bet it's already helping, isn't it? There's no way the royal family hasn't checked in to you. Ever come home to find your apartment's been searched? Your office?"

His chin dips. "Several times."

"That's them being nice. With everything you've written so far, a journalist without your connections would have suffered much worse."

A strange current runs between Jasper and Petra. Her anger rises as his dwindles. He clears his throat as he turns to her and says, "I can help. I want CP to get what's coming to him just as much as you both." He turns back to me to make that statement. It's like he's waiting for me to do something. "I brought this." He finally breaks our eye contact, and I resist the urge to exhale. He pulls a thick envelope out of his soft leather messenger bag and holds it out to Petra, who clearly makes an effort not to snatch it from him. "It's every story I've ever done on CP, complete with sources and whether they've agreed to go on the record."

Petra lays his documents out on the table while Jasper orders tea from our server. She swallows and says, "All of these people are willing to testify?" She skims the documents before looking up at Jasper. He nods. "That's good." Her face struggles for a moment before she adds, "Thank you."

"What are these?" I say, dipping my hand into his briefcase. He doesn't make any move to stop me when I pull out another few folders.

"Ones that still need work."

Pulling the story out about Tonya's disappearance from LeMar, I notice additional images. "These weren't in the paper?" I say, finding a group shot of the party. There must be a hundred people in the room, all in various states of undress or in their shifted forms.

"No. We couldn't use all of them, of course. But there were two recorders at the party," he responds.

My eyes return to the images. There are a few detailed ones, but most of them are blurry or only focused on one or two people, likely because of the recorders' sobriety or lack thereof. Matt and I looked at the original investigation file. My suspicion had been right. Two novice corners handled it. They took statements from her friends, checked the requisite boxes, and closed it as a dead end.

Tonya's face smiles back at me from one of the images. Her lime-green wings aren't broken, and there are no ugly bruises across her throat like the last time I saw her. She looks excited and happy, her arm thrown around a woman with blond curls. They both hold drinks with pink, sparkling liquid. I flip to another one. Tonya stands at the edge of a circle surrounding CP as he takes a shot from a woman's navel.

Squinting, I pull the image closer to my face. Just behind Tonya, speaking to someone the recorder didn't capture, is Bellanie Nichols. It's not surprising. It's exactly the kind of party Bellanie would go to, especially if she was there at Carter's request.

"Can I take these?" I ask Jasper, holding up the images.

"Are you going to give them back?" At my "what do you think?" look, he nods. "Be my guest." He looks across at the tower of files Petra's spread out. The two of them lock eyes for a moment before returning their attention to the table.

There's a pause, as if we're all acknowledging not only the danger and potential futility of what we're doing but also the strange truce that will be necessary for Petra and Jasper to work together.

"Shall we get started?" Petra says at last, tying her long black hair out of her face like she's preparing for war.

After four hours, my brain is mush. Petra requires intense levels of organization, and instead of being as irritated by this as I am, Jasper is energized. He has that look again, like he's excited by a new adventure. I suppose he has been fighting his own battle against CP for so long; it must be nice to have someone take it just as seriously. They're meticulously color-coding things and have provided me with half a dozen lists of things to check, people to interview, locations to investigate.

At least I'm full. Around noon, Jasper spoke to the server and ordered a bunch of things that weren't even on the menu. Petra's eye twitched as he did it, but she said nothing. Dish after dish of roasted vegetables, spiced meat, and steaming bowls of soup appeared. I even got a top-up on my power from the chef. When I went to use the bathroom, I could hear the staff screaming at each other about some game. I ducked my head through the beaded curtain separating the kitchen from the hallway, and the woman let me have a taste.

If it wasn't for all the tedious paperwork and mounting evidence of CP's crimes, which are increasingly feeling like mine by association, it would have been a nice afternoon.

I'm used to the guilt. It's always been there, eating away at me like a ravenous parasite. But I used to be able to compartmentalize. The same way I shove all my feelings about Linnea away when I'm feeling too vulnerable to think about her or keep my face neutral when Draven looks at me like he might start being friendly.

Now it's impossible to ignore what Alaric is. I didn't get involved with him out of some misguided idea that I could change him. Alaric was who I deserved, who I might still deserve.

But his victims don't.

"Sugar?" Petra's voice breaks through the haze in my head.

"Sorry, what is it? I'm paying attention." I sit up straighter. "Please don't tell me there's another list."

Her light brown eyes narrow, but her lip quirks in amusement. "No. Not yet. I asked whether you think any of the evidence collectors or necros would be willing to join our cause?"

I puff my cheeks as I blow out a long exhale. "Corinne and Victor are who I work with most often. They don't seem dirty, but I'm not sure they're into building secret cases." Petra gives me a pointed look. "Why, of course I will add feeling them out to my list," I say in an emotionless tone. She nods, satisfied.

Jasper is looking at the image of Tonya and her friends. "I really hope you figure this one out." His anger is only a low simmer now as he uses long fingers to brush a crumb from the image. I briefly wonder if he has his nails manicured or if they simply grow perfectly when you're born to privilege.

"Certainly getting closer," I reply, refusing to volunteer any of the information we've discovered about Tonya, Sigrid, or their potential connection to Carter. "What do you think happened to her?"

He runs a hand through his red hair and leans back, crossing his arms over his chest. "I don't know. It's easy for my thoughts to turn to CP." He waves his hand at the papers on the table. "But there were so many people there. Her friends didn't see her leave, so she might not have even been killed at the party. Maybe she overdosed on whatever blends are making the rounds these days or was the victim of a botched deadgasm and someone broke her neck to cover up the real cause of death. Maybe she was just in the wrong place at the wrong time on her way home."

"All plausible theories." I drum my fingers on the table. Corinne didn't smell any drugs in her system. It'd be impossible to tell if she had a deadgasm before having her neck twisted.

Petra gathers up the case files. An image of the restaurant CP burned down falls out. She glares at it. "I honestly can't believe nobody's tried to off him yet."

Jasper's lips twist before he schools his expression and focuses on me again. This time, I stare back, challenging him to say whatever he's been thinking.

"Sorry," Petra says. "I didn't mean that. I don't want him to die. What I want is for him to rot in prison for several long decades." She puts the image away and the rest of the files into her briefcase.

"It wouldn't be so bad, though. We'd get Fenrik," Jasper muses. "What's he really like, Sugar? You used to date, didn't you?"

Petra's head snaps up so fast I'm afraid she might have broken something. "What? You used to date Prince Fenrik? How is this the first time I'm hearing of it?"

My relationship with Fenrik isn't a secret, but I know what Jasper's doing now, what he must have been doing the whole time. He knows about Fenrik, which would have been a simple thing to unearth. But all his inquisitive looks during this lunch make me suspect he knows more than that.

Moneybags knows about CP and me.

My heart pounds the way it always does when I think of how it'd feel to have that deeply shameful part of me exposed. There isn't a soul who would understand. And they shouldn't. It's disgusting.

"It was years ago, Petra. And it was nothing serious," I say, willing my heart to beat slower, my skin to cool, and my voice to take on a bored tone.

"Is it going to be a problem? I don't want your romantic history getting in the way of getting justice for these people." Her gaze dances over me, looking for signs of something—heartbreak maybe?

Too bad for her. I learned to lock that away a long time ago. At least when I'm not trapped in a room with Fenrik after an exhausting night keeping his youngest sister alive.

"My relationship with the prince—" I let my eyes slide to Jasper and drop my voice to something dangerous. "—can only help us. It's not anything either of you needs to worry about."

He gives me another one of those assessing glances before turning away. I haven't convinced him, but the message in his eyes is clear. He'll let it drop for now, but he's not going to give it up.

"Good." She snaps her briefcase closed. "This was productive. Thank you both," she says, her voice a little more clipped than necessary when she looks at Jasper.

With that, she gathers up the rest of her things and strides out of the restaurant. The two of us follow, Petra having apparently paid the bill without either of us noticing. I take off before Jasper tries to engage me in any further conversation regarding either prince.

Chapter 24
Sugar

"Let's take it from the top," Matt says. "You ladies were getting ready to go out?" He adopts a casual pose, trying to put Tonya's friend at ease. Difficult to do in one of the department's interview rooms. The slate-colored walls and metal chairs don't provide a lot of comfort.

Normally, I'd stand behind him, but today, I sit slightly to the side so she doesn't feel like it's us against her. She came as soon as we asked. Desperate to find justice for Tonya's killer, or feeling guilty?

Celia, the blond siren from the image with Tonya, folds her hands in her lap and sits up straighter. She's a children's teacher and came here straight from work. Her hair is in a tight bun, and she's wearing a respectable pencil skirt and sweater. I almost didn't recognize her from the images. The night of Tonya's murder, her hair was down, and she was wearing a skintight blue dress with several strategically placed cutouts.

"Right. Tonya, Maurice, and Kiki came over to my apartment to get ready around nine. We had a few drinks. All of us were really excited to go to the party."

"Who invited you?" I ask. CP's parties weren't exactly exclusive, but he normally has people at the door to ensure the right kind of people attend.

"Kiki's cousin works in the Luminous Palace. He was going to get us in," Celia replies.

Matt gestures at her to go on. She takes a steadying breath. The news of Tonya's death had made the papers, complete with a gruesome image of her body. It was taken from far away, but a recorder paired with a Seelie with enhanced vision made for enough detail to be damaging to those who knew her.

"Tonya was probably the most excited. She was always going on about some friend of a friend who dated CP for a few weeks and got to go on amazing vacations or ended up with fancy jewelry." Celia makes air quotes with her hands around "dated." CP doesn't date. He attends official occasions alone, and I've never seen him take a woman to a restaurant. "She was dying to hook up with him." Celia's eyes pop open, and she chokes back a sob, realizing what she said.

I pull a tissue from my pocket and hand it over to her. "Did she say how she planned to get close to the prince?"

The siren dabs at her nose and sniffs before responding. "She didn't really have a plan other than looking hot and being in the same room with him. Tonya didn't have to try that hard to attract attention." Celia smiles wistfully. "She was really pretty."

"She was," Matt agrees. He's sitting low in his chair, trying to make himself as nonthreatening as possible. Among the stale air, I catch a whiff of his aftershave, sun and seagrass. "Did anyone else in your group have a thing for CP?"

Celia shakes her head. "Not like Tonya. The rest of us were just going for the party."

"Was Tonya planning to come back to your place afterward?" I ask. I'm jumping around, which Matt has told me not to do, but I'm antsy to rule out some of the theories Jasper had.

"No. We never talked about it. I would've let her, of course, but no. I thought she'd just go home."

I nod at Matt in apology, and he continues. "Anything happen on the way to the party? Did you meet anyone?"

"No, we got there right away. Kiki's a transport fae." Celia shrugs.

"On that note, what about Maurice?" Matt asks, making a note about the group's abilities.

"He's a solinaire," Celia says.

"Does he work at the factory?" I ask. Solinaire are Seelie with the very useful, if unglamorous, power to infuse light. Many of them work at the orb factory just outside Drahma City. It's hard, uncelebrated work.

"No," Celia scoffs, offended. "He works at a coffee shop."

"Understood," Matt says. "Thank you for telling us. So, you arrived at the party at what time?"

"Around ten-thirty, I think." Celia says, scrunching her nose in thought. "There were already a lot of people there for it being so early."

Matt's eyes flash to mine, and I resist a smile. For a manatee shifter of his age, the only reasonable thing to be doing at 10:00 p.m. is sleeping. I hope he's getting enough of it. His face looks a little drawn today, and he's been stretching a lot like he's sore.

"Was CP there when you arrived?" I ask.

"Yes. He was there. I think." She pauses for a moment. "Maybe. I'm not sure. Tonya said she saw him and headed into the crowd, but I didn't see him until later. She was sitting on his lap on the couch. There was a lot of hair tossing, if you know what I mean." Celia smiles again before sniffling and falling silent for a moment. "Did he kill her?" she whispers so low I barely catch it.

"We don't know." I lean forward. "But we are truly trying our best to get your friend justice. Did you see Tonya go anywhere with CP?"

Celia hesitates. "I thought I saw her go into a room with him, but now I'm not so sure. Maybe it wasn't him? There were a couple of bedrooms. CP had guards on two of them, and it seemed like nobody was allowed in except him. But later, when we were looking for her, I definitely saw him go in with some girl—not Tonya—but that's it."

"You didn't recognize the girl at all? Was she a butterfly?"

"Not a butterfly. I didn't see her face at all."

"Did you see her again?"

"No." Celia shakes her head. "Not that I remember."

Matt's been writing quietly as I question, but he looks up and says, "Did you see Tonya with anyone else at the party?"

She shakes her head again and shrugs. "Not anyone memorable. Nobody she was paying attention to like CP. She stuck to him like a puppy."

"When was the last time you saw her?" he asks quietly.

Her face falls, and she swallows as tears gather in her eyes. "I didn't know it would be the last time. If I did, I wouldn't have... She was just being so stupid. She wouldn't shut up about the prince. Like he was all that mattered. We were getting tired of it. It was around one in the morning. Tonya had just come back from the bathroom and was bragging about how CP had felt her up on the dance floor." She takes a deep breath before blurting, "And I told her to stop being such an obvious pick-me. She stormed off." Celia screws up her face and cries, blotting her eyes with the tissue until it disintegrates. I hand her another.

"Hey," I say. "You were a good friend. And you would have made things right with her. That anger and regret you're feeling will drain you every day until you don't recognize yourself anymore. Save it for the right person, the person responsible for her death." My voice comes out more tense than I intended, and I sit back, trying to relax my shoulders.

She takes a few shuddering breaths before straightening again and nodding at us to continue. Matt's gaze slides toward mine for a moment before he turns back to Celia. "Do you recognize the woman CP went into the bedroom with from any of these images?" He lays out the ones I got from Jasper.

She looks them over but frowns and shakes her head.

"Do you recognize anyone?"

"Oh, sure." Celia points out various fae she knows—actors, minor royals, and socialites, including Bellanie Nichols.

"How do you know Bellanie?" I ask.

"Just from around. Everyone knows who her dad is, and I used to read Carter Fox's paper. Before he died." Her head snaps up to us. "Did they catch anyone for that?"

"Not yet," I say. "Do you recognize this woman?" I show her an image I have of Sigrid. It's from Tradimento the night of Carter's murder. One of the many Carter's recorders had given me.

"No. I don't know her. Is she a suspect?" Celia looks at the image with accusation.

"No, she's not," I reply. I start to put the image back in its folder when Celia reaches out and stops me.

"I don't know her, but that's Bellanie's boyfriend, or maybe bodyguard. He was there that night, too. At LeMar." She's pointing to Bradley, the usher from Tradimento.

"Her boyfriend or her bodyguard?" Matt asks.

"Not sure. He was at the party with her, and they seemed like they were friends, but I don't know. It felt like a professional thing. Maybe he worked with her on Carter's stuff? Kiki tried to hit on him, but he turned her down. Said that wasn't what he was there for." Celia pushes the image back across the table to me.

"Thank you. One last question, I think," I say after wordlessly checking with Matt, "Do you know any Seelie with the power of ice?"

***

Immediately after Celia leaves, we head to Tradimento to speak to Bradley. The chef I'd seen using his magic to peel potatoes meets us at the back door. The name "Sonny" is embroidered on his coat.

"He's not here. It's Wednesday. Club's closed tonight," he grunts before returning to his prep work. He leaves the door open, though, and we follow him inside. There's another chef working, an enormous mound of chopped onions beside him while a mountain of mushrooms awaits his knife.

Sonny has disappeared through a thick door, and I follow him to the opening. "Is Stone here?" I go to rest my hands against the wall but yank them back when I see it's covered in the same glowing red goo that cools the bodies in the morgue. A kylan demon.

"Nope," Sonny says, pulling a clipboard off a shelf and making a note. He scans the shelves of produce, meat, and cheese, and makes more notes. "Sometimes he comes in on Wednesdays to make sure we're on schedule." Sonny rolls his eyes, presumably at Stone's audacity. "But not today. Just been me and Sunset here since this morning." He pauses his writing to jab his thumb in the other chef's direction.

I examine the walk-in freezer. "How long does it take the kylan demon to freeze something?"

Sonny glances to the red walls before returning to his clip-board. A ripple runs across the wall closest to me, as if the demon understood my question. "Well, lady, that would depend on how big a thing you were freezing. Small thing, shorter time; big thing, longer time." He mimes pinching his fingers together and pulling them apart.

I clench my jaw and curb the instinct to say something snappish. "Right. How about something around one-hundred and forty pounds?" I say, estimating Tonya's weight. If she was kept here, it'd connect all three murders. Even if she was frozen initially by an ice-wielding fae, using the kylan's power would reduce the strain on their power.

"Hmmm," Sonny tips his head to the side. "What do you think, Midnight? Twenty-four hours? Give or take."

I turn my head toward the undulating walls. Midnight? Sonny speaks to the demon just like Victor does. "Does he ever answer back?"

"In his way," Sonny says, replacing the clipboard back on the shelf and pulling down a crate of strawberries.

"How do you know his name?" I step aside to let him through. The door falls shut behind me as I follow him back into the kitchen. He drops the strawberries onto the counter.

"I gave it to him. Can't just call him nothing now, can I? He's clearly got some kind of brain in there." He points to his head with the knife he's just retrieved from a magnetic strip along the wall.

"Do the staff ever leave things in the walk-in?" I ask as he sets to work hulling the strawberries. The knife moves under his power while he turns and leans against the counter, facing me. Matt and Sunset are chatting quietly over at his station.

"Yeah, sure. They'll leave meals they bring from home sometimes. We have family meal around five before the club opens, but if you're working until three in the morning, that's a long time to not eat."

"How about anything bigger? Ever seen anyone leave anything really big in the freezer?"

The knife pauses in midair. "Really big?" Sonny says, his brows furrowed in confusion. "Like what?"

"Like a body?" I keep my eyes on Sonny, knowing Matt is doing the same with Sunset, assessing their reactions. Anyone with access to this freezer could have kept Tonya's body here.

The two chefs startle before sharing an incredulous look. Sunset's hands are dark with dirt from the mushrooms he's peeling. He raises a hand to scratch his face, blinking at me, then turning to Matt as if he might explain my strange question.

"Detective, nobody has been storing bodies in my freezer." Sonny speaks slowly, like I'm a little deaf or a little stupid.

"Did you ever hear Stone talk about new nightclubs in the city? Competition, maybe?" Matt asks, changing the subject. He steals a cleaned mushroom and pops it in his mouth.

If either of these two are involved, we need to make them think we're taking their answers at face value. But Sonny, with his potentially throat-slitting knife and close relationship with a kylan demon, has definitely moved up my list a few notches.

"No. He doesn't talk to us about that stuff with the staff," Sonny says, the knife moving again with alarming speed. The strawberries pile up, perfectly hulled and quartered.

"Okay. Thank you. One last thing. Are there any Seelie with the power of ice working here?" I ask. Celia knew a few, but none we recognized from our investigation.

The two share another look before Sonny answers. "Other than Stone?"

Chapter 25
Draven

The early morning sun pierces the blinds in Captain Gibson's office. There's a frantic energy in the department today, courtesy of more protests last night. Every corner is poised to dive into a portal and head off to the under city at any moment. Fear of the ulgashen is seeping into everything, coating everyone's nerves like the beasts' sticky black blood. The attacks are still only happening in the Hollows, exposing the intentionally overlooked line between the haves and have nots.

The door creaks open, and Gibson slams it behind him. "Oh, Draven, good, you're here," he says, taking a seat at his desk. I've been waiting for over twenty minutes for a meeting he scheduled, but I'm not a fool, so I say nothing. "How are you holding up?" he asks.

I inhale and give him a convincing smile. "Better, thank you." Maria and the kids are doing well, really well, even though Lira's only paid me half the money. It'll still be another few weeks until we can be sure the Making was effective. Of course, we won't know how much it shortened her lifespan until she dies, but that's one thing I don't have to worry about. She knew the risks, and that one was certain.

"How's Maria?" Gibson pulls a dark cigarette from his desk and lights it, sending a thread of bluish-gray smoke curling around his head. He's a Seelie with a thick head of wavy brown hair and enhanced healing power. It's odd. Most fae with that ability don't end up as corners. Before all the ulgashen attacks, I'd be surprised if he had used his power much at all while on duty.

"She's okay. Surviving." I rub a palm down my leg. "I'll be checking in on them tonight."

The captain blows smoke from his nostrils before tapping the ash into a glass ashtray etched with the name of a hotel in the west of Eddahn, not too far from Ensame. He waves a hand, healing himself from the lung damage. "Good, good. Please give her my best."

"I'm ready to go back to my regular caseload. I can work alone," I say, leaning forward in my chair. A memory swims into my mind—sitting before my uncle, trying to make him see reason when he started implementing rules that made Ensame inhospitable to anyone who wasn't a vampire. Hopefully, I'll have better luck with Gibson.

He nods. "All right. If you think you're up to it. Not alone, though. We'll need to see about getting you a new partner."

The words hit me harder than I thought they would. A dull ache spreads through my chest at the thought of replacing Kurt. My eyes find his desk out the window in Gibson's door. I haven't touched it. I try to picture someone else sitting there, and heat spreads across my shoulders. My jaw hardens as I continue to glare at the empty desk.

"Maybe not quite so ready, then?" Gibson says, his voice gentle. I snap my gaze back to him. He gives me an upside-down smile. "There's nothing to prove here, Draven. You and Kurt were partners for a long time. I'm sure you want to throw yourself back into work, but it can do more harm than good. Sad corners are sloppy corners."

The anger recedes, leaving me drained. "Yeah, I guess you're right." I run a hand through my hair. A breeze ruffles the blinds, sending the strips of light and shadow bouncing back and forth across the room.

"Take some more time. When the thought of another partner doesn't fill you with the need to punch someone, we'll talk." He waves a hand to dismiss me, and I stand. As I reach for the doorknob he says, "And just give your cold case back to R&E. It'll still be cold next year."

A rock sinks to the bottom of my stomach, and I'm sure the blood drained from my face faster than it's ever moved in my five hundred and two years of life.

"Draven?" Gibson says, clearly wondering why I've frozen, hand outstretched like a mannequin in the world's most depressing window display.

"Will do," I croak before escaping his office. All those times my mind tugged at me, reminding me of lost threads and something to do with CP.

I storm across the office floor. Tindra smiles at me as she steps into my path. Faster than she can speak, I lift her by the biceps and move her out of my way. She makes a small "oh" sound and blushes as I continue on to Kurt's desk.

Linnea Faroe. Kurt died the day we were assigned to her case. Still, I shouldn't have forgotten her, not when everyone else clearly has, too. I rip open the bottom drawer of his desk, and the rock in my stomach instantly becomes a boulder.

The case file is gone.

***

I head down the stairs to R&E, my nerves sparking like a defective orb light. Who would have taken her case file? I wrack my brain for the memory of anyone even speaking to me about it and come up blank. As soon as my foot hits the bottom step, I can hear Nelson and Catriona going at it, as usual. Victor's words come back to me, and I scrutinize the pair of them.

"Stop chewing so loud, you insufferable ballbag," Catriona snaps as I approach the door. She towers over her desk, holding a stack of case files.

"Get fucked, you malevolent stick insect," Nelson replies in singsong. He casually flips the page of the paper he's reading as I stick my head through the opening.

"Hey, you two. I could use some help."

Catriona won't let the backup file out of her sight. So, a few minutes later, I'm sitting at a table next to her desk like a school kid suspected of cheating. Linnea's case is just as thin as I remember it, but it still takes me a bit to organize the witness statements and evidence lists.

Considering how little time they had, the detectives didn't do such a bad job. There are statements, albeit brief ones, from both Stanley and Jacqueline Roman, as well as several of the servants and, interestingly, two employees from the Nest. Apparently, Stanley had been having one of his infamous private parties.

Dispatch received anonymous note of fae in distress. Arrived on scene just after 0645. Butler answered, and myself and Det. Peterson were granted entry. Jacqueline Roman seemingly unaware of why we were contacted. Body of a human female in upstairs bedroom. Evidence collectors were called. Healing and raising were unsuccessful.

Stanley Roman entertaining on sublevel. Also informed corners he was unaware of any disturbance in the home. Deceased name is Linnea Faroe, a maid. No known family.

Reading Cowper's notes paints a depressing picture, one made only grayer by my failure to remember the case. Nobody saw Linnea get stabbed, and no one admitted to sending for help. She was a quiet girl who got along with everyone.

But as I read the statement from one of the servants, my breath catches, and my eyes narrow on a single line.

Linnea didn't work the party, but she helped Madame Writh out.

"There's no way that's a coincidence," I mumble.

"What?" Catriona says, her blond hair grazing the ceiling as she files paperwork in the row of metal filing cabinets behind her desk.

"Has Detective Writh ever reviewed this case file? Or the copy?" I watch Nelson and Catriona. They can't hide the quick look they give one another. "Well?" I roll up my sleeves and grab the statements from the other Roman employees. That familiar feeling of a good lead sparks inside me.

"She has," Nelson says, avoiding my eye as he studies the paperwork on his desk.

"What about any of the other corners? Anyone besides her and Kurt request this file?" I lean back in my chair, crossing my arms.

Nelson's tanned throat bobs. "No, not to my knowledge."

I glance at Catriona. She shakes her head quickly and returns to her filing. Nothing makes me more suspicious than this unusual united front from the two of them. I let the silence stretch out a little longer before returning to the file.

None of the other statements mentions Sugar. The detectives don't mention her being there at all. They do mention several other people by name who slipped away in the morning and refused to be questioned, including our beloved crown prince. Of course he'd be at one of these parties. The man does nothing but drink and fuck when he's in D.C.

There's a sharp jab in my mind at the thought that I'm also avoiding my responsibilities to my people in Ensame. Not like CP, but the feeling of similarity is uncomfortable nonetheless.

"Catriona," I say with feigned nonchalance, "bring me every-thing you can on Sucrelia Writh."

Catriona's shoulders hunch, but she says nothing as she joins Nelson at the cages so they can insert their keys together. Once the door is unlocked, she disappears inside.

"It might take a while," Nelson sniffs before sitting back down at his desk.

I grin. "Not a problem at all. I don't have a single thing else to do."

Chapter 26
Draven

"So she's been looking for her killer? For all these years?" Maria's face is a mixture of horror and devastation. "That's awful." She puts the coffee cup to her lips before remembering it's empty. She stands and makes her way over to the percolator to pour herself another cup.

I run a hand down the back of my neck. "That's my theory. I can't be sure she took it. But it makes sense." She's checked out the file three times already, but knowing it wasn't going to be missed for a while, she probably couldn't help herself from taking another look.

Thanks to Nelson's digging, I know Sugar worked Roman's parties pretty often, and if what that other servant had said was right, she and Linnea would have spent a lot of time together. I can't be sure, but I'd bet she was the one who alerted the corners.

Maria sits back down again at the kitchen table. Soft murmurs can be heard from the living room, where the girls are doing their homework. The house is warmer again. It looks exactly the same, gleaming countertops, jackets hung by the door, the smell of coffee and bread lingering in the air. But Maria's relief at not having to leave her home, at not needing to traumatize the girls further after the death of their father, imbues the place with an intangible lightness.

She had asked me about the money, of course. Wanted to know why all the creditors had suddenly dried up and she'd received a deed to the house. She even tried to give it back, didn't want me to "waste" my money on them. Seeing the girls leaning over the books, safe in their own living room, with the images of their father on the wall and a crackling fire in the hearth, was worth it. Even if it did put me off Making anyone ever again.

And it was only half the money I'm owed. Because Lira still isn't out of the woods. It'll be a few weeks before we know if the change truly took.

The snow is falling outside. Drahma City never gets a lot of snow, but it's pretty. Especially during Soven, the holiday to celebrate Soveh, the goddess of slumber. Even the most cynical fae in D.C. will step out at midnight, candles lit, and sing the goddess to sleep for her long winter nap. Shops and restaurants stay open until one in the morning, serving fire-roasted food and handing out moon- and star-shaped chocolates and sweets for the children.

People decorate their houses with spinning ornaments of Soveh and Neve, the goddess of dreams. I wonder if the residents of Sugar's apartment will decorate their fountain with the statue of Neve, and whether Marco will fix the water.

I usually spent Soven here, with Kurt's family. This year will be different, worse. Who did Sugar spend the holiday with? At the Nest? With Matt?

"Are you going to ask her?" Maria says, refilling my cup.

"To Soven?" I ask, confused. Maria cocks her head, a bemused smile on her lips. "Oh, right. About the file, you mean." I clear my throat. "Yes. I'll have to at some point."

"Draven." Maria sits down, her face full of compassion. "You'll go easy on her, right? Her heart's in the right place. It must have been so awful to lose a friend like that." Her eyes gloss over a little before she shakes away the hurt.

I offer a consoling smile. "What do you think I'm gonna do? Put the screws to her? Just for looking at a case file she has every right to look at as a corner?" Maria shrugs and smiles. "I'm just going to talk to her. Maybe we can help each other and find Linnea's killer." I stand and walk to the sink to wash my mug. Surely Matt knows about this? Has he been helping her?

"No, I didn't think that. But at the reception, you did seem terribly irked by her presence. All that bluster about vampires and succubi. I'm glad to see you've put that old prejudice behind you," she says with a teasing tone.

"I'm not that evolved. It's still there, but I'm working on it." I dry my hands and walk toward the door, pulling my coat off the rack. I smile a little at the box of paid bills on the counter and run a hand over it, noting all the places Maria's written "PAID" in big black letters. She has them neatly alphabetized, just in case a creditor comes calling and she needs to show immediate proof of payment.

Sloane comes marching into the kitchen. "Mom! Keisha won't stop trying to read my homework!"

Keisha yells from the living room. "Why would I want to read your stupid baby homework?"

"It's not baby homework!" Sloane says as she whirls around, hands on her hips. Her elbow knocks the box of bills, sending it tumbling down. Envelopes and letters scatter across the wood floor, causing an immediate gasp from Sloane. "I'm sorry, I didn't mean to do that."

"It's okay, baby. Please, just take your homework upstairs if your sister is bothering you," Maria says, putting a hand on her youngest child's cheek.

Crouching down, I scoop everything back into the box. I snag an errant bill from where it's slid under the counter. It's addressed with slanted, tight script, so different from the official block letters favored by bill collectors.

A dark suspicion creeps up my spine as I look from the bill to the hastily scribbled writing on the envelope. "When did you get this, Maria?" The sick, familiar feeling of betrayal swirls inside me.

"Which one?" Maria steps over, eyeing the envelope.

"The one that's addressed to you. The *only* one addressed to you and not Kurt." I've seen this handwriting before. Written by a hand flecked with blood as it took notes on Lira's transformation. The image of Sugar sitting in the chair in Lira's bedroom, her eyes half closed as she watched the sleeping princess, pops into my head. Fury rolls down my neck, heating my skin.

Maria squints, thinking. She brushes her red hair from her face and taps a finger against her chin. "I got it that same morning you came over. Not long after the reception for Kurt. Why?"

I don't have to ask what morning she's referring to. It was the same day I'd run into Sugar at the diner. The same day I went to her apartment to hear her outrageous proposal. Maria had been waving the bill around, frantic with worry that she was going to lose her home. It was probably the first bill she'd seen, because I'd hid the others or told her not to open them. It's what caused her to go digging and discover all that her husband had never told her.

My eyes fall closed as I crush the paper in my hand. Anger floods my veins along with my venom, primed for a fight. My blood pounds, and my fangs extend.

She sent this to Maria. That conniving demon heard Kurt's confession and sent this to Maria to be sure she found out exactly how dire their financial situation was. All so she could manipulate me into Making Lira and earning her the Crown's favor.

"Fuck!" I slam my hand into the wall, cracking it and sending bits of plaster floating down onto the box of bills.

***

I pound on Sugar's door, letting every ounce of anger and irritation I've ever felt for her or anyone pour out of me. Every muscle I have vibrates with pent-up energy. I hate her for this, and I hate it even more that my uncle was right about succubi. They're all emotionally manipulative parasites. I knock so hard the gold number 3 on her door tips to the right, hitting the D beside it.

Sugar pulls open the door, looking irked. "Yes?" she says, tying a long black robe around her waist.

Her silver hair is in a bun. Loose strands frame her face. The hint of rosemary and oranges floats out to me from the apartment. The idea that she was about to take a bath, to relax in the knowledge of how easily she played me, ignites a ferocity I haven't felt since leaving Ensame.

"What the hel is wrong with you?" I demand. "What kind of psychopath preys on a widow and her children?" I wave the crumpled bill in front of her before hurling it to the ground. My rage only increases as she barely reacts, merely glances down at the paper before leisurely bringing her eyes back to mine.

She lets out a long exhale and crosses her arms. "You were planning to...what? Hide it from her forever? Or just until the debt enforcers came to toss her and her children out on the street?"

"They never should have been on her that quickly. I should have had a few months at least." Cold fury narrows my vision until her face is all I can see. "Did you send Puck? Did you send that lowlife to harass her the day of her husband's funeral?"

"No, I didn't. But seriously? A debt collector showed up at the house, and you still didn't tell her?" Sugar shakes her head slowly as if I'm a misbehaving child. "Tsk, tsk, Draven. That's not being a very good friend."

I grip the trim of her door, cracking the wood. I'm an idiot. She handed me poison, and I willingly drank from it because she was beautiful? Confusing? "You know damn well I would have told her! Once I had a plan, I would have done it properly." I also would have fixed it if I'd had more time, if Sugar hadn't come slithering in, screwing with my life and Maria's.

She arches an eyebrow. "I don't know you at all," she says coldly. "All I did was tell her the truth instead of coddling her like a child. What kind of man keeps his wife completely in the dark about their finances?" Her voice remains impassive, but she takes a step toward me like she's readying to throw me back into the hall.

"Don't you dare," I growl as I whip my hand out and wrap my fingers around her neck. I twist her around, dragging her back against me. Faster than she can breathe, I thread my fingers through her hair, tilting her head so she's perfectly exposed for my fangs.

Sugar does nothing to stop me. But I can hear her heartbeat quicken. I contemplate everything I could do in this position to wring some kind of reaction from her. "Don't you dare talk about Kurt. He was ten times the fae you are." Her cuff spins as I wrap my fingers around her upper arm.

"A good man with a gambling problem he hid from his wife," she scoffs, her voice only slightly less indifferent than when I arrived. She arches her back, driving her ass against me and tilts her neck, offering it to me. "Go on, Draven. Try it and see what happens." Her voice is a dangerous purr.

Even without her power, Sugar knows how to break my grip and hit me where I'm exposed. Every corner does, but she doesn't lift a finger, just continues to taunt me with her apathy. I almost expect her to examine her nails. My fangs lengthen, and I imagine how good her blood will taste on my tongue. She's powerful, but I'm faster.

My gaze travels down the column of her neck, her exposed collarbone. The robe slipped when I grabbed her, revealing a bare shoulder. It's not low enough to see them, but I know those three freckles are just out of sight. If I moved my hand, slid it down an inch, I'd see them waiting for me to put my fingers between each one.

Heat caresses my neck as I struggle to regain my composure. My fingers tighten in her hair, my jaw clenching, before I push her away, hard. There's a flicker of surprise on her face as she turns to face me, not bothering to straighten her robe.

I shake my head at her. "You're not worth it. You're a cold-hearted monster. Your blood is probably as sick as you." She's probably not even looking for Linnea's killer. A terrifying thought shoves its way into my head. She could *be* Linnea's killer.

Emotions dance across Sugar's face. For a split second, I think she might break, lash out at me or yell, before her eyes harden and there's nothing but amused cruelty in her expression.

Her smile becomes saccharine as she slides toward me like a wraith. "Poor Draven. Did you really think that maybe deep down, I just needed a friend? Her voice burns to a low hiss. "Perhaps you thought you could use your dick to find my soft, gooey center?" Sugar's fingers trail down my shirt, the small lengthening of her claws the only sign this conversation is affecting her. "You think I haven't felt your lust when you look at me? Think I don't feel it even now?" She scoffs.

My anger rises to the surface. I itch to touch her again, to shake her until genuine emotion falls out, but I don't. Not even when she leans up, an inch from my face, and breathes, "You're so predictable. You don't even know how much of a monster I really am."

This was a mistake, all of it. I got played. Once again, I let a woman exploit me for her own ends. I could fucking break something. Like her damn neck. But before I do, a noise downstairs has Sugar's entire demeanor transforming. Alarm flashes in her expression as her eyes shoot behind me to the dark hallway. Footsteps sound on the stairs three floors below us.

"Damn it," she whispers. She grabs my upper arms, her lips terrifyingly close to mine.

"What are—" I don't get the rest of the sentence out before a flush comes over my skin. There's an internal flurry inside me, like a storm twisting in my bones, swirling and rushing up and out of my body and through Sugar's lips. My fingers, my eyelids, nothing on my body responds to my command. Everything is wrapped in a warm cocoon of her power.

Something inside me struggles, furious at her for her lies and for using her power on me. The cocoon wraps tighter, like a straitjacket, the warmth turning my will to mush. She pulls me into the room, silently closing the front door behind me.

"Get in the closet and do not come out until I tell you. Don't make a noise or do anything to draw attention to yourself," she whispers before adding, "And no matter what, *don't* be a hero."

Part of me wants to fight her, to ask who I'm hiding from. I'm not afraid of most things. I think. It's hard to remember when her soft hands are leading me to a thin closet door. My thoughts melt away. Her silk robe brushes against my legs, and I ache to feel it slide through my fingers. In the closet, I turn around, and she slams the door in my face.

Coats brush against me, smelling distinctly of Sugar, but my hands don't reach up to move them. Instead, all I can do is stare through the slats into the dimly lit living room. Sugar bends down, grabs Maria's bill, and shoves it into the trash just as the front door opens.

Chapter 27
Sugar

Shit, I think to myself as I hustle Draven into the closet. I don't know how long my control over him will last. A fae of his power, with the amount of anger he was radiating? I'd normally have at least a day. As a vampire, though, what's the conversion rate? One hour? Two?

If Alaric finds him here, I'm not sure what he'll do. That's not right. I know what he'll do. The question is whether Draven will survive it. He beat someone to death for walking in on him with a girl. I'm not sure if he'd ever get that jealous over me as a person, but as something he thinks belongs to him? That, he might kill for.

I'm still shaking inside. I know what I am, the things I've done, but Draven's words prick at a wound I've long ignored. Shame clogs my throat as I rush to throw Maria's bill in the trash.

Alaric opens the door and smirks, his expression predatory. "Another hard day with zero responsibilities?" I say, hoping my voice sounds calmer than I feel. I turn my back on the prince and stroll into the kitchen to pour myself a drink.

Alaric is behind me in seconds, his hands tightening around my waist. "Get me one too." For a minute, I consider telling him to fuck off, but I suddenly can't remember how to treat him, how not to arouse his suspicion. I compromise and pour the drink but leave it on the counter. Alaric runs his nose up my neck as he grabs it.

My skin used to crawl when he'd touch me. When I was with Fenrik and Alaric would slip his hand up my dress under a table or run a finger down my chest, I'd have to stop myself from skewering his eyeballs with my claws. Then Fenrik and I fell apart, and I was nothing but bitterness, furious at myself after all my training at the Nest. The Dame always told us to keep our emotions to ourselves.

Everything we do is carefully curated to match the client's needs. There's no room for the real you in this production.

Fenrik was never my client. But I was a fool to open my heart to him. A pleasure worker and the prince. It's fucking laughable that I ever thought that we'd be anything more.

So, of course, rage fucking his brother was the only appropriate choice.

I slip out of his embrace and head for my bedroom. There's no way to avoid Draven finding out about Alaric and me, but that doesn't mean he needs to see it. Just as I pass the closet, being sure to avoid looking at it, Alaric grabs my arm.

He pulls me closer, and for a moment, I consider how much safer I felt with Draven at my back than Alaric right in front of me. "Why are you still investigating that dead butterfly?" His voice has an edge I've not heard before.

"Tonya?" I ask, taking a leisurely sip of my wine. "Why do you care? Oh, that's right, because her body was found on your beach." His anger increases. The feeling is less personal than Draven's but more potent. "Why do you own the beach?" I extract myself from his arm. The light outside dies a little more, and the weak orb lights in the living room brighten.

He snorts. "What don't I own? That dismal strip of sand has been in my family for generations. I don't want you working that case anymore." He downs his entire glass.

My blood stills. Not once in all this time has he ever asked me to back off a case. I've only had a few where he was personally involved; those accusations were minimal, nothing like Petra's trove of malfeasance. A few days after any incidents, the witnesses would dry up, all of them probably a little richer.

"Well, that doesn't sound like me," I drawl. My plan had been to distract him with sex. After my meeting with Petra and Jasper, the thought of it is nauseating, but I cannot risk him being here when my control over Draven wears off.

"Why should I back off? I am an officer of the law and all. Anything you want to confess?" I turn and tilt my head, waiting for him to explode and give me something, anything, I can use. This night doesn't have to be a total loss.

"Don't fucking play with me. This is serious. More serious than your little corner act." He walks back into the kitchen and pours himself another glass. My spine locks, and my legs refuse to carry me into the bedroom. I roll my neck, my cuff spinning in agitation. His words fill me with undiluted violence. He's never taken me seriously, and it's never mattered before, but knowing Draven heard his words is beyond humiliating.

"Is it, though? Is anything in your life serious, Alaric?" I drain my drink, setting it down on a nearby table. A strange exhaustion settles over me. My limbs are suddenly heavy. I'm so tired of all of this. If I goad him enough, maybe he'll leave. I've never tried it before, but the way my every nerve is a sharp needle from this situation is making me desperate.

He rounds the corner, his glass floating before him before landing on the table by the couch. "I said"—he wraps both hands around my neck, using his thumbs to push up my chin—"don't play with me. My future is riding on it."

A little thrill goes through me. I'm right. Tonya saw something that somehow threatened his place in the line of succession. There were at least two other people in that room, including him, a guard, and our mystery girl.

Could she be another royal child? One born before Alaric? That would definitely make him concerned. Perhaps she was blackmailing him. That would explain why she wasn't dressed for the party.

"Your future? That's a lot of power for one little butterfly."

"Nobody has power over me, Sugar." His voice is cold and callous as his eyes trail down my face and neck. His arousal rises like a tide, almost overpowering the anger. He removes a hand, dragging it down my chest and untying my robe. Draven can't see my face, but he has an excellent view of what Alaric is doing. Nausea roils inside me, and I bite back the bile rising in my throat.

Now he knows exactly what kind of monster I am. The crown prince's whore.

"You are going to close that case." He pushes a hand inside my robe, his fingers sliding over my breast. He pinches hard enough to make me wince. "And I don't want to hear another thing about it. I'm going to own this country soon, and you can be my good little helper. I'll even let you sleep in the palace, unlike my idiot brother. Won't that be nice?"

The words hit their target, and I snap. "How gracious of you. Will I get to use the servant's entrance, or will you hide me in a bag of flour and have them throw me in the cellar?" I've been to the Luminous Palace as much as anyone in D.C. has. I took the tour, saw the ornate murals and the gold thrones that are nearly always empty since the king and queen prefer to stay in Zavrik.

"Oh no, baby." He grins. "I'll let you march straight through the front doors. And then I'll have you crawl across the throne room and show me how much you love your king."

"King? You planning on offing your parents? Not really something you should mention to a corner." My claws extend, and I push them into his chest, which I know only turns him on, but the desire to draw his blood is too strong.

Alaric chuckles. "All in good time. What's a few more years?" He brushes his thumb across my lip as his other hand roams lower.

Maybe she's not another child, but someone who's planning to help him assassinate the king and queen?

"I'm actually thinking of leaving Eddahn." The words fall from my mouth before I've consciously thought them. It isn't something I've been thinking of, not until I solve Linnea's murder. I don't even know why I said it.

He focuses on his fingers digging painfully into my neck. "No," he says slowly, his arousal dancing with rage. "No, you won't be doing anything of the sort. In fact, this shitty apartment is a little too far away for my taste." He drags my face forward, crushing my lips and my body to his, before releasing me and hissing into my ear, "I'm going to have you a lot closer from now on, Sugar. Get used to it."

He walks me back into the bedroom, his drink dutifully following behind. When he slams the door shut, I breathe a sigh of relief that Draven won't see this.

***

When Alaric finishes dressing and walks out of my bedroom, I hold my breath for several long, agonizing seconds. I stand, recover my robe from the floor, and wait for the sound of him discovering Draven. I picture the creak of the closet door, then flesh on flesh and power against power, ending with blood staining my floors and my hands.

When there's nothing but the sound of the front door opening and closing, I exhale, collapsing back down on the bed. I cradle my head in my hands as I try to forget the feeling of Alaric's skin against mine. It was nearly identical to the first time I slept with him, knowing the whole time what a mistake it was and trying to distract myself from how awful I felt. I wonder when that feeling went away, when I started craving the brutality of his affections.

I don't want to go out there.

I don't think I can stomach the disgust in Draven's eyes. When he called me a monster, I nearly crumbled. It's been so long since I felt anything but sadness and rage, but Draven's face felt like a mirror, showing me all the things I hate about myself.

All the light inside me died when I found Linnea's body and learned how insignificant I really am. How pointless my power was when it really mattered. How easily I pretended it wasn't that bad when, deep down, I knew it was.

The wood floor is cold against my feet as I walk out of my bedroom. I put on my best mask, vow to ask Ms. Plichen to clean the apartment again tomorrow, and hold my head up high as I throw open the closet door.

Draven is gone.

Chapter 28
Sugar

My head pounds, no longer capable of doing the intense gymnastics to necessary compartmentalize my life. I've spent the morning running down the endless list of tasks Petra has assigned me to imprison the man who was inside me last night. The shame is sticky, like the summer months in Drahma City, when even the pavement sweats. Bile rises in my throat as I climb the steps to Matt's door.

His house is in the style favored by many water-based shifters—two stories, entrance on the second. The first story is just a big pool. When I step through the front door, I'm greeted by the sight of him sweating through a T-shirt as he crouches over the far side of the water. He holds up a glass vial, squinting at the contents in frustration.

"Little bastards," Matt mutters, his bushy mustache twitching in irritation. His skin has that worn look it gets when he's ill.

"What's wrong?" I say, crossing over the wooden walkway that extends from the front door and branches off to different parts of the house.

"Algae. It's the bane of my existence. Been tossing and turning all night. It's just so hard to deal with in these enclosed systems." He pours the vial out and gets a clean one from a metal box beside him. Inside is an array of testing solutions, powders, and weird instruments.

I peer down into the water. It looks clear enough to me, but I don't sleep in it. There are rock walls and a sandy bottom rich with seagrass and tiny crustaceans. It smells like the warm, empty beaches on the southern coast of Eddahn. "I don't know if you've heard, but we live quite near a large river." I nearly trip over a small alligator blending in with the wood. It scurries off the walkway, bellyflopping back into the water.

"The Fugue is way too crowded." Matt grunts as he gets to his feet. "And the boats are always hitting me right when I get to sleep." He motions toward the kitchen, and we walk over the bridge onto a sunny yellow room with a solid floor. There's a towel hanging up that reads "Manatee or Manacoffee?"

I sink down at the light wooden table, feeling lost. His sketchbook sits open in the middle, showing multiple plant sketches and a reminder to buy soap. Matt pulls out a mug and holds it up. "Drink?" he asks.

Giving him a wan smile, I say, "Manacoffee, please."

He smirks in response before bustling around the kitchen while I replay the events of the other night in my head. Draven's face featured prominently in my dreams last night. The anger, the guilt, all swirling with the uncomfortable feeling of enjoying his hands on me. Like I really need to be turned on by another man who wants to hurt me.

Shaking the images away, I turn to look out the window. It overlooks a garden mostly dead since it's winter, but there are two children playing. Fae children aren't very powerful, but I'm still surprised nobody is watching them. Especially when the younger one hurls a fireball at the other. The older one meets it with a ball of ice. They collide in midair with a small explosion of steam.

It's been two steps forward and one step back on the Carter/Tonya/Sigrid investigation, especially since Stone's alibi for the time of Carter and Sigrid's murder checked out. I'm not yet convinced he wasn't involved, though. He has the power of ice and unlimited access to the cold storage at Tradimento. Anistemi has been backed up, but he's going to raise Sigrid in two days, which should help.

Matt uses his elbow to push his notebook out of the way and sets a steaming mug down in front of me. It smells wonderful. After the coffee at the department, anything is an improvement, but it tastes perfect. He's even given me a little caramel cookie.

Matt waits until I've finished the cookie and half the coffee before he says, "Well?"

"Well what?" I dust my fingers on a blue striped napkin, one eye on the kids next door.

I can feel his eyes roll when he says, "You are the unfriendliest person I know. You expect me to believe you just stopped by for coffee and a casual chat?"

"Hey. I'm not unfriendly. I just don't have a lot of friends." Crossing my arms, I frown at my partner.

"That's because you're unfriendly."

"That's because my friends wind up dead," I snap.

"No need to get so dramatic."

"I—" I snort and choke at the same time, the laughter spilling out of me. Matt grins as I lean my elbows on the table and cradle my forehead with my hands. I need to get it together. Now is not the time to lose control. "I'm just feeling a little stuck."

"I thought you said you had a lead on Linnea's case?" Matt smooths his mustache with his thumb and index finger.

"I do. At least, I will." Lira was fine with parting with the first half of the money, but nothing else until we're sure the change isn't going to kill her. And since Draven will probably never speak to me again, I'll need to wait for her word.

"So it's about prince dickball?" Matt stands and pours himself another cup.

I give a hollow chuckle. I told him about Alaric after we'd been partners for a year. We'd been called in to do security from some big gala and were stuck on the roof, just watching the party through a glass dome. The entire royal family had been there. CP had been on his best behavior since his parents were in attendance. Then the king and queen left, and he reverted to his typical shitty antics.

"He's such an asshole," Matt mutters, watching CP chug four glasses of wine in a row.

Blowing out a breath, I say, "He is an asshole. An asshole I don't like and won't ever compromise a case for, but one I occasionally sleep with." The words tumble out of me before I can take them back.

He wasn't overjoyed. But I told him about Linnea that night, too. And since then, he's never hidden his dislike of the crown prince, but he doesn't mention it often. Treats him like a pet I never should have adopted who constantly pees on my floors.

"Draven saw us together. He came to my apartment right before CP showed up. I had to use my power on Draven so CP wouldn't see him. Then he...had to watch."

Matt whistles low. "Wow. That must have sucked for him."

"For him? It wasn't a picnic for me either, *partner*," I say, glaring at him.

"Ah, but you had a choice. Poor Draven didn't. What'd he say afterward?" The table creaks as Matt leans forward.

"Don't know. He left. Haven't seen him." I fall backward against the chair, exhaling. Somewhere in the house, something big splashes in the water.

"So what? You're worried he's going to tell the world you have a thing for jackasses? That you enjoy being with people who have fewer than three brain cells to rub together?"

"Hey! I didn't come here to be ridiculed." Standing, I turn uselessly, frustrated the kitchen isn't big enough for me to pace.

"Tough." Matt leans back, hands on his knees. "Just because we're friends doesn't mean I approve of your poor choices.

People like CP give free rein to the worst side of you. He's like a disease, and the longer you spend with him, the sicker you get."

My mouth falls open, and I blink. Matt has never spoken to me so harshly.

"I tried to let you learn for yourself, Sugar. But you can't seem to pull that leech off. Soon, you won't be alarmed by his behavior. After a few years, it'll become banal. After a little more time, you'll think it's impressive. And then you'll be the one hanging waiters out the window." He pushes up from the table. "And just so we're clear, when it gets that far, we won't be friends anymore."

There's a stiff twisting in my chest. My skin tightens like a prison I can't escape, and a cold flush works itself down my back. Swallowing, I try to find something, anything, to say in response. My fingers tingle, but my cuff stills, sensing the only threat is me and my inability to drag myself out from under this mountain of regret.

I want to tell Matt I'm not sure I deserve anyone but CP and the way he treats me, but instead, I whisper, "He won't give me up easily."

"He's not your biggest problem, Sugar. You are." He stands, tidying away the coffee cups and napkins.

I blow out a breath. "Wow. You start going to therapy or something?" I wrap my hands around the back of the chair, tightening and loosening my grip until I can feel my fingers again. It groans under my strength. My lungs constrict like I ran a mile.

Matt smiles, his eyes crinkling. "You're a good kid. I just want what's best for you."

"Once again, I am older than you," I sigh.

He chuckles. "Why are you worried about Flint, anyway? He doesn't strike me as the gossiping type." Matt takes the dishes to the sink. Tiny bubbles float into the air, popping and releasing the smell of eucalyptus as he washes up.

He's right. Draven isn't likely to go spreading my business around. My face scrunches as I turn back to the garden. The kids are gone. Just an empty yard, dusted with a thin layer of snow.

Chewing my lip, I consider what bothers me most about Draven knowing my secrets. I hated the way he looked at me. It was humiliating, but he never needs to know that. When he held me against him, I could feel his emotions, the twist of arousal with anger. It was so similar to Alaric. For a moment, I really thought he'd try to bite me.

Then he just pushed me away. And told me all the things I already knew about myself. If he'd attacked, I could have dealt with that. It would've been a relief. He'd get a few hits in, and both of us would feel better. Something in me squirms at the idea of that never happening, of never feeling that relief. I am afraid he won't forgive me. But that's ridiculous. I don't need his forgiveness. Since Linnea, I've tried very hard not to need anyone. Matt wore me down over time, like water. But why am I considering Draven's feelings at all? He's a vampire I barely know.

"Damn it," I mutter to myself.

"Why, Sucrelia Writh, do you care what that vampire thinks of you?" Matt stares at me while holding a hand to his chest. "I need to check with the astrologist, because surely the gods are returning if you're developing actual feelings for someone."

"Okay, okay, enough of that." I hold up my hands. "Giving a shit about what he thinks and having feelings for him are very different things. No more discussion about the vampire. Or I'll start talking about your complete lack of romantic relationships," I say, raising my brows in challenge.

Matt hasn't dated since his divorce twenty years ago. It wasn't even acrimonious. They're still friends. Which confuses me to no end.

"Deal. Let's discuss something less contentious. Like the murders we still haven't solved."

Chapter 29
Sugar

Bellanie Nichols flips her blond hair over her shoulder as she smiles at the man who has approached her. She's sitting at an outdoor table under a canopy of camellias, having brunch with her friends. A fae from a nearby group has split off from the herd to shoot his shot. She's receptive, at least from what I can see from where Matt and I are watching from a bookmaker across the street.

Her mouth opens in a laugh as the man finishes what I'm sure is a riveting tale. Bellanie extends her hand to him, giving her name and tacit permission to send her messages. He grins as he shakes it before heading back to his table. Bellanie and her friends immediately lean toward each other, no doubt discussing the entire interaction.

"It's a long time for brunch," Matt huffs beside me. He's cranky because it smells of sweat and cheap gray smoke in here, but at least it looks like he's sleeping better. And he's right. We've been watching Bellanie drink with her friends over pastries and eggs for the better part of two hours.

"It's a long time for anything," I say, arching my back despite the surprisingly comfortable chairs. The red leather seats are designed to encourage patrons to sit and gamble as long as they want. It's mostly empty in here at the moment, just a few grizzled hopefuls pulling levers on ancient artifacts that are almost certainly charmed by the owner to never pay out.

"Not too long for some things," Matt says wryly as he sketches in his small brown notebook. He's drawing the older fae sitting on the other side of the room.

"Didn't realize we were at the sex joke part of our friendship." I roll my eyes, but inside, I exhale with relief. After our conversation about CP, I was afraid things would be different between us. My worry makes me even more aware of how much I value Matt's friendship. I once again have something good that can be taken, perhaps forever.

Matt chuckles before he looks across the street and his smile drops, face snapping to attention. "Oh, here we go," he says as he stows the sketchbook in his jacket pocket.

We stand as Bellanie gets up from the table, purse in hand. Once they've exited the little wrought-iron gate separating the outdoor seating from the sidewalk, Bellanie and her friends linger for another twenty minutes, chatting.

Matt and I exit the bookmakers, inhaling the cool air outside, and inch closer to the councilor's daughter. It'll be Soven soon. The shops are filled with sparkling clouds, ornately carved candlesticks, and every kind of fluffy blanket and comfortable pillow imaginable.

I usually spend Soven at the Nest, but I'm not sure I'm up for it this year. Matt leaves town to visit family on the west coast. As one of Bellanie's friends squeals at the sudden memory of some vital piece of gossip, I briefly wonder what Draven does for the holiday.

Based on everything I discovered about his family, he definitely isn't going home to Ensame. He must spend it with Kurt's family. The thought of Maria and the kids having their first holiday without their father makes my chest constrict. I forced Draven's hand by sending Maria that bill. I know I did. But she was going to find out eventually. And I did it for a good reason.

At least, I hope it was for a good reason. I've heard nothing from Lira since we parted ways at the house by the river. I want as little evidence of this as possible, so I've resisted sending her a note, but the waiting is undeniably painful.

Finally, Bellanie breaks off from the group and heads down the opposite street, toward her father's office. She stops to look into a store window, and I slide up next to her.

"Bellanie, got a minute?" I dig up a friendly smile I haven't used in years.

Her eyes widen in surprise. "Detective Writh?" She notices Matt on her other side and frowns. "Are you two following me?"

"We don't follow, we surveil," I say, dropping the smile. It was hurting my cheeks anyway. "We just have a few questions. Headed to your father's office? We'll walk with you."

She folds her arms. "Have you found Carter's killer yet?"

"No," Matt says, giving her a genuinely kind smile. "But we're getting closer and still need your help." He gestures forward, and she drops her arms and starts walking.

"How are you holding up?" Unlike with the smile, I don't have to fake the sympathy. I know what it's like to lose a friend.

"Okay, I guess. I'm trying to continue the paper. It's important to preserve his legacy." She quickly inhales and sniffles.

Handing her a tissue from my pocket, I say, "That's a lot of work. Are you still working with his two recorders, Cathy and Sarah?"

"Sarah quit." Bellanie scrunches her nose in distaste. "Said she didn't want to work for some nobody. But Cathy stayed with me. It's hard work, but it's worth it." She brightens. "I've been making good contacts, getting invited to the right things. The paper is going to succeed." She says it like a mantra she's been repeating to herself.

"Do you remember going to a party at LeMar? One of CP's parties?" I ask. Matt holds out a hand to stop her from crossing the street as a bunch of transport fae all materialize with their numerous passengers right in front of us.

"Yes," she says. "Why?"

"We're looking into some potential connections with Carter's murder. Who did you go to the party with?"

"I met a few friends there. And my bodyguard escorted me." She rolls her eyes. "His name is Bradley. My father met him somewhere, and now he tags along with me at events where my dad wants to make sure I don't get into any trouble."

"What kind of events?" Matt asks at the same time I say, "What kind of trouble?"

"Mostly anything where CP is going to be there. My dad doesn't really trust him. He thinks I'm going to be some kind of royal groupie." She pretends to gag. "Yeah right. Could you imagine where his dick has been? I bet the women he's with have to get healed of weird sex diseases every week."

Matt does a terrible job covering his laugh with a cough. I take a fortifying breath to stop myself from reaching around Bellanie and smacking him.

"Yeah, that doesn't sound like something you'd do," I say flatly. "Does Bradley work anywhere else? Or just for your father?" As we get closer to the council offices, the city's decorations become more elaborate. We step under a canopy of real clouds charmed to sit just above the tallest buildings, glowing with pink, blue, and yellow stars.

"He does a bunch of things. He works at Tradimento, the nightclub. And runs errands for my dad sometimes." She pulls blond hair out of her face as the wind rushes past.

"Did you see this girl at the party?" Matt pulls out the image of Tonya, the one where Bellanie is in the background.

"Oh," she says, stopping to take the image. "I look so weird in this memory. Was the recorder drunk?" She doesn't seem to expect an answer as she holds the image closer, looking at Tonya. "She doesn't really look familiar. There were a lot of girls hanging off the prince—wait." She pauses, squinting at the image before her mouth falls open. "This is the dead butterfly? The one they found on the beach?"

"Yes," I reply.

"You think she was killed by the same person who killed Carter?" Her eyes are round with shock.

"We're not sure yet. You don't remember seeing her at the party?"

Bellanie's eyes dart back and forth, as if searching for the memory. "No," she says, frustrated. "No. I really don't." She looks like she might crumple from failing to provide information that could help her late boss.

I change tactics. "Did you see CP go into the bedroom with anyone?"

Bellanie hands the image back, exhaling. "Yes. I did actually. We were standing near a bedroom when CP went in with some brown-haired girl, but her back was to me. I really only remember because Bradley said something like, 'Oh, that's interesting,' and I thought it was weird because it wasn't interesting at all. She was just a girl, and he's as easy as scrambled eggs, so what's the big deal?"

"Did you see them come out?" Matt asks, barely controlling his smile as he delights in Bellanie's continued assassination of my character.

"Nope. I left a little after that." She shrugs.

"Did you notice anything at all about the girl?" I say, shooting Matt a glare.

Bellanie pushes her lips to the side in thought. "No. She wasn't really dressed up, but that's not that unusual. Some people don't take as much pride in their appearance."

Matt and I share a look, and I deliberately don't look down to see what I'm wearing.

"Did Bradley go with you, or did he stay at the party?" We've crossed the street, headed toward the steps of City Hall.

"We left together. He took me home, then came in and spoke to my dad for a bit, I guess. It was late. I didn't hang around."

"Has Bradley ever gotten handsy with you? After all this time you spend together?" Matt asks.

"What?" Bellanie snorts in disbelief. "I could drown him in a heartbeat." She holds up a hand and creates an instant whirlpool in her palm. It dissolves just as fast, and she says, smiling, "He wouldn't dare."

"Water runs in the family, huh?" I say. According to Research & Evidence, Nichols is a crocodile shifter and Bellanie's mother is a water fae like her.

She smiles and nods.

Matt raises his eyebrows at me, and I glance over Bellanie's head to see Councilor Nichols marching our way. He doesn't look pleased. We were pretty sure he'd stop us from interviewing Bellanie without him or the family lawyer being present, hence our new intimate knowledge of Bellanie's brunch order.

"Did you ever speak to Carter about Tradimento? Was there ever a discussion with him partnering with Stone on his night-club venture?" Matt says.

"No." Bellanie shakes her head quickly. "He wanted to partner with CP because he needed a lot more capital."

"Why?" I say as Nichols gets closer. He's derailed for a moment by a constituent, but even as he smiles and shakes hands, he's watching us.

Bellanie opens her mouth and hesitates. "He wanted to build a nightclub in the Hollows." She tugs her lip with her teeth, lost in a memory.

"The Hollows?" Matt says, brows raised. "He wasn't concerned about the ulgashen attacks?"

Bellanie nods and plays with a small charm on her purse as she says, "Yeah, I said it was a bad idea. Told him he should look somewhere else."

"Detectives!" Nichols says from a few feet away. Bellanie's head snaps up at the sound of her father's voice. She immediately steps away to stand next to him.

"Afternoon, Councilor. Love the decorations," Matt says, gesturing to the clouds above us.

"Thank you. The staff always works very hard this time of year." He puts his arm around Bellanie and gives us a politician's smile. "Anything I can help you with, Detectives? I hope Bellanie hasn't been talking your ear off." Bellanie stiffens beside her father but says nothing.

"No, not at all. She was just letting us know how protective you are, especially when it comes to CP. I take it your opinion of the crown prince has not increased with the amount of time you spend together?" I say, keeping an innocent look on my face.

"According to our research, you two do have to meet frequently. All that city business."

Nichols frowns as he glances between the two of us. "Of course I have to meet with the prince. And his younger brother too, occasionally. And I am protective of my daughter, so if you'll excuse us." With that, he marches off, Bellanie tucked securely under his arm.

"What do you think?" Matt asks, turning to me when they're gone.

"She's a great actress if she's lying. We've gotta find the girl CP went into that bedroom with—and why bodyguard Bradley thought it was so interesting."

I'd told Matt everything I suspected after my conversations with CP. The more I think about it, the more I'm convinced Tonya was murdered by him, his guard, or this girl because she saw something that threatened CP's position as next in line for the crown. Mystery girl being a long-lost older sibling looks less likely if Bradley recognized her but not impossible.

"I'll get his address from R&E and meet you there?"

I nod, and a note bearing the royal seal of Eddahn appears in front of me. I tear it open. My heart seizes, and my stomach bottoms out.

"Oh fuck."

Chapter 30
Draven

The note appears on torn and crumpled paper, as if it was written in a hurry. It's late. I was just about to go to bed, but after reading the message, I'm on my feet in an instant. I knock over the crane lamp in my haste to grab my weapons and get out the door. The orb light hisses angrily at me as it rolls across the floor before going dark.

There are no fae available at this time of night to transport me. And none of the stone portals will get me close enough to make it worth it. Instead, I run faster than I ever have, sprinting past closed shops, shuttered restaurants, and dark houses. My lungs burn from the effort. It's been a long time since I've had to move so quickly.

As I round the corner, the scent of blood fills my nose. To non-vampires, blood smells of little more than iron. They can't sense the bouquet like we can. Subtle notes of vanilla, butter, and fear waft from the fresh droplets littering the street as I get closer to the house with the blue shutters. There's a generous spray on the wall next to the door, the kind made when a vampire hastily rips their fangs from someone's throat. It's a rookie mistake.

There's a bang from inside, and I circle the house, slipping down the side. I enter the backyard just as the sound of breaking glass reaches my ears.

"Hey!" a voice calls from above me. I move into the shadows before I look up at the woman hanging out of her second-story window. "What's with all the noise?" She's wearing a pink robe pulled tight, her hair hidden by a blue silk bonnet.

"Sorry, ma'am. I'll have this dealt with shortly." She gives me a look like she doesn't expect me to be able to handle an unruly kitten, let alone whatever's happening inside the house.

"See that you do," she huffs, snapping the window shut.

There's a thin gap between the curtains, and I lean in, trying to see what awaits me. The furniture is everywhere—broken chairs, shredded cushions. Fenrik and Lira stand in the middle of the room, facing another. Lira's holding a young man tight around the shoulders. His head lolls to one side, eyes closed.

She tries to dart to the side, and Fenrik throws another obstacle, a side chair, to block her escape. Lira snarls. When she tries again, I slip through the backdoor, thankful my hand still unlocks it. Just as I dart inside, the front door opens, and Sugar runs in.

"Oh gods," she breathes. Her hair lies limp on her shoulders, sweat beads her brow, and her chest rises and falls with exertion. She must have been in bed, too. There's only a thin camisole under her jacket, and she's wearing loose cotton pants.

Lira spins, backing up so she can see the three of us. "He's my kill. Get your own." Her voice is raw, as if she's been screaming.

Her eyes are wild, pupils blown, but they focus on me, recognizing the competition of another vampire.

A small moan comes from the man, and I breathe a sigh of relief. He's still alive.

"Lira." I hold my hands up in surrender. "Are you still hungry? It looks like you've fed a lot. How does your power feel?"

"I feel amazing." The princess grins at me, blood coating her teeth and lips.

"Yes, it's good, isn't it? You haven't been able to do this before, to feel your magic refilling, that surge of power." I take a small step toward her. "How is your eyesight? Better?"

Movement in the corner of my eye. Sugar is circling, heading behind Lira. She was holding her daggers when she came in, but she's stowed them away. Lira is a young vampire. Her power is strong and chaotic. I have no idea how well Sugar's power will work on her.

"I can see your lashes from here. Each one." Her grip loosens a little, but the man's face is almost completely leached of color. He's wearing an apron covered in flour and smeared with his own blood.

"Good, that's good. There's a limit, unfortunately. Once you get enough, drinking more won't make you stronger. Would you like to try some things? Compare your fae strength with your vampire strength?"

Her eyes light. She's meant to be the academic one of the family. But she hesitates, not wanting to let go of her meal.

Fenrik approaches my left side. "We used to arm wrestle. Do you want to see if you can beat me now?" He rights the overturned kitchen table and pulls over two chairs. "I'm not as strong as Mother, but I bet I could last at least five minutes."

Her eyes widen at the word "mother," and I know it was the wrong thing to say.

"I need all the strength I can get." She moves with lightning speed, digging her fangs into the other side of the man's throat. She sends the furniture flying toward Fenrik and me. A table slams into my knee, breaking on impact, the pain sharp and nauseating. Fenrik only just dodges a lamp, and it shatters against the wall.

Sugar attacks, slipping an arm around Lira's neck and pulling back. Blood sprays the room as her mouth dislodges. Lira reaches behind her and grabs Sugar's hair. There's a moment of internal struggle on her face as she wars with Sugar's power.

Sensing the bigger threat, she drops the body. Fenrik dives for the man, hauling him backward and immediately holding his hands out, healing him. But the wounds are many and deep. I grab a piece of newspaper from the table, mentally inscribing the words and hoping Anistemi is a night owl.

Lira manages to flip Sugar, slamming her against a wall, but Sugar recovers quickly. I sprint behind Lira just as Sugar reaches for her. Sugar's eyes lock on the princess, power seeming to pulse from her skin as she grabs the new vampire.

"Stop." Sugar's voice is ice cold, and the command brushes my skin. Lira freezes, and I take the opening, pulling cuffs from my pocket and restraining her wrists behind her back. The cuffs are imbued with potent magic—not enough to hold her forever, but hopefully until the bloodlust stops.

"Sit." Sugar points to a chair, and Lira sinks down.

"The wounds have closed, but he's not breathing anymore," Fenrik says. "We can't let him die. Lira will never forgive herself."

There's a hesitant knock, and four pairs of eyes dart to the door.

"Fenrik, take Lira into the back bedroom now." If the prince is offended at my ordering him around, he doesn't show it. Instead, he lifts his sister, whose face has fallen into utter confusion, and swiftly exits the room.

I'm more worried about the royals seeing Victor than I am about the reverse. I don't want them to think of him as a loose end if this gets worse.

I give Sugar a nod, and she furrows her brow but opens the door.

"Victor," I say as the young necro squints against the light of the room before glancing from me to Sugar. "We need your help." I motion to the body, and Sugar closes the door behind him as he steps inside.

"How long?" He doesn't hesitate, just drops to his knees beside the dead man. His chest has stopped moving; his half-lidded eyes are unfocused and still.

"A few minutes," Sugar says, coming to stand across from me, Victor, and the body between us.

"Less than ten? It matters." He snaps a little on the last two words, but I'll overlook just about anything right now as long as he helps.

"Yes," I reply.

Victor raises his hands, and a weak blue light emanates from the body.

Sugar gives me a look, an acknowledgment of everything that happened the last time we saw one another. It took me an hour to shake off her compulsion, at which point I'd heard enough. My anger swells at the memory of being trapped inside her closet, listening to everything CP did to her and everything she did to him. Witnessing the possessive way he pushed aside her robe and slid his hand down her body made my fangs ache for violence.

Clearly sensing my emotions, Sugar returns her attention to Victor. The blue light surges before seeping back into the man's skin. Relief washes over me as the color returns to his face. He opens his eyes, blinking slowly at Victor, then us. His face pales again as he takes in the room, the blood.

"Everything is okay. I'm Detective Flint. This is Detective Writh and Mr. Anistemi, necromancer. What's your name?"

"Sundar."

"How do you feel, Sundar?"

"Okay, I guess." His voice is weak, but he sits up.

"What do you remember?" Sugar asks as Victor helps him into a chair.

Sundar studies his hands. "I was putting the last of the bread in to rise for tomorrow. I stepped outside to feed the cat. Someone grabbed me." He rubs his neck. "Kinda ironic. I was just telling my sister it isn't safe for her to live in the Hollows anymore, to come stay with me." He looks up at me. "Was it the ulgashen? Are they coming to this side of the river now?"

It's right there, a perfect excuse. Using it will increase the unrest, instill even more fear in the people. I'm about to answer when Sugar says, "No. A new vampire. We caught them."

When a human is Made into a vampire, there is a period of bloodlust. It's something I expected with Lira, but it's usually not so strong. I've been told it's like having someone else inside your head, a voice that tells you to drink everyone in sight, but you can mostly ignore it until you mature and it fades. Lira's Seelie power must be amplifying it.

Sundar nods, and the movement is slow and heavy.

"Here," Victor says, waving a hand to remove all the blood from Sundar's clothes and body. There's a line between Sugar's brows as she looks at Victor like she's trying to place him. She must feel my gaze, because she looks at me again, but I turn away and help Sundar to his feet.

"I'll walk you back to your bakery," I say.

"Is it Luminous Bread?" Victor asks. When Sundar nods, he says, "I can walk you. I live nearby." He turns to us. "Unless you still need me?"

"Thankfully, no. Appreciate your help tonight, Victor," I reply.

"Yes. Thank you," Sugar says.

Victor purses his lips like he might say something else, but he just bobs his head. "Of course."

When they're gone, Fenrik and Lira step out of the back room. Her eyes are red, as if she's been crying, but her voice is strong when she says, "I can't thank you enough. If something had happened to that man..." She trails off before flicking her wrist and removing the blood from everything in the room. We'll need a repairer fae to fix the furniture, or an industrious human.

"You feeling better?" Sugar asks.

"Unfortunately, I feel amazing right now." Lira sighs. "But yes, the overwhelming need to bleed you all dry has subsided." She holds out her hands, and Draven hesitates for a moment before removing the cuffs.

Fenrik puts his arm around her. "I'm going to take Lira back to the palace. I've sent for one of our transport fae. She should be outside by now." He holds out his hand to me, and I shake it. "Thank you."

He looks so much like CP, but his eyes are kinder, the skin less drawn from drinking and drugs. He seems both older and younger than his brother somehow, even though I know, much to the country's chagrin, CP is first in line.

I should walk out with them, but my feet fail to move. There's a weighted silence as the door closes, leaving Sugar and I alone.

She doesn't speak, waiting me out. I clench my jaw in annoyance. I want to force her to say something first, but she's clearly better at this game.

"So what is it? Your kink is to fuck the worst guy you can find?" I say, scowling at her.

Her eyebrows jump ever so slightly, and I'm proud of myself for getting the smallest reaction. And then I curse internally for still giving a shit about her reactions.

"I'm sorry I used my power on you. But if he'd found you, things would have gotten messy. I figured I could get him out of the room long enough for you to leave."

My mouth almost falls open at the apology, but irritation slices through me, and I cross my arms instead. "Oh, I see. You screwed the evil prince for *my* safety?"

She swallows, and I drop my gaze to the pale column of her throat.

Sugar glances away, brow furrowed in thought. "I can't explain that to anyone's satisfaction." She turns to leave, and I shoot forward, grabbing her arm to stop her.

"You're not even going to try?" I demand. Her skin is warm under her jacket. This close, I can see the full outline of her body under the silk, the narrow strip of skin between the shirt and her pants. When she doesn't respond, I ask, "And what about my case file? Planning to give that back?"

She inhales sharply, her eyes falling closed before settling on me again. "Yes. I'm sorry for that, too. I never meant to keep it so long."

"Were you the one who called the corners for Linnea?" I'm unable to resist pulling her closer. There's nothing sweet about her scent. It's deep and complex, like the darkest chocolate, and I picture what it would feel like to run my tongue from the swell of her breasts to her lips.

"Yes," she breathes. And I catch her eyes flicking to my mouth. It fills me with twisted satisfaction, even though I know she's a perfect actress and probably feels nothing. She had to be, working for the Dame.

Dipping my head toward hers, I think of every lie she's ever told me, about Maria and the debt collectors. I think of the sound of CP's skin against hers. His groans as he took her while I stood powerless to escape. I remember another sweet smile that turned sour as I whisper, "That file better be on my desk tomorrow. And then I expect you to stay the fuck out of my life."

I force myself to look away from her face as I push past her and slam the door behind me.

Chapter 31
Sugar

Matt moves quietly for such a big guy, but I can still hear him on the floor above, starting down the stairs. I lean against the wall next to the entrance to the morgue, my eyes closed, fighting exhaustion from the night before.

Guilt rests heavy in my gut as I think of the baker's lifeless body. I definitely owe Victor a drink. It could have been so much worse. When I considered the dangers of Making Lira, I carelessly only considered the harm that might come to her. I've never heard of bloodlust like that. Then again, documentation on successfully Made Seelies is scarce.

When I arrived and Draven was already there, relief had poured through me. And now, in the cold light of day, something sweet still burns inside me at the memory of Draven's lips so close to mine, his hand around my arm. He was angry, for sure, but it wasn't as strong as it could have been. He was hurt. And underneath it all, that same current of arousal still reached out to me. He hates that he wants me. I'm confident he'll soon learn how to shut it off.

"Do I want to know why you're so tired?" Matt's voice echoes in the empty concrete hallway.

Dragging my eyes open, I let my head roll toward him. "It's not because of my usual unsavory habit, if that's what you're asking."

"A different unsavory habit, then? Good to see you're maturing." He jerks his head toward the door. "You ready?"

"After you." I grab the door handle and open it, ushering Matt through. At least he looks better. His brown eyes are clear, and that drawn look has disappeared. He must have eradicated the nefarious algae at last.

Victor is waiting for us next to Sigrid's body. He's done a good job sewing up the lacerations on her face and putting her jaw back in place. The blue sheet is tucked over her arms and under her body, hiding the worst of her injuries. Her lips are blue, courtesy of the weeks she's spent in the metal box with the kylan demon.

"Good morning," Victor says. "Body, names, and badge numbers?" He holds out a clipboard. He looks just as tired as always but gives us a smile. It's worse because I know, this time, it's my fault. I look at Matt expectantly, a smirk playing on my lips.

"You have got to be kidding me," Matt huffs but gives our names, badge numbers, and the victim's name. We both sign the clipboard, and Victor tosses it on the nearby counter and pulls back his sleeves.

Sigrid's hands grip the sides of the metal table as she curves into a sitting position. I swallow bile as her limbs move in ways they shouldn't under the sheet. The blue light wavers around

her, and she lets out a string of curses when she sees her surroundings.

"Be so fucking for real! Over godsdamn food?" she shrieks,
looking around the room. "I can't believe it." She buries her face
in her hands and sobs, her pale shoulders shaking. Matt and I
share a look. She's upset, but this isn't the reaction we'd expect
from someone who just experienced such a violent and painful
death.

"We're very sorry, Sigrid. Do you remember us? Detectives
Diaz and Writh," I say, motioning to Matt and back to myself.
"It sounds like you know who killed you?"

The blue light flickers, and my eyes shoot to Victor in surprise. He's already sweating. We had to wait a little longer to get
on the schedule because he's been so busy, but Sigrid shouldn't
be fading already.

The necro gives me a grimace and says, "Sorry. Late night.
Keep going."

Well, fuck. Shame thickens in my throat. "Sigrid?"

She's still crying, holding the blue sheet against her face. Matt
hands her a tissue from the box sitting on the counter. She
immediately balls it into something useless and dabs at her nose.

"We're not sure how long we have with you. Can you please
tell us what happened?" Matt asks.

Sigrid sniffles. "I was at work. It was after the late show, and
I was pretty hungry. I went into the cold storage, said "Hi"
to Midnight, and thought I'd look to see what food people
brought from home." Neither of us says anything, but she

twists toward us, her arms crossed. "Don't give me that look. Everybody does it. It's no big deal."

"You were murdered. We're not judging you for stealing someone's snacks right now. Go on. Please," I say, watching the increasing furrow on Victor's brow.

"I grabbed someone's lunchbox."

"Do you know whose it was?" says Matt.

Her cheeks pink only a little, but it's bright against her pale skin. "No. I didn't really check for a name." She picks at a damp part of the sheet, creating a hole. Her skin shows through, and she digs a nail into it. "I can still feel pain," she whispers. "I'm really alive right now, aren't I?" She asks Victor, tears welling her eyes again.

"For just a bit longer. Please," he says, tipping his head toward us to get her to keep talking.

"What happened next, Sigrid?" I prod.

"I don't really remember. One minute, I was staring into the box, and the next, it was like the lights went out." Her chest heaves, and her gulping sobs fill the room. "There was a sharp pain and then nothing."

I glance over at the recorders hidden behind the one-way glass before grabbing her a tissue.

"Did you hear anything? Anything to tell you who it might have been?" Matt asks.

"No, not really."

The light flickers again, and Victor says, "I'm sorry. You've got maybe three minutes." His eyes meet mine, and I swallow.

Making Lira is already causing far more trouble than I anticipated. If I can't solve this case because Victor is too drained, it'll be one more on a growing list of regrets.

"Who was in the kitchen when you came in?"

She wipes her cheek with the back of her hand and gasps, touching the stitches.

"Sigrid, please. We're running out of time." I glance toward Victor again. Sweat drips from his temples.

"Just the chefs, I think, Sonny and the other one. It was late. Maybe some bussers?"

"I'm losing her," Victor says through gritted teeth.

"Can you think of anyone who would want to hurt you this badly? Who would be this angry at you?" I wave my hand at her mangled body. It's impossible that someone could do this kind of damage to her in the kitchen without anyone noticing.

She shakes her head, clenching her eyes shut. "No. Maybe..." She trails off as the light pulses twice and dies. Sigrid falls back, her eyes closed, skin once again dull without blood flow. I grab her arms at the last minute and gently lay her down.

Victor clutches his water and chugs it, his face covered in sweat. His hand braces against the counter as he puts the bottle down. "I'm sorry. I really thought I had longer."

"It's okay. I know you've had a lot of bodies recently." Next to me, Matt's eyes pop in surprise. "We'll leave you to it." I turn and try to walk like I'm not keeping secrets from my partner. I send a message to Stone, requesting a list of everyone who was working the night Sigrid was killed and reminding him we still have more questions for him.

"Is there any chance you're going to tell me what's going on?" Matt asks as soon as we're back in the hallway. His leather shoulder holster creaks, his daggers probably freshly sharpened, as he crosses his arms and stares at me.

Inhaling, I wonder what I can even tell him that won't put him in danger, too. I hate lying to him, but after involving Victor, even if he doesn't understand the whole story, has already compromised this case.

"I made a deal. To get a lead on Linnea." Which Lira hasn't given me yet. "It's not something I want you involved with."

"And you needed Victor's help?" Matt raises an eyebrow. "Don't think I didn't notice how weirdly understanding you were back there."

"That was an unforeseen complication." I shove my hands into my pockets and head for the stairs. Matt follows, but I know the conversation isn't over.

"Do you need help?" he asks, his voice low as chatter reaches us from the next floor.

I pause on the landing, turning to someone I never would have met if Linnea hadn't died. A man who has been a constant in my life, day in and day out, for years.

And I lie.

"No. Thank you. I'm fine."

***

We climb the stairs to our floor. As we cross the checkered tile, my eyes studiously avoid the mossy green shirt and dark hair in my periphery. I haven't given Linnea's file back. I crashed when I got to my house after dealing with Lira and barely made it to work on time. The attention burning a hole in the side of my head tells me Draven is well aware I haven't followed his order to deliver it to his desk.

I'm steps away from my desk when Tindra steps into my path. She's a lot stronger than she looks when she checks my shoulder with a snide "Watch it, mind fucker." I see the satisfied smile she gives Draven as she walks past me. She's clearly hoping to gain favor with him by adopting the insult most favored by the vampires.

It's not the first time one of the other corners has tried me with some smart remark or physical reminder of why they don't like me. It's never really bothered me. I'm not here to make friends. One of the reasons I was promoted from your everyday street corner to a detective is my ability to get the work done without creating a lot of drama.

Maybe it's the letdown of having another victim who can't identify the killer or the way I know I've burned my last bridge with Draven, but I'm suddenly craving a bit of drama. The power rolls through me, reaching out to taste the animosity she's left trailing behind her like my favorite perfume. Matt shifts on his feet beside me. After all this time, he may not be able to sense emotions like I can, but he can certainly read my tells.

"Tindra," I say, pinning her with my eyes. I flex my hand, the cuff spinning beneath my sleeve.

"What?" She turns, hand on one hip, and a surge of hatred rushes to greet me.

Several of the other corners have stopped working, watching us with jeering smiles as I take a step toward her. When I look at Draven, I have to stop myself from sucking in a breath.

His head is down, intentionally ignoring Tindra and me. His clothes and hair are rumpled. He looks how I feel. I have the most irritating urge to touch him. I turn back to Tindra, but don't move.

"Well? No cutting remark?" she says, smirking at her audience.

Instantly, the fight drains out of me. Maybe it's the way she's trying so hard to look casual, but I can see her bracing, readying herself for a fight. And after last night, I don't think I have one in me to give her.

"No. I was just going to say you look nice today," I say with sincerity. "That color really compliments your eyes."

Matt makes a quiet, strangled sound beside me.

Tindra frowns and looks from me to Matt. "Okay..." She scoffs before walking back to her desk, where she pulls a miniature brown bag from her pocket. She waves her hand, returning it to a normal size, and pulls out a seriously squished sandwich and a banana.

Matt must come to the realization at the same time I do because as my head whips around to him, he snaps his fingers and points at Tindra, who is unaware of the revelation she's caused. We both turn to head back to Tradimento, but the sound of a slamming door and a familiar voice has my feet sticking to the floor.

"Where the fuck is she?" CP barks as he storms in, wearing a black wool suit and sucking all the air from the room. Corners and other employees make themselves scarce, even the ones I know are on his payroll. My heart thrums in my chest as he spots me.

"Sugar." He smiles, his eyes like chips of ice.

The captain steps out of his office, spots CP, and mumbles, "Shit," under his breath. But he raises his head and says, "Good afternoon, Prince. How can we help you?"

CP stalks forward, ignoring the question. He grabs me by the arm and hauls me into the captain's office. Before he slams the door in Gibson's face, Matt steps forward and Draven rises from his desk. I give them both a look to back off.

CP sets a silencing charm on the table by the door. It's a small jade globe that'll cocoon us in a soundproof bubble. They're not cheap. I raise an eyebrow. It's really not like him to care whether people think.

I open my mouth to ask why he's here when he grabs me by the neck, lifts me up, and slams me down on Gibson's desk, scattering papers, ashtrays, and assorted memorabilia. The pain stabs into my spine, shooting up my neck. I have years of experience feigning indifference to his moods and block the instinct to cry out even as he holds me down, squeezing my neck.

CP bends down, his nose almost touching my skin. I can smell the alcohol on his breath. His clothes stink of smoke, and there's more red than white in his irises. "What did I tell you, Sugar?" he breathes, spit landing on my cheeks. "You're not supposed to be digging into that godsdamn butterfly."

"Gods, Alaric," I say, my fingers digging into the hand around my throat. "You look like shit. Week-long bender?" I dig my heels into the wood and push up, twisting out of his hold and jumping behind the desk.

"I told you to back off." His eyes flash with anger, and I inhale. It tastes different. It might be whatever designer substance he's got coursing through his veins, but it's far more chaotic than normal.

He rounds on me, using his power to throw the desk out of the way. It slams into the wall. The window rattles but doesn't break. A tremor runs down my back. My power is thirsty, dying to absorb the sheer rage rolling off him. Whether because it's sick of being denied or my survival instinct is kicking in, it takes so much more strength to hold it back this time.

Matt is outside, and Draven, and plenty of other people CP will take it out on if I put him in his place. Gods know Victor can't do another raising right now.

The idea slams into me at the same time CP's power throws me back against the wall. The royal family doesn't use necros because it would fuck with the chain of succession. Our mystery girl isn't a missing older sibling or a blackmailer. Tonya couldn't see either of those just from walking into a room. What she could have seen, what could cost CP his crown, is a *raising*.

"You seem stressed, Alaric. Maybe you need a good deadgasm." I regret the words as soon as they're out of my mouth. I know I'm about to pay for my pride in figuring it out.

He moves like a viper. His fist shoots out and collides with my face, and I hear the crunch of the bone as blood streams from my nose and over my lips.

The door bursts open, Draven and Matt standing behind it. Their eyes collectively move around the room, taking in the blood on my face and the state of Gibson's office. Matt's jaw clenches as he straightens to his full six feet, six inches.

Draven has gone dangerously still, his eyes narrowed on CP like he's seconds from driving daggers through his sensitive parts. For a moment, we share a look, and my breath catches. His stormy eyes are filled with something other than anger or disgust. But it's not pity either, and I allow myself the tiniest moment of comfort.

"Detectives. I don't remember inviting you to this party." The cool smile CP gives them sends alarms ringing through my head. Sheer terror seizes me as his eyes move from Draven to Matt before settling back on the vampire. His psychotic smile grows, and the skin on my neck flushes with hatred that would feed me for a week. What was I thinking, accusing him like that?

Wiping the blood from my nose, I say, "Go home, Alaric. I'll come see you later." I catch his eye and try to silently convey that I'll keep my mouth shut.

CP's voice dips. "See that you do, baby." He keeps his eyes on Draven as long as possible before he slams his mouth to mine, clamping my face with his fingers. There's a smear of my blood on his cheek as he pulls away. He grins, straightening his jacket and grabbing the silencing charm as he walks out.

"At least the window held," I say to the silence, avoiding Draven's eye. He opens his mouth, and I interrupt. "I'm going to run to the healer."

As I step out of his office, I ignore the captain, who could easily heal me, and stride across the floor. Instead of going straight to the department healer, I head for the bathroom to clean the blood off my face and think for a moment. My knuckles turn white as I grip the sink and take deep, long breaths.

The orb lights in the bathroom give off a strange brassy glow, making my skin less pale and my hair a dirty blond. I sniff, the breath catching in my throat as I stare at the stranger in the mirror.

CP will hurt them to keep me from ratting him out. I squint to remove the image of Tonya's broken wings and sightless eyes from my memory. Losing Matt would break me. And if he does something to Draven... My stomach hollows out. He already thinks I'm poisonous. Several tears roll down my face and join the blood in the sink.

The sound of the door has me hastily wiping my face and stepping back from the sink. My hand drops to my side on instinct, even though my whip is less helpful in such a tight space.

Tindra eyes me from the door, a line etched between her brows. Her mouth is shut, but her lips move as if words are struggling to get out or stay in. We eye one another warily before she says, "My healing isn't great, but here." She jerks her hand toward me, removing the blood from my face and clothes.

I try not to insult her by looking surprised. "Thank you."

With a jerk of her head, she walks out.

I turn on the faucet and rinse the blood away before squaring my shoulders. Tears couldn't bring Linnea back or keep Fenrik. They damn well aren't going to help now.

Chapter 32
Sugar

My breath visibly unfurls in the frigid night air. I stuff my hands deep into my fur-lined pockets, grateful for the heavy wool coat. Pulling the wide hood over my head, I bounce on my toes and search the street before returning to the same dark window. I need this gamble to pay off.

This morning, I stopped by Ms. Plichen's to replace the protection charm I'd provided for her and her granddaughter.

"You haven't come around here recently to ask me to clean your place," she says, her tone curious.

"I cleaned it myself. For once. Can't promise I won't ask again, but figured it was time to learn that skill." I straighten under her assessing gaze. She makes me more nervous than the Dame sometimes.

"Everyone should know how to take out their own trash," she says with a condescending but not unkind smile before thanking me for the charm and closing her door.

Lira is still not doing great, according to Fenrik. It's not terrible, but he's apparently had to keep her confined to the palace. I still haven't demanded my favor. As far as I'm concerned, Draven and I held up our end of the bargain, but she and her brother may not feel the same as long as she's still trying to drain the palace guards.

Lira has the power to get Jacqueline Roman to submit to questioning. Both she and her husband refused during the original investigation. Stanley's too wealthy to be forced into much of anything. But Lira can effectively kill Jacqueline's social standing. There's no way to make her tell the truth, but being friends with people who feed off emotions means I'll have a pretty good advantage.

Stanley was downstairs when it happened. His wife, the one who regularly beat Linnea, is the one I want.

Matt and I have been trading surveillance for days. Turns out, Sonny the chef lives in the same building as Sigrid. He's handy with a knife and could have been in the kitchen alone with Tonya. We've trailed him back and forth to the club, the market, and, occasionally, his brother's house. It's only to cover our bases.

We know it was Bradley. After Tindra's demonstration of how easy it is to crush something small, the pieces fell into place. Bradley isn't the only employee at Tradimento with size manipulation, but he is the only one with a connection to all three victims.

Without better evidence, I can't pin Tonya's murder on anyone, even CP. But we still have a chance to lock up Bradley. After reviewing the recording from Carter's raising, and a little trip to R&E, I developed a theory. Which is why I'm once again freezing my ass off in an alleyway outside the usher's apartment, like I've done for the past several nights. I don't think Bradley is going to suddenly give up after all the effort he's made and people he's killed.

Movement to my left has me spinning, dagger out.

"Easy." Draven holds up his hands. "It's only me."

I keep my weapons out. "You haven't spoken to me since you told me to stay the fuck out of your life. And now you show up unannounced to my stakeout? Try again." It's not like I've been around the department to speak to, but regardless of what I saw on his face after CP's face-damaging visit, the vampire has kept his distance.

"That's fair," he says, blowing out a breath. A lock of his dark hair falls over his forehead at the movement. "Matt asked me to take his place tonight." He steps closer, into the minimal yellow light afforded by the orb at the far end of the alleyway.

I don't appreciate the tendrils of warmth that whisper inside me at having him so close. Our eyes haven't even met in the last five days, and now he's two feet away, acting like we regularly work together. It's unnerving, and I really hate being unnerved. A note appears in my pocket. I keep my dagger pointed at him as I retrieve it.

I needed the sleep. He's not so bad. Stop pouting.

"Rude," I huff, stowing my dagger and Matt's note. "Fine. That's Bradley's apartment." I point up at a third-story window. "That's the back exit. If he comes out the front, he'll pass us there." Draven's eyes follow to each place I point.

"Got it." He blows into his hands, rubbing them together. I stare at them a little too long, remembering what it felt like when he held me against his chest.

Shaking myself, I turn away. It's just exhaustion and the monotony of watching this place night after night. It's messing with my libido. And sure, maybe I'm a little relieved he showed up despite everything that's happened.

"I didn't realize you and Matt had become friends," I say, keeping my tone casual and my eyes off him.

"He's a good guy," Draven says.

It's a non-answer and doesn't invite further questions. That's fine by me. I'm here for one thing only. A half hour passes with nothing more exciting than a cat chasing another down the alleyway. It's one in the morning. Normally, I'd leave and Matt would cover the place until daylight. But I don't move from the stack of crates I'm using as a chair, burrowing into my coat and ignoring the loss of feeling in my backside.

Beside me, Draven rifles around in his bag, and I watch from the corner of my eye when he pulls out a thermos. He pops off the attached tin cup and pours a steaming cup of coffee for himself. I stare straight ahead, arms crossed and face impassive.

Fine.

He's clearly still mad, and with good reason. I lied and used my power on him. His attitude is understandable. I console myself with the fact there's still a low level of arousal coming off him.

"Does that happen often? What he did to you?" His anger is a thick blanket around me as he bites out his words. I'm not sure if he's angry at CP or angry at me for being with him.

"Skipping the small talk, are we?" Draven remains quiet, waiting. I avoid looking at him when I answer. "He doesn't usually hurt me...without my consent." His outrage spikes and splinters like lighting. He doesn't know who to hate. I completely understand the feeling.

Draven frowns and takes another drink. He opens his mouth to speak but closes it, wrestling with the words.

I decide to put him out of his misery. "You want to know why," I say, sighing. "But you're not sure if you're asking why someone like me would be with someone like him because you're not convinced I'm all that great to begin with. Seeing CP hit me inspired your hero complex, but you also think I might be a villain. And that's stirring up all kinds of issues for you because you thought you found a sweet girl in Ensame who turned around and fucked your uncle because she wanted to be with a lord. Does that about sum it up?"

He freezes, the cup halfway to his mouth as I finish speaking.

"I looked into you, remember? But even before that, I knew all about Lord Salvatore's marriage to Lady Eliza and his fun views on fae other than vampires from working with Duft. It was nice to put a face to all that drama."

He's silent for so long I think he's going to keep ignoring me, and I shake my head and turn back to Bradley's apartment.

"If you know all that, then you know I ran away. Got my heart broken and left my people to deal with my uncle and all his bigotry." His voice is bitter, and the wrath circling him seems purely self-directed.

"Life is long, Draven. You'll do something about it when you're ready." I rub my hands together and blow into them.

We fall quiet again. A light goes on in another building, and we watch the shadow of someone getting ready for an early morning shift through the curtains. The night deepens around us, a gentle giant crouching among the apartment buildings and shops.

"Coffee?" he asks.

I blink in surprise as a cup appears in front of me. "Thank you." I pull the tin cup from his fingers, relishing the way it burns in my hand. I've only had a sip when Draven speaks again.

"I don't think you're a villain. Then again, in a place like this, everyone is so gray it's hard to tell."

He isn't wrong, and it stings a soft place inside I thought I'd lost. My voice is quiet as I say, "I am a villain in someone's story, Draven. But not in yours.

He nods and blows out a breath before reaching into his bag and pulling out a wrapped package. The scent of warm meat and pastry floats between us. "I guess you can have this, then." He holds out a crescent-shaped hand pie. Tremors run across my shoulders as our fingers touch.

I smile down at the peace offering. "Thank you, again."

I don't have any food because I finished it before he showed up. Because I'm supposed to be gone by now, but instead, I'm sitting here for no reason. I'm about to take a bite when he puts a small pouch of pepper down on the crate between us.

"If this isn't enough, I'll have serious concerns about you."

"Don't you have those already?" I say as I take a small bite before dumping in all the pepper. The familiar flavor pricks at my tongue, and I groan as it mixes with the buttery pastry. "This is delicious, thank you."

"Welcome." Draven pulls out two white napkins and hands one to me before using the other to wipe his face.

I arch an eyebrow at him. "Should I expect you to pull out a finger bowl and a palate cleanser next? Perhaps a small glass of port?"

Draven grins, his eyes flashing dark silver in the shadows. A forgotten feeling, a lightness, stirs in my belly. The nearness of him casually leaning with his elbows on the crate behind him is causing something inside me to open. Like a closet stuffed with items that are all about to come tumbling out.

The smile falls as he turns to me. "I haven't forgiven you for Maria. It wasn't how I wanted her to find out. She'd had enough bad news."

Brushing the crumbs off my jacket, I nod. "I'm sorry. It was thoughtless of me."

"But..." He blows out a breath. "You were right. Kurt put her in that mess with his dishonesty, and I shouldn't have let my determination to preserve his memory keep me from telling her the truth. And now that I know how desperately you required me for your own selfish desires, your burning, insatiable need…" Draven takes a solemn, deep breath. "I understand how you couldn't control yourself."

I roll my eyes. "Might wanna stretch before you make that leap, buddy."

He moves toward me, a smile playing on his lips. "Sugar—"

"Shh," I hiss, standing and slapping a hand over his mouth. His eyes widen, and I hastily remove it. "Look."

A light glows in Bradley's window.

***

Draven's lips are a brand on my palm as we trail Bradley through the darkened city. Snowflakes fall from the cloudy sky, small at first, then heavier as we approach the river. My fingers twitch as each of his furtive steps confirms my theory.

Draven and I use hand signals to communicate as we avoid the glances our prey tosses back over his shoulder. The night is near black, save for the streetlamps. Their glow dulls the closer we get to the Fugue. The pavement becomes rough under our feet, and the snow turns grimy as it mixes with the puddles among the sunken cobblestones.

Bradley approaches the East Bridge and pauses at the edge. We pull up, watching from among the trees on either side as he pulls something from his pocket. It's too far to see, and I look to Draven to confirm. The vampire nods. Whatever Bradley's holding is bloody. He holds it out over the water, and I risk leaning over the side while his back is turned. Bradley floats it down and across, directly into a cave at the base of the wall.

I pull back. We can't risk following him onto the bridge. He'd definitely spot us. Draven follows me further into the forest, and we come out in Lekotto Park, which runs the length of the plateau bordering the Fugue and across into the Hollows.

Nobody uses this route into the under city. The bridge is far more convenient than the carved stone steps. Draven is a blur as he steps in front of me to descend first.

"My eyesight is better than yours," he whispers, even though there's nobody around to hear us. It's hard to argue with him when I have to ensure each of my steps is secure before shifting my weight for the next one. The stairs and the wall on our right are wet from the snow but thankfully covered in some branches I hold on to for balance.

Draven stops suddenly. I grab his shoulder with one hand and an exposed tree root with the other. My chest bumps into the back of him. He reaches back and puts a hand on my waist, pushing me toward the wall while holding a finger to his lips. We're almost at the bottom, and I squint into the blackness, ignoring the heat of his hand seeping through my coat.

An ulgashen, a juvenile from the size, lumbers past us before soundlessly dropping into the river. Draven removes his hand and silently continues his descent. I focus on my surroundings and not on how his muscles tensed when my hand slipped from his shoulder.

Luckily, as the only thing moving, it isn't hard to spot Bradley as he advances into the Hollows. He doesn't get far before the street pushes him back. But he's not dissuaded and moves between houses like the clever rat he is.

Based on the previous attacks, I'm pretty sure I know where he's going. It's the most densely populated area of the Hollows and the farthest away from the Fugue. There have been no ulgashen attacks this far from the water. He's clearly trying to change that.

Draven touches my elbow and gestures to the ground. Bradley didn't just give the beasts a hint. He's dropping blood as he goes, leading them exactly where he wants them. We move on, watching as he arrives at his intended destination.

He scans the area, and we duck into a slim alleyway. There's just enough room for both of us to stand at the entrance and watch Bradley as he searches for any lights in the nearby buildings. The ground rumbles beneath us, and the walls shift, pushing Draven closer to me. He ignores it at first, unwilling to acknowledge the under city's intentions. But once the wall has pushed him far enough that his hands bracket my head, his chest firmly against my back, he curses under his breath.

"The magic here favors you, Sugar." His mouth is level with my temple. A shiver runs down my back as his arousal spikes. A slow warmth climbs inside me as he murmurs, "Doesn't it?"

"Sometimes," I whisper, watching Bradley pull something else from his pocket. "I appeal to it by anointing myself in blood and dancing naked under every full moon."

Draven's lust expands, swiftly blanketing me. I inhale, my body loosening in satisfaction. Regardless of what else he may think, he still wants me. And this time, he doesn't try to drag it back. It caresses my skin and teases my power. His fingers curl against the brick.

Bradley flicks his wrist, and the item he placed on the ground grows. It's a dead goat, freshly slaughtered. He whistles like he's calling to a dog and looks around.

Draven bends his head, his mouth inches from my neck. I suck in a breath as the sharp points of his teeth graze my skin. His arms are a cage of heat, deliciously contrasting with the snow falling around us.

"It's only fair, isn't it? After you took from me without even asking," he murmurs. He drops his hand to my hip, holding me in place. I haven't even fed off him and yet can feel his lust, heady and languorous, inside my veins already. I tip my head back, and he tightens his grip.

"It is only fair," I breathe. "But you'll have to save it for next time. We're on."

Draven yanks his head away as the walls noiselessly shift back into place. An ulgashen lumbers up the street. Bradley grins at it in satisfaction.

"Which one do you want?" he asks, unsheathing his daggers.

"I get Bradley." I revel in all the pent-up energy, anger, and humiliation of the last few days as I drop my arm and unfurl my whip.

A wave of lust hits me before Draven charges out, not wasting a moment. He easily slides his dagger into the ulgashen, who was too busy eyeing the carcass to notice. The strike severs the beast completely in half, and it topples over, its black blood blending in with the dark street. Draven pivots, eyes peeled for further attacks. His eyes narrow on Bradley, who stumbles back, mouth falling open.

Bradley turns to run, but I'm already there, cracking my whip, wrapping tight around his neck and dragging him toward me. His fingers scrabble at the leather closing off his windpipe as his knees scrape against the pavement. I yank him up until we're face to face and I can absorb all his violent feelings.

"Drop your hands, Brad," I command.

He lets go of my whip, and I release him, retracting the leather back into my cuff. Draven's gaze flits around the surrounding area, searching for more threats, but continues to return to me. I don't miss the hunger still playing in his eyes when I order Bradley to turn around. Draven puts the cuffs around his wrists, and Bradley's shoulders lock in defiance.

I recall my whip. "We raised Sigrid. You really did a number on her, didn't you?"

"I didn't mean—" He stops talking and shakes his head. "I don't know what you're talking about."

"Really? She said she was hungry. Just looking for something to eat. Stealing your turkey on rye doesn't seem like a crime worthy of killing your friend." I pause and lower my voice. "But it wasn't food, was it, Bradley?" He grinds his teeth, chest heaving. "You shrank Tonya and kept her in your lunch box. Easy to freeze something that small. And easy to hide, right? And Sigrid found her, so you shrank her and stomped her to death." I shake my head with disappointment. "Some friend you are."

His face contorts, and a tear gathers at the corner of his eye. But he shrugs as if she meant nothing. "It's her own fault. Why didn't she ever just bring her own food?"

Draven makes a face of disgust. I agree. Bradley doesn't deserve to cry. But emotional people are careless with their words.

"Tonya, Sigrid, Carter. Quite the little serial killer, aren't you?"

"Shut up! I didn't kill Tonya." His eyes widen as he realizes his mistake, and he swings his gaze between me and Draven, who's stepped up to stand by my side.

"Did Stone help you freeze Tonya?"

Bradley barks a laugh and wipes his nose on his shoulder. "Stone doesn't have the power of ice—not to freeze things. He has the power to *make* ice. Like cubes."

"Not as useful as your power, at least not for killing people. Did Carter discover your fun hobby? Is that why you did him in?" I wave my hand toward the dead ulgashen.

He starts, his red-rimmed eyes landing on the dead goat before coming back to us. "I'm not saying another word." He straightens and gives us a self-satisfied smirk. "You can't touch me anyway."

"No." I step closer. I've got a few inches on him and stare down before caressing his cheek. He flinches. "You have friends in high places, don't you, Bradley? That's why you dumped Tonya's body on the royal beach."

"That wasn't my idea. That was—" Bradley abruptly shuts his mouth, finally catching on to his predicament. "I'm not saying another word. I want a lawyer."

I sigh. Why couldn't he have run his mouth a little longer? I still don't know how Carter fits into this or why Bradley's fishing for ulgashen. Is it just cruelty? Entertainment?

"Fine. But first—" I clutch the dregs of his animosity and exert my power over him so I can remove his cuffs. "—be a good boy and shrink that dead goat and the ulgashen. We're gonna need them as evidence."

Chapter 33
Sugar

We haul Bradley down to the department and throw him into a holding cell to wait for his lawyer. I really hope it doesn't end up being Petra. Matt meets us there.

"Theories?" I ask as the three of us step into an unused office.

I take off my jacket and hang it on the back of an empty chair. Moving from the cold streets into the warm office has my skin feeling sticky. The adrenaline of catching Bradley, and maybe those few moments with Draven, hums in my blood, softening a few of the sharp edges of the last few days.

Matt removes his overcoat as well and combs his mustache with two fingers before saying, "He admitted to killing Sigrid and didn't deny Carter but claims he didn't kill Tonya. But he was clearly helping to cover up her death." He cocks his head. "You're thinking your shitty boyfriend killed her and Bradley swooped in to save the day?"

I ignore the boyfriend comment and avoid looking at Draven. "Either him or his guard. He's a viable suspect but also a somewhat untouchable one." I pluck at my shirt to get some air into it.

"No more than normal," Matt replies. His jaw ticks when I blow out a breath and give him a comical grimace. "Is there yet another thing you're not telling me?"

"I've been working with Petra and Jasper, that reporter, on building a case against CP."

Matt and Draven give me identical looks of surprise.

"What? Do they both know about you and him?" Draven asks. His eyes are like stone, but the anger is mixed. Some other emotion is bothering him. The man who gave me pastry is gone, replaced by this guarded version.

"Petra doesn't. Jasper suspects. If they ever get around to hate fucking each other, I expect he'll tell her."

Matt makes a queasy face and shakes his head as if the idea of hate fucking is completely incomprehensible. "Thanks for that visual," he says. Draven rubs his fingers across his forehead and doesn't look at me.

"Petra's keeping a tight rein on the cases she wants to pursue against CP. She was specific that she doesn't want him to know we're preparing to charge him until every piece of evidence and all the witnesses are solid. This case doesn't fit the bill, especially since we don't have any evidence he killed Tonya.

Matt mumbles something under his breath before pacing the room. "Fine. Let's focus on the usher for now."

"I should go," Draven says abruptly. I look at him in surprise. "I'm not really supposed to be on active duty." He shrugs like that isn't the lamest excuse.

"Thanks for your help," Matt says, giving him an easy clap on the back.

"Yeah, thanks," I say. I shouldn't have expected one conversation to have changed everything between us. It certainly didn't change me or the things I've done. Draven gives me a tight smile before walking out.

After he's gone, a thought jumps to the front of my mind. "What made you come in? To the office? CP had a silencing charm."

"Didn't stop Draven from smelling your blood," Matt grunts, leveling a look at me.

A frisson of warmth goes through me. "Oh? Was he afraid he was missing out on a good meal?" I lean my hip against the table and examine my nails. When Matt doesn't respond, I look up to find him looking at me like I'm a tiresome child.

Clearing my throat, I push away from the table. "Right, well, let's walk through it. Tonya is at a party with CP when someone kills her. Bradley offers to use his fun-size abilities to help the killer conceal her body until she can't be raised. Two months later, he kills Carter for unknown reasons and, shortly thereafter, kills Sigrid for finding Tonya and throws her in the same box, causing one of Sigrid's jewels to end up in Tonya's clothes. Someone tells him to dump Tonya's body on a beach belonging to the royal family, and he leaves Sigrid in her apartment."

"Because they're friends and he wanted her to be found."

"Maybe. Or he couldn't risk hiding her at Tradimento or didn't have the power to keep her small the whole time, so her apartment made sense because everyone thought she was sick and it was less likely to incriminate him. Or, you know, the power of friendship works too." Matt gives me a snarky look, and I respond with a tired smile. "You might be right," I concede. "He didn't seem to care at all about the others."

"And Sigrid didn't find her."

"Sorry?"

Matt shakes his head. His anger swoops through the room like a rare bird. "Sigrid didn't find Tonya. She never mentioned it. He only thought she did. She didn't have to die."

***

The morning light assaults my senses as I step out of my building. I sway slightly on my feet, having only had a few hours of sleep after Bradley's arrest. The walk does me good, cold air rushing past and bringing promises of a cozy winter while Soveh sleeps.

I head into the upper city, letting the smell of snow revive me, until I reach the Second Circle. I pass high-end boutiques and stately homes. The smell of expensive shampoo beckons me as I dodge several people exiting a beauty salon. I'm almost to the First Circle when I veer off a side street with a row of metal doors. They have various business names on them, healers and the like, but Jasper's door says nothing.

"You sent for me, m'lord," I say, curtsying as he opens the door.

"Please come in," he says, rolling his eyes and gesturing to a deep red leather chair in front of a dark wooden desk.

Jasper's office is small and organized. Shelves and file cabinets cover every wall, and a few journalism awards sit on a windowsill next to a healthy-looking plant and a silencing charm. On his desk are a few framed photos of what must be his family. The red hair seems to be as dominant a trait as the money.

He pulls a folder out of his briefcase and puts it down in front of me. "I think I've found her."

"Really?" I grab for the folder and pull out the contents. The mystery girl from the party at LeMar stares back at me from several images. Some are okay, but she's mainly in the background, her face cut off or half hidden. But it's definitely her. My hope falters as I look at the locations.

"I recognize these places," I say. The priceless art, enormous chandeliers, the fae dripping with jewels... "This is Stanley Roman's house." I point to an image where the girl is half hidden by a towering plant. I give the names of the other rich fae whose homes I recognize.

"I thought you might. These were all from private parties."

"Explains the quality." Stanley, like most of the fae who hold these kinds of events, makes recorders wear charms to prevent them from capturing anything. People slip through, of course, or the host simply forgets. I pick up the best image of the dark-haired girl. She has a pointed chin and thick brows. If she passed me on the street, I'm not sure I'd recognize her.

"Her name is Roberts. Ingrid Roberts," says Jasper.

"And let me guess, she's a necromancer?"

Jasper's eyebrows jump. "How did you know that?"

"A combination of deductive reasoning, experience, and poor choices." I toss the documents back on his desk.

"Then you know if CP was having deadgams, the royal protocol dictates that he died and is therefore no longer first in line."

I dip my chin and narrow my eyes at him. "Yes, I do. And it's something I think you should try very hard to forget. Without proof, talking about it will get you a dip in the Corvid with an anchor necklace."

He leans on his crossed elbows and glances out the window before giving me a quick nod. "I'm confident she's not in any danger from my inquiries." He pulls the image of Ingrid toward him. "But it's clear she doesn't want to be found."

"I bet." She probably has too many secrets and gets paid way too much to bother helping us. Even if we could physically track her down, I can't be responsible for something happening to her, too. I push the images back at him. "You need to get rid of these."

I leave Jasper's office and run straight into the person I've been thinking about almost from the moment the Dame told me about Lira's proposition.

Jacqueline Roman stops, the door to the beauty salon swinging shut behind her. She got her money's worth. Her chestnut hair is spectacularly shiny. Under my sleeve, my cuff spins as my blood heats at the sight of her.

My eyes flick up at the salon's black and white awning. "Doing a little self-care?"

She runs a hand through her hair, the sun glinting off her enormous emerald wedding ring. "You should try it. You're not looking nearly as fresh as you did when you were being passed around among my husband and his friends."

"Maybe I will. I have been feeling a little lackluster lately. But I don't need a salon. How about I just tell you about every fae your husband fucked and feed from that mouth-watering hatred you're feeling?" My claws ache for release as I stare down the woman who left bruises on Linnea's neck and once made her clean her own blood from the floor.

She pales, and her emotions are thick on my tongue, like aged red wine. "Well, like Fenrik, he must have tired of fucking you. You can't imagine the conversations the ladies had when the prince dumped you and you ran off to the corners' department. I, for one, am enjoying your desperate attempt to crawl your way out of the trash. Do you think you'll just move your way down the line? Lira's still single." She smirks before snapping her fingers twice. A transport fae appears beside her, already laden with shopping bags.

I swear I can feel how easily her skin would tear under my whip. The memory of a hardwood floor under my knees and blood soaking into my slip has cold fury sweeping over my skin. But I've never let Jacqueline see how I feel, and I'll be damned if I start now. "Funny you should mention Lira. You two are close, aren't you?"

She hands her bags to the waiting fae and adjusts her dark gray fur coat. "The princess and I are on good terms."

I smile. "That's nice. I've only met her a few times. But she's sweet, isn't she? Just so accommodating."

Jacqueline gives me a scathing look. "If you think for a moment that Princess Lira would give a damn about whatever little complaints you're still obsessing over after all these years—"

"Oh, don't worry, Jackie. Like your husband, Lira never talks about you either."

Chapter 34
Sugar

When I step out of my apartment the next morning, Draven is leaning against the wall next to my door, freshly shaven and holding two cups of coffee.

"Thank you." Our fingers barely touch as I grasp the cup, but something passes between us at the contact. Not friendship, not partnership, not even a truce. Simply an understanding of the continued unavoidable overlap of our lives. The coffee is delicious, full of cream and cinnamon, and Draven watches me as I take the first sip.

"It's no problem," he says as we head toward the bridge.

His hunger from the other night is gone, replaced by something more cautious. I can't blame him for what he did in the dark or under the influence of ancient magic. Despite my exhaustion, the streets don't shift to make our journey faster, and I side-eye the cobblestones. The power doesn't favor me, not really. I believe it protects its people but otherwise often does things for its own amusement.

"Did you meet me at my house because you're worried I'm going to double-cross you? Take your cut of the money?"

"Shouldn't I be? You've really given me no reason to trust you." There's no hostility in his words, no anger. Like trust is something he forgot to pick up at the market. He takes a drink of his coffee, briefly scanning the surrounding area, then tips his head toward the street. "Shall we?"

Draven keeps pace beside me as we head toward the river house, where I've agreed to meet the princess. "Lira is helping you with Linnea's case, isn't she? Helping you with a witness?" he asks.

I inhale sharply. "Yes. Now keep your voice down." We slip through a crowd of people who've just appeared on the street. The transport fae among them disappear again to collect more passengers somewhere else.

"Who is she helping you interview?" He drops his voice, speaking into his cup.

"Jacqueline Roman." There's no point in lying. He's seen the case file. Or at least the backup of the case file. I still haven't returned the original.

Thankfully, we reach the river house before he asks any more questions. I should want his help. He's got a good reputation, and until Gibson gives him a new partner, his workload is light. But I resist the conversation, unwilling to look closer at my reasons.

Lira and Fenrik both rise from the sofa as we enter, and my mind stumbles over itself at seeing him. I was so distracted by catching Bradley and figuring out CP's motives that I didn't stop to think about what that meant for Fenrik.

Before they can open their mouths, I say, "I believe CP was getting a deadgasm and that he or his guard killed a butterfly for witnessing it and had someone else hide her until she couldn't be raised."

Gulls call to one another outside as the two of them share a weighted look.

"You knew?" Draven asks, his words sharp.

"Oh, no, not about the butterfly," Lira says quickly.

"But yes, we know he's been getting deadgasms. We just can't prove it." Fenrik adds, moving toward me. "It's something we've suspected for a long time."

Lira comes closer. "We've been trying to do something about it. He finds necros from all over and pays them to keep their mouths shut. It's unacceptable. Fenrik would obviously make a better king." There's a fire in her eyes, her outrage like sparks from a forge. "As far as I'm concerned, he is the crown prince." Fenrik's eyes meet mine, and an understanding passes between us.

He left me because he's going to be king.

Something ugly twists inside me. I never once thought of what dating Fenrik could do for me, never simpered like the rest of the minor royals hoping to become consorts or princesses. But knowing he cared for me but deliberately cut off that path because I'm what, Unseelie? A Nest worker? The insult eats at me like acid.

"Anything you can do?" Draven asks, and I dismiss Fenrik with my eyes and focus on Lira's response.

"Not without proof of the raisings." Lira clasps her hands in front of her.

"I mean about Tonya, the dead butterfly." Draven's voice is like frozen steel, and I have the urge to smile. "Can you find out the name of the guard? Can we interview them? Would you stand in the way of their arrest?" he continues, crossing his arms.

"My brother employs his own guards. They're notoriously loyal, and the ones who aren't don't last long," Fenrik says. "We, of course, wouldn't stand in the way of you interviewing or arresting them. But we don't know who it was. And knowing my brother, he may have tied up loose ends already." His voice is full of frustration, and my irritation ebbs slightly.

Fenrik would be a better king. Honestly, there are probably few people who wouldn't be better than CP. I don't know how the king and queen really feel about their firstborn, but they've certainly never put a stop to his antics in D.C. Fenrik and Lira probably feel just as angry as the rest of us at a future of kneeling at his feet.

Draven doesn't seem to have a similar sympathy for the siblings, as he demands, "Are you trying at all? Why don't you confront him?"

Fenrik looks taken aback and turns to me for an explanation, but I give him a look to let him know I'd also like an answer.

"If I confront Alaric with anything, he can accuse me of staging a coup. It will set certain things in motion for which we're not yet prepared. The majority of the members of the

Senate like the way he does things. They don't want them to change." There's a flash of fire in Fenrik's eyes as his ire builds.

A beat passes while we acknowledge that there are potentially worse and likely smarter people in Eddahn than CP.

Draven purses his lips to one side, unconvinced, but turns back to Lira instead. "How are you feeling? How is the bloodlust?"

"Better. Not gone, unfortunately. But the periods between episodes are getting longer. And I feel great, which is why I wanted to bring this." She bends down to a metal box on the coffee table and flips it open. The coins clink noisily as she hands each of us a bag of money.

"Thank you," Draven says before looking at me expectantly. It's the expression Matt would give me to indicate I should take the lead in an interrogation. He's also stepped closer, like he's subtly conveying a united front. Curious. And...confusing.

I keep my eyes focused on Lira as I say, "I need you to help me get Jacqueline Roman in for questioning regarding the murder of Linnea Faroe."

The similarity between the two siblings is more obvious when they both raise their eyebrows. I never told Fenrik why I became a corner. I wanted to keep my continued interest in Linnea's case as much a secret as possible, afraid that if too many important people got wind of it, I'd be forced off the job, maybe even out of D.C.

The princess drums her fingers on her cream linen pants. She's wearing a soft blue sweater, her hair perfectly curled at her shoulders. When she addresses me, it's with the voice of a royal, a woman accustomed to being heard.

"If she's the killer, why would she agree?" Lira asks.

"Because you're going to make her a social pariah if she doesn't." My voice is thick with the loathing I feel for that putrid woman. My power vibrates at the thought of getting my claws into her. Even if she isn't the killer, there are so many bruises and harsh words I could extract from her in blood. "If she is the killer, she'll be confident she can outwit me. After all, to her, I was always just one of her husband's playthings."

Lira furrows her brows, her expression thoughtful, as if she's mentally dissecting the problem I've given her. "The Romans are powerful, Sugar. I can get Jacqueline in a room, but when she comes out, I won't be able to prevent their retaliation forever."

I wave a hand, brushing off her concerns. "Power is an illusion, Lira. Everyone can be knocked from the highest pedestal or lifted from the deepest pit. Once I find Linnea's killer, I don't plan to hang around." Again, the words are out of my mouth before I've thought them, but they're true. Her death has been a tether to a life in this city—hel, in all of Eddahn—that I don't need. When I came to D.C., I never meant to stay here this long.

Out of the corner of my eye, I can see Fenrik's surprise and Draven's confusion.

Lira assesses me for a moment before nodding. "I'll see what I can do."

***

Draven and I part ways as I head back to the department to meet Matt so we can talk to Bradley again. We reach the holding cells right as Bradley walks out with a woman I don't recognize.

"Hey, who the fuck are you?" They both half turn to look at me. She's wearing an expensive-looking red suit and has her dark blond hair pulled back into a sleek bun.

"I'm his attorney," she says curtly. Her card appears before me, and I grab it out of the air. "And we're leaving."

Bradley's cuffs have been removed. Instead, there's a thin ring of glowing red around his neck that'll keep him from using his power or leaving the city. Instead of being happy to be getting out, his face is drawn, mouth slack. He looks scared.

"Who hired you?" Matt asks, glancing over my shoulder at the thick card. Her name is in bold, fancy lettering.

Delaney Cross

"That's really none of your business," she says, taking Bradley by the arm and marching out. "Oh." She stops and looks over her shoulder at me. "And Detective Writh? My condolences. Dumped by two princes? That has to hurt. A thing like that might make someone do all kinds of things for revenge." She gives me an impressively wintry smile and walks out.

"Two? I know punching you wasn't a particularly romantic gesture, but it didn't look like he was breaking up with you," Matt says, confused.

My insides twist as chills run down my arms. "The royals hired her to defend Bradley. If we throw around allegations about CP and Tonya, that's going to be the line. I'm a bitter ex desperate to get back at them both for breaking my heart." My skin flushes with embarrassment. "They've probably already sold the story to the papers. Fuck!" I shout into the empty hallway. I push the card into Matt's hand to avoid tearing it into smithereens.

There was always a good chance we'd be unable to charge or convict CP. That's not on me or my poor choice in sexual partners. But if CP's meddling causes us to lose out on a perfectly good conviction of the murderous usher? That's unacceptable.

"She could be bluffing to get you to back off. Do you think CP told her? Because only Draven and I saw him kiss you."

Just then, a message appears in front of me. When I open the blood-red paper, there are no words, just two kisses.

"She's not bluffing," I say, crushing the Dame's angry note in my palm. "*Everybody* knows."

Chapter 35
Draven

I pull my coat up against the freezing sleet as I head to Maria's house. The streets are lively despite the rain. Some people hold colorful umbrellas, but just as many have purchased a charm to keep them dry in the onslaught. I duck into a small shop, intending to purchase one myself.

Steam rapidly escapes my clothes as I step in, courtesy of whatever enchantment the proprietor has in here. I'm dry in an instant, but I shake my coat anyway out of habit. There's a large display of Soven decorations on an end cap, and I browse for a few things for Maria and the girls.

Two women pass me, a vampire and a human. The vampire has one of the city's many gossip rags open as she walks and talks. "I knew there was something going on. Didn't I tell you that one time I saw the three of them at Aurelie's party?" She readjusts the purse on her shoulder, giving me a flirty smile with a subtle hint of fang as they pass.

Her friend, holding a different paper, responds, "I know! And remember when I passed CP that one time and he picked up the book I dropped? He's really not as bad as people make him out to be. People just make stuff up to sell their stories about him. And you know, he has feelings too." Their words have my jaw ticking in annoyance. As if CP deserves the benefit of anyone's doubt.

The memory of him with Sugar in her apartment taunts me. While I'd like to think something has shifted in our relationship since the stakeout, I'd be naïve to think that means she's done with him or that I really know her any better. She's proven to be single-minded when it comes to what she wants, which makes her untrustworthy.

It feels like Eliza over again. She'd been parroting my uncle's talking points about concubi and other Unseelie for months. I knew what was happening. I knew what kind of person she'd become, but I hid my head in the sand because I thought I loved her. And because I didn't want to be the kind of person who was so easily tossed aside. She took advantage of that. She's still trying to take advantage of that by sending me all those letters, trying to get me to come back. My uncle is getting old. She no doubt thinks she can just switch to me and maintain her place in Ensame's ruling class.

My mood has soured considerably. I glower at the shelves as I search for the right weather enchantment, one that will only make me resistant to rain and snow for the next hour. Last winter, I accidentally bought one that lasted a week. Kurt, with his enhanced sense of smell, wouldn't sit next to me after day three.

I ignore the racks of papers, having no desire to learn any more than I already know about the prince's exploits, and approach the counter. The women reach the front only a second after me, and I step aside to let them go first.

"Thank you," the vampire says, giving me a once-over. I smile politely in response.

Her friend has her nose buried in a paper and gasps. "Do you know she wrote them both hundreds of messages?" She giggles. "They're all really unhinged and dirty."

"What? I didn't see that one." The vampire grabs it from her friend's hand, short, spiky nails covering her mouth as she reads about whatever poor woman is trying to get CP's attention.

"Anything else?" The thin man with dreads behind the counter asks as he mentally calculates what they owe.

"Just these," the human says, pointing to the snacks on the counter and the collection of papers in her hand.

While she's paying, the vampire turns to me. "Don't I know you from somewhere?" She toys with the fur lining her dark coat.

"Not that I recall," I reply, giving her a tight smile. Her friend steps out of the way, and I put my purchases on the counter.

"I'm sure I do. You look so familiar," she says, her voice playful.

It's not impossible she has seen me before, given my current profession, but I don't recognize her, so I just shrug. "Maybe."

I pay for my things and step to the side of the door so I can push up my sleeve and apply the tattoo. As I do, my coat falls open, and the vampire gasps. My holster is showing, one hilt of a dagger visible beneath my coat, but it doesn't usually garner that type of reaction. I glance up at her in confusion.

"I knew I'd seen you before!" she shouts, grabbing the paper from her friend's hand and furiously thumbing through it.

My stomach bottoms out. No good ever comes from being in the paper. Panic seizes my chest as I prepare myself to see an exposé on the Making of Princess Lira. The vampire shoves the paper into my face.

"Look! That's you, isn't it?"

A strange tension coils inside me as I process the image before me. In it, I'm standing at my desk, watching CP as he grabs Sugar and prepares to haul her into Gibson's office. The angle doesn't show his face, only her insouciant expression. Recording images within the department is prohibited. My jaw ticks as I mentally narrow down the suspects. There are only so many corners on our floor with that ability.

My eyes widen in shock as I read the story.

Crown Prince Begs Stalker to Back Off!

Detective Sugar Writh has allegedly been harassing Crown Prince Alaric for years, culminating in a stand-off today at the D.C. corners' department. Writh, a succubus who can use others' emotions to steal their autonomy, was previously in a relationship with Prince Fenrik. Prince Fenrik could not be reached for comment, but sources say he never took the relationship as seriously as she did. He broke it off when he discovered Writh had the misguided impression she would someday be queen.

"I felt bad for her. Getting dumped by the guy who would pity fuck anyone has got to be rough," CP said from an interview at the Luminous Palace today. "At first, I thought her behavior was a little erratic but fun. Not anymore. She won't stop following me, sending me messages. It's like she'll do anything to connect her name to mine."

CP met with Writh and her captain today to discuss the avenues he and the entire royal family are prepared to pursue if Writh doesn't cease her unwanted attention.

"Hello…" The vampire waves her hand in front of my face, breaking my concentration.

Turning to the rack of papers, I see Sugar's face staring out from at least three more. Two look recent, but in one, she's standing in a gorgeous dress next to Prince Fenrik, smiling as he whispers into her ear. A balding man wearing a suit picks it up, but when I glare, he hastily puts it back and heads to a different part of the shop.

"Yes, it is me. And this is all complete bullshit." I shove the paper back into the vampire's hands, and she scoffs indignantly.

I storm out of the store and down the pavement before my steps slow. What am I doing? Sugar's not a stalker, but there is no reason I should vouch for her to complete strangers. Kurt's absence is like a gaping hole. This is exactly the sort of thing I would have discussed with him. I clench my eyes, trying to imagine what he would have said but come up blank.

The rain can't touch me, but the icy wind stings my face. These stories are too concentrated to be anything but a targeted hit. It's slimy and heavy-handed, exactly the thing my uncle would do. I run a hand through my hair, incapable of forcing my feet in any direction.

A cart rolls by, sloshing water toward my shoes. The water bounces off an invisible dome, causing droplets to scatter like a fountain. I stand there for another five minutes before muttering, "Screw it" to myself and firing off a note. The response comes back quicker than I expected. I glance at the street sign, then turn and head in the opposite direction.

The papers are everywhere as I make my way through the city, sticking out of bags and being read by people on their way home. Sugar's face is crumpled on the floor next to bins and posted inside newsagents. Each one makes me more suspicious. CP wouldn't go through all this effort to sully her name for nothing.

I take the stairs two at a time to the second story and knock on the weathered wooden door. Matt opens it after a moment and silently beckons me inside. I follow him across a floating walkway, marveling at the extensive underwater environment he's created.

"This place is amazing," I say, stepping onto the solid floor of a kitchen. I take a seat at the kitchen table. It's dimly lit by only a single orb light, but it's cozy, not stark.

"I'm glad you like it. Sorry I don't have more ornamental birds. Heard you like those." He leans against the counter and crosses his arms.

Snorting, I shake my head, surprised Sugar even mentioned my apartment to him. Of course, now he must be wondering why Sugar has been in my apartment. "It isn't like that," I say.

"No? What is it like?"

Matt towers over me, and I regret sitting down. I've walked right into a trap. I can't explain why Sugar was at my apartment and don't know how she explained it to him, so whatever I say, he'll know I'm lying. When I stay silent, he huffs and turns back to the cupboards. He sets two glasses on the table and pours us both something that smells strong.

It burns my throat, leaving a slightly grassy but not unpleasant aftertaste. "Thank you."

He grunts. "Take it you saw the papers?"

I nod.

"Did you come here to ask me if it's true?"

"No. I know she's not stalking CP. The whole thing reeks of a smear campaign."

Matt raises an eyebrow. "She tell you why?"

"I overheard him tell her to lay off that butterfly case. Is that why?"

"When did you overhear that?" he asks, glass halfway to his mouth.

Fuck. I feign deafness at my second slip of the evening. I'm usually much better at this.

Matt pinches his nose between two fingers and mutters something under his breath before downing his drink and pouring himself another. "How can the two of you be so old and still so stupid?"

Chuckling, I say, "Funny. A friend of mine recently said something very similar to me." I turn my glass, letting it catch the light. My anger bubbles to the surface when I think of Sugar willingly giving herself to such a terrible person. Does she crave his cruelty? Is that what she wants? It wouldn't surprise me at all to find she'd double-crossed me with Lira as well. And yet, here I am, concerned about her.

"How long have you known?" I say. "About CP?"

Matt runs a hand over his mustache, his face strained. Worry deepens his dark brown eyes. "A while."

His words send a sudden stab of anger through me. "And you didn't tell her to stop? Look what it's cost her. And you and your case!" I clench the glass, the muscles in my wrist straining.

He doesn't take the bait, just shakes his head slowly and grunts, "Case isn't over yet. And she knew the risks."

"Of all people, why him?" I fall back in the chair and rub my jaw. I don't want to hear that CP is a great lay. Or maybe I do. Maybe I need to hear that Sugar is shallow and only cares about the sex and money.

Matt inhales through his nose and lets it out slowly. "It used to confuse me too until I knew her better. And I did tell her to stop. She's just…" He pauses, eyes searching the kitchen ceiling for the right word. "Everyone has their demons. Sugar just likes to keep hers visible."

Chapter 36
Sugar

"How could you be so naïve?" the Dame hisses from behind her desk. The smoke curling around her is red today, to match her red silk blouse and matching wide-leg trousers. Thin gold hoops hang from her ears and catch the light as she shakes her head at me. "What have I always said?"

"I didn't get emotionally involved with him," I bit out. "It was never about that." I cross my legs and lean back into the chair. I dig my nails into the armrests to keep from raising my voice.

She taps the cigarette on a jade ashtray and rounds on me. "Don't be obtuse, Sucrelia. There's more than one emotion. I know you don't love him, but any emotion is powerful. *We* know this," she says with a look that could wither stone.

I'm thrown back to the first time I sat before her, feeling ignorant and out of my depth. It's like there are two of me, one who blindly continued on thinking I was immune to the consequences of my actions. And the other, who was content to silently watch me bury myself deeper. She's a pretty chatty bitch now, though. Nothing the Dame says can be worse than what I've been calling myself for the past several hours.

The Dame paces toward the fireplace. "When?" she asks, red smoke flowing from her nostrils in the shape of perfect spirals.

I don't bother asking what she means. "After Fenrik left me. It was never supposed to continue, but he kept showing up." I hate how weak my voice sounds.

My memory of the first night is hazy. I was at the Nest but not working, just looking for my self-worth at the bottom of a wine glass. CP almost never came here. Some kind of line he didn't like to cross, or perhaps there were too many eyes. When he first approached, I thought he was Fenrik, and hope had surged inside me. I felt pathetic when I realized my mistake. Which is possibly the only reason he stood a chance in that moment.

"I told you not to waste your time with my brother," CP scoffs, grabbing a puff pastry filled with caviar off a passing tray and tossing it into his mouth. "Spineless little shit." The bartender hands him another glass of wine, leaning over so he gets a good view down her top. He winks at her.

"Pretty sure you told me I wasn't good enough for him. And apparently, you were right. Cheers." I tip my glass at him before throwing back the rest of my drink.

CP's lust is bold, predatory, and layered with hate as he moves into my space. His presence makes my skin crawl, but my power coils, ready to pounce. I haven't been working. Instead, I've been spending my days trying to find out why the corners' department is so unbelievably incompetent. They couldn't possibly have done less to find Linnea's killer. I'm not sure I can face Stanley Roman again without wrapping my whip around his neck until he turns a satisfying shade of purple.

"I said he couldn't treat you like you deserve." His voice is low in my ear as he slides his hand down to my ass. "He humiliated you. Treated you like a queen when he knew he couldn't make you anything but a—"

I slap him hard before he finishes the sentence. He grins. The skin on my neck flushes, and angry splotches pepper my chest. The alcohol is affecting my control. I bite down on the inside of my lip and taste blood.

"It's embarrassing, really. He's never going to be king, and yet, even as a lowly spare, he still thought you'd mar his precious reputation. That has got to hurt." He wraps his hands around my waist and drags his lips across my neck.

Rage cracks inside me like lightning, and my nausea transforms into something heavier, something dark and bitter. The wine swirls in my blood, dulling the memory of my conversation with Fenrik, erasing the words he said and the hurt in his eyes as he said them. Everything becomes a twisted mess of pain and disgust.

"And the worst part? All his power, and he did fuck all to find out who killed that maid you liked."

The tether inside me snaps, and I lose myself.

Apparently, I'm still lost. The Dame glares at me from across the room, and I meet her gaze. She blinks first.

"He kept showing up because you kept letting him in," she drawls. "And the worst part is you didn't tell me. He went all the way to your shitty apartment in the Hollows. Was that not enough to tell you what kind of power you have over him? We could have used him, Sucrelia! We could have squeezed him for so much information!" Her fists clench, and she opens her mouth to say something else but shuts it and turns away like she can't bear to look at me.

The Nest deals in all kinds of things, but information is one of its most lucrative commodities. And she's right. I could have used CP for something more than my own self-destruction. She'd drool if I told her what I think I know about him and the mystery necro, but nothing will drag that information out of me if it'll put my friends in danger.

Deep, pervasive sadness cascades through me. Lira still isn't out of the woods, and who knows if she'll hold up her end of the bargain now that her brother has dragged my name through the mud. I may have lost the only chance I had to get justice for not only my friend, but for Tonya, Sigrid, and Carter, too. Petra is probably livid. Even Matt is tired of my bullshit.

At least Draven got away. I wonder if he's sitting on his ridiculous red and gold couch, staring at his crane lamp and laughing with relief. He's probably got his arm thrown over the back of the couch, swigging from a beer, sighing in gratitude that he can safely ignore me for the rest of his days. I almost smile at the thought.

"Sucrelia?" the Dame asks. Her brow is still furrowed with irritation, but the tone is soft.

I swallow, looking up to where she's leaning against the edge of the desk. She sucks in a breath at whatever she sees on my face.

"Knock it off. We do not wallow," she huffs, standing and going back behind her desk. "Take your old room. There are probably reporters at your apartment." She turns to the wall of mirrors on the wall, resuming her watch over her domain. "And fix your face. I can't have you scaring the customers."

I inhale and straighten my shoulders as I rise from the chair. "If it makes you feel any better, he wasn't going to keep coming to my shitty apartment anymore. Said it was too far. Maybe I didn't have as much power over him as you think."

The Dame turns, a line between her eyebrows. "He broke up with you? You didn't tell me that."

"No..." I trail off, tipping my head and blowing out a breath as I try to remember CP's words. Shaking my head, I say, "He just said he was going to have me a lot closer from now on." I shrug. "Maybe he was going to make me meet him somewhere more convenient for him."

"Like his brother?" She arches an eyebrow.

Her words sting as desired. "Yes. Like his brother, who I also should never have gotten involved with. You were completely and totally right about everything."

"Hmph," she says. "As long as you acknowledge it. Have Helen give you a top-up. She just found out James stole one of her best clients." She waves her red-and-black-tipped nails, dismissing me.

I step into a small powder room across from her office. There's an ornate gold mirror and dark blue wallpaper with gold veins. With my dull hair and puffy eyes, I look distinctly out of place. After splashing cold water on my neck, I lean back against the wall, hands behind my back, and try to take a deeper breath than I have since I walked out of work to find CP had purchased every journalist he could get his hands on.

I'm not safe in here. But it feels good all the same to have the tiny room to myself. I can almost pretend nobody can find me. Pressing my lips together, I entertain myself by imagining who I'll eviscerate for leaking Bradley's arrest. There's no way CP did all of this in the time between Bradley getting to the department and his snake of a lawyer showing up.

Unless, of course, this was his plan all along. Another wave of boiling shame at my stupidity runs through me. He could have had those stories ready for months, primed for him to use if I ever stepped out of line.

My power twists, begging to be fed. I send a message to Helen, asking if she's got time to help me out. She comes down the hallway a few minutes later to where I'm leaning against the wall, having dragged myself out of the powder room.

"Hey, Sugar. Bad day?" she asks, giving me a sad smile. She wears a dark blue lace gown, her hair in a sleek updo.

"Not at all. Why do you ask?" I keep my face blank, grateful I can still control something.

The left side of her mouth twists, and she tips her head down and shakes it. "Nobody who knows you will believe any of that bullshit." She gestures down the hall toward my old room.

"Ah, yes, but that's the problem, isn't it? Who knows me? You, the Dame, a few others here. But not the other corners, except for Matt." The image of Draven resting on his couch enters my mind again, unbidden. But this time, he's got his elbows on his knees, staring right at me with those burnished eyes of his, judging me.

Before I feel the intent, or perhaps because her intention is to help and not harm me, I don't dodge before she reaches out and smacks me upside the head.

"Ow! What was that for?" I rub the back of my head and shoot her a dark look.

"Because you are getting on my nerves. People don't need to be your best friend to know you didn't stalk CP. He's dug a massive hole for his reputation. Most of D.C. would trust a complete stranger over our crown prince. Give the people some credit, Sug."

"I'm not just concerned about my reputation, Helen. His lies will compromise multiple murder investigations," I huff, pushing open the door to my room. Everything is exactly as I left it. The Dame allows me to store all the fancy clothes and costumes that have no place in a corner's wardrobe.

Helen sits down on a chest at the end of the four-poster bed and runs a hand over the velvet comforter. It's been a long time since I've been here, even to grab something. I moved to the Hollows because I needed to get away from the palace and because having a corner around regularly wouldn't be good business for the Nest.

There are necklaces hanging off the mirror, shoes lined up in the closets, and a halter dangling off the bathroom door. It smells expensive. It's a scent I no longer recognize. The perfume of someone who really thought they had their shit together.

The malevolence emanating from Helen starts small, then grows as she tells me all about James and the poaching of her long-time client. I move close to her, inhaling as she speaks, relishing the warmth that floods my body. Sparks of power move under my skin, and chills run up and down my back, infusing me with strength again.

"Thank you," I say, pulling back.

She smiles up at me before leaning back on her hands. "What's your plan?"

Flexing my fingers and rolling my neck, I reply, "Don't have one yet. Denying it won't help." I walk over to my vanity and inspect the contents of the drawers. I pull out a black diamond ring surrounded by tiny emeralds. "Bradley killed Sigrid and Carter, but we think someone else killed Tonya and he just helped."

"And by 'someone,' you mean CP?" Helen frowns at the ceiling. "CP has done tons of horrible things, and they've never been able to pin anything on him. Why would he even bother asking someone to cover it up? Especially someone who doesn't work for him?"

Twirling the ring on my finger, I consider her question. "You're right," I say slowly, trying to catch all the errant thoughts in my head. Did Bradley know she was a necro and that's why he thought she was "interesting?" "Bradley worked for Nichols, and I know CP and Nichols worked together, but that's still a lot of trust to place in the councilor's lackey."

"Not if CP had something on Nichols," Helen says.

I tuck my lips as I consider her theory. If CP had something on Nichols, the councilor would want to even the leverage. And CP would trust Bradley not to say anything because if he did, it'd be mutually assured destruction.

"What does the Nest know about the councilor?" I ask, pulling out a long red glove and running the silk through my fingers.

She shakes her head. "He's been here to play cards and to use the pool," she says, referring to the giant aquatic environment in the Nest's basement, which is favored by water shifters. "Obviously."

I frown at her. "Why obviously? Just because he's a crocodile shifter?"

She cocks her head at me. "No. Because he built it."

"I didn't know that." I put the glove down but keep the ring.

"All that stuff—the grotto, the tide pools—that's all him. Hel, the water even changes color when he touches it."

"What kind of charm is that?" I pick up a bracelet with emerald clovers lined in gold.

Helen shrugs. "I don't know, but the Dame was a little pissed about it. She wanted it to change for her as well, but he said it was tied to his blood."

"I'll bet she was," I say, frowning. "Nichols is certainly talented. I'll give him that. Was there always a pool down there? Or access to the river?"

"Nope, it was just a bunch of rock. Blew a big hole and let the sea find its way in."

Later that night, I stare up at the familiar ceiling. The Nest's stone walls mute the sounds from the gaming floor downstairs and every other room. So different from my apartment. The noise of a message arriving in my jacket pocket is like a thunderclap in the eerie silence.

I climb out of bed and cross the floor, relishing the feeling of the blue silk nightgown. I remind myself to do a meticulous search through my wardrobe here before going home. Just because I can't wear any of my fancy clothes to the department doesn't mean I can't keep a few things for other occasions.

Even though it doesn't bear the royal seal, the expensive paper gives Fenrik away more than his name on the bottom of the note.

Can't stop thinking about the last time I saw you. Obviously, I don't believe anything he's saying in the papers. But if something did happen between the two of you, it's none of my business.

Even if it does make me insanely jealous.

I made some inquiries. Just after Tonya Penn's body was found, CP spoke to the senators about the approvals necessary to subdue the magic in the Hollows. It's something that has come up a few times before but generally doesn't get much support. It'd be necessary if Drahma City's council ever decides to build over the under city.

Nobody would testify to this. Senate hearings are confidential, of course. But I hope it helps.

I'm trying, Sugar. Please believe me.

Love, Fen.

The note should soothe me or inspire that familiar warmth. But even though the information is helpful, something stings. I've been so angry at myself for so long, and I thought self-hatred pushed me toward Alaric. But the memory of his words about Fen not helping me with Linnea has exposed a pit of resentment. I've ignored it all this time because I didn't want to ruin my memories by blaming him.

None of his business?

I told myself I didn't want Fen to find out about me and his brother. But as I crush his note in my palm, I know that's not true. I wanted him to hurt. Not just because now I know he didn't consider me queen material, but because this note shows he could have helped back then and didn't. I put my faith in him, and he let me down, made me doubt my ability to rely on anyone else.

I throw the note on the ground. If he truly cared, everything about me would have been his business.

Chapter 37
Sugar

A quick trip to R&E shows Councilor Nichols has purchased nearly all of the recently vacated homes in the Hollows. Matt and I stand in the hallway, a thick folder of paperwork split between us.

"Nichols had his minion bait the ulgashen to drive the people so he could buy up the land," I say, flipping through the deeds. I'm not positive, but the rising water levels, the bridge collapsing, and Nichols's abilities with water engineering make me suspect he has plans for the Hollows that don't involve high-rises.

"The Crown still owns most of it, though. Did Nichols think he was going to pressure CP into selling?"

"CP was in on it." I whisper the particulars of Fen's note to Matt. "The only way CP would have let Bradley help him out is if he had something on Nichols to even the score. It's not illegal for Nichols to want to develop the Hollows. It had to be something else. CP had to have known what Nichols was doing to drive away the residents."

"Can we prove that?" Matt holds the folder at his side as he leans back, arms akimbo, and stretches. "There's nothing to connect Bradley to CP other than Bradley's testimony, and something tells me he's going to be real quiet, whether he wants to or not."

Bradley looked terrified when he left with Delaney Cross. Delaney was the last person seen with him, so it'd be her ass on the line if something happens to him. That gives me some confidence that CP won't kill him.

"We need to get him to turn on Nichols. He doesn't have to talk about Tonya." My heart sinks at the thought. "Do we have to keep CP out of it?" I look at Matt with the question in my eyes. "Is there another way?"

"Only one way to find out."

***

Matt and I dodge the flood of people moving in and out of the Rettirness building and climb to the third floor. The black and gold marble walls are just as light-eating on the inside as out. When we reach the dark cherrywood door with Petra's name engraved on the glass, I don't bother knocking.

We freeze at the scene before us. Sitting in front of Petra's neatly organized desk is none other than Councilor Nichols. He's wearing a solemn expression. A man I don't recognize sits next to him, but from the open briefcase at his feet, I'm guessing it's Nichols's lawyer. Greta, Petra's assistant and a recorder, sits at a table near the window. She's older, nearly eight hundred, and doesn't bother to hide her look of disapproval as she stares at the two men.

The room smells like Petra's apartment but with an undercurrent of coffee and aged paper. She wears a cream silk blouse. Her gold necklace glints in the morning light as she swivels toward us in her chair.

"Good morning, Detectives." One hand drums on the dark gray blotter as she speaks. "Your timing is impeccable. Councilor Nichols has come forward with information regarding Bradley Thorn."

"Did he now?" Matt says as he takes a seat next to Greta. She gives him a warm smile.

Walking behind Petra's desk, I lean back and prop my foot up against the wall. She turns ever so slightly toward me, an eyebrow raised, and I put it down. It's a subtle display of dominance I can appreciate.

Her office, her show.

"Now that everyone's here, why don't you start at the beginning?" Petra nods to Nichols.

Nichols, dressed in a dove-gray suit, crosses his legs before speaking. "Yes, well, as I was saying, I hired Bradley to escort my daughter to events to ensure her safety. He was very eager, always asking if there was any more I needed done. I thought he was ambitious." He stops, inhaling as if gathering strength.

It takes me more strength to stop from rolling my eyes.

"He knew I was interested in developing the Hollows, repairing streets and housing, making things safer for the community."

Matt loses the battle with his expressions. He and Greta share a look of disbelief, but unlike me, they're not in Nichols's eyeline. I grit my teeth as he continues.

"He told me he had some great ideas about how to jump-start that project. He said he wanted to do some community outreach to help people understand the project." Nichols sucks in his breath and runs a hand across his face. His lawyer pats him on the shoulder and murmurs at him to keep going. "I don't know how I didn't see it. The attacks...those poor people." He takes another steadying breath. "I believe Bradley's been baiting the ulgashen to come to the Hollows in some misguided attempt to help me." His lawyer gives him a bracing smile and another pat.

"Why would he think driving people out of the Hollows would help you?" Petra asks, her voice as smooth and unbothered as a river stone. But her knee bounces under her desk.

"I'm not entirely sure. I only recently heard he was arrested and started putting it together from offhand comments he made..." He looks down before speaking again. "When the people started leaving the Hollows, I bought the properties. The planning commission can take ages when you're dealing with individual homeowners. I thought if I bought them, we could speed through the process." He holds his hands out, palms up. "I would have sold them back—at the same price, mind you—whenever there were buyers. My efforts to cut through the jungle of bureaucracy might have given Bradley the wrong idea."

"The idea that you wanted him to wield the ulgashen as a weapon to drive out the rightful for your own gain?" I drawl.

Nichols shifts in his seat and gives me a patronizing glare. "I don't expect anyone who hasn't been elected by the people to understand the pressures of public office. The Hollows has more crime than the upper city, more accidents from unsafe buildings, not to mention the erratic nature of the magic down there. I'm the one who receives the complaints, Detective Writh, the one who has to answer the press's questions when things go wrong. I had no idea that man would twist my good efforts into something sinister."

"Bradley hasn't just been accused of baiting the ulgashen, Councilor," Petra says, leaning forward. "Do you have thoughts on why he allegedly murdered three people?"

"Anything I say on that account would be pure conjecture. I don't pretend to understand the mind of a madman. I only wish to tell you what I suspect regarding the attacks."

If Nichols spoke to Bradley after we caught him, he'd know Bradley essentially confessed to the killing of Sigrid and Carter but not Tonya. Which means it's likely Delaney and the Crown have Bradley locked down tight. We have to assume Bradley told Nichols about the killings in the moment, about finding Tonya at LeMar. But Nichols won't go up against CP unless he has to.

I glance at Matt, who sucks a tooth in annoyance.

"Councilor, Detective Diaz and I raised Carter Fox. He told us how he had to wait outside your office and overheard you talking," I say.

"Yes, he said he spent the time answering fan mail." Nichols narrows his eyes on me, the slightest smirk playing around the corner of his mouth. He's letting us know he knows exactly what Carter said. Which means he bribed someone for the recorder's transcript.

"He also said he thought you might have something to do with the West Bridge falling into the water."

"Oh, please," Nichols scoffs. "That bridge had been disintegrating for decades. It's one of four avenues into the Hollows, entirely unnecessary."

My voice drops, the tiniest hint of violence threading through my words. "As someone who just recently took the rock stairs from Lekotto Park down to the Hollows so I could watch your employee draw hungry animals into populated areas, I can assure you some routes are more desirable than others."

Nichols stretches his neck and smothers his rising irritation. He's been a politician too long to let his feelings run away with him. "I'm sorry. That must have been difficult to witness. The council is committed to keeping the East Bridge in good repair."

"Do you think Bradley shared his plans with anyone else? Bellanie, perhaps?" Petra says.

"Bellanie knew nothing about this. She's not terribly interested in the daily trials of a civil servant." He gives her a "what are you going to do?" look, as if Bellanie is a small child and not a fully grown adult.

"I think the councilor has done his duty in telling you his suspicions," Nichols's lawyer says with a voice reminiscent of bacon grease. "If you have any other questions, you may direct them to my office." The two of them stand and stride from the room.

"Well, that was both disgusting and entirely predictable." Petra stands, lacing her fingers together and stretching them back and forth as she takes measured steps around her office.

I look up at her from where I've sat in the seat vacated by Nichols. "You have to make a deal with one of them."

Matt takes the seat next to me. "What a choice. The mastermind, the murderous patsy, or the cancerous growth that infects us all?"

Petra rubs a hand across her forehead. "You think Nichols would turn on CP?"

"To save his own skin? Yes. He's too recognizable for CP to do much to him. He won't take the risk if Bradley doesn't cooperate, though," I reply.

"Bradley isn't too recognizable. Once things are settled, CP could easily arrange for him to have an unfortunate accident," Matt says.

Petra turns to her assistant. "What do you think?"

Greta adjusts the yellow sweater around her shoulders. "When it comes to CP, you have some big ambitions, Pet. Involving him at all could compromise those."

Petra leans on the edge of her desk, assessing me as if I'm a dish she's not sure how to clean. "And what about you? You once said your "activities" could only be a benefit to us. Still true, or will it turn this trial into a circus?"

The shame still digs in its fangs, but it's not as painful. I can't allow my choices to fuck up our chances, not when it's already going to be such a difficult balancing act for Petra.

I tip my chin up at her. "No circus. You don't need me to testify. Matt and Draven are more than enough." Matt turns, his eyes mournful but understanding. He knows how much I like testifying. Trials are a performance, and I'm nothing if not a skilled actor.

"I wish I could say I was surprised he made such an impressive effort to ruin your reputation. You must have done something to really piss him off." Petra raises her eyebrow in question.

"Yes. I did. It has to do with Tonya, and for your own safety, we won't be discussing it."

"Of course we won't," she says flatly.

Before I lose my nerve, I add, "I'm sorry for not telling you about my involvement with CP," I say. Beside me, Matt shifts in his seat. "It wasn't my intention for you to find out like that." I wave my hand to encompass the countless salacious hit pieces.

"I knew. Jasper told me after that first meeting." She doesn't look at me as she says it, toying with something on her desk.

"He did?" My eyebrows shoot up. I expected no loyalty from Jasper, but I thought his animosity toward Petra would make him hold out a little longer.

Her lips purse, and her eyes take on an unfocused look like she's remembering before glancing back at me. "Yes. I wanted to cut you off completely, but you continued to work the files, and I required the help. I figured I didn't need to trust you or approve of your choices to get the work done." She shrugs.

I blink, taken aback at her cold logic. My gaze bounces from Matt to Greta and back to Petra. "Anyone ever told you that you'd make a great dominatrix?"

A line appears between her brows, but the corner of her lip quirks. "No, I can't say that they have. Besides," she says, pulling her thick hair into a bun on top of her head, "if anyone knows what it's like to regret a relationship, I do." Matt and I simultaneously open our mouths to speak, but she holds up a finger to silence us. "And no, we will not be discussing that."

Chapter 38
Sugar

Petra takes slow, measured steps as she walks across the dark wood floor of the courtroom. She wears long green robes identical to those worn by the accused, the three judges watching from an elevated dais in the center, and Donahue, the defense attorney. Her heels echo in the hush, ensuring the eyes of everyone present are on her when she finally speaks.

"Please state your name for the recorders."

"Bradley Thorn."

"When did you first meet Councilor Nichols, Mr. Thorn?"

Bradley folds and unfolds his hands in his lap before putting them on the table in front of him. "About a year ago. At Tradimento. He was there with his wife and Bellanie. I tossed out this guy who was hitting on Bellanie."

"Did you see him after that night?"

"Yes. He sent me a note a few days later, asking me if I wanted a job. I came to his office, and he asked me if I wouldn't mind looking after Bellanie."

"Why did he believe Bellanie needed looking after?"

Bradley looks puzzled by the question for a moment before he responds. "She was going to parties. Nichols wanted to make sure that nobody took advantage of her, I guess."

"Isn't Bellanie quite a strong water fae? Wouldn't she have been able to take care of herself?"

From the corner of my eye, Nichols smirks.

The courtroom is a half circle surrounded by rows of raised, black leather seats. An entire row at the top is filled with press, including Jasper. Bellanie and the councilor's wife sit one row behind Nichols. Draven, Matt, and I are in the same row, behind the marble-topped desk reserved for the prosecution. The defense attorney, wearing an insufferably smug expression, lounges at the one for the defense across the aisle.

"Yes, that's true." Bradley tugs at the collar of the suit Petra found for him to wear. "He wanted extra help, I guess."

"Did he send you to every party with Bellanie?"

"Objection. How would he know if it was every party?" Donahue drawls, his voice just as greasy as I remember from the first time we met in Petra's office. He barely rises from his seat to speak to the judges.

"Quite right. Did you *believe* he sent you to every party Bellanie attended?" Petra asks slowly, enunciating the words for opposing counsel, who purses his lips in response.

"No, I don't think so. Mainly the ones where CP might be there," says Bradley.

"Did Bellanie ever express any romantic interest in the crown prince?" Petra's voice is smooth and confident as she leans against the desk. From beside Petra, Greta watches the questioning and the judges for their reactions.

Bradley makes a face. "No. Never. She was not into him." His ears pink, and he glances around, afraid CP will hear him, but the crown prince hasn't yet made an appearance.

I join the rest of the crowd as they look around for CP. I swallow and shift in my seat. Next to me, Draven's knee bumps mine. I don't look over at him but dip my chin slightly to acknowledge the gesture. The reticence he'd had seems to have melted, but we've kept things professional for the two months since Bradley's arrest. I resist looking over to appreciate the sight of his broad shoulders filling out the dark blue suit.

Matt and I both wear black, our standard for court, but I've paired mine with four-inch stilettos and dark red lips. I got a top-up from some asshole who thought it was cool to yell at someone else's kid at the market. He's enjoying the next several hours building the girl a treehouse. By hand. I had to be sure I was looking my best for everyone who showed up hoping to get a glimpse at CP's crazy stalker. Just because I'm not testifying doesn't mean I'm hiding.

"Did you ever perform any duties for Councilor Nichols other than being Bellanie's bodyguard?"

Bradley puts his hands back in his lap before speaking. "Yes. After a few months, he asked me if I wanted to make some more money. He taught me how to bait the ulgashen to get them to go to the Hollows."

"Where did you lead them?"

"To the graveyards. I'd dig up the newer bodies so they'd keep coming back. Nichols also gave me something to sprinkle on the bodies to make them wilder, I guess."

Gasps ring out in the courtroom. Several people boo. The judges let it go on for several minutes before one of them waves their hand for silence.

"Did he tell you why he wanted that?"

"Said the under city was dangerous and it would be better if only good fae like us lived in Drahma City."

Nichols leans back from his chair at the defense table, raising a green-robed hand in a gesture of "do you believe this?" as he rolls his eyes for the crowd.

"Community outreach, my ass," Matt whispers for my ears only.

"You are aware that the ulgashen attacks have resulted in the deaths of twenty-four people, are you not? Including Detective Kurt Copper, Detective Flint's partner." Petra raises her voice on the number and stands up, letting the crowd see her face as she dips her chin toward Draven.

There are more boos and hisses. Draven tenses beside me. My hands rest on my thighs. With the slightest movement, I graze his leg with my pinky. He barely turns his head, but I know he feels me.

Sweat beads on Bradley's forehead. "Yeah. I heard that. But they could have left after the first attack—"

"Thank you," Petra interrupts as she moves closer to him. "Tell me about Tonya Penn."

Matt turns his head, searching the courtroom. I meet his eye, and he shakes his head.

"I found Tonya dead at a party at LeMar." His voice is hard, like he wants to fight a little more about the sensibilities of the people of the Hollows, but he continues. "I thought she would be good bait for the ulgashen. Thought finding a really fresh body would attract a lot of ulgashen at once. Figured the more people I could get to move at one time, the more impressed the councilor would be."

"Monster!" a woman yells from her seat. There are loud grumblings of agreement. The judges ignore it, all three of them leaning forward to listen to Bradley. One of them, a butterfly, struggles to maintain a look of passivity as Bradley explains shrinking Tonya's body and keeping it in the cold storage at Tradimento.

"You wanted to make him proud?" Petra holds the silence after Bradley nods in affirmation. "Did you ever kill for Councilor Nichols?"

"Yes." The courtroom erupts with calls for him to be executed or worse. Petra doesn't flinch or look back at the spectators. Her eyes are locked firmly on Bradley's.

"Who?"

He swallows, and there's a moment where I can see him wonder whether he has to go through with his deal with Petra before he gives up.

"I killed Carter Fox. Councilor Nichols said Carter overheard him talking with—" He checks the room again and steels himself. "—CP and might figure out his plans. He told me to get rid of him." He shrugs, which only incites the crowd more.

"Objection." Nichols's lawyer stands. "The record of Carter Fox's raising has been already admitted into evidence. The witness cannot contradict what Mr. Fox claimed he heard."

"The witness did not testify regarding what Mr. Fox heard," the judge closest to me, a man with a bulbous nose and shiny forehead, responds. "He testified as to what Councilor Nichols told him he thought Fox heard. Go on." He inclines his head at Petra, and Donahue sits down. Nichols leans over and whispers into his ear.

Petra steps close enough to touch the witness table. "But he wasn't the only one, was he, Bradley?"

"No." And now his voice wavers a little, and his eyes find his hands on the table. "I killed Sigrid."

The councilor leans forward, hanging on to Bradley's every word. Sigrid is a strong point for the defense.

"Did Nichols order you to kill her?"

"No," he says weakly. "She found the box where I'd been keeping Tonya. I thought she saw her. I didn't mean to. It just happened."

There are more jeers and shouts. Petra looks out into the crowd, her eyes slowly sweeping across. The crowd quiets, eager to hear what she'll say next.

She's still looking at them when she says, "It didn't just happen, did it? You found her, shrank her, and stepped on her, snuffing out her life like she was no more than a bug. Didn't you?" Bradley wheezes and nods behind her. As if she can see him, Petra continues, "And then you put her body in the same box with Tonya?"

"Yeah." It's barely a whisper. "I took her to her place afterward, though. I didn't want her to be fed to the ulgashen."

Petra ignores him. That was off script. She's walking a tightrope between showing Bradley as a hired mercenary and a fool Nichols exploited for his own game.

"Whose idea was it to leave Tonya on the beach in the Hollows, Bradley?" Petra raises an eyebrow at the crowd, daring them to make a noise and interrupt her flow.

"Councilor Nichols told me to do it."

Petra's eyes find the councilor in his seat next to Donahue. The crowd's attention immediately follows hers, and I can't help but be impressed by her control. Tendrils of lust reach out to her from the spectators. I don't blame them. She's in her element.

Nichols is the center of attention as she stalks toward him, stopping when she's right in front. "Why did he do that?" she asks Bradley while standing a few feet from Nichols.

"He said he wanted to send a message to CP. Said he was supposed to be helping with, like, royal permission or something. He wanted him to hurry up."

"Did he?" Petra turns to the judges, who have been whispering behind their hands, a sound charm blocking their voices from us. "Was it your understanding that CP knew what

Nichols was doing? What you were doing?" Petra glances at the crowd, a frown playing on her lips as she asks the question.

"No. Based on what I heard, I think CP and Nichols just had a business deal and Nichols wanted to speed up the timeline." He memorized the words, and it sounds like it. But Nichols and Donahue won't bring up CP.

She turns back to him. "Bradley, you're going to prison for a very long time, aren't you?"

The crowd stays silent, and he gulps. "Yes. Fifty years. But maybe thirty with good behavior." He bobs his head like he's convincing himself. Nobody jeers; the crowd is too busy murmuring.

"And in exchange for this court's leniency—" She nods at the judges as she walks back toward her witness. "—you've agreed to testify against Councilor Nichols. Is that correct?"

"Yes."

"But Bradley." Petra leans over his chair from behind, and he twists his neck to look at her. "Why should we believe anything out of your horrible, murderous mouth?"

A sliver of arousal stronger than the others sweeps out from the audience. I tear my eyes away in time to spot Jasper hungrily watching Petra. I turn back, filing that information away for later and focusing all my mental energy on Bradley. He'd better get it right. On either side of me, Matt and Draven lean forward. Draven rests his elbows on his knees, his eyes like steel blades on one of the men responsible for his friend's death.

"Because—" Bradley takes a deep breath, his voice wavering. "—if I don't stop him, he'll just find someone else like me. And he'll keep using them until he gets what he wants."

"What does he want?"

"Everyone in the Hollows to be gone or dead."

***

Matt testified about Carter, Sigrid, and Tonya, and Draven testified about catching Bradley with the ulgashen. The audience loved them. Especially Draven's side story about the walls moving in on us.

"He can shove me up against a wall anytime he wants," a woman behind me sighed when he told her of our heroic resistance to the old magic. "Better than wasting it on that slutty barnacle."

Matt shifts, twisting toward her, but I stop him with a hand on his elbow.

"No circus, remember?" I murmur.

She doesn't bother me. I've been called worse, and she can't sense Draven's feelings. Eager, like deft fingers plucking at my clothes, as he describes watching me capture Bradley. I involuntarily search the crowd again for the absent prince before moving my gaze back to Draven. His eyes find mine, and the hope that swirls inside from just that glance is frightening.

CP has come looking for me a few times. Keeping him accommodating while refusing his advances has been beyond challenging. For now, he's convinced my refusal is a temporary punishment for his stalker allegations. But his patience is about as durable as fog; once it's gone, nothing will stand between him and what he wants. Including, and especially, a rival for my attention. As long as CP is around, anyone I'm with will feel the effects of his violent possessiveness.

We adjourned for lunch, eating in a sad, beige, windowless room inside the courthouse, before returning to our places in the courtroom.

Petra's nails drum on the marble, her eyes flitting over the people filing back into their seats. I smooth down my pants for something to ease my nerves.

"Any sign of him?" Petra asks, her robe open a little at the top. I shake my head, and she purses her lips but turns around, reorganizing her already precisely organized desk.

Matt stands and paces the length of the floor, examining the life-size painting of Rett, the god of justice, on the wall. He's rendered in gold and silver, giving the assembled masses a shrewd smile.

"Hey." Draven's voice sends an involuntary shiver across my shoulders. I exhale, wondering when that started. I turn to see his elbow on the seatback, his fingers almost grazing my shoulder. "It's going to be okay. No matter what happens, you got Bradley."

My mouth prepares the words of something snarky, but I stop before they come out. "Maybe." I swallow. "CP is..." I huff at the memory of Stone's words at Tradimento. "Mercurial."

Draven cocks his head, nodding, but I know he doesn't get the reference. Those pewter eyes search my face before pausing on my lips.

"You remember when I asked you if you ever smiled?"

I arch an eyebrow in response. The seats are filling up, and I know he's distracting me from searching for CP, to see if he's come to doom or save us all. Draven leans in closer, the scent of his soap, pine and clover, mingling with an undercurrent of lust.

"I'd really love to earn one of those. A real one, aimed right at me."

"A smile?" I give him a bemused look. "That's it?"

"A smile from anyone else is as common as water, but from a woman like you? That's worth something." Draven holds my stare for a beat. Heat that has nothing to do with my power expands in my chest and travels down my body. He gives my shoulder a light squeeze as Matt returns to sit beside us and the judges take their places.

Chapter 39
Sugar

"Councilor Nichols," Petra begins. "You hired Bradley to keep an eye on your daughter, Bellanie, when she went to parties. Is that correct?"

"Yes." Nichols smooths down the front of his robes. They're meant to show how little difference there is between the accused and the attorneys and judges. That anyone, if they make the wrong choices, can wind up at the defense table. But unlike Petra, he's not used to the robes and can't hide his discomfort at having to forgo his favorite sharp suits.

Petra rubs a hand across her neck as if she's already bored with his conversation. "And he was a good employee? Brought her home safe, etc.?" She picks up some papers and rifles through them, not looking at him as he answers.

His jaw ticks. "He was adequate." Nichols throws a glare to his attorney, who gives him a bracing nod.

"You heard Bradley testify that Bellanie didn't like CP and wasn't interested in him romantically. Is that correct?"

A smug grin grows on his face, and I'm ready for it when he looks directly at me and says, "Yes. Unlike some people, my daughter has much higher standards." I can feel the other eyes on my back, but my expression is nothing but bored contempt.

"Well, it's good to know Bradley was telling the truth about that," Petra says, and he whips his head back to her, face reddening.

Sucker.

"I assume you deny Mr. Thorn's testimony?"

"Yes! Every word was pure lies." He sits up straighter and aims the remark toward the judges.

"Well, not every word, as you just admitted. And do you believe he was telling the truth about baiting the ulgashen to come to the Hollows?"

"Well, yes, because he admitted it. But I think—"

Petra cuts him off. "You must have been pretty upset to hear about that?"

He relaxes a little. "Yes, I was. Terribly dangerous for our citizens. Just despicable."

"Not only that, but you own a pretty sizable chunk of the Hollows, do you not?" Petra hands him the deeds Matt and I dug up. "These are yours, correct? Nearly thirty percent of the existing Hollows."

The lie slips out as smooth as butter. "Some of those, I purchased years ago. But truly, the council has been discussing rehabilitation of the Hollows for decades, and nothing has ever happened. When people began moving away, I saw it as an opportunity to speed up the doldrums of bureaucracy. By buying the properties myself, when it came time for the permissions we'd need to repair streets and improve schools, I would be able to provide them. And then, I would sell those houses back to new owners. Without making a profit, of course." He places a hand on his heart. "I had no idea Bradley was behind the attacks in some misguided attempt to help me. I thought I was buying the properties because the ulgashen drove the people away, not because Bradley was driving the people away so I could buy the properties. That would be insane." He gives the audience an incredulous look.

The crowd doesn't look convinced, but they aren't booing either.

"Some of these properties weren't abandoned by their occupants because of the ulgashen, but because of flooding. Do you know anything about that?"

"Water levels rise. Drahma City is built in a cove, after all. But a little flooding is nothing." He turns a doting eye on Bellanie, who chews on her lip and looks less than enthused at her father's attention. "My daughter and other water fae could have it removed easily."

"That's very generous of you. Future landlord, current councilor, and prior engineer. Isn't that right?"

"Yes." He pulls his chin up, stretching it out from his collar. "I am an engineer."

"Forgive me, *current* engineer. You built the pool under the Nest, correct? I heard it's amazing." She casts a quick glance at me like we've just been gossiping in the hall.

"I did. I hear people enjoy it." He manages to look gracious.

Dread creeps into my stomach. It's still Nichols's word against Bradley's right now. A well-respected councilor versus an admitted murderer who has no proof he was acting on someone else's orders.

"It must have been difficult," Petra says.

"Yes. It was tricky. We had to create the space from scratch."

"Without bringing down the existing building?" Petra smiles, and a few people chuckle.

"Of course," Nichols says indulgently, but a muscle in his eye twitches.

"That's some talent. You must be quite skilled with explosives, soil analysis, and structural engineering, not to mention understanding all the ins and outs of water flow, right?"

There's a long beat of silence before he replies. "Yes, that's correct."

Murmurs break out, but not enough to give me much confidence. The judges make a few comments to one another before looking expectantly at Petra.

"It's all just a coincidence, then?" Petra walks in front of him and back again, letting the audience follow her. "You buying up all that land right after the ulgashen began their unusually frequent attacks? It's a coincidence that you would know all about how to flood a space that large for a massive underwater housing division? It's a coincidence that you are a crocodile shifter and your wife and daughter are both powerful water fae? Just a coincidence?"

Nichols's face slides from menacing to patronizing in a second. "It all sounds very salacious when you say it like that, Ms. Kohl, but politics are rarely so dramatic. I am a servant of the people, just doing my best to assist where I can. I did not have anything to do with Bradley's ambitions." He makes a face of disgust but doesn't look over at his former employee.

When Petra dismisses him, he strolls back to his seat, looking around as if he's merely tolerating this before getting back to his good work for the people of D.C. Petra is doing an amazing job with what we have, but one look at the judges tells me they're not convinced. The hatred in the courtroom is still focused mainly on Bradley.

"The prosecution calls Bellanie Nichols."

A vein leaps in Nichols's forehead as his daughter stands and gives her mother a reassuring hand squeeze before descending. Her eyes are wary, but her back is straight as she walks to the witness table.

"Thank you, Bellanie. Can you tell us how you came to work for Carter Fox?"

She pushes her shiny blond hair over her shoulder, and a small smile touches her lips. "I sort of just hounded him until he agreed to hire me. He knew who I was—who my dad is—but I don't think that's what persuaded him. I'm just really stubborn."

The crowd chuckles. Petra gives it just a moment to sink in. "You must miss him?"

Bellanie's chin wobbles, and she gives a strained smile. "He was a good boss. And I was good at my job."

"His killer, someone you trusted, is sitting right there." Petra motions to Bradley, who snaps back in his chair, looking terrified. His gaze bounces to his guard, no doubt wondering if he'll lift a finger to stop Bellanie from attacking him.

Bellanie's blue eyes turn icy as she stares him down. "I don't understand you. What kind of person could do something like that in cold blood? Carter never did anything but bring happiness to the world, and you snuck up behind him like a coward. You disgust me." She waves a hand, and a jet of water blasts into Bradley's chest, knocking him backward and onto the floor. His guard glances down, takes an annoyed breath, and rights his chair.

"Did that help?" Petra says.

"A little. But not really." Bellanie swallows, and a muscle jumps under her lip as she struggles not to cry. To my right, Nichols is furiously whispering to his lawyer.

Petra approaches her, her steps light. "You heard what Bradley said about your father. Do you believe him?"

Nichols's lawyer leaps out of his seat. "Objection!"

The heads of all three judges swivel in unison. The butterfly frowns at him. "What are the grounds for your objection?"

"It's..." He fumbles. "Inappropriate."

Nichols looks murderous. I can see Petra struggling to control the withering look she wants to shoot at him while trying not to distract from Bellanie.

The judge does it for her. "Denied."

"Bellanie?" Petra pulls the audience's attention back. "Do you believe him?"

"No." She shakes her head, silver earrings dangling. "He wouldn't do that. He knew how much I liked my job."

"And you didn't find it odd that he now owns quite a lot of the Hollows?"

"Like he said, he was just doing it to help people." But her gaze flits to me as she says it. There's a question there, and I'm not sure if she's wondering whether she can trust her father or whether she's just wondering if what all the papers are saying about me is true.

"Does your father think you're clumsy?"

The question throws everyone. Bellanie blinks up at her. "What?"

"Your father. Does he think you're clumsy? Do you break a lot of things at home?"

"No." Bellanie looks between Petra and her dad. "I don't break things. And we have a repairer on staff, so what would it matter?" She's not stupid. She looks at me again, this time with suspicion, like I'll give away whatever Petra's getting at. I stare right back.

"Indeed. Why would it matter?" Petra taps a manicured nail—black today—against her chin. "Bring in the exhibit, please."

From stage right, Matt floats in the giant vertical river from Nichols's office. Draven keeps a hand on it, ready if Matt's strength waivers. Matt gently guides it to the ground, turning it so the crowd gets a good look.

Nichols stands, face reddening. "How dare you remove that! It's mine!"

"And it's amazing," Petra says. "Truly. You built this as well, correct?"

"Yes." His voice is weak, and a thin layer of sweat beads on his forehead. His lawyer seems to have given up and watches the proceedings like one of the audience.

Petra claps her hands together. "Almost forgot the best part. Lights." The entire room darkens, illuminated only by the glowing blue water. "Councilor, could you do us a favor and activate the enchantment for the other lights?"

"I don't have to do a damn thing," he spits.

"That's disappointing. You've frequented the pool you built in the Nest, have you not?"

Nichols's eyes slide down and to the side, as if he can see his wife sitting behind him. Her face, a mirror image of Bellanie's, remains impassive, but I can feel her anger.

"I did, purely for quality assurance."

"Of course," Petra says, her voice dripping with condescension. "I've heard the water responds to you, changes color. A benefit of being the creator—you can do whatever special things you like. Why don't you come up and show us how that works?" She waves a hand toward the water feature.

My gaze flicks between Draven and Matt. Their expressions don't give anything away, but the three of us are collectively holding our breath, hoping this is going to work.

"I will do no such thing. This is a courtroom, not a theater."

"And yet you're such a good actor." The words slip out before I can stop them. The people behind me laugh. I grimace and throw an apologetic look at Petra. Nichols looks apoplectic.

"That's all right, Councilor. You can sit down. Nobody is going to make you do anything." Petra holds his gaze while he slowly sinks to his seat.

"Bellanie. You said you believe your father, that he had nothing to do with Carter or with Bradley baiting the ulgashen. But you also said he doesn't think you're clumsy. Has he ever let you touch this?"

The whispers buzz behind me, reaching conversational levels. The judges cover their mouths with one hand while gesturing as they talk to one another. My eyes find Draven's, and there's a slow, barely discernible smirk on his face. Maybe, once today is over, I'll let myself picture what we might be, just for a moment.

"No." Bellanie's voice is hesitant.

"If you believe he had nothing to do with the death of your boss, the deaths of all those who died at the hands of the ulgashen, please dip your hand in the water."

The room goes silent. Even the judges freeze. The only sound is the steady dripping of water coming from Bradley as he, too, watches with rapt attention.

This could end very badly. When Helen told me Nichols could change the water in the pool at the Nest, I thought of his water feature. It is amazing but wildly over-engineered. So many enchantments for such a trivial decoration that most people would never see. When we were in his office, Nichols pulled his daughter away from the vertical river but wasn't bothered at all by Matt's proximity.

He wasn't worried about her breaking it, so he must have been worried about her touching it, especially in front of Matt and me. Nichols is an engineer; he'd want a model of his plans for the Hollows.

I think. I hope.

Bellanie looks at her father, then her mother, then at Petra. She swallows and slowly stands from her chair. Draven steps out of her way as she approaches.

She dips her fingers into the water. The light in the pool changes to red, revealing a map of roads and homes.

"That's the Hollows!" someone shouts. Everyone begins talking and pointing. The judges don't bother to shush them. They're muttering to one another, not even bothering to hide their mouths.

"Now why do you have a gorgeous water feature such as this with a map of the Hollows in it?" Petra asks in a casual voice. The tone, so at odds with the chaos, hushes the crowd.

Before he can speak, his lawyer remembers his job and leaps from his chair. "The councilor is not currently testifying. And once Ms. Nichols is done, I request a recess."

Chapter 40
Sugar

"What a load of shit," Matt grumbles, his jacket off and feet propped up on the table. "Do you think anyone actually bought his claim about repairing the Hollows?"

We're back in the beige room. Draven leans against the wall with his arms crossed. Petra stabs her paper with a pen on the other side of the table.

"Unfortunately, even with the water feature, I think a lot of people will buy it." She lets out a long breath. "He's going to say it was all part of his rehabilitation plan, that he planned to unveil it once they had everything completed." The room is stifling, and she sends a current of air around, ruffling our clothes and hair.

"How's he going to explain all the water on top?" Draven asks. He's loosened his tie, and that lock of hair keeps falling onto his forehead.

"Whatever he needs to—that it was just to keep it hidden, that he didn't want to waste a good model while the work on the Hollows was still being done," Matt replies. Petra points at him in agreement.

"Bradley is a murdering nobody. I need to prove Nichols did it. Being an opportunistic politician isn't a crime. Without a solid connection between him and the destruction in the Hollows, we've got nothing," she says, giving me a pointed look.

I have never, ever, since the day I met him, wanted CP to show up. Regardless of what may have happened afterward, there has never once been a moment when I desired his presence.

Until today.

My mind runs through our conversation again, trying to find the point at which he decided to play me.

"We'll keep your name out of it when it comes to Tonya. Bradley didn't see who killed her." I phrase the words carefully. We're in his townhouse again, thankfully without the additional naked body. CP isn't high this time. He's freshly showered and wearing a dark suit and sits behind an ornate jade and black desk.

"If they can't testify about her, why would I need your help?" His anger is cold today. Like a chilled glass waiting for me to fill him up and give his rage purpose.

"Because it's not her death you're worried about." I cock my head to the side. "No, I think you're hoping Bradley keeps his mouth shut about something else entirely."

He leans forward, his expression one of naked malice. "He didn't see shit. You're bluffing."

This is where it could all fall apart. I am bluffing. Bradley walked into the room at LeMar and saw CP, one of his guards, and Ingrid, the mystery girl, standing over Tonya's dead body. Being the industrious young man he is, he told CP he could help him on behalf of Nichols. We still haven't been able to track down Ingrid.

But CP doesn't know that. Bradley followed her in because she looked out of place, and CP was acting strange by keeping their interaction so hush-hush. He hit the jackpot or sealed his doom, depending on the view.

"Fenrik and I started talking recently," I say casually. "We might start spending time together again." I examine my nails and let a small, secret smile play across my lips, hoping CP takes it for a reaction to my memories of his brother.

He launches out of his seat and hurls a small table out of his way as he rounds on me. It smashes against the wall, raining splinters onto an opulent gold rug. "You won't go near my brother, not for any reason. You will make sure my name and that butter-fly's are never mentioned in the same sentence and that reporter forgets all about that night at LeMar. Am I understood?"

I step closer, trailing my hand over his lapel. "As long as you tell the truth about Nichols."

"I'll testify that Nichols came to me with his plan to flood the Hollows to make his ridiculous water community. And that he told me he'd hired Bradley to help, including dumping a dead butterfly on my beach because he thought I was taking too long to get him the Senate approvals he needed to subdue the under city's magic. But I won't be saying shit about the ulgashen or the other murders."

It was enough. At least, I hoped Petra would think so. "Why would you even get involved with Nichols?" I ask.

"Money." He snorts like it's obvious. He gives me a cruel smile. "But the added benefit of fucking up your apartment so you'd have to move back to the upper city also appealed. In fact, I think I'll make that a condition too."

Leaning my elbows on the table, I run my hands over my face, exhaling. "I thought I pulled it off. I thought he would come. Stupid." Draven's face is open in something like surprise, but he quickly schools his expression. Petra tries to nod in understanding, but it looks almost painful. I'm quickly learning that she hates to lose. I look back at Matt. "I'm sorry."

He shakes his head. "Let's not throw ourselves off a bridge yet."

When I found Linnea, I was panicked and sick. The grief came in waves, hitting me when I least expected it. This feels similar, but without the blood. Like a moment I'm going to regret over and over again. If I'd never gotten involved with CP, I don't know how this case would have turned out. But it wouldn't be this. It wouldn't be the four of us, stuck in this fucking coffin of a room, about to allow the man who orchestrated the death of twenty-four people—twenty-six, counting Sigrid and Carter—to go free.

"What about Bellanie?" Draven says. "Can you lean on her a little more? She must have been upset to see that map."

"I'm sure they've given her all the explanations she needs. It's much easier for her to believe Bradley's a deranged killer than admit she's living with one," says Petra.

A clerk pokes her head through the door. "Twenty minutes, counsel." Petra dips her head in acknowledgment. The clerk is about to duck back out when she barks, "Get your feet off the desk." Matt drops them instantly, and she shuts the door behind her.

"Good boy," I say, and he glares. Draven smirks, and the sight curls around me, sending enticing visions of a future devoid of men from the royal family of Eddahn.

Petra looks between me and Matt before jumping out of her seat. She grabs her things and crams them back into her briefcase. "Get up, Sugar," she demands. "You're testifying."

Chapter 41
Draven

"And did Mr. Thorn ever tell you someone had ordered him to lead ulgashen to the Hollows?" Donahue asks Candy, one of the other servers at Tradimento. She was friends with Sigrid, and her eyes are pure murder as she looks at Bradley.

"No. He never said anything like that. He said he was "making moves'" and all the other bullshit guys'll say to get into your pants."

"So he never mentioned Councilor Nichols?" Donahue stands with his hands behind his back, head bent and eyes half closed, nodding as Candy answers. He's a pretentious piece of shit and reminds me of the sycophants who surrounded my uncle.

"No. He told me about Bellanie, but I think it was just to make me jealous. That's it."

Candy is the fourth witness for the defense, all of them Bradley's coworkers or friends. Each of them testified to the fact that while they knew Bradley worked for Councilor Nichols, he never said anything about Nichols's plans for the Hollows or the ulgashen.

"Candy, just a few questions." Petra stands. "You said Bradley got you the job at Tradimento, correct?"

"Yes." She draws the word out and leans slightly away from Petra.

"Do you know how long he worked there before you started?"

"About three years."

"And you've worked there for two?"

She nods.

"Did you start as a server?"

Candy's dangling earrings swing as she shakes her head. "No. You have to start as a dishwasher, then a busser, then usher, then a server. If you've got any talent, you can earn a place as an actor."

"Interesting. What you've achieved in two years, Bradley still hasn't managed to achieve in five. Are there any other employees who have taken so long to advance?

She thinks for a moment, a line appearing between her eyebrows. "None that I know of."

"Does that sound to you like the brains behind a criminal enterprise or just the hired muscle?"

Before she can answer, Donahue leaps up. "Objection—"

"Withdrawn. Thank you for your testimony, Candy. You're excused. I believe she's the last of the defense's witnesses. As such, the prosecution would like to call a rebuttal witness. Detective Sucrelia Writh."

Gasps and whispers break out as Sugar stands from her seat. I can practically feel the recorders in the top row lean forward. Sugar brushes her silver hair over her shoulder, making sure the audience gets a good look as she strides across the room. She takes a seat at the witness table, curling her fingers around the armrests and crossing her legs. Her eyes focus on Nichols for a beat before she lowers her lids, dismissing him with a blink.

"Detective, can you tell us about the night Carter Fox died?"

Petra takes Sugar through it all again. The murder at Tradimento, finding Sigrid on the beach, trailing Bradley with me into the Hollows. Sugar's calm demeanor never falters. She answers every question calmly and with impeccable detail.

"Thank you. And now I think we need to address something else before we go any further." Petra pauses.

The courtroom is silent. Nobody shifts in their seat; not a single pen scratches. The judges watch as Petra backs up to give Sugar the floor. "There have recently been some rather unsavory articles about you in the newspapers. When did you first meet Prince Alaric of Eddahn?"

Petra didn't prep her. There wasn't time. Sugar arches a single brow before answering. "I met him when I worked at the Nest."

"When you were dating his brother?"

"I'd met him before that, but our interactions became more frequent during that time, yes."

"And were those interactions pleasant?"

The smell of popcorn wafts over to me, and I whip my head around. A man in the third row shoves something out of sight as I glower at him before turning back to Sugar. There's a nearly imperceptible downturn to one side of her mouth. If I hadn't spent so much time searching her face for evidence of emotion, I'd have missed it.

"No. They were generally not pleasant. He didn't approve of my dating his brother."

"And why was that?" Petra clasps her hands in front of her as she leans against the dais, ensuring all attention is on Sugar.

"At the time, I just assumed he thought I wasn't good enough for him, but now I know better."

"What do you know?"

"That he wanted me to be with him instead. He was envious of his brother's relationship with me." She gives a delicate shrug.

"And you understood that when you became involved with the crown prince, isn't that correct?"

"Yes."

The moment the words are out of her mouth, a flurry of murmurs and activity takes place behind me. It's Matt's turn to scowl at the audience.

"It must have been quite a surprise to see the stories, then? The interviews he gave claiming you're a stalker?"

"Infuriating but not truly surprising. I've always known CP is capable of anything."

"Including ruining your reputation?"

Sugar laughs. It's throaty and seductive, a glimpse of her as one of the Dame's darlings. "I don't think there's a soul in this room who thinks he isn't capable of doing worse than that."

The whispers whip around the room like a trapped bird. Matt mutters under his breath about gossipy idiots.

"CP sought you out at the Nest when your relationship with Prince Fenrik ended?"

Sugar nods.

"What job did you perform for the Dame?"

"I was a dominatrix. People paid me to create the fantasies they couldn't even whisper to themselves. I'd coax those desires from their most secretive depths and free them from inhibition." Her voice captures the crowd like a riptide, pulling everyone further out until they're trapped in the apex.

"And you'd receive more than coin in return, would you not?"

"I fed from their emotions, allowing me to exert the control they needed."

"*They* needed?" Petra's voice drops as she takes the tiniest step back. A moment of understanding passes between the two women.

Sugar's lips twist. Her expression shifts into something dangerous. If she was hinting at her past profession before, now she becomes her. Madame Writh. Her back straightens, and she narrows her eyes at everyone and no one at once.

"Every person who has knelt at the end of my whip, begged me for pain, or watched my nails drag across their skin craved my control. Outside the Nest, they couldn't achieve that level of freedom. They couldn't want those things. But without me, they have no one to make them crawl, no one to serve. Without their dom, a sub is motionless, powerless to act."

To his credit, Nichols catches on, his eyes blinking in sudden understanding.

"A sub needs the permission, the order, to do what they already want to do. They want to give me their choices, to bend to my will. They need me to exercise their desire." Sugar's eyes cut to Nichols, who is too late as he grabs at his lawyer to do something. "They might want to kill, to hurt, but without their dom, they won't. Someone more powerful needs to hand them the knife."

"In your professional opinion, based on your past experience at the Nest and your current knowledge of both Councilor Nichols and Bradley Thorn, would you say this is a dominant-and-submissive-type relationship?"

A quick intake of breath is all the audience gets before Sugar replies, "I would."

Chapter 42
Sugar

"Well done, Petra," I say, clinking my glass with hers. She practically glows from all the adrenaline, her eyes bright with the thrill of victory.

"Thank you. It was truly a team effort." Matt and Draven raise their glasses before taking a drink. Callahan's is packed. The band is playing something upbeat, and Callahan has two other bartenders helping him out.

We managed to snag one of the midnight-blue velvet booths, with Matt stealing a chair from another table to sit at the edge. Conversation around us buzzes with talk of the trial. Petra perks up anytime someone mentions having lost money by betting on the defense.

The door swings open, and Jasper walks through, shrugging off his expensive coat and dropping snowflakes on the ground. I give him a wave and don't miss the side-eye Petra gives me as he walks over.

"Congratulations. That was a great show," Jasper says, his gaze lingering on Petra before he nods to the rest of us.

Draven sits across from me. He's removed his suit jacket and tie, and his sleeves are rolled to his forearms, one arm slung over the back of the booth. He raises his eyebrows over his drink as he catches me appreciating him.

It felt good to be in my comfort zone again, being a woman filled with certainty instead of shame. Nailing Nichols and Bradley to the wall and doing it without CP's help will be a moment I'll relish for at least a hundred years. I'll probably have to deal with some pathetic revenge plot from the two of them when they get out, but that's a problem for fifty-plus years from now.

Will I still be in Drahma City? Escaping seemed like such a viable option before the trial. CP is like a rusty fishhook in my side, infecting and dragging me down. My eyes flit back to Draven, then Matt, and then Petra, who looks like she's desperately trying and failing to maintain an air of distance from Jasper. Until CP tires of me, he could use any of them to keep me in line.

It surprises me I've so easily slotted Petra into that group and can't help punishing her a little for it. "I suppose we go back to work tomorrow?" I look between her and Jasper. "Building cases, spending all those late nights working things out?"

Petra kicks me under the table, and I wince. I glare at her, but I deserved it. Matt chuckles into his drink. Jasper gives me a disdainful look he probably learned from a wealthy fae's guide to commoners before looking around for a waiter.

"I got it," Draven says, offering Jasper his seat. Jasper thanks him and gives him his order before sliding in next to Petra.

I shuffle out of the booth, ignoring the knowing look from my partner, and join Draven and the crush of people at the bar. His forearm presses against mine, skin to skin. A tremor dives from the connection to settle between my thighs. There would be something deeply satisfying about taking him home after this.

"Good job today." He leans over so I can hear him above the noise. I give him a genuine smile, and his eyes widen like I punched him in the gut. "What did I do to deserve that?" he murmurs into my ear.

I lift my lips. My breath just grazes his skin. "You did a good job, too. And it wasn't even your case." My hair falls to his shoulder, and his eyes dart to where it rests against his shirt. "Catching two out of three killers isn't bad. And soon I'll have a lead on a third." His breath mingles with mine. If he turned slightly, our lips would almost touch. And I want them to. I feel so much lighter than I did a few months ago, like having a life without constant guilt and finding Linnea's killer are within my reach.

"What do you think his excuse will be? For not showing up?" he asks. I can see the lie in his question. He doesn't want to hear about CP's excuses. He wants to know if I'm going to see him again.

I lean closer as I say with cold certainty. "I could not give less of a fuck about him or his excuses."

His eyes drop to my neck before trailing back up to my lips as if he's trying to decide where to taste me first.

A bartender breaks the moment, and we give our drink orders, then carry everything back to the table.

Matt entertains us with stories from before we joined the department, and Jasper is a wealth of knowledge on what he calls "unverified stories" and I would call gossip. Petra describes some of the most amazing trials she's seen in and outside of D.C. At eleven, we call it a night. Everyone has to work tomorrow.

The others seem to disappear into the night by the time Draven and I step out of the bar. He buttons his heavy coat and asks, "Can I walk you home?"

I want him to. I want this high to last. Shivers run their delicate fingers over my neck, promising me how good it would feel to have all of Draven's skin against mine. But not until I deal with CP.

"No." He doesn't mask his disappointment, and my lips quirk. "But you can walk me to the bridge." I turn, and he falls in step beside me.

We don't speak. The snow is falling again, and it lands in his hair, stark against the dark strands. When we reach the bridge, I pause, memorizing the look in his eyes, the way his desire curls around me, pulling me closer. "Thank you. I can make it from here."

"Are you sure? It's pretty dangerous out there."

"You're concerned for my safety?" I ask, my chin dipping.

"No, for mine. I might be set upon by all manner of creatures. You wouldn't want anything to happen to me now, would you?" He's joking but unfortunately has hit the nail on the head.

"You don't have much of a sense of self-preservation, do you, vampire?" I brush snowflakes from his hair before letting my hand rest on his lapel.

"Apparently not." He toys with the seam of my coat, leisurely sliding a hand up and down. When I make no move to stop him, he slips his fingers underneath, between the buttons. The heat from his fingers reaches me through my silk shirt. The shivers of need become more insistent, begging me to take what he's so willingly offering and screw the consequences.

But ignoring inevitable consequences is why I still need to worry about a vicious prince.

"You make me constantly wonder whether I should fight or flee." A dark expression, savage and thirsty, crosses his face as he slowly undoes several of my buttons. He opens my coat wide enough to slip his hands around my waist and pull me closer. "Let me walk you home." Draven's voice is like rough rope, but his scent is black silk against my neck. My blood throbs in every place I want him to touch. But when his lips brush my temple, I force myself to grab his wrists.

"I saw the way CP looked at you in Gibson's office. He thinks I belong to him. And if he catches you playing with his toys, they'll never find your body." I step back, finding my balance and giving him a small smile. "And I would find that less than ideal."

The primal part of him must tense at the threat; the muscles of his neck tighten. "You're not a toy. And you're not his." His voice is so dark, and my power stretches like a cat.

I let my thumb brush over his pulse as I shake my head. "No, not anymore." Every part of me, especially the lower parts, screams at me to drag him back to my apartment. "Goodnight, Draven. I'll see you at work." I turn away and walk down the bridge, throwing the words over my shoulder.

As the ramp hits the street on the other side, the magic opens a portal directly in front of me. Not just a direct route to my building, but actually inside my apartment. I don't have time to contemplate what a bad sign this is before something pinches tight around my neck.

Chapter 43
Draven

A single blade of light slices through the thick red curtains in my bedroom. Part of me wants to get out of bed and head into the department so I can see Sugar. The other part of me knows how ridiculously frustrating that will be. I kick off my sheets and run both hands down my face before folding them over my chest.

It's impossible not to compare them, but Sugar isn't Eliza. For one, Eliza wanted me, at least for a time. Sugar has been pushing me away since we met.

I shouldn't feel this discombobulated over a woman. Not at my age. This restless energy, this desire...it's like I'm strung out on one of those illegal mixes everyone's snorting these days. Every hit of Sugar I get is going to make it worse. The silk of her shirt is a ghost between my fingers. I rub them together, picturing how soft her skin would feel. A breeze passes through the window, rustling the curtains. The light hits my eyes, and I wince.

Dragging myself from the bed, I head into the bathroom and stand under the shower until the water moves from ice cold to scalding hot. With the work I did with Sugar and Matt, Gibson will probably deem me ready for a new partner. I hope they're a total asshole.

I shut off the water and run my hands through my hair, then go through the motions of my morning routine, not even trying to get those navy eyes and that silver hair out of my head. I throw on some clothes and head into the kitchen. As I wait for my coffee to brew, the newspaper appears on my kitchen table.

CROWN PRINCE ALARIC OF EDDAHN MUR-DERED.

FORMER LOVER SUCRELIA WRITH ARRESTED.

***

Thank you so much for reading! If you enjoyed Sugar in the Blood, please leave a review! And if you want more of this world before the next book comes out, sign up for my newsletter and get a bonus alternative chapter from Sugar's POV. I've also got some other great bonus content lined up to tide you over before you find out what happens next!

Acknowledgements

As always, first and foremost, thank you to my husband Brendan and my two boys for their love and support. Nobody has it all, but with you three I come pretty close. Thanks to my awesome parents and family, who keep buying and reading my books even though I tell them not to, because how embarrassing is that? To my wonderful critique group—Sherri, Christa, Liz, and Mary—I'm so glad our paths crossed in Vegas. Your helpful comments and encouragement keep me going every week. Thank you to all my ARC readers and my steadfast beta reader, Whitney! Endless appreciation to my editor, Victoria, for her expertise and to my spectacularly talented cover designer, Idil.

And thanks to you for reading this book! I'm exceedingly grateful you spent your precious free time with my words. And if you're so inclined, please leave it a review so I can pull other unsuspecting readers into Drahma City.

About the author

L.M. Dodds is the author of Sugar in the Blood, and the fantasy romance series, the Chronicles of Lim. She's also an attorney, voracious reader, avid cookbook collector and occasionally provides legal advice to fictional characters. She reads and writes in order to live many lives from the comfort and safety of her couch.

When she's not writing or embarrassing herself on the internet, you can find her at home in Virginia with her husband, two rambunctious boys, her loyal hound, and a lot of unfinished DIY projects.